SHORT
STORY
AMERICA

VOLUME VII

EDITED BY T.D. JOHNSTON

SHORT STORY AMERICA PRESS

Volume VII

Short Story America
35 Great Contemporary Short Stories
Edited by T.D. Johnston

ISBN: 978-1-7923-8997-9
Library of Congress Control Number: 2022936869

Published by
Short Story America Press
www.shortstoryamerica.com
editors@shortstoryamerica.com
843-597-3220

FIRST EDITION

Printed in the USA

Book design by Soundview Design

TABLE OF CONTENTS

Introduction • vii
Tim Johnston

Acknowledgments • ix

THE ALMOND TREE • 1
Lawrence Buentello

A GLITCH IN TIME • 15
Doris Wright

WE LIVE HERE • 32
Jarrett Kaufman

LIFE LIST • 44
Ray Morrison

THE FAIRY HOUSE • 53
Katie Sherman

OUR UFO • 62
John Engell

BLESSING • 72
Martin McCaw

MONKEY MOUNTAIN • 82
Kali VanBaale

**THE NEVER-FAILING
VICE OF FOOLS** • 89
James Kearney

MODEL A • 93
James Kearney

**WHAT HAPPENED TO
MRS. ELEONORA VALDEMAR?** • 101
Carmelo Rafala

THE CUSTODIAN • 111
John W. MacIlroy

SEPARATION • 117
Steven B. Rosenfeld

PERCH • 128
James D. Balestrieri

PAROLE • 136
Mathieu Cailler

A BURDEN OF TRUTH • 142
Tim M. Ruth

A DAY AT THE CREEK • 147
Vernie Singleton

NEW WORLD • 157
Scott William Woods

THE TOKEN COLLECTOR • 173
Jayne Adams

THE TELEPHONE CALL • 178
Skip Robinson

THE TANNER GRAVES • 186
Douglas Campbell

FOG • 198
Jean Rover

**OF HALF-HOUSES,
WITH VERNON** • 208
Gregg Cusick

**WHAT THE
SEASONS BRING** • 220
Heather Luby

**THE SEARCH FOR
ST. FRANCIS** • 233
Lawrence Buentello

A PRACTICAL WOMAN • 246
Ginny Hall-Apicella

HECTOR RAMIREZ • 252
Sean Winn

**THE BABY JESUS IN
PHNOM PENH** • 263
Nim Stevens

THE NO WAY WAY • 273
Marjorie E. Brody

**ELSIE "PEACHES"
BOULWARE, AGE 69** • 275
Jon Tuttle

**THIS KIND OF
HEARTBREAK** • 278
Kathryn Brackett

THE WORKSHOP • 296
Martha Weeks

IN HIS IMAGE • 305
Joel Shulkin

SWAT! • 332
Katherine Tandy Brown

A REAL MOTHER • 336
T.D. Johnston

INTRODUCTION

It has been the privilege of a lifetime to edit and publish the seven volumes in the Short Story America anthology series of contemporary short fiction. The authors in this series stand among the very best of the short-story writers of the early twenty-first century. The friendships forged with these accomplished men and women, like those with readers who deeply appreciate this great original American literary art form, will remain current and dear to my heart for the rest of my life.

While I must turn the page in my own writing life to full-time creation of long and short fiction, the seven volumes that culminate with this book will continue to be available, as will an occasional special volume focused on a popular genre, like horror or science fiction or fantasy. Who knows what today's great authors will produce when invited to offer a story in the future?

For now, enjoy this final installment in the seven-volume Short Story America series, and please keep in regular touch. I can be reached at tim@shortstoryamerica.com, and on Instagram (@tdjohnston) and Facebook. I look forward to continued mutual love for the short story. Thank you, friends.

Affectionately,
Tim Johnston

ACKNOWLEDGMENTS

Many thanks to Amy Vaughn, Steve Thompson, John W. MacIlroy, Jayne Adams, and every contributing author for your roles in making this a very special final volume in the SSA series.

THE ALMOND TREE

Lawrence Buentello

i

She didn't understand; her husband's anger confused her, because he seemed so accessible at other times, even loving. He assured her that it wasn't because of the alcohol. His father had been a connoisseur of liquor and never succumbed to alcoholism, a talent his son surely had inherited. But Allan was a man with shadows in his mind obscuring memories she wished she had the ability to penetrate—

Mona sat on the steps leading from the kitchen door of the small house into the backyard, snapping green beans in a large stainless steel bowl as she stared out over the pale green grass toward the small tree standing alone between the fences. *I made him angry, but I don't know what I could have said.* When she'd moved into the house as his wife she felt as if she were starting her life over, a necessary revival. But after a few weeks the old feelings returned, the old fears, and they remained. Perhaps that was why he was angry now. Her state of mind had always been a problem.

The tree began flowering the first week she'd arrived, twenty feet tall and thin, its buds painted delicately on crooked branches, white petals with rosy accents. He'd told her that it was an almond tree, that it had been lurking in the backyard like a vagrant when he bought the house. He'd kept intending to cut it down, but also kept forgetting it existed; but he would cut it down immediately if she wanted to use more of the yard. She'd protested, uncharacteristically, telling him that it was a beautiful tree and to please let it stay in the yard. That was the first time he'd stared at her with a subtle hatred in his eyes, an animosity that flared more and more frequently.

She balanced the bowl between her legs and wiped her hands on her dress. The breeze had freshened and pulled through the branches of the tree, then fell against her face and lifted the strands of her long brown hair. The blue California sky refused to hold any clouds that day, the warm sun shining on the blossoms as if they were firing up a light of their own. She noted her solitude, accepting that it was the one state in life that most eased her suffering, but hating her isolation. Why did she have to always feel this way?

Allan wasn't a handsome man. On the contrary, his gray eyes pressed too closely to his nose and his lips were thin and color-less. His pale skin left an impression of poor health, though he often declared himself to be fit and athletic. Perhaps her husband had been handsome at one time, but Mona had witnessed what persistent drinking had done to her father, dulling his eyes, turn-ing his flesh to cheesecloth, sinking in his cheeks, and finally clos-ing his eyes forever—so she knew Allan's face might be bearing the artifacts of premature aging brought on by the alcohol.

But she wasn't a beautiful woman, either. Her large brown eyes were parted by a small nose and set above a continually pouting mouth. Allan once called her a grieving cow, though she wasn't heavy. He'd laughed, and she laughed, too, but afterward she realized he wasn't only teasing.

After requesting that he leave the tree unmolested, she'd asked him if it produced many almonds. He explained to her wearily that most almond trees needed to be pollinated in order to bear fruit, and since the tree wasn't part of an orchard it would never grow any almonds. As far as the greater philosophy of trees was concerned, it was a useless ornament, a vagabond taking up space. She thought she would conduct her own research to verify this information, but she didn't tell him this. She had more than sufficient time to read about almond trees while he was gone—he often left the house for days at a time.

During these times Mona paced between the rooms of the house, stopping to stare from the windows into the sunlight, though immediately feeling her shoulders tense, her stomach jump at the thought of passing through the front door. This same fugue also overcame her while living in her parents' house, causing panic attacks and tears. Therapy had helped in small ways, but she still felt like a prisoner of her own mind. *Did I marry a hypochondriac?* Allan had asked her. Yes, you did, she'd wanted to say, but didn't. She knew it was a rhetorical question—he was well acquainted with her problems, and he'd still married her, just as she knew of and accepted his drinking. Broken people also had their desires.

Their union hadn't been forged in some romantic setting. Her mother had met Allan at the office supplies business where she worked as a bookkeeper and had subsequently introduced him to Mona. In their initial conversation, Allan had told her mother that he was unmarried but would like to have a wife one day; and her mother, in turn, had told him of her daughter, describing Mona as terribly shy, and also unmarried. Later, Allan came to her mother's house to visit, always speaking soberly, never reeking of beer or liquor. And when he'd broken through Mona's reticence, which was the diffidence of a woman who had lived a life tortured by irrational fears, they went dining together, to movies, or shopping, when she could momentarily break the psychological chains that kept her imprisoned in her room. Soon, the three were talking about marriage, and her mother enthusiastically encouraged the possibility—her mother was an older woman, after all, and had often spoken of being unburdened of the responsibility of living her daughter's life for her.

When Mona exhibited resistance to the concept of marrying him, her mother insisted that it was a miracle any man would actually want to take on the responsibility of having her as his wife and to stop thinking so selfishly—

Mona stood up on the steps, the stainless steel bowl in her hands, wondering if he was still angry with her, or if his anger faded as the liquor diminished in his glass. She wanted to believe she would find happiness in her marriage, but she was afraid of making him angry again. Why had he married a woman like her, anyway? She didn't understand, but perhaps he wanted love, too.

The leaves of the almond tree glittered beautifully in the fading light.

ii

Two months later, on the evening of the day her husband first beat her, Mona's mother finally came to the house, after protesting for many hours that what transpired between a husband and wife wasn't any of her business. *It is your business*, Mona insisted, *because I'm your daughter—*

Only after Allan left the house would her mother come to console her, though she really hadn't come to offer her sympathies. Mona met her at the door of the little house, her face washed of blood, but her blouse still stained with it. Mona's cheeks were swollen where he'd slapped her, her left eye blackened, the pain throbbing in her face and jaw. Her tears stung her eyes, especially the eye he'd struck, but she wasn't sobbing—the tears were a purely reflexive gesture by her body. She was too shocked by Allan's violence to be in control of her emotions.

Why did he hit you? her mother asked as she searched for ice in the freezer above the refrigerator. *What did you say to provoke him?*

Mona sat at the kitchen table. She accepted the dishcloth her mother had wrapped around a handful of ice cubes and gently applied it to her eye. *I didn't provoke him. I only asked him to stop drinking so much.*

Why did you do that, Mona?

You don't understand, Mama. He gets in his car and leaves on his sales trips, he's gone for days and days, sometimes a week at a time, and when he comes home all he wants to do is drink. He sits in his chair and watches the television drinking one beer after another and after a while he can't even talk coherently to me anymore. He falls asleep in his chair, and I have to wake him up to put him to bed but he always gets so angry with me because he thinks I'm interrupting his television watching, but he's never awake, he's always drunk—

Listen to me, her mother said as she sat in the chair across from her daughter, *you don't understand what working does to a person. Mona, you're selfish! You've never worked a day in your life, you've always let someone else take care of you. Allan works hard, so he wants to drink beer and watch television. That's the way of the world. Do you think I berated your father for drinking after he came home from work? Of course not! I knew he worked hard, and so I let him have his time.*

Mona stared down at the table, and then into her mother's eyes. At one time, her mother had had a beautiful face, symmetrical and fair, and her glowing blue eyes lit magically when she smiled. Her auburn hair was always elegantly styled. Now her mother's cheeks lay sunken on her face, and wrinkles had imprisoned her beautiful blue eyes. The auburn hair had grayed, and clung to the woman's head like a crown of silver nettles.

Daddy never hit you, Mona said. *He never hurt you when he was drunk.*

I respected him. Her mother straightened in her chair, as if she were proclaiming an immortal truth. *Now, you must have disrespected Allan to have angered him so much. Why did you have to criticize him?*

I wasn't criticizing him. I want him to spend time with me when he's home. I get so lonely, and he's away so much of the time. I want him to talk to me when we're together, I want to do things with him.

He shouldn't have hit you, it's true, her mother said. *But you shouldn't antagonize him, either. You're his wife, Mona, you have a wife's responsibilities. Be grateful for what you have.*

Mona pulled the dishtowel from her eye. *What do I have, Mama?*

You have a home, and you have a husband who provides for you. Do you know how many women don't have as much? Do you know how many years I spent praying that one day you'd live your life like a normal woman? Now that my prayers are answered, you're trying to ruin everything!

I only want him to want to be with me. I want him to love me, not just use me when it's convenient.

Her mother raised a remonstrative finger. *How many years did you use me because it was convenient for you? You let me do everything for you, because you cried and said you couldn't face the world, that you were too afraid, that you had too much anxiety. And then you had all those doctors agree with you, placate you. So who was it that worked to give you a life after your father died? Your mother! Now you want me to take you back home. Yes, I see it in your eyes. You want me to take you home and protect you from the world again, but I can't, Mona, I won't. I can't do it anymore, this you have to do for yourself.*

Mona felt her lips trembling and could only stop them by placing the cold dishtowel over her mouth. When she could speak again she said, *But he beat me, Mama, what can I do? What if he does it again?*

Her mother, perhaps feeling more sympathy for her daughter's situation, rose from her chair and hugged Mona's head to her breast. She stroked Mona's hair and said, *Make yourself happy by keeping him happy. Whatever he wants to do, do that, and he won't hit you anymore. You have to make your marriage work for you, Mona. You have to do whatever it takes to please your husband so he'll treat you well. Don't you know that what I'm saying is true?*

Mona didn't answer, but pressed her cheek into her mother's breasts, needing the warmth of her mother's care and not wanting to lose it by disagreeing. *I'll try to make it work, Mama. I will.*

This is your home now, Mona. You must make it work for you. I won't live forever. You have to have someone to take care of you.

Mona found herself staring past her mother's thin shoulder through the kitchen window at the distant shadow of the almond tree. In the early evening darkness it was not an actual tree, but had transformed into a shadow of a tree, a thing that was there, but not there, silently meditating on the nascent night. And she was there, too, in her husband's house, she was there and not there, and the two had only each other to keep each other company. Perhaps a shadow was all she ever was—

But whether she was a shadow or a whole person, she knew she had to find a way to live peacefully with her husband, because her mother didn't want to bring her home.

iii

She couldn't remember when she began singing to the almond tree as she sat on the back steps meditating on the day, or sometimes in the evening when her husband was traveling. Why she should want to sing aloud at all was a mystery to her, though she did possess a passable singing voice, or so her mother once told her when she was a child. The tree was a captive audience, and offered no criticism.

Today was a good day. The previous night, before he packed his suitcase for his trip, Allan confessed to her that he knew he wasn't being a good husband, that he wanted to treat her with more compassion. And that he wanted to curb his drinking so that his life wasn't ruled by alcohol, as he feared it might be. This admission he gave with his face turned away from her as he folded shirts into an open suitcase. She assured him that he was a good man, though by his body language she knew he didn't believe her. Over time she had almost become used to his violent outbursts and knew when to leave the room when he seemed ready to unleash his anger on her.

Allan apologized to her, for all the pain he'd caused her, and told her he'd try to be a better man, better than his own father, at least. She embraced him in tears, and they made love that night, and for a little while she could envision her life becoming happier with his sobriety, perhaps even to the point where they could consider starting a real family together.

After he left that morning she brought a cup of coffee to the back porch steps and sat singing to the tree, a love song meant for her and her husband. Though she'd always considered herself handicapped by her mental fragility, she couldn't help feeling wonderfully optimistic now. The light in the sky brightened, the sound of the wind in the tree was a whispered congratulations, and the birds seemed to dance in the air for her. How silly she felt for singing of the love she found in the moment—

As she sat and stared at the little tree, though, she realized that it would never bear fruit, that because its blossoms would have to be pollinated, and that the bees in the hives of the area would have no access to the pollen necessary to perform this act, the tree would always remain barren of almonds. Her joy of the moment was tempered by a sudden empathetic melancholy; the tree would never fulfill its purpose for being a tree.

But it is only a tree, she said to herself, it is beautiful in other ways. Its static beauty gave meaning to its existence because her recognition of it grew its beauty inside of her. She didn't want to feel sad. She wanted to know that the future held the promise of so many other beautiful things. And she would try, too, to break free of the fear that held her in place, she would travel with her husband and see wonderful places. She would conquer her fear and they would share a wonderful life together.

When she was a little girl, before the world seemed to close on her mind with shadows and dark foreboding, she kept a scrapbook filled with pictures of all the places in the world she wanted to travel to: to the stately churches of Italy, to the stony white castles in Germany, to the river Thames in London and the mountains of Switzerland and the Aztec and Maya ruins in Central America—she would pore over the pictures of mysterious artifacts and women dressed in exotic dresses and children laughing in the shadow of the Eiffel Tower and see herself among them, laughing too.

But then the panic attacks began in her adolescence, her irrational fears, her agoraphobia, all closing in on her and locking her away in a small room where all the frightening feelings of the world couldn't steal her breath away, where she felt safe and protected. A cell to lock herself away, a place that all the dreams in the world couldn't trespass. She was home-schooled by her mother, and her mother and father were the only people she had to relate to—and then only her mother.

Such was her life, lived vicariously through television, books, computers, devices that allowed her to appreciate all the things that she would never do or experience for herself. But she hated that life, she didn't want it anymore. She wanted her own experiences. She wanted—

She wanted what the little almond tree couldn't have—she wanted to fulfill her purpose in life. She wanted to do more than just live in suspended animation while the world spun past her eyes in all its grandeur. If she couldn't do anything else because of her anxiety, she could live up to her feminine potential; if she couldn't master a profession, if she couldn't even bear to be among great numbers of people in conventional employment, that was something she could do.

She began singing again, another love song meant to bring back the joy she'd felt before sympathizing with the almond tree's unfulfilled potential. But the old fear returned, creeping like a shadow toward the terminal night. She felt it in her heart, and was afraid.

But if Allan kept his promise, if he truly meant that he wanted to change, there was still a possibility her life would change, too.

iv

She watched while her mother dug the hole before the trunk of the almond tree with the spade Mona normally used for tending her small garden. The flashlight lying by her mother's knees where she knelt silhouetted the woman's body, giving her the appearance of an apparition. Mona sat on the stair steps wrapped in a blanket, her mother having helped her bathe and change her clothes. She still felt sick to her stomach, and weak from losing blood, or perhaps only feeling weak from the sight of it. *I'll dig the hole deep*, her mother had said, *so there'll be no question of finding the remains*. That is how she phrased the word — remains. Her mother refused to take her to the hospital; she would take care of Mona herself, she'd said. She would say a prayer and consecrate the remains, and care for Mona while she healed.

Allan's sobriety had only been temporary. While he was sober, though, they had managed to live a fairly happy life. Over the last year she'd observed his mood warming, the influence of whatever demons he harbored loosening their hold of him, and in that time they enjoyed their evenings together free of the anger that had seemed second-nature to him. She also managed to quiet her fears long enough for them to dine together, see movies, or even walk through the town holding hands. She found herself enjoying her life, even planting a garden by the almond tree to occupy her time, flowers only because she wanted to see the little tree ringed by pretty colors and rich green leaves. They made love more frequently, too, if only because the impotence brought on by the alcohol subsided along with his drinking. When he held her on those nights his breath was free of the unpleasant smell of liquor. They laughed together more often than not — he seemed to have really changed.

But his sobriety didn't endure, no more than the beautiful red, yellow, and white petals of the flowers in her garden; they both bloomed brightly, were beautiful for a season, and then fell corrupted again. The smell of liquor lingered on his breath more and more frequently, and his temper flared in accompaniment. She had her demons and he had his, but hers only wanted for love, and his demanded someone suffer for their existence. When he began hitting her again she wanted to leave, but where was there for her to go? Her mother wouldn't have her. She had no friends, no way to make a life for herself.

She tried to save the world they had made together — that morning she'd resolutely gathered all the bottles in the house and emptied their contents down the kitchen sink. When he discovered what she'd done he slapped her, and then struck her with his fist in her stomach. *Now you feel what I feel every day*, he'd said to her as she lay struggling to breathe on the kitchen floor. Then he told her, *I'm going where I can drink without having my bitch of a wife try to run my life for me*. He left her lying on the floor in grotesque pain, but she managed to stand up and walk to the bedroom. She lay in bed for hours crying softly to herself. Toward evening, still alone in the house, she'd started to hemorrhage.

She called her mother, and her mother came reluctantly, though when she recognized Mona's physical condition she ceased complaining and addressed the seriousness of the circumstances.

Mona hadn't known she was pregnant. She suspected she might be, but had been too afraid to visit a doctor to verify her suspicions. She was also too afraid to let Allan know of the possibility. She had no idea how he might react when she told him. She couldn't have been pregnant long, not from the dimensions of the child she'd miscarried. She'd sat on the bathroom floor in her own blood staring at the surreal remains until her mother found her. Sometime later, in an awful series of actions that seemed more dream than reality in Mona's dissociated state of mind, her mother washed and dressed her, and then, while Mona sat staring blankly at the bedroom wall, gathered the physical artifacts of her dead grandchild in a towel and cleaned the bathroom floor.

You can't call the police, her mother told her. *This was only a terrible accident. I'll take care of you until Allan comes home.*

He killed our baby, Mona said, her voice a soft monotone.

You told me he hit you when you poured out his liquor. Why did you do that, Mona? Why did you do something so foolish?

I was trying to—

You were trying to ruin everything you have with your husband! You'll never learn, never. You only want things your own way. Your father died trying to take care of you, and I went back to work to support you. When I'm dead, what will happen to you? I'm only trying to do what's best for you, Mona. You have to listen to me!

He hit me. He hit me and now our baby's dead.

You provoked him. You're to blame, too. Don't try to pretend you're not. There's nothing to be done now but make things right, to make things like they were before. He doesn't have to know. We'll be the only ones who do. We'll bury the remains.

Mona wondered if her mother was right, if what she'd said held some truth. Did she really provoke her husband? Wasn't he responsible for his actions? But what could she do—he hadn't known she was pregnant. What would she tell the police? They would arrest him, put him in prison. Then what would she do? She had no money of her own, she wouldn't be able to make the house payments, or even buy food for herself. But could she ever only think of losing her child as an accident?

Now Mona sat on the back steps watching the shade of her mother trying to excavate a hole deep enough to bury the memory of the events of that horrendous day. She felt like singing a

9

dirge for her child, but no song ever composed could relate the sorrow she felt in her heart as her aging mother pressed the folded towel down into the hole and then began scooping black earth back over the tiny grave. She wondered if she should name the child, but she hadn't noticed whether it was a boy or girl, and her mother never told her.

When her mother finished wiping the dirt from her hands she rose from her knees and joined Mona at the back door so they could say a prayer together.

v

The cool December air chilled her face where she stood in the back yard. She held a small wooden canister in her hands. The flowers of her garden were long dead, and the almond tree spread its long, bare limbs to the sky in hibernation, a stark reminder of the effects of time on all living things. She wore a light coat over her dress, a scarf over her hair which she'd bound respectfully for the dispersal of her mother's ashes. Two years had passed since her miscarriage, and now her mother was dead.

Neither old age nor an accident had taken her mother's life. Her mother wasn't terribly elderly, nor had she carelessly died. She'd suffered a catastrophic stroke while sitting in a chair in her own home, but days had passed before a neighbor found her. Mona and her mother had spoken infrequently on the phone after the woman had buried her grandchild's remains beneath the almond tree. Neither seemed to want to risk having the subject come up in conversation, though Mona suspected her mother simply had an aversion to the bad news her daughter always seemed to have for her.

The memorial service had been brief, and as inexpensive as they could manage. Allan resented having to pay for the woman's burial, which was the reason why her mother had been cremated. There wasn't any insurance money to make up the difference for the funeral service her mother had desired for herself. A lawyer was still processing the legal documents concerning her parent's property, but Mona simply wished to leave everything in place right now—she didn't have the wherewithal to dispose of her mother's belongings. She would inherit the house, but selling the property could wait. Processing her feelings was not something she felt she could do in a timely fashion.

Her mother was dead, her child buried, and she knew of no more living relatives that might bring her comfort. The only person she had in the world to care for her was her husband, and she felt that he didn't love her anymore, if he ever loved her. He often complained that she was his impossible burden. When she told him that her mother had died he responded by remarking that now he would have to bear the whole of her care. What did it matter? she wondered. He was too often a ghost in their home, absent more often than present. She'd grown accustomed to being alone.

She never asked him where he went when he was away—she knew he wasn't off on business trips. But asking him would only provoke him, and she'd also grown tired of his abuse. She simply let him do as he pleased.

She didn't know what to feel about her mother's passing. Her mother had protected her for so long, but then cast Mona out of her house. She must have loved her daughter—perhaps she felt she'd demonstrated her affection by finding another home for Mona, even if it wasn't a loving home.

Her coat was long enough to prevent her dress from staining, so she knelt in the rough brown grass before the almond tree and stared at its stark beauty. Such an ugly display of ash-colored branches would give way to a new blossoming in spring, and the lovely flowers and rich green leaves would decorate the branches again. This renewal always gave her cause for a brief but sincere expression of joy. She pulled off the canister's lid and opened the plastic bag holding her mother's ashes. Then she spread the contents of the bag around the base of the tree—what ash wasn't carried away on the wind would remain, grandmother and grandchild lying together by the fruitless almond tree.

Mona began singing softly, not to the tree, but to the child that lay beneath its shadow, and not a love song, but a lullaby. Every so often she would walk out in the middle of the night and kneel in perfect darkness to visit the tiny grave and sing to her child in a clear voice so she could be heard through the vale lying between this world and the next. She often dreamed of her child, and in her dreams she held her little girl, and sang lullabies to her as she drowsed. These dreams always left her happy, but sad, too, and that was their enigma. Now she wished that she had kept her child, that she had never poured out her husband's liquor bottles, but it was too late to redress history.

She knelt in the grass singing for a long time, though it grew cold and she began to shiver as she sang.

She sang for her child, and then for her mother, and then even for the barren almond tree, and when she finally walked back into the house she didn't remember her sense of the cold, she only re-called the darkness of the night and the sensation of tears falling from her chin and striking the folds of her coat.

vi

In March, just as the almond tree fully bloomed with white petals glowing in the warm spring sun, Mona's husband left her.

He didn't have the courage to tell her directly, so he left a note for her to find after packing up his well-traveled suitcase and walking out the front door for the last time. Mona brought the note with her to the steps of the back porch and sat read-ing the lines over and over again, trying to find some variance in their meaning, but their meaning was singular and perfectly clear. *We'll never be happy, Mona. I tried to love you, but you're not a normal woman and you'll never be a normal woman. If I can't help myself then I'll never be able to help you. I think I found someone who can help me, and I want to be with her. She's not crazy, Mona, she's not a burden to me. I need someone to care for me, not the other way around. I'll contact you again when I've found a lawyer. I won't be coming back.*

Her husband hadn't bothered to sign the note—perhaps he couldn't bring himself to accept that much responsibility.

A wave of loneliness overwhelmed her where she sat, chilling her shoulders, her arms. Her dull brown eyes stared at the beau-tiful little flowers bursting in lovely patches on the limbs of the tree, their unspeakable beauty juxtaposed with the grief she felt for losing her husband. Still—what had she lost? Had she really loved him, or only the comfort he provided, the barrier he repre-sented between herself and the greater world?

Now she'd lost her child, her mother, and her husband, and nothing stood between her and the requirements of living in a world that terrified her. The medications only provided so much relief. She was alone.

The mortgage payments would go unpaid; the money in the bank account would dwindle, if Allan had even left any money for her to access. She would have to leave the house—she still had her parents' house, which remained unsold, a relic gathering dust across its fading memories. But she had no job of her own, how would she pay taxes, support herself?

Was it even worth continuing to live with the crippling fear and anxiety that had made all the decisions in her life for her?

She thought: *I don't know what to do now—I've lost everything and I don't know what to do—*

Mona felt, in that moment, that the only choice left for her was to follow her child and her mother into silence.

But the almond tree had bloomed so beautifully that to leave it now would seem like she was leaving her only friend. Perhaps she should wait until all the blossoms dropped away. When they fell, and nothing remained to represent the uncommon beauty of the world, she would have no reason to stay.

vii

Mona had never seriously considered the presence of God in her life—she couldn't believe a loving God would place in her mind the curse that would ruin it from so early an age. And so she never believed in divine mercy or miracles. After her father's death her mother rarely mentioned God, though she'd been a religious woman at one time; they'd ceased attending church as a family because of Mona's disability. For Mona, there was no good or evil, only the endless recurrence of painful experiences.

But on that morning in May, when she walked down the steps to say goodbye to her child and the solitary almond tree that stood sentry over it, she wondered if she'd been wrong—

Since her husband had left her, she'd spent her time moving through the small house like a spirit taking an inventory of the life it was forced to abrogate. A terrible anxiety for the future held her like physical restraints, and so she spoke to no one, lay in bed all day waiting for help that wouldn't arrive. When the documents from Allan's lawyer were delivered, she left them unread, too intimidated to examine their contents. She'd spent her evenings sitting on the back steps of the house singing to her child, weeping foolishly over her emotional breakdown, incapable of doing anything else, as if the soul of her child would rise to her and comfort her. When the petals of the almond tree began to fall, she knew her time was coming, and that the only way to stop her pain was to kill it where it lived inside herself.

But after that morning, she decided against silence.

She visited the bank that held the mortgage on the little house and arranged to receive a loan for her mortgage payments using her mother's house as collateral. She told the manager at the bank that eventually she would sell her childhood home, repay the loan and use the rest of the money to continue making payments on the house where she now lived. Then she told herself that she would find a job—any job that would let her support herself, no matter how painful she found interacting with other people. After settling with the bank, she retained a lawyer to negotiate her divorce settlement for her—she threatened to bring criminal charges against her husband if he didn't agree to let her have sole ownership of their house. Perhaps he was desperate to finalize their divorce, or perhaps he genuinely felt guilty over his treatment of her, because he agreed to her terms without an argument. Either way, she would keep the house, she wouldn't have to abandon her child.

She didn't know yet if the social anxiety that had found her in her youth was still an immovable obstacle, that if she ignored her racing heart and trembling hands she could move through the world with purpose. Conquering her fear had always seemed impossible, and attempting to do so a waste of time. How could she possibly negate the effects of her subconscious on her body when that subconscious chose to fill her conscious thoughts with one frightening scenario after another? All the cognitive therapy she'd endured had only allowed her to keep the worst of its symptoms at bay. But perhaps not all conditions in life were eternal. There was still too much to consider, but she believed she could solve her own problems, if she only worked to solve them day by day. *It is possible,* she'd told herself, *isn't it possible? I can make a life for myself.*

No, she still didn't know if she believed in God, or miracles, but during the long days and nights she'd sat watching the almond tree's petals slowly collect over her child's grave, she'd begged for a sign to affirm that ending her life was the right decision.

On that May morning, as she stood before the tree to sing one last song, she realized that on the flowerless branches small green pods were growing together in groups of four or five, fuzzy velvet green fruit containing the hard-cased almond seeds within. She reached to touch these unprecedented additions to the tree, understanding from everything she'd learned that without the tree's pollination the fruit she held in her fingers should never have existed. Was it a miracle? Or a process she simply didn't understand, as much as she didn't understand the processes of her own life?

But it really didn't matter if she knew the answer to this beautiful mystery.

In that moment, she understood that a miracle could also happen inside of her, a great and wonderful transformation, if such a miracle had come to a lonely, solitary tree that shouldn't have born fruit.

A GLITCH IN TIME
Doris Wright

Irene turned the corner onto her street, glad the walk home from the bodega was almost at an end. The grocery bags were heavier than usual today since she had treated herself to an extra large can of Dinty Moore beef stew. She shifted the bags from both arms to one, and with her freed hand searched for her keys amid the linty tissues in her pocket. As she approached her building, she noticed people—ones she didn't recognize as tenants—standing on the sidewalk in front of it. They were whispering and pointing at the building. And then they looked at her, and continued to stare as she approached, which made no sense at all. Irene knew from long experience there was nothing about her that merited attention. Most of the time, she might as well have been invisible. It wasn't unusual for people she had met before to introduce themselves to her, as if this was a first encounter. She maneuvered her way through the crowd and climbed the stairs to the entrance.

By the time she got to the top step, breathing heavily, she saw that the entrance door had been propped open. This was both strange and annoying to Irene. Tenants were reminded regularly that this was something they must not do under any circumstance. She always took her time, making sure the door swung solidly shut behind her, but some people were not that careful. It was sinful how careless they were. She would never dream of propping it open, not for a minute. Anything could happen in a minute, as she well knew from reading the Metro section in the paper every day. The city was just not safe anymore.

People were milling about in the lobby—this time they *were* tenants, whispering and looking worried. She speculated that the social security checks might be late again this month. She herself was not on social security—she was only 58, after all—so it was really not her concern. If her mother was still alive it would have been, but three months ago she had died. Irene had moved into her mother's apartment months earlier to take care of her during her illness. Finally she died. Her time had come. The trouble had been one of those bad types of cancer. Irene had trouble remembering the name. So complicated those things were. Why couldn't they give diseases nice, simple names, she wondered.

She decided to wait until later to check for her mail. It would be too difficult to deal with the locked mailbox since her arms were burdened with groceries. She pushed through the crowd, but before she could make her way to the elevator, Millie made a beeline for her. Irene considered Millie a busybody who suffered from some sort of compulsive talking disorder, leaning in too close when she spoke and spraying spittle as she did so. Millie had frequently stopped Irene to ask how her mother was doing, but in truth, Irene thought, she did so just to have news to spread through the building. When Irene's mother died, this woman, who had been oh-so-concerned, had not bothered to attend the calling hours at the funeral parlor just a block away.

"Now they're questioning everybody. They're starting at the top," Millie stage-whispered to her.

"Some sort of survey?" Irene responded, taking a precautionary step back. She always took the time to demonstrate interest, for she believed in good manners, though in truth she rarely had any interest in the goings-on of these drab, commonplace people. But regardless of how much of a hurry she was in, it was her practice to take the time to be polite.

"Oh, my gosh, no! Didn't you hear? It's the most terrible thing. Mr. Catswold is dead! Poor man. Murdered, most likely. They think it happened last night. You didn't hear anything, did you? Mr. Catswold's place is right above yours—3B and you're 2B, right? The policeman said we should be in our apartments when they come to question us."

Irene laughed. She had a tendency to laugh reflexively in extreme situations, an embarrassing affliction. Millie, though, took it to mean Irene thought she was joking.

"No, no. Really. He was murdered. You can ask any of the others. There's Mrs. Worthy. She'll tell you."

Irene shook her head, thanked Millie for the news, and continued on her way to the elevator. When she arrived at her apartment door, she made sure before she entered that it had been twice locked. Once inside, she double-locked it behind her. She was a little skittish entering, but decided that was foolishness. She was always careful to lock at least two of the three locks before she left, and her mother had paid a small fortune to have that dimwitted janitor install iron bars over the windows. And no one had any reason to be killing her. She had little money, made no costly purchases, or allowed fancy displays. Most importantly, she never did anything wrong.

Now Catswold was a different story. He was a rude man. Just plain rude. Not in the least little bit a gentleman. He would let the outer door swing shut even when she was just a few steps behind him, struggling with her arms full of packages. He had to have recognized her as a tenant by now. How much more effort would it have cost for him to hold the door for her? Like a minute of his time would cost him a fortune. Why, time didn't cost anything at all! And when she passed him now and then, he never responded when she said "Good Morning" or "Good Afternoon." Never nodded. Not even the slightest dip of his chin. What would that have cost? No, he wouldn't have a bit of it. He was a rude, rude man. Just like her ex-husband, she thought. Rude and selfish, through-and-through. Irene decided on the spot that the murderer was someone he was involved with intimately, some woman who couldn't stand even one more minute of his rudeness and selfishness. It was those domestic things that were the problem in most homicides; the kinds of things that a decent person didn't have to be concerned with. It's not like those lowlifes would be coming after you, not when you don't even know them, and you took care to mind your own business. When you didn't make it a practice to get involved with unstable people. Drinkers and suchlike. Catswold, she figured, had gotten his due.

After she put away the groceries, folded the brown paper bags, and put them in the side slot of the broom closet where they belonged, Irene looked around the apartment, making sure it was tidy for her expected visitors, the police officers. She smiled with satisfaction. It was always tidy. She never made any messes to begin with. She always put things away just as soon as she was finished using them. Every morning, after she had her breakfast, like clockwork, before she took her shower and got ready for her shopping trip, she dusted and vacuumed the apartment. It was small. Just big enough for one, really. Perfect for her.

When she was taking care of her mother, her mother had the bedroom, of course. Irene slept on the pullout couch with its metal rod down the middle that took after her with a vengeance. It was the right thing to do, to be there to take care of her mother, even though her brothers would have nothing to do with it. They thought it was enough to call once a week, or send a greeting card, or send flowers on Mother's Day. Now, how in heaven's name did those things help? How did they compare in any way to what she had done? Given up her job, her life, her acquaintances, and her routine, to come and be by her mother's side. Make all the arrangements for doctors' appointments, chemo treatments, traveling back and forth to radiation. It was a full-time job just managing it all. She arranged for aides to come in to bathe her mother, dress her, and change her Depends. She expected that some people might say that she herself should have been doing those things. It made her blood boil to think how vicious people were, if that's what they thought. Just dealing with aides alone took the patience of a saint. Late half the time, wanting to leave early on some flimsy excuse, and sometimes not bothering to show up at all. Well, it should have been clear she couldn't do those things. After all, she had a bad back, didn't she, and, besides, wasn't she doing enough? Wasn't she doing more than her brothers, more than the average person would do? It had been like that all her life, always doing the right thing when everyone else just looked the other way.

Satisfied that the apartment was tidy, she thought she should put on water for tea. That's what people seemed to do on her crime show when the police officers came to question them. That showed that you didn't have anything to hide, that you didn't mind being questioned and that you appreciated the hard work the police had to do. Sometimes on TV the people they were questioning just kept walking so the officers had to walk fast to keep up with them. Or they just kept doing what they were doing before, washing dishes or cooking dinner, as if they weren't the least bit fazed by being questioned by police. She, herself, would not be disturbed, as she didn't have anything to hide. But she believed it was proper manners to give people your full attention.

She got out her mother's tea service. The pretty roses on it had faded and the silver trim had worn off in places. Such a shame, that was. The nurse aides, not knowing any better—ignorant, low-class women, really—had probably put it though the dish-washer. Maybe she would get a new set some day.

After her mother died, she had decided to treat herself a little to some nice things. Do nice things for herself. She had always taken care of others, waiting for her time to come. Thinking the people she had done so much for would hold her in high regard and finally . . . *finally* . . . realize how much she had done for them. They would appreciate her and start doing things for her for a change. But it hadn't happened. Not with her husband (of course), nor with her children, certainly not her brothers, her co-workers. Not a bit. They were all just plain selfish. They always relied on her, never once thinking, "Oh, Irene, honey, you have spent your entire life doing for others, now you just sit back and rest. Let us take care of things. What can we do for you?" You'd think it would occur to her brothers to give her their share of her mother's small estate, seeing as they did nothing but send greet-ing cards when their sister was giving her life's blood to take care of their mother. And shouldn't it have occurred to her own moth-er to have changed her will, leaving it all to Irene, who was there every day, listening to her moaning and complaining? No, things didn't happen that way.

Just look at her children. She'd raised them single-handedly. Even while her husband was still around, he might as well not have been, because what had he done, in terms of earning money, or fixing things around the house, or helping them with their homework? Nothing, that's what! Nothing except hug them, play with them. "Oh, Daddy's so great. *He* loves us." Well, what are hugs and games when the electricity is about to be turned off and she had to go borrowing money, humiliating herself over and over, to just keep a roof over their heads? I would call *that* love, thought Irene; not tossing a ball back and forth. And when he ran off with that ugly-as-a-mud-fence woman, you'd think, then, finally, they'd see what a ne'er-do-well he was. But, no. That didn't happen. One of them told her he could understand why he'd left! So, so cruel! How could a child, a child you'd done everything for, be so unkind?

Well, no use now waiting for anyone to bring her justice, the fairness she had been hoping for. She was going to stop taking care of others and start doing for herself. It was time. She was taking charge of her life from here on out. It was just the right time.

Irene looked at her watch. It had been nearly an hour. What was taking them so long? She wondered if they had found a suspect in one of the other apartments and wrapped up the case. She didn't know whether to start watching her show or not. It was coming on in five minutes. She watched it every day. Thanks to re-runs she could watch it twice a day. It was on at noon, when she normally ate her lunch. It was on again at seven, when she ate her supper on a little TV tray she set up in front of the couch. It was on again at 11 p.m., but she rarely stayed up that late. Once in a while, if she was feeling a little restless, just not sleepy enough, she would watch the 11 o'clock show, even though it repeated the episode that was on at noon. It didn't matter. She had seen them all anyway. The "all new" episodes were on Wednesday nights at 10:00 p.m. She watched those, too, though she didn't think they were nearly as good as the old ones. The new ones—they said they were "ripped from the headlines"—seemed slapped together. Those new writers must be lazy, she thought, taking something that happened in real life, tweaking it a bit, and calling it a show, when real life was never as interesting as made-up life.

She liked the very oldest ones best. Her particular favorites were those that had that one district attorney. He had been brilliant. Took his work very seriously. The new fellow they had now, he acted just plain foolish sometimes; always posturing, making faces. She liked honest, straightforward people. And the head district attorney—oh my, that man was plain wonderful, she thought. If only they could bring them back. Men of principal, they were. Some were better than others, but there wasn't a lazy one in the bunch.

She looked around the little apartment. The afternoon sun was streaming in through the curtains, and it felt cozy. But she had plans to spruce it up some. Her mother had let it get dowdy and run down and—ugh—that old people's smell! Add to that the odor of soiled diapers and antiseptic that took her weeks of airing out and scrubbing to get rid of.

But now that she had the small inheritance her mother left her, she was going to fix it up. Get new curtains, have it painted, for sure. Maybe get a rug, perhaps even a record player. She could afford to stay here because it was rent control. She knew that some people would say she should notify the rent control people that her mother had died. But it didn't seem that way to her. She was entitled to a break now. For taking care of her mother all those months. For taking care of everyone all her life. Though her pension was small, she could afford this apartment and still get some things for herself. *Do* some things for herself. Like taking a trip. She had always wanted to travel, and now she could. Oh, nothing extravagant, really. But she figured she could afford to join one of those tour groups and go to Ireland or the Grand Canyon. She pictured herself with a group of laughing, bright people, on a boat maybe, all enjoying themselves, with her right in the middle of the fun. They seemed to really like her.

She heard voices in the hall and went to the peephole for a look. They were just going into Mrs. Ferguson's apartment, so she would be next. Everything was set. She had put a paper doily on a plate and put some Oreos on it. She knew officers weren't allowed to drink alcoholic beverages on the job, but she didn't think there was a rule against a snack.

Then it occurred to her to think about what, if anything, she knew about the crime. She should have thought of that sooner. She had assumed she didn't know anything about it, but—like she had observed on the TV—sometimes you thought you didn't know a thing, when you really did. It would come out when they asked the right question.

And what question would that be? She was home last night, as she always was except for bingo nights down in the community room. She had watched television until...let's see, did she watch the late episode or not? No. She hadn't. She'd turned it off after the news. Which news, they might ask. Why, the channel 10 news with that handsome, gray-haired anchor, same as always. Then she had turned off the TV, checked the locks, pulled down the shades, did her nightly toilet, and gotten into bed to read. She fell asleep reading. She woke up during the night and looked at the clock. It was 1:20 a.m. Had something awakened her? Perhaps. Now wait a minute! This could be significant. Had she heard anything unusual from upstairs? No, she rarely did. Catswold must have had really thick rugs in his apartment. Fortunately, he never bothered her. If he had, she would have reported him to the Super. She liked her peace. She herself was quiet as a mouse.

At last there was a knock on the door. She checked the peephole to be sure. Yes, it was them. She was pleased that they were the "suits" — the detectives — and not uniformed patrolmen. She asked them to hold up their ID's, as proper police procedure dictated. Their badges looked fine to her.

"Come on in, detectives. I've been waiting for you."

"Oh? Why?"

"Well, I heard you were conducting interviews throughout the building."

"Who told you that?" the older one asked. He reminded her a little of the older detective on her show, but he seemed more brusque. Her show's detective could be a bit sarcastic, but was always gentlemanly to innocent people, especially women.

"Why, a lady in the building. Millie something or other. She lives in 4E, I think. 4E or 6E. I'm not sure."

The older office made a note of it. The younger detective was looking around the apartment, at her mother's wedding picture hanging on the wall, and then at other framed pictures on the mantle over the fake fireplace.

"Could I offer you gentleman some refreshments? I've made a pot of tea, and I have some cookies. How does that sound?"

"No, thanks, Ma'am," the young one said. "We just ate."

Irene was disappointed. "Well, how could that be? You've been here for hours. You must have missed lunch."

"You're Maria Dispensenza?" the older detective asked.

"No, that was my mother. She died recently. Cancer. I forget what kind. I'm her daughter, Irene."

"You live here?"

"Yes. You see, when Mother died, it took time to make the arrangements, and then there was all the paperwork. Finally, I did some long hard thinking. Should I go back to Omaha, or...."

The younger one cut her off. "Were you home last night?"

"Why, yes."

She wanted to tell them the rest of it: what time she had gone to bed and how she had awakened at 1:20 a.m.

But the older one got up and said, "That's all we need for now, Ma'am. We'll be in touch if we have further questions. Here's our card in case you think of anything significant." And they left.

Irene was disappointed. She studied the card while she idly nibbled a cookie and thought about the interview. The card was printed in elegant italics. Detective Maury Klimko. Scribbled in pencil on the bottom was "Daniel Lyon." Klimko must be the older one; Maury was an old-fashioned sounding name. Suddenly she realized that her show wasn't over yet. She could still catch the last half. She poured herself some tea and got comfortable on the couch. She turned on the TV and instantly recognized the episode. It was an especially good one.

The next morning Irene was almost ready to go out and do her daily shopping. If she shopped only once a week, she would have to call a cab to get home with all the bags. She could have the store deliver, but the fee was outrageous and she didn't like having a stranger come into the apartment. What did she know about the delivery boy anyway? What did the store know? She doubted they bothered with background checks.

She had just put on her everyday tweed coat and picked up her pocketbook when the doorbell rang. She looked through the peephole and saw it was the detectives. She brightened, thinking they might now conduct a satisfactory interview. When they came in, the older one sat down again, but the younger one went over and stood by the window, looking out onto the fire escape. She noticed that he looked a lot like that cynical hothead on her show, though not quite as handsome.

"Did you install these bars?" he asked.

"Mother had them installed. For security reasons, of course."

He took the bars in his hand and tried to shake them. "They're pretty secure, alright. What if you needed to get out?"

Irene laughed. "Why then I'd go out the door."

Both men looked at her now.

"What if there was a fire in the hallway?" the younger one asked.

"I don't know. I never thought about it. What's this got to do with...?"

"Thanks, Ma'am. That's all we need for now." And they left.

Irene stood by the door for a full minute, trying to figure it out.

"What in the world?" she thought. "What kind of cockamamie interview was that?" She could conduct a better interview herself.

The following day Irene had just settled down to eat her lunch in front of the TV. The same lunch she had every day, peanut butter and red-raspberry preserves on whole wheat bread with a glass of milk. She had never liked peanut butter as a child, but now she couldn't get enough of it. Her mother used to shake her head every time she saw Irene having peanut butter for lunch.

"You're backwards," she told Irene. "What kind of lunch is that for a grown woman? You do everything backwards. You're going backwards through time. Pretty soon you'll be wanting a baby bottle."

And then she laughed that loud, offensive laugh of hers that always set her off into a coughing fit. Irene ignored her. After all, her mother was old and was expected to die at any time, and Irene wouldn't have to endure her ridicule much longer.

Irene hadn't taken the first bite of her sandwich when there was a knock at the door. It was the older detective. He was alone. She was not happy. She had learned not to expect much from their bumbling interviews.

"Sorry to disturb you, Ma'am. There's something we forgot to ask you."

"Yes, go ahead. As you can see I was just about to eat my lunch."

"Have you seen anyone around who has red, curly hair?"

"I suppose you mean a woman?"

"Yes, of course, a woman."

"No, can't say that I have. Is she a suspect?"

"Sorry, Ma'am. You know we can't answer questions like that."

She did know. She felt she was pretty much an expert in these matters. But how did he know what she knew?

"Well, that'll be all. Sorry to disturb your lunch. Peanut butter?"

"Yes, why do you ask?"

"No reason. Thanks for your help."

After he left, she ate her lunch, though she no longer relished it. Her show had gone to commercial, the bread was slightly stale, and the milk no longer crisp-cold like she liked it. She tried to shake the memory of his questions, but they kept coming back. Who was the woman with red hair? Did peanut butter have anything to do with the case?

And so it continued. The officers, one, or the other, or both, stopped by each day. Each day they had a new, seemingly ridiculous question. On Sunday, she had just been leaving to go to church. Sunday, for God's sake! You'd think they could take a day off, leave her in peace. They had asked if she owned a purple dress. Now, did she look like a woman who would wear a purple dress? She hated garish colors, sticking always to browns, and grey, and occasionally a navy or a deep burgundy, but nothing that you would call flashy. People laughed when she told them her favorite color was beige. Why? It was such a beautiful, subtle color.

Then yesterday, she had just laid down for an afternoon nap. She didn't usually take a nap, but she hadn't been sleeping well lately. For some reason, she found herself waking every night at 1:20 a.m. Then she couldn't get back to sleep, wondering why she had awakened. Why 1:20?

She answered the door in her robe, something she wouldn't normally do, but she was fed up with these interruptions. It was the younger one. He looked at her hair and seemed to be stifling a laugh. She patted it down, guessing it was ruffled up from lying down.

"Yes, what is it?" she asked, sounding, she knew, somewhat discourteous.

He asked her if she'd heard anything the night of the murder. Finally. You'd suppose that he would have asked her that right off the bat.

"No. Not that I know of. But I did awaken that night, and I looked at the clock, and it was 1:20 a.m. I'm not sure what woke me up. Is that significant?"

"One-twenty you say?" And he wrote that down in his notebook.

"Yes. 1:20 a.m. Is that when he was murdered? Surely you must have the M.E.'s report by now. At least a preliminary TOD?" She waited, thinking he would be impressed by her knowledge of police lingo, even compliment her.

"I'm afraid we can't reveal anything like that. You know that, but you persist in asking us questions."

"Well, I didn't mean anything by it. I'm just getting so tired... so frustrated... every day, day in and day out. Just how long is thing going to go on?"

"As long as it needs to. We're just doing our job."

"I'm surprised my neighbors aren't raising a stink about it. They're real complainers. I'm surprised they haven't called the mayor's office."

"Why should they?"

"Well, I just assumed that if you're questioning them like you're questioning me..." But she stopped in mid-sentence. She realized by the look on his face that they weren't questioning her neighbors. Just her! She felt like cold water was running through her body, trickling down her legs. What was this? What was going on?

"Do I... do I need a lawyer?" she asked. She had heard suspects ask that question time and again, and she had always thought, "Well of course you need to get a lawyer. Lawyer-up, you dummy!"

"Do you think you need a lawyer?" the detective answered. But he was staring at the iron bars on the windows. She stood frozen, not knowing what to say. Finally, he left, without even saying, "Good day, Ma'am."

Irene stayed in the rest of the day and never changed from her robe to her day clothes. She didn't vacuum. She wanted to be sure she would hear a knock at the door. If the police returned, what would they think if she didn't answer? They might even break in, and she would probably have to pay to repair the damage. Who was responsible for such damages was never made clear on her show. She didn't go grocery shopping or even cook the supper she had planned. Instead, she had a bowl of cereal with chocolate milk. Lately she'd had a craving for chocolate milk and on her last trip to the grocery she had bought some. She imagined the checkout woman thought she had a grandchild visiting. She had no grandchildren. "Why should children have all the fun?" she asked herself, justifying the purchase in her mind.

She pulled over the TV tray and turned on the 7:00 p.m. show, paying strict attention, hoping it would help her understand what was going on. It was one of her favorites, the episode where the limousine driver killed the coke-addicted model he was in love with. At first, everyone thought he'd killed her because she gave him the brush off. But everyone was wrong. It wasn't the right motive at all. It was a touching story, but it didn't seem to give her any insight into her own situation. She got up to wash out her cereal bowl. She was still a little hungry and thought about making popcorn.

As she stood over the sink, finishing the cleanup, it hit her. *Motive.* Of course! Everything hinges on motive. What possible motive would she have to kill Mr. Catswold? None! None at all. People just didn't go around killing other people without a motive, unless they were on drugs or were drunks like her ex-husband, or were crazy. She certainly wasn't crazy. They could test her if they liked. It would show them she was perfectly sane. And she never did drugs (only her blood-pressure medication). She had maybe four glasses of sherry a year, on special occasions only.

So that was that. She was in the clear. She had absolutely no motive. Sure, Catswold was rude, but that was no reason to kill the man, not if you weren't married to him. On TV she'd seen her share of perfectly good cases with lots of evidence get stalled because they had no motive. And there couldn't be any corroborating evidence in her case; she had never even been in the man's apartment. No fingerprints. Nothing.

Irene felt much better. She felt she could sleep now. A day of worrying had tired her out. She'd never showered that day and it felt kind of funny to go to bed without having showered. She was nothing if she wasn't clean. But she could just as well do it in the morning. Tomorrow would be a new day. She could start all over new, and get back on track.

The next morning she returned to being more like herself. Eating her usual breakfast, reading the morning paper, straightening up, vacuuming, dusting, and then taking her shower. Feeling so much better, with freshly shampooed hair and a bright clean apartment, she put one of her better everyday dresses and made out a grocery list. Irene wondered if she should wait to see if they would come again. She didn't want it to look like she was avoiding them. But no...no, she should resume her normal routine. They hadn't told her she couldn't leave the apartment or anything like that. They could leave a note if they stopped by. What had she to do with them anyway? Let them go about their business and she would go about hers.

When she returned from shopping, there was no note. Maybe they'll come later, Irene thought. And, so what if they didn't? She wouldn't trouble herself to care. But nagging thoughts kept coming back. When will they come? What are they thinking? Am I in the clear?

By the end of the day, she had a headache and felt, once again, that she didn't have it in her to cook. She closed the blinds to keep out the afternoon sun, and lay on the couch without even changing out of her dress. When she awoke it was dark. They had never come. What did that mean? Was it over, finally? She thought about eating something, or watching TV, or getting ready for bed. It all seemed too much for her. She got off the couch, turned out the lights, and went to bed, once again sleeping in her clothes.

The next morning she awoke and her headache was worse. She made coffee and a piece of toast, but did not bother getting the newspaper, thinking it would hurt her head to read. She took two aspirin and thought she would wait until her headache subsided to start getting into her routine. While she had such good intentions of doing that yesterday, something happened. The day had fallen apart. She had lost control of it. Well, she wouldn't let it happen again today. As soon as her headache went away, she would start over.

But it persisted even though she took more aspirin and drank more strong coffee. It was bingo night but she didn't feel up to going downstairs. She didn't even feel like watching TV.

She couldn't go on like this, she thought. Tomorrow she would take positive steps. She just needed to know what was going on and then she could get on with her regular life, which she now recalled with some nostalgia.

She awoke late the following morning, having forgotten to set the alarm. She recalled disturbing dreams but couldn't figure out what they could mean. In one she had shrunk, still a grown-up person, but only knee high. She went down to play bingo, but found she wasn't tall enough to climb up onto a chair. No one offered to help, but she finally managed to crawl up herself, and found that the bingo caller was Mr. Catswold. He kept repeating 3B, 3B, 3B over and over. It was a relief to be awake with daylight streaming in.

As she had resolved to take control today, Irene decided the best way to do that was to call the precinct and find out what was going on. Despite her fear of what they might say, it was better to get on with her life. She felt better just thinking of it. She couldn't recall where she had put their business card, so she looked up the police department number in the phone book and asked to be transferred to Detective Maury Klimko. She was put on hold. Finally the receptionist returned and asked what precinct Mary Klimko worked in.

"It's not Mary," Irene said, testily. "It's Maury." And she spelled out his name, both first and last. The woman told her that no such person was listed with the police department.

"That's ridiculous," Irene laughed. "Well then, give me his partner, Daniel Lyon." Again she was put on hold, and again was told there was no such person there."

Irene was stunned. "Try the regular policemen, not just the detectives."

"I did, Ma'am. There are no such people here. Are you sure you have the right city?"

Irene gave the woman her address, and the woman confirmed she was calling the right place for crimes in that area. Irene was exasperated. Near tears. What was going on? She wished she was one to swear, but she wasn't.

"Please," she begged. "I need to find out the status of a murder in my building. I need to know. It's a matter of life..." Her voice trailed off.

She was transferred to the desk sergeant who, she was told, would have access to information on all the crimes, but he said there was no listing for a murdered person named Catswold. She spelled it different ways in case they had listed it wrong—they were not very bright, after all. She asked him to check by the address. Still nothing, he said.

Irene began crying. She couldn't remember when she had last cried. Not when her mother died. Even as a child she had been one of those children who just didn't cry. The sergeant asked her if she had someone she could talk to.

"About what?" she asked.

"About your problems, lady. You seem really mixed up."

"I am not!" she yelled into the phone. "I am not mixed up at all. But I know your kind. You, sir, are just plain rude," she said and hung up.

Irene stared at the bars on the window. What was going on? Then it occurred to her to look for the detective's business card. For a good hour, she searched her apartment, looking for the card, not caring where she threw things. But she couldn't find it. She had just been too neat. She must have thrown it out.

What was going on?

Of course! She could ask her neighbors. The detectives had visited Mrs. Ferguson across the hall just before coming to her apartment that first time. She rushed out, forgetting she was still in her robe, and knocked on Mrs. Ferguson's door. Mrs. Ferguson opened the door a crack, leaving the chain latch on. You'd think the old bat would see she was harmless and open the door, Irene thought. But Mrs. Ferguson acted like she didn't know what Irene was talking about. Like she couldn't remember any of it. Not the detectives, not even the murder. Irene kept trying to make her remember, but the woman just shook her head, and closed the door. Irene stood there, puzzled, wondering what to do next. It occurred to her that Mrs. Ferguson must have that Alzheimer's condition. Half the tenants in the building seemed to have a touch of it.

Irene ran down the stairwell, not waiting for the elevator. There was almost always someone down in the lobby. She saw Millie. Oh thank God, Irene thought. Millie would know. She was the one who first told her about the murder. And she wouldn't forget. She collected rumors, even telling Irene old gossip that was two, three years old. But to her amazement, Millie, too, acted like she didn't know what she was talking about. The other women standing around, overhearing their conversation, looked at Irene strangely. One of them said, "You should know better than to be down in the lobby in your bathrobe. It's against the rules."

Irene looked down and realized that she was not properly dressed. She ran back to the stairwell and started making her way up slowly, because stairs always winded her. When she was almost to the second floor, she heard someone enter the stairwell from the floor above, whistling a cheerful tune and hurrying down. She had just started to open the stairwell door to her floor, when she looked around at the person who was rushing past her. It was Catswold!

Irene screamed, but he just gave her a strange look, shook his head, and kept running down the stairs, still whistling.

Irene rushed into her apartment and locked all three locks. She sat at the kitchen table, trying to catch her breath. What was going on?

"I can't be...*crazy*," she said aloud. "I just can't be. I refuse to be." For it was her turn now. It was her turn to enjoy herself, treat herself well, and have a little fun. And how much fun could a crazy person have? She was supposed to start over. But everything was all mixed up. Turned around.

She sat at the table for what seemed like hours, trying to sort things out, make sense of it all. But there was no sense to be made. Only that one thought kept coming back to her: everything was all mixed up; turned around. She could see that plainly. Everything was out of order.

She recalled her mother saying she was going backwards. Liking peanut butter now when she hadn't as a child. Chocolate milk, too. Looked at it that way, things began falling into place. The detectives had investigated the murder *before* it happened. Backwards, again! It was like time was all mixed up. There had been some sort of glitch in time and she was somehow caught up in it. She had been trying to fix things—trying to go ahead with her life. Now she saw that was not the way to fix things. You had to go backwards to go forward! That only made sense. The signs had been there all along, and now she could finally see it. It was up to her to fix it. Like always, she had to step up and take responsibility. Who else would, when they didn't really understand what was going on? No, it clearly fell on her.

She sat for another hour thinking how best to straighten things out, until that, too, became clear. There was no use waiting now.

She began her preparations. First she straightened the apartment. Wrote out her grocery list. Took a long shower. Then she looked for the box of her mother's things that she had planned to give to the church rummage sale next month. In it she found her mother's purple dress and the curly red-haired wig her mother had insisted on ordering when she was going through chemo. Irene had tried to sway her mother to get a lovely, dignified, silver-haired wig, but her mother, always one who liked attention, settled on the red wig. She had wanted to be buried in them, the red wig and the purple dress. Irene had promised her mother she would abide by her wishes, though she'd had no intention of doing so, and didn't take them to the funeral home. She didn't want her mother to be as ridiculous in death as she had been in life. If people laughed at her mother, they would surely be laughing at her as well.

At 11:00 p.m., Irene fixed herself a peanut butter and jelly sandwich, eating it while watching her show. She had a few more things to do. She turned off the lights in her apartment. There would be enough light from the moon and the street lamp to work by. She took a screwdriver and removed the iron bars from the window by the fire escape. Thanks to her lazy husband, she had of necessity learned to be handy. When she finished, she turned the lights back on. Then she pulled out her father's gun from its locked box on the closet shelf. He had bought it for protection when the neighborhood started going downhill, and her mother had just put it away after he died. There was even a package of bullets in the box. Irene had seen enough on TV to know how to load it. It was easy. Then she put on her mother's purple dress, a bit of a squeeze. Irene looked in the mirror and shuddered. How anyone could wear purple she didn't know. Then she pulled on the wig and looked at herself again, this time getting a good laugh. She got out the white gloves that her mother wore to church. Irene hardly recognized herself. Chuckling, she practiced different poses in the mirror.

Once again she turned off the lights. At 1:15 a.m., she went out the window onto the fire escape; as always, quiet as a mouse. It was a hot night and Catswold's window was wide open. That was really not a safe thing to be doing. In addition to being rude, the man was just not very bright. He was sleeping on his bed in his boxer shorts. An open book lay across his belly. He had fallen asleep reading, like she sometimes did. She smiled. She had not realized they had anything in common. She stood watching him until his alarm clock read 1:20 a.m. And then she picked up the extra pillow, and in one sure movement put it over his head and shot him through it. The head, she had decided, would be much more effective than the heart. Then she went out the window, back down the fire escape, and into her apartment.

Before turning the lights back on, she put the bars back on the window, securing them tightly in place. She put the white gloves and the red wig and the awful purple dress in a brown paper bag. She would dispose of them when she went grocery shopping tomorrow. Some dumpster out of the neighborhood should do the trick. She picked up the gun with a paper towel, wrapped it in another paper towel and put it and the box of bullets in her purse. She knew a nice spot in the park where a little bridge crossed the lake, and she could drop it in there, sight unseen.

She washed the dishes from her late-night snack and went to bed, feeling much better about everything. Now, time would be on track again and she could go forward. Go on with her life. Tomorrow she would book that tour she wanted to take. No use waiting. She lay in the dark considering Ireland and Italy, and decided on Italy for sure.

She pictured her attractive and well-dressed tour-group friends, all of them in the back of a large gondola, their arms around her. They were so enjoying her company; there was much laughter and sharing of stories. Perhaps the gondola would stop soon and they would get out and go into a well-lit restaurant—she gazed admiringly at the crystal chandeliers—where they would eat and drink and the merriment would continue. She was wearing a light gray silk dress, subtly revealing just a hint of cleavage but fluidly skimming over her other bulges. A white shawl—no, cream-colored would be more elegant—was gently draped over her shoulders. Oh, but she loved imagining like this! It brought her such peace, such contentment. It always had. So much nicer than her ordinary, boring life. She imagined various scenarios until she fell asleep, falling ever deeper, moving in perfect rhythm with time, forward, forward, surrendering, yielding, toward her own proper destiny.

WE LIVE HERE

Jarrett Kaufman

1.

The barefoot girl is tossing rocks into the shallow creek when she hears a car approach on the dirt road. She looks above at the beam bridge. She sees the janky gold car pass by and she catches a glimpse of an old man with a nest of silver hair hunched behind the steering wheel. The car kicks up dust that hovers like a brown cloud over the creek. The girl lingers at the bank and looks down at her mangled foot and she looks at the meaty stubs. She stopped wearing shoes after the operation because they hurt her bad foot. She knows her parents hate that foot. The girl is certain the gray scars remind them of the accident. She can see that shame in their eyes.

It happened at a Motel 6 a year ago near St. Louis during a snowstorm. The girl's mother woke her. She was shaking her. The girl could hear her father yell. She saw him and a masked-man grapple over a gun at the door. The mother took the girl from her bed and she pushed her out the window. There wasn't time for her to grab a coat or her boots. The mother told the girl to run. "Run," she yelled, and the girl sprinted barefoot in the icy snow. She scurried through the frigid night air and the whirling wet snow and she went to a Dairy Queen across the street. It was closed and the girl panicked. She banged on the windows. Then the girl heard the gunshot. So she ran. She ran down the street and wept and she found a dumpster in an alley behind an abandoned K-Mart and hid in it. She buried herself in the soggy trash and in the brown snow.

They found her 2 hours later. "Here," the police officer said. "Over here," he yelled.

EMTs pulled the girl out of the dumpster. They carried her to the ambulance.

"I want to go home," the girl stuttered. Her face was blue. "Can I go home?'

The girl lay bunched in covers on a stretcher in the cabin. "Home," an EMT said.

* * *

The old man parks. He sits in his Chevrolet Caprice and he watches the girl leave the creek. The hot August wind gusts and it rolls over the dirt road and the girl's brown hair moves over her shoulders like breakers in the ocean. "That's it," the old man says. "This way."

He coughs. The old man fumbles a bottle of methadone out of his shirt pocket and he chews down a tablet. He grabs the 7up from the center cup holder. He takes a gulp of the soda to wash down the chalky medication. Then he flips down the visor mirror. He wipes the sweat off his yellow skin. The jaundice has gotten worse. The old man gazes at the dark scar on his face. Parker did that. He marked him after he'd went 10K in the hole in one night of bad blackjack.

The old man rolls the car window down. He takes out his wallet and sits there and he waits for the girl. The old man breathes in the humid air. He exhales with a moan. He is tired. He is sick. He told Parker that but there was no use. He owed Parker. This was all that mattered.

The old man wags a dollar bill at the girl. "Do you want it?" he asks. "Little girl."

She shrugs. The girl considers the old man. She ponders his scar. "Yes."

"Here," the old man says. He holds out the dollar. He holds it there.

When the old man opens the car door, the girl springs off the dirt road then bolts into the cow pasture. The tang of wet dung clings to the dank country air. She cuts across the meadow. The girl keeps moving. She crosses the gully that's teemed with blackberry cane. She looks back at the creek and the gold car is gone. So the girl runs into the woods. She walks towards the rail fence and the ramshackle farmhouse that she and her parents have lived at for 2 months now.

The girl rushes to the wrecked porch but stalls at the backdoor because the kitchen window is cracked open and she can hear her mother yell at her father. The girl steps back. Her gut coils. The father shouldn't be home. He should be at work. The girl punches her fists into the front pockets of her khaki shorts and she strolls gloomily to the magnolia tree. She sits down in the grass next to the tree trunk. She stretches out her legs over the grass and over the leaves and the twigs that clutter the ground. The girl listens. She hears the parents. She can hear them argue.

2.

The father paces the kitchen floor. His hair is tussled. "Just listen to me," he says.

"I could hit you," the mother howls. She clutches a skillet in her hand.

"They're here. I saw a man in town. Why can't you believe that?"

"No," she pleads. "Parker doesn't know we're here. Why can't *you* believe that?"

The mother wanders to the sink. There's a load of dirty dishes and a pile of grimy pots stacked on the countertop. She tosses the skillet in the sink before she drifts to the breakfast table. She sits in the chair. Her hair is frizzled from the wet Midwestern heat. There's a rusted box fan positioned in the corner next to the living room. It pushes hot air over the linoleum floor. "No," she frets. It's impossible. She believes that. They stayed on the move for ten months.

"No," she says. "We disappeared." The mother pulls a Marlboro from her purse and lights it. She takes a drag. "You're wrong," she says. She blows smoke. She says, "You're always wrong."

The father looks for the daughter. He glances in the living room. "Sweetheart?" he calls.

"I let her go to the creek. I let her go," the mother says. "She's fine."

The father smirks. He sits in a chair next to the mother at the breakfast table. He gawks at the mess—the shriveled orange peels and the dirty plates and the soiled napkins. He fingers his head where the bullet grazed his scalp that night at the Motel 6. He looks at the mother. He knows he didn't see anyone in town. He knows she's right. He knows it's his fear and paranoia.

"You said it would be different here," the mother reminds him.

The father says, "I know what I said."

"Do you?" she says. She draws on her Marlboro.

"We can't pretend like nothing happened," he says.

"You're the only one pretending," she broods.

They say nothing for some time while the father fiddles with a dry orange peel.

"We can't go back," the mother says. She scratches her neck. "I won't go back."

He worked as a clerk for 3 years at Ten Pin Bowl in St. Louis. It was the hub of Parker's racket in Midtown where the gambling profits were laundered. The father learned that the dirty cash was stored in a chest freezer in the basement office. He and the mother planned for months and the father heisted the cash on a Tuesday

night like they'd decided when Parker had left to visit his ill
mother in Miami. He broke into the freezer with bolt cutters. He
grabbed the cash in an excited frenzy. He would never have to
feed his family Ramen for dinner again and he would never have
to buy his daughter a birthday gift at Goodwill again. The father
filled the duffle bag with 60 bricks of cash that totaled $300,000.
Then he sped home. Everything was in order. The mother had
packed their bags. She'd destroyed the credit cards and checks
and their cell phones in the oven. They drove to a Motel 6 across
the Mississippi River where the mother and the father celebrated.
They sipped on box wine and played with the cash on the floor
and their daughter lay on the pull-out bed and watched *Three
Stooges* on TV until she fell asleep.

The father drops the orange peel. Hey says, "If you think
frostbite is the worst—"

"Parker," the mother yells. "Parker Parker Parker." She
screams. She yells, "Stop."

The mother stares at the father in a pitiful gaze as she recalls
with a miserable clarity all the cities they've lived in this last
year—Indianapolis, Chicago, Milwaukee. After that, there was
Louisville and Kansas City and now there's Eldora in Iowa. She
looks at the father yank on the collar of his uniform. He's worked
at the Suzuki factory in town for three weeks now. She knows
the game. She understands his need to run. It's what he does.
He'll rush home. He'll say he saw someone. He'll say they've been
found and he'll demand they leave. But that was supposed to end
here. He vowed that'd stop. He even got on his knees at a Denny's
parking lot in Kentucky and he swore it. He kissed the mother
and he hugged the daughter. "I swear," he'd said.

The father watches the mother smoke. He says, "I hate that
you smoke. It's—"

"It's what?" she asks. She sparks the lighter twice.

"It's—" the father hesitates. "It's damned filthy that's what it is."

The mother takes a wicked drag. "Fuck you," she hisses.

3.

The old man drives the Chevy into the woods and parks the
car near a clearing in a knot of pine trees. He turns off the engine.
He opens the glovebox. The old man grabs the 38 Special and
he checks the safety lock. He tucks the revolver into his belt. He
opens the car door and he walks through the woods to the rickety
rail fence. The old man stares at the girl. She reminds him of his

daughter Tina. The girl looks just like her sitting crossed-legged like that underneath the magnolia tree in the glimmering sunlight. The old man rubs his eyes. He looks at the girl again.

"Hey," the old man says. He shades his eyes from the sun. "Little girl," he shouts.

The girl eyes him. She remembers now. She saw the old man at the hospital.

It was morning. The father and the mother took the girl from the hospital bed. They sat her in a cold wheelchair. The father said, "Ready?" and kissed her before he pushed her into the hallway. The girl knew that they'd have to leave because a police officer had questioned them the night before about the incident at the Motel 6. He'd sat on a chair and he scratched at a red mole on his chin while he scribbled in a notepad. Then a woman from Child Services took over.

The father and the mother rushed the girl to the exit near the cafeteria. They pushed the girl through the exit, but an orderly followed them outside. "Go," the father said and the mother rolled the girl to the Windstar. When the orderly reached for the father's arm, he lunged at him. He struck the man in the neck and the man buckled and he writhed on the icy concrete. The father bolted. He dove in the van and started the engine and he skidded out of the parking lot. The girl peered out the back window and she saw the old man. He stood in front of a red brick building. He was talking on a cell phone underneath an awning that said: PICKLE'S DELI.

The father passed the Arch on I-70. He said, "I had to do it. He was bad."

"How do you know that?" the girl asked.

"Sweetheart," the mother said. She grabbed the girl's nose. "They're all bad."

The old man dawdles in the quack grass. He stares at the girl. He says, "Hey."

The girl peels a chunk of bark off the tree trunk. She smells it.

"Hey," he says again. He grips the rail fence with both hands. "Little girl," he says.

The old man steps into a thicket of orange tiger lilies that sprout near the rail fence. His wife used to garden lilies at their house in Cleveland. "Tina," he says and recalls a day in 1979 when she was 9 years old. He and his wife were lounging on the patio. She drank Lipton's iced tea and thumbed a *Redbook* and he smoked a cigar and watched his daughter chase grasshoppers in the backyard. He called her. "Tina," he'd said. She ran to him and he tried to hold her in his arms but she twisted free. So he yanked her arm. He yelled, "Tina," but she raced to the mother.

"Let her be," the mother said and took the girl into the kitchen for a Popsicle.

"Fine," he said. He grabbed his cigar. "Jesus Pete," he said. He hollered, "Fine."

That night, he left when the mother and the daughter were asleep. There was a three-day $75,000 poker game at St. Louis. He packed his bag in the dark next to the window. He swiped the emergency cash that was stashed in the sock drawer. He walked 4 miles to the Greyhound station. He boarded the bus and sat in the back row. He sat alone and the bus departed and didn't know at that moment he'd never return to Cleveland or that he'd never see his daughter again. He gazed out the window and he watched the city buildings fade to a glow on the horizon. The glow shrank to a speck and the speck turned to nothing but the black of night and he felt joy.

The old man coughs again. The searing pain in his chest blots out the memory of Tina and he is grateful for that. He hacks and this time there's blood in his spit. The doctor said this would happen. He'd said, "Hemoptysis," at the last appointment in July. The old man wipes his mouth clean and chews another methadone tablet. Then he waves at the girl but she turns her head and looks away and the old man flares with rage. He looks at the farmhouse. He hears the mother's shouts echo out the kitchen window. He hears the father holler, too. The old man touches the handle of his .38 Special and he says the girl's name. "Valerie," the old man says.

4.

The father reaches for the mother and he touches her arm in a delicate way as if she is a fragile doll but the mother pitches her cigarette at him. Fiery ash explodes in the air. She huffs and she lights another Marlboro. "It will be a risk if we stay here," the father says as he struts to the refrigerator. He grabs a carton of 2% milk. The mother huffs again so the father slams the door closed and returns to the table. "What?" he says then takes a loud nasty slurp of the milk.

The mother sags in her chair. She punches out her cigarette in a piece of old burnt toast that lay on a frayed napkin. She looks at the husband searchingly. The mother has a basic need: she wants the father to feel safe so that he can make her feel safe. "It will be a risk if we *don't* stay here," she finally says and these are bitter and mad words. She grabs the bottom of her shirt. She knots the fabric and twists it in her hands. "I'm tired," the mother says. "I'm so tired."

She pulls at her collar and she digs her fingernails into the hives that color her neck. Her mother had suffered from them as well. She can remember how her mother's neck swelled like a turkey wattle when her father grabbed the scotch. He was a mean drunk who spent much of her childhood hungover in the city jails. Her mother liked to say he was cursed with Cherokee blood.

The mother scratches the welts and the father grabs her wrist and he pulls her clawed fingers off her neck. She gazes up at him. He'd suffered, too. She knows that. She can see the flicker of an old agony in his eyes. It's the same dark pain that she can find in his eyes when he was a boy when she used to study the St. Joseph's Foster Home Polaroids from his childhood.

"We can live a decent life. We just need to give ourselves that chance," she says.

"Please," the father says. A blue vein forks over his forehead.

The father unbuttons his work uniform, then doffs the nametag. The image of the cash they stole from Parker, piled in a heap underneath their bed, fogs his mind like a daydream. He's stood in a daze at the conveyor belt at work now everyday riddled with dread as he bolts support brackets to the metal bumpers. He's considered taking the money that's left back to Parker. He could drive back to St. Louis. He could dump the cash—all $197,541— onto Parker's desk. The father could drop to his knees and he could beg for mercy. He could tell Parker he'd do whatever it took to fix it. "Tell me," he'd say, kneeling on the cold floor. He'd say, "Just tell me."

The father takes a swig of milk. He says, "Do we deserve this chance?"

"Our daughter does," the mother says. "She's eleven years old. She's only eleven years old."

"Yes," he says. "I know that." He sneers.

"You're a good father," she says.

"I'm many things but that sure as hell isn't one of them."

"Don't say that. I mean it," the mother says.

"It's the truth," the father tells her.

She rubs her hand through his hair. She plays with his curls. "You're a good man," the mother says.

He sips the milk. He sets the carton down and says, "Yeah?"

"We're good people," she says.

"We're good people?" he says.

5.

"Little girl," the old man bellows. He coughs. He winces. He coughs again.

"What?" the girl says. She spots a leaf in the grass. She nabs it and breaks off the stem.

"Come here," the old man says. "Just come here." He says, "Come here."

The girl lowers her head and she fondles her brown hair. She stuffs a wad of it into her mouth and sucks on the strands. The girl's parents said it would be special at the farmhouse. They wouldn't move again. They wouldn't sleep in hotels anymore. They promised that. She only had to listen. Her father warned her to never leave the backyard and now she's ruined it. He'd just yelled at her a week ago when she had wandered off to the meadow after breakfast. She'd seen a doe. So she wanted to watch it eat the wet alfalfa near the bean fields. The father chased her down. He grabbed her arm. "You can't do that," he yelled. He shook her. "There are bad people out there who want to hurt you." He hugged her. He said it again. "Bad people."

The old man mills in the thistle. He says, "Come here," and the girl stands. She drags her feet through the dry grass. She rubs her bad foot into the ground. The patches of scar tissue that sock her foot feels nice buried in the warm grass like that. When she finishes, she lopes across the backyard. Her heart pounds—like it did that night in St. Louis—as she moves towards the old man. The girl stops at the rail fence. She looks back at the kitchen window and she looks over at the backdoor. Then she climbs the fence. She crawls down the other side. She leaps into the tall and bushy chickweed that hums with the chirps and the chatters of crickets and of katydids.

"My name's Valerie," the girl says. She moves closer. "My daddy calls me Pretty Girl."

"Well," the old man says. He says, "You are pretty." He says, "Yes you are."

The old man tromps across the wild grass and he urges the girl to follow him. He says, "Over here," as he enters the woods. "This way," he says. Sweat beads over his shaggy eyebrows. Gnats swarm his head in a blade of yellow sunlight that splinters through the branches of the tall oak trees. He turns to face the girl. She lulls at the edge of the woods. Her hands touch at the red wildflowers. The old man lowered himself to a knee. He coughs and spits in the weeds. "Come here," he says. When the girl backs way, the old man yelps, "No." He says, "Please."

The girl stops. She warily plods into the woods. She walks towards him.

"Sit," the old man says and points at his knee. "It's alright."

She sits on his lap. She doesn't say anything. The girl just stares at his dark scar.

"You can touch it. I can tell you want to touch it," the old man says.

He takes the girl's hand. He places her finger onto his face. The girl touches the scar and the old man shuts his eyes. She traces the scar tissue down the side of his face. The old man pretends that the girl's finger is Tina's finger and his face and his skin begins to tingle. A blissful warmth fills him but when the girl takes her hand back, the old man is rattled. He opens his eyes. He is burdened by a heavy sadness that aches in the marrow of his bones. The girl lifts her bad foot out of the tall grass and the old man takes her foot into his hands. He is gentle with her.

"I got frostbite," the girl says. She presses on his dark scar again.

"I'm—I'm sorry," the old man mutters.

The girl looks at his wrinkled hands. She likes how they cradle her dead foot.

6.

The sun cuts into the kitchen window. It shines a red luster over the messy table.

"I know you hate your job but you can't quit," she says.

The father frowns. He says, "Yeah?"

"I could cut hair again," the mother says.

"That would be nice," he says.

"I can work at that salon in town."

"You were good at it," he tells her.

"I saw a sign the other day," she says. "They're hiring."

The father trots to the cabinet. He finds the Jim Beam and two cups.

"I need you to promise me something," the mother says.

"Alright," the father answers.

"You can't talk about Parker anymore," she says.

"Fine," he says and fills the cups.

She says, "You can't *ever* say his name.

"I won't," he says then grumbles.

"You have to promise. You have to promise," she demands.

"I promise," the father says coolly.

"I want to believe you," she tells him.

"You can believe me," the father says.

The mother raises her cup. "To second chances," she cheers.

The father raises his cup. He says, "To second chances," and they drink. The mother grabs for the Jim Beam but knocks it over. "Shit," the father barks as the mother fumbles the bottle, spraying more whiskey over the table and onto the floor. She gets control. Then she pours another cup with a grin on her face. The father stares at the spilled whiskey. It streams over the table. It collects at the edge. He notices the whiskey is about to overflow. He sighs. He can't take it. So he grabs the old newspaper off the table and he lays it open over the spill.

They drink. The mother pours out two fingers of Jim Beam in the cups.

"I want a new car. I like those Subarus," she says.

"How about a TV?" he says. He says, "I want a flat screen."

"We could buy a house," she says. She laughs. "You know?"

They drink the whiskey and the father refills the cups and the mother gazes down at her drink and she smiles. They'll enroll their daughter in school. She'll take classes like children are supposed to do. The mother can take her shopping for new clothes at the South Ridge Mall in Des Moines. It's only a 50-mile drive. They can have lunch at the Cheesecake Factory. Then she'll call that salon in town. The mother stands. She hurries to the sink and turns on the faucet.

"What are you doing?" the father asks. His face is red.

"I'm cleaning," she says as she soaps the dirty dishes.

The father titters. "Cleaning?" he asks. He caps the Jim Beam bottle.

"Yes," she says. She scrubs at the skillet.

"Ok," he says. He grabs the dishes off the table. He brings them to the sink.

7.

The old man tucks the girl's long brown hair behind her ears. He buries his face in her hair. He grabs a bundle of it and he clenches his hand into a fist. He squeezes tight. He should break her neck. He should do that right now. But the old man doesn't. He lets go of her hair. The old man cradles the girl on top of his knee. "Do you know who I am?" he asks. He touches her cheek. He says, "It's okay." He touches her cheek again. "It's okay if you tell me," he says. "It's okay."

The girl shrugs. She says, "I don't know." She touches a flower. Her head lowers.

He lifts the girl off his knee and he tells her, "Don't move." He tells her, "Be good."

The old man takes out a flip cell phone from his back pocket. He calls the only number listed under "Contacts." The line rings but he wants to hurl the cell phone into the ditch. When he hears Parker's voice, he glances at the girl. He watches her pull up purple milkweed. He looks over at the gold Chevy parked behind a grove of pine trees. He could take the girl. They could go west. They could travel west to Utah or to Montana. He could take the girl away from this place.

"I was wrong," the old man tells Parker. He turns his back to the girl. "It's not them."

Then it happens. The girl clubs the old man over the head with a pine log.

He collapses. His face is tweaked. He mumbles. He says, "Val—"

"No," the girl screeches. She drops the pine log in the grass.

"Honey," the old man cries. His eyelids twitch. "Honey Honey Honey Honey."

The girl lugs a rock out of the ditch and she stands over the old man. She stares down at him with a cold gaze. Then she shuts her eyes. She pictures in her mind a time her parents took her to Forest Park in St. Louis. They often walked there from their apartment in the Delmar Loop on the weekends that summer. They followed the rock trails past the sculpture gardens to the playground near the sandstone cascades. The mother always sat in the red gazebo and she always munched on fruit that she'd totted in a picnic basket. The girl sat on the swing and her father pushed her. The girl soared and the wind slid through her hair like fingers. She said, "Higher."

"Higher," the mother called out. "You heard her." She yelled, "Higher."

"Higher," the father said. He laughed. "Higher," he said and pushed her.

"Higher," the girl said as she kicked her feet into the yellow sun and the blue sky.

The girl opens her eyes. She hefts the rock above her head and a black wave spills over her. She heaves the rock down onto the old man's face. He groans and his legs kick and his feet pedal in the weeds. "Little," the old man babbles. "Little—" The girl brings the rock down again. She hammers his head and she strikes him harder with each blow. The old man's skull finally gives and the girl tosses the rock onto the ground next to his body. There's blood everywhere.

The girl claws dirt over the face. She piles leaves and weeds over the feet and she stacks pine branches over the body. She cleans the blood off herself in the ditch water. Then she runs. She runs out of the woods and she climbs the rail fence. She runs across the back yard and she runs past the magnolia tree. The girl runs. She runs to the backdoor. But she stops. She turns and searches the porch for the Nikes her parents bought her at an outlet mall in Chicago. She finds them. She tugs them on and she ties the laces. The girl grabs the doorknob. She lets go. She grabs it again. The girl turns it. She turns the knob real slow and like that she opens the door.

LIFE LIST
Ray Morrison

I was surprised to find Teresa already in the kitchen, pouring water into the coffeemaker. I glanced out the window that overlooks the backyard. In the nebulous predawn light the oaks were barely visible, more the suggestion of trees than actual ones.

"You're up before the sun on a Saturday," I said. "What's the matter? Couldn't sleep?"

Teresa didn't turn or look at me. She scooped coffee into a filter. "I've got a lot to do this morning."

"Like what?"

"A pet adoption fair this afternoon. I told the director I'd help get everything set up."

The scent of coffee begins to fill the room. "You certainly have become a busy bee," I said.

Teresa, usually a homebody who many times over the years I've teased about bordering on agoraphobic, had recently become involved in several activities outside the home. In the past ten months she'd joined a biweekly book club, helped deliver meals to seniors, and volunteered for a local animal rescue group.

"Besides, I thought you said you were going bird watching this morning?" she said.

"Birding."

"What?"

"It's called birding," I said. "'Bird watching' is looking *at* birds. Birders go and look *for* birds."

"Well, excuse me."

I walked over to the cupboard to retrieve my thermos, whose lining is coffee-dyed from years of use.

"And I might not be home for dinner," Teresa said.

"Why? Do people adopt pets at night now?"

"No, smartass. But there's cleaning up, paperwork, things you wouldn't know about. In any event, I'll probably be late, so while you're out you might want to grab something to fix for dinner."

"It's getting so those shut-ins you deliver meals to have dinner with you more often than I do."

Teresa looked at me then, frowning. "All those years you complained I never left the house and now that I have interests, you complain."

"I'm not complaining," I said. "I'm just not used to it, is all. Besides, it's the weekend and I was thinking we might have dinner at Bernardin's. We haven't been there in ages."

She looked at me for a moment and didn't say anything, but then she nodded and turned away. "I'm going up to get dressed. I hope you have fun and see lots of birds."

I watched her walk out of the kitchen. The room was still except for the gurgle and drip of the coffeemaker. I thought about when Teresa and I met twenty-eight years ago. Back then I often spent my free time in the woods and fields of the North Carolina Piedmont. I'd become adept at identifying even distant birds by only a faint snippet of a song or call. Teresa, who never had any particular interest in the hobby, had seemed enamored of the bookish seriousness with which I pursued my pastime. It was a large part, I'd always thought, of what drew her to me. But as the years evaporated and our lives picked up the tedious rhythm most marriages achieve, our time became filled with prosaic needs—jobs, bills, and all the banal requirements of everyday survival. With no children in our lives to provide the shared burden and bond that parenthood brings, we'd come to not so much live together as exist together.

I headed to the den to gather my things: knapsack with frayed straps, twenty-year-old Swarovski binoculars with lenses as crystal clear as the day I bought them, my creased and dog-eared field guide, my lucky ball cap I credit for many first sightings. On my way back to the kitchen to fill my thermos, I heard the shower running upstairs and Teresa singing.

After I filled my thermos and stuffed a Ziploc to stretching with pretzels, I headed for the kitchen door. Teresa's pocketbook was on the counter, and I noticed a scrap of paper jutting out from underneath it. It was a store receipt, on the back of which she'd scribbled a grocery list. On a whim, I snatched up the list and shoved it into my pants pocket, figuring I'd save her the errand when I stopped at the store on the way home that afternoon.

As I drove along empty roads toward the park, the newly greened trees stood silent in the gauzy dawn light, watching me, it seemed, as I passed. I powered down the car window to let cool air rush against my face. I figured that by the time I arrived at the park in another hour, the sun would be just rising above the horizon, and the air would start to warm. When I pulled up at a stop sign before turning onto the county road that leads to the park's entrance, the mingling songs of the dawn chorus immersed the car's cabin, lifting my spirits, exciting me with anticipation. The spring songbird migration was near its peak, and I'd hoped to add to my extensive list of sightings. Perhaps my first Philadelphia Vireo or Connecticut Warbler, rarities in North Carolina that I'd read had been spotted in the nearby foothills.

In my brightened mood, I summoned the memory of driving along the very same road one evening many years before, when Teresa and I had been married less than a year. We were heading to a Christmas party hosted by her boss at the small podiatrist's office where she was the receptionist. Teresa was dressed in a dazzling, tight red dress. Neither of us had been able to keep our hands from caressing the other's legs as I drove, and by the time we were only a few blocks from the podiatrist's home, I pulled the car off onto a darkened side street where in short order we were in the back seat grappling in a tangle of hastily removed clothing and slick limbs.

It was hard not to smile when I remembered we never made it to the party. But my smile faded quickly. It had been a long while since Teresa and I kissed in any way. How long *had* it been, I wondered as I made the turn onto the narrow county road, since Teresa and I shared the singular electricity of holding our naked selves against each other? Or delighted in the slippery pleasure so common in those early days of our marriage?

Twenty minutes later, movement on my left drew my attention and I spotted a pair of crows silhouetted against the roseate sky. I found even their strident caws pleasurable. It was 6:50 when I slowed the car at the state park's entrance gate. I saw a ranger shuck off his jacket and dump it into the backseat of his vehicle. He tossed a quick wave in my direction. I drove up to the padlocked barricade and lowered the passenger window. The park ranger, a young man who I pegged at no older than twenty-five, leaned down and flicked the brim of his campaign hat back from his face.

"Good morning, sir."

"Sure is."

"Looking to take an early morning hike?"

I lifted the knapsack resting on the passenger seat. "Gonna do a little birding. Hope to add to my life list."

"Well, your timing's perfect. I've seen quite a few migrants in the past week." The ranger pointed to a line of chokeberry shrubs edging the entrance road, just past the barrier. "There are a number of redstarts hanging around right over in that thicket near the parking area.

I glanced where the ranger pointed and nodded.

"The park doesn't open for another ten minutes, sir," the

ranger said. "But... I'm going to make an executive decision. Hang on a sec."

I watched the ranger jiggle a ring of keys he took from his pocket. He then unlatched the padlock securing the bar blocking the park's entrance road. He swung the fulcrum and signaled for me to drive forward. I eased off the brake, tossed a quick two-fingered salute in the young man's direction. I drove to the parking area and chose a space from the empty lot closest to the main trailhead. I tossed my cellphone into the glove compartment before grabbing my binoculars and knapsack. I got out and stood quietly for a moment, all alone in the still, peaceful morning. I hooked the strap of the field glasses around my neck and breathed deeply. The air brimmed with fecundity, saturated with the spring scents of new life. The brightening sky held only scattered shreds of clouds. Somewhere to my right, beyond the trailhead, I heard the choked gurgle of a rock-strewn creek.

And everywhere around me, there were the songs of birds.

I stripped off my sweater and left it in the car. For the first hour or so within the lush confines of the forest, the air would still be clutching the remains of the night's chill, but I knew as the sun crested the upper limits of the canopy, the day would warm comfortably. I hoisted my pack onto my back, jigging the straps snugly across my shoulders. My field guide was at the ready behind my back, tucked in the waistband of my pants.

Walking toward the trail, I studied the hedge line along the road. Immediately, I caught a flitting movement and lifted the binoculars, training them on the bush. A series of sweet, high-pitched notes emanated just before a male redstart popped into view in a gap among the leaves. I made fine adjustments to the focus wheel, admiring the beauty of the bird's brilliant orange shoulder patches and wing bars before the bird darted away. Immediately to his left, a hooded warbler sharply voiced its distinctive call. It didn't take me long to find the bold black and yellow bird and hold it in my gaze until the migrant hopped from view. I lowered my binoculars and started again for the trail. By habit, I tilted my neck back and scanned the pale expanse of the morning sky. Directly above, a brace of red-tailed hawks glided along in nimble, unhurried loops. Having taken no more than a couple steps, I noted I had identified three species. I smiled, sensing this boded well for a gratifying day of sightings. I decided to start a list, not trusting my increasingly unreliable memory. From a flapped pocket on the side of my pack I retrieved a pen, but I was momentarily confused when the small notebook, which I habitually carry to record my observations, was not there. I rummaged through the main compartment with no luck. All at once, I remembered taking the book out several days before in order to review my list from previous years' migrations, leaving it on the desk in my den.

I considered retrieving my cellphone to record my sightings, like many modern birders do, but I found it distracting and clumsy, and hate the interruptions from calls and texts. When I shoved my hand in my pockets, searching for anything upon which to scribble notes, my left hand found the crumpled store receipt with Teresa's shopping list. Not a lot of room to write, but I figured I could abbreviate.

Teresa's precise cursive nearly filled the entire space on the back of the receipt. I flipped it over to see if there was any room on the receipt's printed side that I could use. At first, my eyes registered only the blank margins, making a quick assessment of their utility for my purpose. But instinctively, I read the printing on the receipt, which I noticed was from the local Walgreen's pharmacy. There was only one purchased item listed. When I read it I looked up, blinking and confused, and glanced back over at the spot where I'd spotted the hooded warbler, as if I could rewind time to erase the error of my misreading. In the sharp, crystalline light of the new day, I read again the item line on the printout:

EPT PREGNANCY TEST 2 COUNT   14.95

Who, I wondered, would Teresa be buying pregnancy tests for? I stared at the sales slip, the words blurring as my vision turned inward to see my wife in the budding days of our marriage. Teresa was tugging at my clothes, yanking my shirttails free, stripping off my trousers in frenzied desire, shoving me onto the bed or sofa or carpet at all hours of the day before mounting me. I readily remembered the taut softness of her youthful skin as I clenched her waist, my fingertips registering the tensing of the muscles of her back as she arched backward in the final ecstasy of the moment. My wife collapsed beside me, the sheen of sweat on her neck, her satisfied grin. I remembered the confidence in her voice, so certain that was the time that had worked. A hope invariably dashed. Until eventually, despite test after test assuring us we should be able to conceive, the last atom of optimism drained from my wife's heart, and she accepted the bitter reality that her and my journey together would be ours alone.

I stood in the wide empty parking lot, staring at my solitary car, confused. In the downy light I eyed the store receipt like an Egyptologist deciphering obscure hieroglyphics. There were, I told myself, many potential explanations for this mystery. My mind enumerated them (all the while repelling the one prickly concern pushing its way to the front of my thoughts)—the receipt was not Teresa's, but one she found littering a sidewalk and felt it her civic duty to pick up; the purchase was for a friend to whom Teresa had mentioned she'd be out shopping; perhaps an improperly scanned bar code of a different item she had purchased. I struggled to think of more options. Then, ceding at last to the unthinkable, there was the possibility that there *was* no mistake, and my wife needed to know if she was pregnant.

The air, which had moments before filled my nose and lungs with the pleasant thrill of springtime, now felt thick and heavy—nearly unbreathable. I squeezed the shred of paper into a tight ball in my fist and thrust it back into my pocket. I took one step back toward the car, knowing I should go home and clear up the mystery, but I stopped. Instead, I moved toward the trailhead, my steps short, leaden, as though my ankles were hobbled. Around me, the exalted melodies of a dozen or more birds proclaiming their territories or wooing mates were lost in the howl of blood in my ears. My concentration severed, I shuffled along the path, oblivious now to the bounteous natural activity in the surrounding woods that I had come seeking.

A half mile along, there was a sharp bend in the main path as it veered abruptly away from the nearby creek. The emphatic burble of the stream held me entranced and, for a moment, I was distracted from my unease. I threaded my way among the thicket in the water's direction. My boots snagged in the vined underbrush, and I had to jerk my feet violently to free them. Just beyond the border of trees, I came to the narrow hem of damp earth that edged the noisy creek. Not far downstream, I spotted the fallen trunk of a broad oak whose top half had snapped off and was dragged away by the current. The spiked crown of the remaining stump rested beyond the bank, the tip barely submerged, pushing large, jagged points just below the surface, causing the water to eddy and churn.

The thick rubber bottoms of my boots sank into the soft, grayish loam, leaving a trail of perfect casts of my soles when I headed to sit on the stump. It was cooler down by the water, and I felt the muted pinpricks as goose bumps rose on my bare forearms. I rubbed them distractedly. Nearby, a Louisiana Waterthrush whistled and bobbed its tail in the shallow mud. As I settled onto the tree trunk, the book wedged in the back of my chinos dug into the small of my back, but I made no move to retrieve it. I let my eyes settle on the place in the stream where the water labored to rush past the enormous spikes at the tree's severed end. I studied how it splashed across the hardwood, sounding like rapid, impotent slaps, as though the water was rebuking this unwelcome intruder.

My heartbeats mounted perceptibly as conversations with Teresa from the past year were recalled with enhanced clarity.

Your book club ran late.

Oh, you know. It was as much the Chardonnay as the discussion about the book.

Which book this time?

Nothing you'd ever read. A girly thing with lots of romance.

Do all the ladies dress up, too?

Women like to look nice.

Then, from just that morning:

And I might not be home for dinner.

In any event, I'll probably be late, so you might want to grab something to fix for dinner while you're out.

I wondered, too, about the evenings when I'd arrived home from work to an empty house, only to find a note saying she'd be stuck at a volunteers' meeting with the director of the animal shelter and that perhaps I should order a pizza. And hadn't I remarked, just last week, how much more my wife was smiling? I'd ascribed it to her enjoying her newfound avocations.

My shoulders sagged. Close by, a woodpecker drummed repeatedly in hope of dislodging some insect or extracting a bit of sap. A thinly leafed branch floated by in the current. The incessant purling of the stream tripping over the fallen tree hypnotized me, and I remained still, as though I was a part of the log on which I sat, an anomalous growth sprouting from the trunk. Soon, I became aware of nothing save the mad pulsing of blood behind my eyes.

The sun rose high. My back ached from the ceaseless hunching posture I had assumed. A great blue heron emerged from its shoreline hiding spot across the creek and stealthily skimmed the water's surface until it disappeared from my sightline. I didn't bother to hoist my binoculars. I kept telling myself I should drive home and simply ask Teresa about the receipt. But, I wondered, had enough distrust already permeated my heart that I would believe whatever she claimed?

It was not quite ten o'clock when I decided to leave. Stippled sunlight freckled the ground of the woods as I maneuvered back between the pines and oaks toward the main trail. Once on the path, I hesitated, looking from one direction to the other—deeper into the woods, to the familiar and comforting forest, or back to my car, which would take me home, to the unknown. I plodded along, away from the park's entrance, and headed deeper into the woods. I knew I'd missed the best shot of seeing many birds, as they had settled in during the warmth of the day after a busy morning of moving about foraging and building nests. There were more people in the park then and I nodded silent greetings when they passed me or I raised my binoculars in pretense at studying some bird in order to avoid contact entirely.

Despite my riven mood, I managed to identify dozens of birds over the next two hours. When I came upon the base of a tall pine abutting the path, I noticed a large patch of chalky white splotches and gazed up to discover a nest lodged in the high tangled branches. Just visible with the binoculars, above the nest's edge, was the distinctive head of a yellow-crowned night heron, the long trailing feathers of its eponymous crown bobbing in the soft breeze of the treetop. I stepped off the path onto the bed of pine needles at the side of the tree in order to get a better sightline on the bird. With my eyes trained upward, I felt my foot press down on a spongy lump and jumped backward. Lying on the tree litter was a dead hatchling. I stared at the bulbous blue-black eyelids and the ragged new feathers that sprouted from the chick's drying dimpled skin.

I peered up at the nest before crouching next to the dead bird. Using curled fingers, I scraped a narrow grave beside where it lay. I nudged the diminutive carcass into the hole with the tip of one boot, shoveling dirt and needles on top of it with the sides.

Finding the dead heron had sucked all my will to continue looking for birds, so I decided to head home at last to face what I'd been avoiding. The midday warmth had drawn out raw earthy scents from the trees and land. As I retraced my trek, I welcomed the return of the creek's song, building as I neared the final bend of the path close to the trail's entrance. The raucous sound of teenage boys laughing and talking broke the spell I was in, and soon I spied a trio of them ahead on the road. As they passed by, one of the boys asked if I'd found anything good, gesturing to the binoculars. I gave a noncommittal shrug, but the boys had already moved past me, not truly interested in any answer.

I approached the trailhead and paused in the last trace of shade where the trees ended before giving way to the sun-soaked clearing of the parking lot. I stood contemplating Teresa's answers that awaited me. But at that moment, I was surrounded only by the unspoken disinterest of the forest. All at once from close behind me, a red-eyed vireo repeated its jeering, undulating call, easily identified by a common mnemonic: *Here I am; Where are you? Here I am; Where are you?* I stared at my feet, and my eyes settled on the dirt smudges from burying the dead chick, and listened for several minutes to the vireo's persistent song. *Here I am; Where are you? Here I am; Where are you?*

I retrieved the balled-up Walgreen's receipt from my pocket and held it in my open palm and stared at it. I knew it was no more than a fraction of an ounce, but I felt the weight of it on my hand. I closed my eyes and once again envisioned Teresa naked, her back arched as she climaxed, but the memory was no longer a happy one. Weariness engulfed me then. I opened my eyes, looked briefly at the receipt and then tossed it into the woods. I turned and headed back into the wilderness, and I walked until I found a small spoor that tracked deep into the woods in a part of the park I'd never explored. The vireo continued to call. *Here I am; Where are you? Here I am; Where are you?* I followed it, deeper and deeper into the forest, until I found the elusive bird resting on a branch of a tall pine. He stayed there a long while. I sat on the cool ground and watched him.

"Here I am," I whispered to the vireo. "Here I am."

THE FAIRY HOUSE

Katie Sherman

MY Mama was known for flinging lies at strangers. She told people on the Amtrak that she was a country singer. She told one of the church ladies in town that Daddy's an Orthodox Jew. "Why else wouldn't he join us on Sundays?" Mama asked with a casual shrug.

I remember her straightening her spine, sitting ramrod tall, and telling a stranger about a fish she'd once caught. We were at the Five & Dime, this big thrift shop with broken toys and chair frames stripped of upholstery, and globes, more globes than I've ever seen. Red globes and blue ones. Globes lit up from within. Globes you could draw on with chalk. All those globes reminded me of the places I've never been but want to visit. Mama was looking for kitchen stools that could be salvaged, though I still don't know what was wrong with the tall kitchen stools we had. We ran into a friend of hers from high school and they got to talking with the owner about how good a fisherman Mama was.

"She caught more whoppers than you've seen," the man said with a sly wink.

"One was bigger than a truck tire," Mama said. "Scales so shiny it looked like a diamond doused in glitter. He was pretty, but that's nothing compared to how he tasted."

Then she barked her laugh, a hoarse sound that sprung from her like a Jack-in-the-Box with a loose spring, and pulled my sister and me tight against her bony hips. Later, as she was tucking us in, Bailey asked, "How big was it really Mama?"

Mama sunk her shoulder into the mattress, nudged her forehead and nose against Bailey's cheek. "As big as my palm." Her lips smacked together noisily as she kissed Bailey hard. "But he did taste good."

The truth in Mama's life was that it was all a lie. She had an unquenchable desire for more. More than her girls or Daddy. More than the two-bedroom house nestled in a deep holler where the soot from coal trucks covered every surface. More than a husband who loved her hard and often but still played pool every night. Sometimes the nagging need for more was a woodpecker on her window that wouldn't go away.

All the wants ate at her, and she called these dips in her personality "the lows." On good days, Mama slunk from her room in a cloud of cigarette smoke with a to-do list a mile long. She made biscuits with sunny side eggs and split sausage patties. Sometimes she'd let us mix three sugary cereals together and eat breakfast in front of the TV. But during the lows, Mama wore a stained yellow nightgown that stretched wide over her breasts and hips. She woke with a migraine, and light and noise and scented candles and sausage patties and everything related to us were triggers. I hid scissors and dishwasher tablets and the kitchen knives, anything that could be perceived as a threat, in the fairy house in our backyard.

The fairy house was a pine cottage Daddy built before they brought me home from the hospital. It smelled like sawdust and new packs of construction paper and finger paint. It was a clubhouse for my *Little House on the Prairie* set and my easel, the best hiding place. As I got older, Mama, Daddy, and I couldn't stand shoulder to shoulder in the fairy house without one of us turning sideways. I had painted the door bright yellow and stacked the window box high with soil and pansies. When Bailey was born, six years after me, no one expected me to introduce her to the fairy house. But when Bailey was three, Mama got the lows. Bailey was pawing at her, and every time Bailey touched her, Mama grimaced, as if her skin was getting singed. I carried Bailey to the fairy house and let her knock over my things. I smeared her hands—wet and sticky with paint—and together, we branded the walls with our handprints. We sat until the firefly wings buzzed around us, and I whispered to her, "This is when the fairies come to paint the sky black." It's what Mama said to me on nights when it was just the two of us. Bailey smiled wide, her peach hand lightly grazing the top of my spine as she patted my back.

In the winter of my senior year, my greatest fear, what I'd been preparing for, happened. Mama tried to commit suicide. Bailey and I found her stretched in a wide X on the black-and-white tile floor of her bathroom.

When Bailey and I were younger, Mama and Daddy would have us pose like misshapen starfish on the hot asphalt in front of our house. The blacktop burnt the chubby undersides of our arms but we giggled as they made chalk outlines. Daddy always had a lukewarm beer and sometimes, while he drew, Mama poured long gulps into the grass and ashed her Marlboro on top. While we colored the shapes, Mama made fried peanut butter and jelly sandwiches. Bailey and I dipped them in milk as she and I ate at the splintered picnic table in front of the fairy house.

So Mama looked like one of those colorless chalk outlines. I knelt to touch her limbs, looking behind my shoulders for Bailey. Mama's arms and legs felt cold. Both wrists were covered in some mixture of dried and wet blood. The razor blade was just out of her grasp. Her tongue hung from her mouth and it looked like she'd eaten a purple lollipop. We'd come home early because Bailey had a croupy cough that rattled her chest and rib cage. Even if we hadn't come early, we still would've found her. A searing anger flooded my sinuses, and hot tears fell swiftly down my cheeks at this realization. A minute later, Bailey walked into the bathroom behind me, nearly tripping over my stalled frame.

"Shit," she gasped, biting hard on her lower lip.

She applied pressure to Mama's wrists with a frayed towel.

"Call 911," she yelled. And again, "Call 911. Hurry."

I brought in the cordless phone, but the hollow voice that spoke didn't sound like mine. I gave our address. I asked them to hustle then bristled as I realized the word was Mama's. Her command as she demanded cooperation. Her plea on mornings when we were hopelessly late. While I lingered on the phone listening to bad elevator music, I looked at Bailey. Her long strawberry blond hair and pale skin, so pale it was basically cellophane, was Mama's. She was prettier than me but I was supposed to be stronger, more in control. The role reversal now was unsettling. Bailey stared at the ceiling and then, looked hard at me.

"I always thought Daddy would go first," Bailey said, her voice low so the operator wouldn't hear.

"Just wander away like a stray cat," I replied through tears and panic, the vocal equivalent of a Jell-O salad.

"It's just us," Bailey said, a bare truth I recognized.

I opened my mouth to say, *What about next year? What about the application I'd mailed for early acceptance to WVU a few months before? What about the rest of the world? The globes?* No sound came out.

We peered at one another, separated by six years and by the thin body of our nearly dead mother and by two pools of blood that seeped into the tile grout. The heat coughed through our house, making my armpits sweat. When the EMTs arrived with their flurry of activity, I stood close to Bailey. Our pink hands were stained with Mama's blood. I squeezed Bailey's hand into my own. Pressure. Release. I'm here. Gone. Adrenaline coursed through me as we stepped into the ambulance and watched them hook Mama to a machine that would fill her with a stranger's blood. I tried not to cry and failed, leaving deep red tracks down my face. Some part of me knew Mama was capable of this. Some part of me wished I were wrong. A foreign voice whispered, *Is this salvation or damnation? A blessing or a curse?*

The drone of the hospital's air conditioner circulated a frigid blast. Both the noise and the cold were imposing. I flattened my palm on Mama's skin. She felt like the day-old snow we used to pack tight when we built snowmen, donning caps of itchy pink wool she had knitted. Mama's legs and stomach and face were bloated from the liquids they'd given her. Daddy arrived just after us, an emergency call summoning him from the bowels of the mine. Bailey and Daddy slumped against one another, shoulder to shoulder on a small gray couch. Bailey had a square stain of blood on one knee. It looked like the state of Wyoming, an ominous square that reminded me of fifth grade when Mama taught me all the state capitols. With a book splayed across her lap, her legs pinched together, she quizzed me. "Cheyenne," I answered and Mama flicked a tongue against the back of her teeth as she spoke. "That's a pretty name," she said with a wink, her blonde eyelashes braided together for a moment. "Smart girl." I basked beneath her subtle praise.

"How did we get here?" I asked, my voice an echo in the cramped hospital room. Neither Bailey nor Daddy answered but the question was a tangible thing, a puzzle piece fitting easily, inevitably into our lives.

Bailey swung her feet, scuffing the blemished floor. Her hands were shoved deep in her pockets, but I could still see her fingers moving, possibly grazing a smooth stone from the creek bed behind our house or a worn and veiny leaf. Mama's room was depressingly bare. No balloons or flowers or teddy bears. There was a phone with a curled tail, wound endlessly around itself. The lights were bright, so bright I squinted to see through them. Mama was unconscious. Not sleeping. Not peaceful. Not dead. Her arm was packed heavy with gauze and tape. Blood was being pumped back into her veins. As it warmed her limbs and brightened her cheeks, it congealed and burped, competing with the sound of the air conditioner.

I couldn't curl myself around her because Bailey and Daddy were watching. I didn't think to build a shield, from either Mama or Bailey. I didn't know whom I most wanted to protect.

Bailey stood, crossed the room in a graceful ballerina glide. She coughed into the crook of her arm.

"We should've known," she said, resting her head on my bicep. She felt warm in contrast to Mama. I shrugged her from me and sat on the floor beside the low hospital bed. I yanked my knees to my chest and rested my head on the bony caps. When I lifted my head a few moments later, Bailey was back on the couch with Daddy. Her eyes were pinched tightly together, her fists accentuated by white rosebud knuckles. *I should hug her,* I thought but couldn't rise to do so. Daddy hiccupped then belched, and an undercurrent of stale Pabst danced lightly around us. I lifted Mama's fingers and snaked them into my thick knot of hair. Hair she had combed and conditioned and braided in a fishtail more times than I could imagine. More times than I would know. I wanted Mama to wake up. To kiss my cheeks. To tell me what a smart girl I was.

The stillness filled the space around us like unwelcome company. Daddy was useless. He wasn't massaging the moment into submission or normalcy.

I don't know when Bailey inched her way back to me, but I felt her before I saw her. She lifted a small, pale hand to my face. Perhaps to brush the loose wisps of my mane from my forehead the way Mama would, but she stopped midway, thinking better of it. On her elbow, I noticed a small constellation of freckles. Mama had those, too. I opened my mouth to say that, then receded, knowing it could only hurt her more. We sat, crisscross-applesauce on the linoleum, and I slid a little closer. Away from Mama. I laid a hand on her elbow, on the freckled star structure. I covered it, erased it, and together we watched Mama's chest rise and fall beneath the thin white sheet.

Later that night, after we visited Mama, I was the one who cleaned the bathroom. My knees throbbed as I cloroxed the tiles. I threw the razor in the trash bin. I threw her clothes in, too, brown pants with pleats and a lavender shirt with delicate pearl buttons. And then, when I got rid of the clothes, I bleached the floor again. This time I scrubbed until my hands were raw and my eyes watered from the smell and my nose itched. I scrubbed that floor every day for a week but there was always a thin gray line laced in the grout, just in front of the tub. It seemed like I could see it even after the tiles were replaced two weeks later with gleaming white squares.

The following week, Bailey started her period. I found her in Mama's bathroom with blood swirling through the bowl. She hadn't called Daddy. She'd spent the entire school day in pants marinated in her own blood. The smell was acrylic and too familiar. She leaned her head against the toilet, her hands propped against her stomach. She looked too small to have a period, to be in middle school, to live without her parents. I walked to Magic

Mart and bought her a large package of pads, then showed her how to position them in her panties, how to fold the plastic wings over to secure their placement.

"You want to talk about it?" I asked. I was washing the jeans in the bathroom sink with a combination of dish soap and water.

"I'd rather kill myself," Bailey said. Even though it was hyperbolic, I stopped, my hands a little sore as the pink water slunk down the drain. "Sorry," she muttered, looking down. She popped her knuckles. "What did Mama say to you? When you started?"

It was summer and I had a yellow two-piece I wanted to wear to the pool. I knew my period would cut into that. I watched my belly grow wide and swollen. I remembered feeling all the water throughout my body.

"Did she say you were a woman?" Bailey asked. Her voice trembled with optimism.

"I don't think so," I said. I paused, thinking hard about the moment without any real recollection to it. "She showed me what to do. She stocked the freezer with icebox cake and Girl Scout cookies. She took me to the gas station. We got Coke in glass bottles and poured peanuts in it," I lied.

"Mama was good at the little stuff."

Bailey ran her fingers along the smooth pedestal sink. She looked down the drain where so much blood had recently gone. "I'm going to lay down," she said but instead of walking down the hall to our bedroom, she headed straight through the French doors in the back, and ducking her head, slipped into the fairy house. She was out there the entire evening. I made chicken pot pie thick with brown gravy and cubed carrots and finally walked out back and hollered for Bailey.

"Dinner," I yelled. Daddy was still at the pool hall. He'd make a meal of Pabst Blue Ribbon and maraschino cherries. "Bailey…" I called again. I walked cautiously out to the fairy house, the frozen grass crunching slightly beneath me.

"I want to see the fireflies," she said as I opened the door. The fairy house smelled like mildew.

"It's too cold, Bails," I said, folding myself onto the plywood. The two of us took up all the space the little house provided. I looked out the square windows that were eye-level, even though we sat. I exhaled. My breath was a visible cloud kneeling at the base of the mountains that hovered against our yard, eavesdropping on our conversation. I shivered against a brisk breeze. "We should go inside."

Bailey was fidgeting, rubbing something in her pocket again. The gesture reminded me of the hospital.

"What's in your pocket?" I asked. She hesitantly yanked out a thin letter on expensive cardstock. The state seal was stamped in the upper left corner, embossed in gold. I ran my fingers over the words *Montani Semper Liberi*. I said it aloud to myself, remembered the phrase from my seventh grade West Virginia History class.

"What's it mean?" Bailey asked.

"Mountaineers are always free," I said, though the walls and the hills suddenly felt a bit claustrophobic to me.

"Are we?" she asked. "I opened it before we found Mama."

Her voice trailed off and I slid the letter from the envelope.

"I was bringing it to you when we found her," she said, an uncharacteristic wavering clashing with her voice.

I read the letter once. Then again.

"I got in," I said, looking at Bailey to uncover what reaction I was allowed to have.

"I know." She smiled and looked out the window, running her fingers against the wooden sill to avert meeting my eyes. "Will you go?"

The question felt aggressive and loaded. I didn't have an answer now, with Mama gone and Daddy gone and Bailey's eyes avoiding mine.

"Will you go with me?" I asked. I needed her and wanted her and yet, I knew the question was a fantasy. A plaything in a play place.

"No," she said simply, her vacant expression fixed on her feet. My heart broke a little. "Let's eat," she said, and I was happy for the distraction. Relieved that no anger penetrated Bailey's voice.

I couldn't sleep that night. It felt like I was drowning within the sheets. The next day, I drove to the mental institute to see Mama, the letter in the back pocket of my jeans. Daddy's maroon Taurus groaned slightly as I took each curve. The institute was a non-descript tan building beside an abandoned Sears. There were no windows on the first three floors. A common room that attendants affectionately referred to as the "game room" was situated in the back. I would have coined it the drool room as all the patients sat in tattered robes with stationary eyes fixated on their flimsy slippers. Its doors opened to a brick patio interspersed with rows of succulents. The garden was surrounded by a tall chain link fence adorned with barbed wire.

Mama didn't rise to greet or hug me. She sat, looking out at the plants.

"Hi, Mama," I said. I leaned down, speaking in a slow, meticulous voice. "You want to walk?"

She nodded and extended her hands for me to pull her up.

We circled the tiny patch of land outside a few times. There were only two wrought iron benches bolted into the bricks, and they were occupied, so we continued to walk in succinct circles. Mama broke the silence.

"In another life, I would be the scuba diver lying at the bottom of a fish tank," she said morosely. "Perfectly encased in water. Buoyant and weightless and unable to talk to anyone."

Her arms were wrapped with gauze that yellowed in the sun. During the two-hour drive, I had folded and refolded the letter until the creases were thin jagged lines against the heavy, fibrous page. I thought of what was under Mama's bandages, the way the cuts formed lopsided V's.

"I never wanted anything as much as I've wanted silence," she said, her face a profile as she pressed her hands against a cactus. "Ouch," she said softly before doing it again.

It felt wrong to talk after that, like something a toddler would do to test her parents. Mama's breath was heavy and ragged, the breath of a jogger rather than a slim, middle-aged mother. Occasionally the breeze would grind against the flimsy metal fence, a needle stabbed into the noiselessness. The only laughter we heard was manic. I thought of Mama's laugh. I thought of the times when I thought she was better, self-corrected. The times when she was wise. I ran my hand against the outline of the square letter still in the back pocket of my jeans. In the end, I stayed for half an hour and drove home. I didn't tell her, unable to see through the fog the institute produced to rescue Mama.

When I got home, I found Bailey in the fairy house. She had uncovered an old Lego set and was constructing a multi-colored tower that brushed the ceiling. She didn't greet me, instead handing me the bag with the blocks. I started adding a layer to the base.

"You have to go," she said, her voice rattling off the walls a little and catching me off guard.

I scraped my index finger against the cuticle of my thumb until a few thin spots of blood emerged.

"It's just us," I said, and Bailey flinched as if her own words were attacking her. She sat next to me.

"What did Mama say?" she asked, though I hadn't told her where I'd been.

"Nothing," I said. I couldn't discuss the drive or the scuba diver or the fenced-in garden with no flowers. I wanted so badly to leave, to go to school, to escape. I wanted so badly to stay.

"It'll always just be us," she said.

We continued to build the tower in silence until the floor was covered in blocks and we no longer fit. Then, Bailey placed her hand in mine. We walked away from the fairy house with its low windows and its piney aroma and the fragments of our childhood.

OUR UFO

John Engell

On the last day I saw my uncle, he became sentimental. Just before I left the summer cottage he broke down and said, "I want you to know you can think of me as a second father. You boys"—he was referring to me and my older brother who had left a few days before; my aunt and uncle had no children—"are like sons to me." He didn't say another word, but wept without a hint of self-consciousness.

My uncle felt a little unworthy. My father, who died when I was ten, had been an imposing man, a prominent lawyer equipped with an immense will and carefully chosen ideas. My uncle was short and squat and ungifted, except for his hands, which were the squarest and gentlest of instruments. With them he molded oak, cherry, walnut, mahogany, maple, ash, pine; and he tied flies. I remember once, years ago, he bandaged a large gash in my leg. His fingers at their first firm touch quieted my blood and healed the wound. "... like sons to me," he said, and enveloped my slender hand in his broad one.

My uncle had no secrets, or so he thought. His opinions were stern and choleric, unthinking and untutored, like those of his peasant ancestors in Germany. He hated disorder, confusion, doubt. Yet he lived without an idea, a child of pure emotion. "They ought to shoot the bastards," he railed about petty criminals headlined in the newspapers. "Damn wops have ruined the place," he insisted concerning his hometown. The Communists, Arabs, Jews, Fascists, Blacks, Mexicans, Catholics, Democrats, Republicans—these and many more he connected in some irrational subterranean conspiracy against the forces of world order.

To the forces of order my uncle gave his one potent weapon— his hands. In them lived generosity, patience, perfection. They dressed and shaved him precisely—he was a dapper little man— and they fed his stomach copiously and well. They displayed his wedding band and masonic ring, the two golden circles of his social life.

And, chiefly, they worked. My uncle's mind preached order and lived chaos. His hands preached nothing and created order. They were his spirit, his genius, his life. I loved to watch him cut a piece of wood, joint a table, or varnish a bed. Then he had skill and infinite patience, and the inept emotionalism of his mind vanished, to be replaced by the simplicity of just and ordered action.

On weekend mornings in the years before he retired, my uncle tied flies. The process was a mystery to me. For though I enjoyed fishing with him, my pleasure came not from the lengthy preparation and patient waiting, but from the momentary excitement of the strike combined with the romantic influence of sunsets on the lake and quiet evening breezes rippling the still water.

Sometimes I would watch my uncle tie the flies, watch his hands and the vacant concentration in his face. Old Doc Tiller, who went out with us once a month or so, raised fighting cocks and would bring a supply of feathers — "the very best" he insisted. The feathers looked colorful but unpromising. I wondered how anyone had ever had the cleverness to make a fly from rooster feathers. The leap of imagination involved — for now I know it must have been just such a leap, a living metaphor — confounded me. But my uncle never wondered or questioned. His hands worked and made the beautiful, useful, necessary thing.

One Saturday evening in late June, perhaps the longest evening of the year, he and I went out alone. The lake was perfectly still, its surface a mirror. I carried the oars down from the cottage and put a life cushion in the boat. My uncle could not swim a stroke. He brought the tackle and our fly rods. Mine was shorter than his and much newer. He had bought it for me three summers before when I was eleven, and he taught me to fly cast — that effortless flick of the wrist which took me three months to perfect.

I rowed to the eastern end of the lake. My uncle sat in the rear of the boat and watched the water. When we stopped moving he cast his fly, flicking it up in gentle arcs against the sunset, each time letting out more line with his right hand until the fly rested against the edge of the lily pads. I straightened the boat and began casting my own yellow and red fly. We were both silent, waiting for a strike, but no fish surfaced anywhere. The water seemed empty, still, without depth or life. I glided the boat further along the shore. My uncle smoked a cigarette between casts. Its tip glowed the color of the sunset.

Soon I felt bored. I whistled. "Don't whistle," said my uncle. I talked. "Don't talk," he whispered, "it scares the fish." I watched the black bats coming out, pirouetting through the empty air, silhouetted by pink clouds. I remembered a story my uncle had told about Doc Tiller and a bat tangled in his fishing line, lassoed in mid-cast. "God was he mad," my uncle had said and we all laughed and laughed, imagining the old man's bumbling, good-natured anger while he struggled with the hopelessly knotted line. I saw the lightning bugs hanging in the black holes below the over-arching foliage of the shore. They would appear, disappear, appear again in the same spot or somewhere else, lazily rearranging themselves in patterns of light and darkness. I found the evening star.

"A strike," my uncle declared. I started. "Wake up. You had a strike. Hold her steady. Now jerk your tip up a little. That's right." We waited. The fish had gone. I cast again in the same place. No luck. "They don't give you a second chance," he said, smiling in the dusk. I smiled back and felt foolish.

The clouds had lost their color except for a lone jet trail high, high in the sky, pointing from west to east, growing into the darkness. It seemed to move among the stars. My uncle did not notice. He was patiently changing his fly, using a flashlight when necessary.

I rowed to the extreme eastern end of the lake where a sluggish outlet carries water into the swamp below and where, as my uncle recounted once or twice a month, he had caught the largest lake bass of his fishing life, a thirty-five incher, mammoth and fat and very, very old, the sort of fish I imagined living under a snag in the Mississippi, trapping in its cavernous mouth smaller fish washed down from the north. Here in the lake that bass would have had to settle for the small fry in the outlet. And so, I conjectured, inventing a longer story to go with my uncle's laconic account, his hunger overcame his wisdom and he ended as dinner for my uncle and my aunt. That had been years before I was born. I had never eaten or seen a thirty-five-inch bass.

For a long time we cast in silence. The light in the west and the jet trail disappeared. Stars filled the sky. I could lee lightning bugs beyond the shore, dotting the mountainside, dancing to the songs of cicadas and bullfrogs. A breeze rippled the water. Perfect fishing weather. My uncle lit another cigarette. I heard his rod whip back, the line arching through the air, and as my eyes opened in the night I saw his bright fly lying close to the lily pads, saw it disappear and reappear near the same spot, a bit to the left or right. I knew my uncle's thumb and forefinger touched the line, holding it gently, waiting for a strike, ready to tighten firmly, to set the hook. One of us, I hoped, would land another great lake bass.

From the boat the whole expanse of the lake, stretching east to west, lay exposed. I had seen it from here many times, in daytime and at night, a small body of water, perhaps a mile long, less than half as wide, surrounded except for the swampy eastern tip by summer cottages, their white docks jutting into the black night water, their lights shining out from among the trees. At night this small lake looked larger than in sunlight, or perhaps only more at peace. The motorboats—ugly and loud—were moored. The power line—necklacing the northern mountain—was invisible. The people—raucous and summer-free by day—were asleep or indulging their pleasures in private.

I was fourteen that summer and in the boat at night look-ing up at the lake to the west, I was stirred by a vague feeling of adolescent longing and expansiveness, the sort of feeling that is revered by some ages, laughed at by others, and feared by a few, but which our present time seems bent on disowning, along with every other idea, adolescent or mature, of transcendence. Disowning in one of two ways: by claiming the mind is no more than a mechanism of reactions, or by claiming the mind is purely, hopelessly subjective.

But at fourteen I was ignorant of such theories. So I felt, quite naturally, the needs beyond the body and the call above the flesh. I wanted to travel, to explore, to study to feel, to love, to believe— and while doing these to reach outside myself into some other realm. Of course this other realm was ill-defined, defined not at all, I suppose. But of its existence I felt as sure as of my own. It had not yet occurred to me to doubt that.

Beside me sat my uncle, fishing. He was fifty-six. He seemed to have, as I have said, no secrets. He lived for his work and for his peace. His hands moved solidly in solid space, the carpenter and fisherman equipped with perfect tools. And now I heard the strike and saw my uncle's hand tighten on the line. "A big one, boy." He gave the fish some play. "Look at him bend that rod." He took in more line. "This is the one." I was excited. Slowly my uncle worked the fish toward the boat. He jumped. In the dark his white belly showed clear for a moment, long and wide, then slapped against the black water, loud. He was near the boat now, thrashing. Suddenly he broke straight for my uncle. I could see his wake. My uncle's hands rushed to take in line. The fish came on. He disappeared. We sat for a moment. "Well, I lost him. He was too fast for me. Gave him too much slack." My uncle pulled in the last few yards of line, looked at his fly, reeled up the loops lying in his lap and at his feet, gently laid the rod across the seat, and lit a cigarette. I reeled in my own line and was silent. This time my uncle's hands had failed. "Too much slack," he repeated, more to himself than to me.

The cicadas and the bullfrogs sounded louder now. The moun-tainside seemed covered with a thousand lightning bugs. And up that mountainside my favorite mourning dove, who visited the lake in every summer of my youth, began her night lament. "Did you see him when he jumped." I said I had. "He was a damn big bass." Yes," I said. "I'll bet he was more than thirty-five inches long." I felt proud of this good deed in the middle of my uncle's disappointment. But in retrospect I doubt he cared about the size of the lost fish. He had caught one giant bass. That was enough for him. Whatever he was thinking, my uncle said nothing. Other than the hand holding his cigarette, he did not stir at all.

I scanned the sky above the northern mountain, above the lightning bugs and mourning dove, looking for shooting stars. They were common in late June and I loved to watch them. I waited, saw nothing, righted the boat which was drifting toward the lily pads and the outlet, and looked up again. Then I saw it. Just above the mountain, moving quickly, coming up across the sky. "Look," I shouted. "Look!" I pointed over my uncle's left shoulder. He turned and I could hear him grunt or gasp, I don't know which.

I will try to describe the thing. It was a disk of light. Perhaps a ball, though it seemed to have no depth. We could never decide afterwards how large it was, how wide or deep or thick, since we had no way to tell its distance from the ground. This disk of light appeared as large as a full moon and as bright. But its light was yellower, at once more brilliant and more diffuse. Radiant at the center, it blurred ever so slightly around the edges, suffusing with the darkness through which it travelled. And it moved quickly, steadily toward us. "What is it?" I whispered. "God only knows," replied my uncle.

Within a few seconds, ten or twelve, perhaps fifteen, it was over us. We could never agree, later, how long the thing remained in view. Then, at the apex of the sky, above our heads, it seemed to pause, or so I thought, and so my uncle diffidently remembered once I made the suggestion to him. There was no noise. None at all. No roar of engines or passing of a wind. It paused before continuing on across the sky toward the south. We stood on one impulse, I think, and followed with our glowing eyes its steady retreat down the sky, through Sagittarius's close-knit starry bow, beyond the southern trees, and out of sight.

When I turned my uncle was still standing behind me. I had never seen him stand in a boat. He was mortally afraid of drowning. "A flying saucer!" I yelled. "We saw a flying saucer!" But though I was an imaginative boy, I disdained the credulous and superstitious, and I feared reasoned rejection. My words were hardly shouted into the dark air before I felt a bit uneasy and embarrassed. The disk was gone. Its spell was broken. My uncle would dismiss it. I sat. To my amazement he did not, but remained standing, legs spanning his seat, feet apart. With one square hand my uncle pointed to the spot where the disk of light had disappeared. "By God," he said, "I think you're right, boy. By God. A flying saucer." He sat down unsteadily. The boat rocked.

We fished no more that night. We were silent for a few minutes. The boat drifted into the lily pads at the mouth of the outlet. "Let's go home," my uncle said. I began to row and the thick lily stems clutched the oars, slowing our progress. I pulled and strained, breaking the stems. When we gained open water I noticed an eerie brightness in the eastern sky, to the rear of the boat over my uncle's head. I held my breath and rowed harder.

Now, reading this account, I realize I have recalled that June evening forty-two years ago in very serious, very mysterious terms. The disk of light was mysterious and serious for me and for my uncle. But there is a humorous side to the story, as well, and it begins with that light in the east over my uncle's head and behind him. I kept watching and said nothing. The light increased while I rowed. My uncle had bent forward, clicked on his flashlight, and begun the methodical tidying of his tackle box, a ritual marking the end of every night's fishing. For some reason I was afraid, and all the peace rising from the lake and the mountains around me and from my uncle's presence could not quiet my heart. Then, as I stared back toward the outlet, a full moon rose majestic and white. The light was explained. I laughed. "Why are you laughing?" asked my uncle. "I don't know," I said, feeling foolish.

At the cottage my aunt seated us around the kitchen table and served up a plate of fresh-baked ginger cookies and mugs of hot chocolate to "warm your bones." It was not a cold night. "Any luck?" she asked, knowing the answer. "No," we replied in unison and glanced at one another. Who would speak first? For a time the three of us blew and sipped in silence.

"We saw a flying saucer, mame," said my uncle, looking up from his chocolate. He was not a man given to practical joking. My aunt stared at him as if he had said, "We drowned tonight, mame, and are come back from the dead." There was another lengthy silence.

"We saw a flying saucer, didn't we?" He turned to me. I nodded. "A flying saucer," he repeated.

"A flying saucer?"

"That's what I said, mame."

My aunt stood and began serving us more chocolate. My patience was at an end.

"Or at least we think it was. I mean, it must have been. It was big as the moon and really, really bright. And it moved across the whole sky without a single sound. And it stopped right over the boat when we were down by the outlet. It had to be a flying saucer, didn't it?" I looked toward my uncle. He placed his palms on the kitchen table and shook his head up and down, slowly and resolutely.

I think my aunt must have feared, for one weak moment, that my imagination, notorious in the family, had punctured my uncle's sanity. She turned on me.

"You're positive?" she snapped.

"Well, yes."

Changing tactics, she smiled and passed me a plate filled with ginger cookies. I chose one and took a bite.

"It couldn't have been an airplane or one of those satellites they're launching these days?" She paused. "Or a searchlight?"

I stared, my mouth full. My aunt was an ingenious woman.

"Or maybe even the moon? It's full tonight." She caught my eye. I blushed.

"No. It wasn't the moon."

"But one of those other things?"

"I don't see how it could have been."

"But it might have been?"

"Well..." I faltered. "I don't think so. It didn't look like anything I've ever seen. And the way it moved..." I stopped.

"So you're not sure." My aunt was determined to make her point.

I had forgotten my uncle. I was sitting between him and my aunt, one at either end of the small oak table my uncle had made, and I had turned away from him to speak to her.

Now I sensed him rise behind me. I turned back. "By God, mame," he bellowed, "leave the boy alone. He said it was a flying saucer and by God it was a flying saucer. And that's the end of it." He folded his napkin neatly, laid it beside his empty mug and plate, and walked into the living room. I did not understand why then, but instead of crushing my aunt or terrifying her, this outburst seemed to clear the air. It was, I realized later, a speech typical of my uncle, unreasonably final, unanswerable. He had accompanied every emotional word with a controlled oratorical gesture, his hands firm and resolute. He was, my aunt must have decided, still perfectly sane.

In the weeks that followed my uncle spoke often of the flying saucer, the unidentified flying object as my aunt insisted on calling it when he was not present. He told his neighbors and coworkers. He told the milkman and the gas man and the ice man and the local grocer. On Sundays he told people after church. On

Monday nights he told the masons. And he told me and my aunt what he had said to all of these other people. I do not know what most of his listeners thought. The one time I was present his audience consisted of the Methodist minister. The old, nearly senile man listened respectfully, smiling and nodding, then walked away without saying a word of doubt or contradiction. My uncle never expected contradiction. It simply did not occur to him.

Near the end of the summer my mother came to spend a few weeks at her sister's cottage. With her she brought my brother, who was twenty-one and in college. On the evening of their arrival, after dinner while we were sitting on the front porch overlooking the lake, my aunt and mother and uncle drinking coffee and my brother sipping brandy, my uncle described the flying saucer. My brother, who was majoring in chemistry—he is now a successful surgeon—listened incredulously. He glanced at me and I squirmed. When my uncle had finished, my brother coughed and asked him to repeat the location of the boat.

"Down by the outlet."

"Near the swamp?"

"Of course it's near the swamp."

After a pause, my brother treated the four of us to a brief lecture on the nature of swamp gasses, their strange behavior and frequent luminescence. He stated the facts between sips of his brandy. My uncle listened, but I could tell he failed to make the obvious connection. My brother was a master of implication; my uncle was a novice at inference.

My aunt, sensing danger, tried to come to the rescue. "That's very interesting," she said. "Would anyone like ice cream? I have chocolate and strawberry."

I was about to order strawberry, but my brother had noted his tactical error and spoke first.

"Don't you see?" he continued, looking at my uncle. "This so-called flying saucer was almost certainly an exhalation of gases from the swamp."

With my right hand I clutched the arm of the glider on which I was sitting. I looked at my uncle and he looked at my brother.

"Gases?" asked my uncle.

"Yes, luminescent swamp gases."

I waited.

"Gases! You mean swamp farts!" My uncle laughed for quite a while and after a moment I laughed with him. Perhaps my mother and my aunt joined us. I am not sure. Of course my brother appeared to take the whole thing perfectly in stride. But he was defeated. I never heard him mention swamp gasses again.

Fourteen summers passed after my uncle and I saw the disk of light, and I spent part of every summer at the lake. My uncle seldom spoke of the flying saucer. Some nights, when we were out on the water fishing, he would watch the sky. "I wish we'd see that damn thing again," he might say between casts. We never did.

But over those fourteen years my life had become complicated and my uncle's health had begun to fail, his back increasingly arthritic. Instead of spending two months at the lake each summer I had gradually shortened my visits to three weeks, two weeks, one, making excuses to my aunt and to myself. My uncle had no interest in excuses. By the fourteenth summer he could no longer go fishing and I had lost interest. Still, my uncle continued to tie flies and to make beautiful furniture. He never suffered arthritis in his hands.

Before that fourteenth summer I had become engaged. My aunt and uncle were ecstatic.

"What would you like for a wedding present?" he asked me over the phone.

I had known he would ask. My fiancée and I had decided on what seemed a perfect answer.

"A mahogany bed," I told him, "like the one your father made, the one in the front dormer room."

"It'll take time," he said, but I could tell by the tone of his voice that my uncle was deeply flattered.

"It's seven months to the wedding."

"I'll finish it in three," he boasted.

He did not finish in three months, and I was not married. Somehow I made a mess of things. When my aunt wrote, all mention of the bed was dropped. I assumed my uncle had given it up and gone back to paying jobs. He was retired from the auto parts firm where he had worked for over thirty years, but all his friends kept asking him to design and make a chair or a table or a bed, and they sent others. They knew that whatever my uncle built would be perfect. As a craftsman he was unequaled. He insisted on using the finest woods, he worked with painstaking care, and he preferred simple designs that reminded me of the Shaker aesthetic.

Fourteen months after I had first asked my uncle for the mahogany bed, I visited the lake. It was my shortest summer stay, less than a week. I stopped on my way back from a trip to England before I moved south to begin graduate school. My uncle had grown weak, but this bodily weakness seemed to feed his emotions. He had become more choleric and more sentimental.

When I arrived he nearly cried. When I asked him about local politics or pollution of the lake, he railed. "Damn fools with their god-damn fancy motorboats. They'll ruin the place yet."

On my first evening, over coffee on the porch, my uncle surprised me. He mentioned the bed.

"It's done," he said. "I set it up in the front dormer room where you'll be sleeping." He could tell I was a bit embarrassed. "I know you're not getting married just yet, but I think you'll really like this bed," he said.

We climbed the stairs while my aunt washed dishes. My uncle had moved the old mahogany frame into the back room and substituted his new work. It was like most things he made, simple and sturdy. The grain was fine, the finish beautiful. He had added no footboard, remembering that I was too tall for a six-foot bed. But there was a headboard. A remarkable headboard. It was high, almost three feet at the sides, and rose another foot at the center in a perfect, classic curve, a mass of dark mahogany dwarfing the bed. And in the center, crowning the swelling curve, he had inlaid a perfect circle of golden satinwood, protruding a quarter of an inch from the mahogany; a disk of light that seemed to travel through and suffuse with the darkness surrounding it. I touched the disk. My uncle smiled.

"I knew you'd like it," he said.

I turned and hugged my uncle. We had never hugged before.

The following winter, twenty-eight years ago, my uncle died. At the funeral I watched his hands, lying on his chest. I watched silently, waiting, then placed my white hand on his ashen hands. I stood back and saw his coffin closed. At the last my uncle's hands were quiet.

BLESSING
Martin McCaw

Ellen put the second pill on her tongue and washed it down with a sip of water. She shouldn't have reached to the top shelf for the butter dish. An ordinary plate wouldn't do, though, not on Thanksgiving.

She pressed her hand against the small of her back. Goofus! As if her fingers could straighten the shattered vertebrae.

Had she forgotten anything? Let's see, the turkey was almost done. The aroma made her mouth water. Sweet potato casserole in the pantry. She would wait till they got here to put it in the oven and melt the marshmallows. Candied pears in the refrigerator. Soon as they arrived Craig would race to the fridge. How he loved his grandma's candied pears.

Little Julie would run to hug her. James would stand stiff as a mannequin while she hugged him, just like his father did. James, her darling boy, though he wasn't a boy any longer, not with that fringe of gray hair on his temples. Should I dye it, Mom? Not on your life, she'd told him. It makes you look distinguished. Janet had agreed with her for once.

The salt and pepper shakers. She would forget her own head if it weren't wired on. She'd quit using salt after Frank died. He loaded it on everything, potatoes, corn on the cob, tomatoes. You're a heart attack waiting to happen, the doctor told him.

Dear Frank. Her eyes misted. Their first walk along the river, his hand brushing hers, the tingle up her spine. Then he'd jerked his hand away and apologized. She'd grabbed it and hadn't let go till they got back to the picnic table. Charlotte Grubb had given her the evil eye.

She put the shakers in the center of the kitchen table so everyone could reach them. Were the settings right? Five big plates, five salad plates, teacups and saucers for the adults—her good china with the pink roses. They had been a nightmare to unpack. She'd got back spasms and had to take more pain pills, but if she didn't get out her good china for Thanksgiving, when would she use it?

A sweet potato lay on the kitchen counter. She took a paring knife out of a drawer, but when she tried to scrape off the skin, she flinched and clutched her back. They would have to do without the sweet potato casserole this one time.

How long since she'd taken her pain pills? Should have written it down. She went to the bathroom and shook two pills into her hand. One didn't do the job anymore. She tilted the water glass and swallowed them, one at a time, little sips so she wouldn't choke.

Her fingernails were blue. Poor circulation, she supposed, but didn't everyone her age have poor circulation?

Sleepy. Better lie down for a while. She left the bedroom door open so she could hear them knock. She smiled. They never knocked. They always came bursting in, Craig making a beeline for the fridge, Julie running to hug her.

She took off her shoes and lay on the bed, propped her feet on pillows like the doctor said. My, how swollen her ankles were.

She couldn't feel her chest move. Was she even breathing? It would be so easy to slip away, join Frank in heaven. No, she couldn't do that to James, not on Thanksgiving of all days. He wanted to hug his mom, not find her dead in bed.

Something nagged at her, something she'd forgotten. Last Thanksgiving James couldn't come because he was sick. So hard to remember, like drifting through fog. Just let go.

A knock.

Her chest lurched, and she sucked in air. They'd arrived.

Another knock, louder.

"I'm coming." Her voice was so hoarse she could barely hear it. Why couldn't she move?

Thump Thump Thump. That horror story, the dead son knocking.

The room darkened. A man peered down at her, olive face, scruffy goatee, a smell like Frank's when they lived in the shack with no running water. He left the room, but a brown-skinned woman rushed toward her. She pushed Ellen's head against the pillow and jammed something up her nose. Vapor saturated a nostril. Chloroform. They were going to rob her.

A low voice muttered outside her bedroom door. The man came back and clicked shut a cell phone. He'd called his cronies to come haul away her things.

What poison was spreading through her body? It couldn't be chloroform because she was wide awake now. *Got to get away.* She rolled sideways, but the woman pinned her shoulder to the bed.

"Not yet. Wait a minute."

For the poison to take effect.

She began to itch. It was already working. The woman stepped back, and she scratched her arms.

"Careful. Your fingernails draw blood." A staccato accent. She was an Arab, and so was he. Our president warned us.

She swung her legs off the bed and stood up too fast. She held onto the headboard till the room stopped swaying. A migraine was coming on, right behind her eyes.

"Lift your foot." The woman was kneeling by the bed, a shoe in her hand. "Can you walk?"

"Certainly." What an insult.

In the kitchen the man was drinking from a glass, water dribbling down his chin. He'd left the cupboard door open. A mole on his neck had a hair growing out of it. Black hairs protruded above the top button of his frayed shirt. He was probably covered with body hair, like an animal, lice crawling all over him.

He rubbed the back of his hand across his mouth. "Where's the food? You promised us turkey dinner with all the trimmings."

"I did no such thing."

The woman took her elbow and guided her to a chair at the head of the table. "Yesterday afternoon. You were sitting in the rocking chair on your porch. We ask if you have work for us. Run errands, maybe. Your car has weeds growing up around the tires."

Yes, the sun was in her eyes, so she didn't know they were foreigners. She'd been about to shoo them off, but then she remembered Jesus' words, if you do it to the least of these you do it to me, something like that. Without thinking, she'd invited them to Thanksgiving dinner. There would be plenty of food. If stuck-up Janet didn't like it, she could just grin and bear it. This was her house, and she could invite anyone she chose.

The woman sat down, to Ellen's right. The man pulled back a curtain and looked out the window. Watching for his cronies?

Her headache was getting worse, battering her left eye from the inside. "Who are you?"

"My name is Maryam, but they call me Maggie. Too many Marys to keep track of."

She had lush black hair, streaked with white. Big, expressive eyes, long lashes. Her dark skin would hide wrinkles, so she could be any age. "Where do you live?"

"Good question. We spend some days in the library. I read the psychology magazines, the back copies. At night we sleep in alleys, anywhere we can."

She should have guessed it. They were illegals, keeping one step ahead of the law.

"We got kicked out of the Christian Aid Center last week. The manager searched his bag and didn't like what he found."

"Liquor?"

"No." She pretended to pop something into her open mouth.

The man dropped the curtain and scowled at Maggie. "She doesn't need to know my life history."

"Everyone else knows. You made sure of that." The woman leaned closer. "He's a regular customer at the emergency room."

He pulled a cookbook out of her bookcase and skimmed its pages, too fast to read anything.

"Has he been in prison?" she whispered. "Because of the drugs?"

"Prison was the least of what he's been through. He wasn't always like this."

"I worked in construction for fifteen years." He crammed the cookbook into the wrong shelf, front first, bending back its cover. "Then I got the call."

"He was a street-corner preacher. He preached that everyone is equal and the land belongs to all of us. No private property."

A socialist! Frank would have run him out of town with a pitchfork.

"Some of us liked what he preached." She chuckled. "We were a ragtag bunch. Homeless people, peddlers, hotel maids, gamblers with no luck. Three of us named Mary."

"You were my favorite. The happy one."

The woman turned her head to smile at him. Why, she was beautiful. When she looked in her own mirror all she saw was wrinkles. She'd unscrewed the bulb above the mirror so the only light came from the ceiling behind her. At least she could brush her teeth now without getting depressed.

"He said nobody should hold power over another human being. Before I met him, a pimp beat me up." Maggie hunched her shoulders and shuddered. "Every prostitute I know lives in terror that a customer will damage her face. Then she can't earn money and her pimp will give her a worse beating. I lay for two hours on a cot in the emergency room before anyone checked me. I heard a nurse say she's a whore, she deserved what she got."

"Your face looked like hamburger." He grinned at her. "You stood there all afternoon in the rain, listening to me."

She could feel electricity jump between them. On her first date with Frank, they were watching a drive-in movie, and his elbow grazed her arm. The loud snap and the shock had startled her.

"I hadn't eaten for three days. He only collected enough money to buy one loaf of bread, and he shared it with me."

A prostitute and a drug addict. What a pair. How could she get them out of her house? Frank would have aimed his shotgun at them, but James didn't like guns. James—something was wrong. The clock on the wall said one thirty-six. If they'd had a car breakdown, he would have called. He had a cell phone.

A siren howled far away. What if they'd got in a wreck?

Maggie squeezed her hand, as if she'd read her mind.

"This all you got? One raw potato?" The man stood by the sink, holding up a sweet potato.

"Turkey's in the oven."

He pulled down the oven door. "It's empty."

She'd forgotten to cook the turkey.

"It must still be in the fridge."

He opened the refrigerator door and slammed it shut. "Pyew! Don't you throw anything away?"

He was a fine one to talk. He probably ate out of dumpsters.

The woman's hand was warm. Her shoulder itched, but she knew if she scratched it the itching would get worse. Her headache was going away. Maybe they hadn't poisoned her.

"What did you spray up my nose?"

"The antidote. To reverse your symptoms."

"What symptoms?"

"Your breathing was shallow and your pupils were little dots. I thought you had a drug overdose."

"I don't take drugs!" Of all the nerve, lumping her in with this addict. "I just take pain pills for my back."

The man had been turning the pages of her wall calendar, glancing at the pictures, but now he looked at her. "What kind of pills?"

"Oxy something."

"I rescued him so many times I lost count. That's why I carry the antidote. The dose I gave you was my last one. It wears off in about thirty minutes, then you need emergency medical help."

She thought she'd done the right thing, bless her heart. They needed baths, but she only had enough towels for her family. The least she could do was feed them. She stood up, swayed, and sat back down.

"I'll get us some food in a minute. We won't wait for my family."

"What family?" Maggie said.

"My son James and his wife and kids."

"You have grandchildren." She beamed. "How old?"

"Craig's a third grader, and Julie's just starting kindergarten."

"You see them often?"

She shook her head. "They live too far away. I used to talk to them on the phone, but I can't anymore."

"Why not?"

"Their mother won't let me talk to them. When I phone nobody answers."

"Caller ID," the man said. "She has caller ID, so she doesn't answer when she sees your number."

"Why is the mother not allowing you to talk with your grandchildren?"

What a nosy woman. She shouldn't be sharing her personal life with these foreigners. Frank always said she was too gabby.

"She said I upset them."

"Yet they come for dinner." Maggie looked at the oven. "But no dinner." She picked up the address book from the phone table. "What's the last name of your son?"

"Evans."

"James Evans." Maggie thumbed partway through the book, then lifted the phone's receiver and dialed.

"No." The man strode across the room and took the phone from her hand. "They won't answer. Use mine." He handed her his cell phone.

"I didn't give you permission to call my family."

"Shh." Maggie tapped her lips with a forefinger.

"Don't you shush me!"

"Mrs. Evans? I'm your mother-in-law's social worker."

What a lie. "I don't have a social worker."

"She accidentally overdosed her pain medication."

The woman was a con artist, planning to extort money from her family. She would put a stop to that.

The siren whined again, closer.

"Can I use your bathroom?" the man disappeared down the hallway without waiting for an answer.

Would he ransack her bedroom? She'd left her jewelry box open.

"She thinks she is not allowed to talk with her grandchildren." Maggie listened. "Yes, yes, I see. Memory loss and delusions are symptoms of opioid intoxication."

What gobbledygook! She must have learned that jargon from the psychology magazines.

"No, I understand totally. I will explain everything to her. Thank you so much." Maggie hung up.

She pulled a chair alongside Ellen, sat down, and clasped Ellen's hand in both of hers. "Your son James died in August."

The ringing had wakened her from a happy dream. She'd been playing on the floor with baby Craig, showing him how to stack blocks. She couldn't get past three because he'd knock over the tower and laugh. As soon as she lifted the receiver and heard Janet sobbing, she knew what had happened.

"I'm so sorry." The woman hugged her.

She felt light, as if she might dissolve into a puddle if Maggie let go.

"Your daughter-in-law said the children got confused when you phoned." Maggie was talking into her ear, so close her breath tickled her neck. "You asked them to call their father to the phone, and they got upset. Finally the mother stopped answering the phone when she saw your number. I think she answers next time you call."

"It must be dementia. I never used to forget things."

"Denial is a powerful defense mechanism, and narcotics add to the confusion. I think the narcotics were causing delusions."

Nonsense! This woman was trying to convince her she was going crazy. She shook Maggie's arm off her shoulders.

"You lied about being my social worker."

Maggie laughed. "I'm a volunteer social worker."

Harlots are social workers? "You said your pimp beat you up."

"Not *my* pimp. I stole one of his girls, placed her in a convent."

"You weren't a prostitute?"

"No. I don't know why that rumor is so persistent."

"I do." The man came in from the hallway. "You got labeled a temptress."

Maggie rolled her eyes. "Don't get him started."

"Religions are the problem. Christian, Muslim, Jewish, they all demean women." He paced back and forth across the kitchen floor. "The first Christian apostle was a woman, but over the next two thousand years the church turned her into a repentant prostitute." He glowered at Ellen as if he knew she went to church.

What a strange man. One minute he's bawling her out for not having dinner ready, the next minute he's talking like a women's libber.

"Prostitutes have nothing to repent," Maggie said. "They're not detestable sinners like the Bible says. Pimps force them to become prostitutes when they're twelve or thirteen."

"Are you immigrants?"

He flicked his thumb at Maggie. "She's from Syria, but I don't think she wants to talk about it."

"If I don't, who will?" She went silent, and Ellen knew why. She didn't want to blab that she was an illegal. If Frank were here, he would have already phoned the immigration enforcement people.

"In our home a female could never bring honor to the family. She could only dishonor it. My little sister and I lived in constant fear. If my veil slid off my nose, my father would beat me." Maggie's accent was more pronounced, and Ellen strained to understand her. "I was sixteen. It was late at night, and everyone else was in bed. When I finished cleaning the dishes, I went into our room. The window was open and my sister was gone. She was thirteen years old."

At thirteen her sister should have known better. Craig was only three when he sneaked out of the house. She'd looked everywhere, inside and outside. Then she heard him giggling behind a rose bush. He'd decided to play hide and seek without telling her. That rascal!

"I looked all over the neighborhood. Then I saw her limping toward me, her hands grabbing at the air. I hugged her. Sometimes I still feel her damp hair."

Maggie caressed her cheek with her fingers.

"Three men had pulled her through the window. She didn't cry out because she was afraid to wake our father and brothers. I took her into the house to wash off the blood. Our mother heard her moaning and came into the kitchen." Maggie's voice changed to a monotone, "When she saw the blood she woke the men. My brothers dragged Fatima outside. I screamed that men had raped her, but it made no difference. She had shamed the family. They tied her hands and feet. My father twisted my arms behind my back so I couldn't help her. He wanted me to watch. My brothers walked around the yard, gathering rocks. Then they hurled the stones at her."

Ellen could feel the father's hands digging into her own wrists, hear the rocks thudding against the girl's body. She put her arm around Maggie and pulled her close. She knew what to do now. They needed a place to stay, and she had this big house. It didn't matter that they were foreigners, that Maggie might be illegal.

"When my father let go of my arms, I ran to Fatima. I threw the rocks away. So many rocks. Pebbles stuck between her ribs. I lay on top of her and cried. A rock hit my head and I saw flashing lights. I ran down the street, men shouting behind me. I ran all night. I made a vow. I failed to rescue Fatima, but I would devote my life to helping other girls."

Maggie's hair felt thick against her neck, not wispy like hers. What could she say to comfort the poor woman?

"What happened wasn't your fault. It was part of God's plan."

"God's plan?" Maggie gaped at her. "God planned to have my little sister tortured and killed?"

"She'll get her reward in heaven." As soon as she said it she realized her error. Maggie's sister was a Muslim and hadn't accepted Jesus as her savior, so she would go to hell. Her stomach cramped. That couldn't be right. She would pray for Fatima.

That awful Sharia law. Frank used to go on and on about it. "Your brothers were obeying Sharia law."

"No they weren't," the man said. "Islamic law doesn't permit honor killings. Very few Muslims believe in them."

"We need to ban immigrants."

"I was a refugee," Maggie said.

"That's what the rapists and murderers would say."

"Most refugees are women and children. They flee for their lives, like me."

"Okay, let women and children in. Just ban the men."

They stared at her.

Why did she have to open her big mouth? Maggie's just re-lived this horrible experience, and she starts prattling about Sharia law. She could hear Frank, you can't keep your tongue from wagging, can you?

The man cocked his head at Maggie. "She might have a point."

Maggie laughed, a throaty laugh that seemed to come from deep inside her.

The tension in her shoulders oozed away. Why, she could say anything she wanted around these two.

He pointed to the wall clock. "The church only serves Thanksgiving dinner till three."

"You are always in such a hurry. We are guests, remember?"

That's right, they were her guests. What could she feed them? She hadn't been to the store for a while. Maggie said weeds were growing up around her tires. Had it really been that long?

A box of soda crackers sat on the second shelf of the cupboard the man had left open. She reached for it, but her back twinged.

"I've got to take a pain pill first."

She weaved into the hallway and slid her right arm against the wall so she wouldn't fall. Inside the bathroom, she locked the door. She opened her cabinet. The little plastic bottle was gone.

How could she be so stupid? He'd been after her pills all along, and the woman was his accomplice. They had conned her, Maggie pretending to phone Janet while he searched the house. She'd recited that story about her sister like a zombie, as if she'd read it somewhere and memorized it. Frank always said she was too gullible.

She paused in the hallway to catch her breath. They would be out the door by now, but she would phone the police.

They were sitting at the table, watching her.

"Give me the pills and I won't call the police."

Had he even heard her? His face looked different, relaxed. He was feeling the rush. It wouldn't last long, but who cares?

"My back hurts. I need my pills right now."

He nodded. "I know." His eyes were gentle, as if he really cared. How could he know what she was going through? He took drugs for pleasure, not pain.

"Okay, I'm calling the police." She picked up the phone and dialed, slowly, to give him time to change his mind.

Had he noticed she'd dialed six nines in a row? He'd been to prison. A con man would know when he was being conned.

She laid the phone in its cradle. She couldn't phone the police. They might find out she was getting her pills from two doctors. She was a con artist herself, just like these charlatans. They were three peas in a pod. Besides, they were her guests. Where were her manners?

"I'll get us something to eat." She wasn't sure they heard her because the shriek of the siren was deafening.

Wheezing, she shook crackers out of their cellophane wrapper into a bowl. She tried to take a deep breath but couldn't. She slapped the bowl on the table and flopped on her chair.

The siren moaned and died. A neighbor must be in trouble.

"We have to say the blessing first." It wouldn't be Thanksgiving without the blessing. She couldn't remember what Frank used to say. She would have to think of something.

"We're supposed to hold hands." His dirty hand would be alive with germs, but it was too late to change her mind. She clenched her teeth and groped for his right hand. Her fingers touched a crusted indentation in his palm. Of course. He was once a carpenter.

She gripped Maggie's warm hand and his poor, broken hand. "Thank you," she said.

Was the pounding coming from the door or from inside her head? She closed her eyes and pictured Frank holding the man's left hand, James linked with Frank, Julie at the table's end smiling at her beloved grandma, Craig peeking over his shoulder at the refrigerator, Janet holding Maggie's hand. The room shifted and a girl with dusky skin sat between Frank and the man, who locked their hands around hers, protecting her from whatever was out there.

MONKEY MOUNTAIN

Kali VanBaale

The brothers first heard the screaming one morning as they fed calves. The piercing cries echoed from the timber above the dairy farm, a bluff the family had called "Monkey Mountain" since the boys were little. Startled by the sound, Eric and Jamie straightened in unison with armfuls of hay clutched to their chests, and turned toward the dark woods.

"What was that?" White puffs of Jamie's breath billowed against the flat pink horizon.

"Shh." Eric frowned.

Seconds passed. A cold gust funneled between the white fiberglass calf huts and swirled late spring snow in Jamie's face.

Another screech splintered the air.

"Is that a woman?" Jamie whispered. "It sounds like someone screaming." He shivered inside his thick denim coat.

Eric shook his head. "It's an animal of some sort."

Jamie's eyes widened. "What kind of animal?" He'd never heard anything of the like before.

Eric tossed the hay into the pen for the waiting, hungry calf and brushed off the front of his winter coveralls. "Sounds like some kind of cat. Bobcat, maybe." He paused. "Or a mountain lion."

"Mountain lion!" Jamie also tossed an armful of hay into the next pen. "You're lying."

"No, I'm not." Eric cuffed his red nose. "We get 'em here sometimes when they wander down from South Dakota. Maybe a half dozen in the last twenty years. Look it up on the DNR website."

Jamie didn't need to. He knew his brother was telling the truth. Eric was only eighteen but had always seemed to be some version of a responsible adult. He could've picked on Jamie any time he'd wanted to with their four-year age difference, but Eric never had. He'd always been kind to his little brother.

Eric pulled an empty bottle from a pen and dropped it into the back of the utility wagon. "We should tell Dad."

"Why?"

"He'll want to kill it. Big cats like that are hunters." Eric mounted the four-wheeler and started the motor. "Let's go," he said. "I got homework to do."

Jamie straddled the back of the seat, trying to imagine a

mountain lion strolling through Iowa hills and pastures, hunting for its dinner, but couldn't. The idea seemed ridiculous.

* * *

Two days later, Eric and Jamie donned their camouflage hunting clothes, loaded their 12-gauge rifles, and started for Monkey Mountain in search of the animal. Once again, they'd heard the screaming during evening chores, and their father agreed with Eric that it sounded like a big cat. Bobcat or lion, he didn't care. He wanted it dead before it started picking off livestock or their mother's beloved dogs.

The boys crossed the frozen creek, trekked up the snow-dusted bluff, and hiked deep into the trees. Eric was a good shot and had been hunting this timber most of his life, but Jamie didn't much like hunting and only did it when his father made him during deer season. He'd never killed anything and hated the sound of gun blasts. Sometimes it has to be done, Eric often reminded him. They needed the meat, rabid animals were dangerous, and dying cattle shouldn't be made to suffer. All part of farm life.

As the brothers picked their way through brambles and naked saplings, Jamie made sure to step in Eric's larger boot prints. The boys silently entered the section of timber that had spawned the nickname Monkey Mountain: a copse of Catalpa trees with brown, banana-shaped seed pods that dangled from branches all winter. Grandpa Chuck always claimed his father had planted the non-native trees for his pet monkeys he let run wild in the timber, and the boys had believed the story until they were old enough to realize Grandpa Chuck liked to tell tall tales.

Eric stopped and brushed his gloved fingertips over a short, crooked trunk. "I love it up here," he said. "This is my favorite place on the whole farm."

Jamie rested his rifle against his shoulder and plucked a pod from a low branch. He crushed it in his gloved palm. Jamie and Eric had camped amid the trees many times on warm summer nights in a little yellow dome tent. A good mile away from the farm and house and completely isolated, it had never bothered Jamie, so long as he was with his brother. But now, standing beneath the same trees hunting for some unknown screaming creature, the thought of camping here again unsettled him.

"Do you really think there's a mountain lion up here?" Jamie asked.

Eric shrugged. "Maybe." He tilted his head back, staring up into the branches. "I sure wish Grandpa's story had been true."

"Which story?" Their grandfather had told them many.

"That his father kept monkeys up here. It was always my favorite story."

"Me, too." Jamie dropped the pod pieces and switched his gun to the other shoulder. His favorite story from Grandpa Chuck had been a claim that once during a dust storm in the thirties, he'd witnessed a flock of birds flying backwards to keep from getting dirt in their eyes.

"Are we resting?" Jamie asked.

Eric exhaled a steamy cloud and blinked slowly, his eyelids droopy and tired. "I just want to take this in for a moment," he said.

He'd been up since four for the early milking. Eric had milked the morning shift before school since he was fourteen, while Jamie and their father milked the evening shift. But soon Jamie would be old enough to take the evening shift by himself. That was the plan. The brothers would slowly take over the farm in a partnership, passing the reins from father to sons.

Last night, Eric and their mother had walked to the milking parlor where their father was finishing up the evening shift, and all three had stayed out there until close to midnight. This morning, no one spoke at breakfast, their shoulders hunched tensely over plates of bacon and eggs. It wasn't like Eric and their parents to argue. He'd never been in any serious trouble and worked hard at home and at school. Jamie couldn't imagine what they'd been talking about for so long in the milking parlor.

Jamie's toes grew uncomfortably cold inside his boots, and he stamped his feet to get some blood flowing. He studied his brother's profile in the fading light, the tense line of his jaw.

An ear-splitting scream startled the boys and Eric reflexively trained his gun in the direction of the sound. Jamie fumbled with his own weapon, struggling to get the safety off and the butt comfortably settled against his shoulder. The brothers waited, fingers on triggers, steel barrels side by side, until another scream tore through the trees.

"God damn," Jamie whispered, "that sounds like a woman being strangled."

"Shhh." Eric shifted his weight and leaned forward.

The screaming continued, a demented, painful growl that echoed off the hillsides. A half mile away, maybe less.

"It's a mountain lion," Eric finally said, his voice low. "Female. She's in heat."

Jamie's hands began to tremble, and the end of his gun barrel wavered. "How do you know?"

"I watched a YouTube video last night. That's how they sound."

Jamie widened his stance for better balance on the uneven terrain.

"Stop moving," Eric said.

Several minutes passed before another screech echoed through the trees, but farther away this time.

Eric lowered his gun. "She's heading east."

"Will it come back?" His voice betrayed his worry.

Eric patted Jamie's shoulder. "It's okay, buddy. You're the one carrying the gun."

* * *

On the second trip into the timber, Eric tracked fresh scat and paw prints in the new snow. The trail led from the creek straight into the heart of Monkey Mountain.

There, the brothers hunkered down in the fallen needles and seed pods, huddling close to a Catalpa with fresh claw marks on the trunk.

It was even colder this evening than the previous, and Jamie wished he'd thought to bring a couple of warming packs to stick in his coat pockets. He shivered and tried to mask the chatter of his teeth by clenching his jaw. While Eric wasn't shivering from the cold, he had burrowed down deep into his coveralls until only his eyes were visible over the collar.

"This is funny," Eric said.

"What's funny?"

"We're in Iowa hunting lions in a place we call Monkey Mountain."

"Huh. Yeah, that's funny."

The sun made its final descent below the horizon, basking the fallow fields and barns in a soft orange light.

"The farm looks so small from up here," Eric said.

"Yeah," Jamie answered. "But I like that you can see it all from one place."

Eric sighed and burrowed deeper.

Jamie adjusted his weight and pulled a large stick from beneath him. "What were you and Dad and Mom talking about for so long the other night?"

Eric didn't respond. The timber was quiet but for the occasional rustle of the wind gently rocking the Catalpa pods hanging above their heads.

"I had to break some news to them," he said.

"What news?"

Eric tensed when a squirrel scrambled across a branch and jumped from one tree to another. He relaxed and settled back against the trunk.

"I told them I'm joining the Marine Corps," he said. "A four-year enlistment. I'll leave for boot camp in California at the end of August."

Jamie slowly lowered the barrel of his rifle to the ground.

The Marine Corps.

California.

Four years.

The words slowly sunk in. Jamie lifted his face to the sky and watched the brown pods sway back and forth. His throat tightened with the threat of tears and he turned away so his brother wouldn't see his face. Unlike Jamie who cried all the time, *a tender heart* his mother called him, Eric hardly ever cried. In his whole life, Jamie had only seen him cry a couple of times. Once, when he had to put down his old sheep dog, Dolly, and once at their Grandpa Chuck's funeral.

"Did you hear what I said?" Eric asked after some time, but Jamie didn't answer. He kept his gaze high in the canopy, blinking the tears away.

"I signed up 'cause I just want to do something different for a while," Eric said. "Something on my own." He tugged his knit cap down further over his ears. "It's hard to explain. Mom and Dad don't understand."

But Jamie didn't understand either. He couldn't imagine the house without Eric, or doing chores every day without Eric nearby, just an arm's length away to tell him what to do and answer questions.

"Are you upset, too?" Eric asked.

"No." Jamie sniffed. "Do what you want. I don't care."

It seemed to Jamie that the air between himself and his brother had suddenly changed. Grown colder, or thinner, making it harder to breathe, like those hikers on the tallest mountaintops in the world where they had to carry oxygen tanks. But Jamie and his brother weren't on a mountaintop. Not a real one. They were only here, in their small little world on Monkey Mountain.

Jamie kicked the snow with the heel of his boot. "Monkey Mountain is a stupid name," he said.

"It's just a nickname, Jamie." Eric stood and brushed snow from the seat of his coveralls.

"It's just a story."

"It was a stupid story," Jamie said. "And we were stupid kids."

As Eric opened his mouth to respond, a screech echoed over

the bluff just above them and Eric ducked as if dodging a bullet. Jamie scrambled to his feet.

"Jesus, that was close," he whispered.

Eric lifted his gun to his shoulder and silently motioned to the top of the bluff. He tapped Jamie's chest and pointed right, then tapped his own and pointed left. Jamie nodded, and the boys split up.

Jamie made his way up the western side of Monkey Mountain, taking slow, quiet steps. His shoulders and biceps began to burn from holding the rifle set. Tiny flakes of snow drifted through the trees, lazily landing on his face. Another cry, this one even closer. Jamie's heart hammered in his chest. He stopped and fumbled with the rifle to double check that he'd taken off the safety, that it was, indeed, loaded.

He hadn't fired his rifle in over a year, since the last time Eric took him target practicing. Had he cleaned and oiled it after the last time? He couldn't remember. He hoped so. Eric had lectured him about gunk building up around the firing pin and causing it to jam. Maybe he would shoot more accurately with his gloves off. He bit the tips and pulled his hands free, leaving the gloves where they landed on the ground. Just as he repositioned the stock against his shoulder, his peripheral vision caught a sliver of movement.

Jamie looked up the bluff and there it was. Ten, maybe twelve feet away. She stared back at him, perfectly still, poised with one front leg bent, ready to pounce. She was beautiful with a light cinnamon-colored coat, dark-tipped ears and black-lined eyes. Six, possibly seven feet long. So much bigger than he'd imagined.

Monkey Mountain was silent. Jamie and the lion both remained still, locked in a staring contest, like Jamie used to play with Eric when they were kids.

Jamie pressed his cheek against the cold stock and squeezed his left eye shut, sighting with his right. His index finger curled around the trigger, his arms trembling with the kind of old man shakes his Grandpa Chuck used to get.

The lion lowered her paw to the ground and took a few steps backward. Maybe she was retreating. If she turned and ran, he wouldn't have to be the one to fire at her.

But in a blurry, split-second motion, the lion launched from the top of the bluff straight at him. Jamie cried out and squeezed the trigger. One, two, three shots, each slamming the stock against his shoulder like a violent punch. The lion screeched and hit the ground hard, front legs buckling, her face plowing into the fresh snow. She tried to stand, staggered sideways, tried again, then collapsed with a thud.

Slowly, Jamie lowered the gun barrel, dazed, his ears ringing. Acrid gunpowder-filled smoke drifted in his face and clogged his nostrils. The lion lay just a few feet in front of him on her side, unmoving. He waited until her shallow breaths ceased and carefully stepped closer. Two small red circles dotted the left side of her neck. Two of his three shots had hit. Her glassy eyes fixed on nothing.

He kneeled next to her and laid his bare hand on her warm belly, stroking her coarse hair.

Footsteps pounded down the hill above him.

"Jamie!" Eric shouted, panting. "Jamie!"

Eric halted when he saw Jamie and the prone animal and stared, mouth agape, his expression disbelieving. He crouched next to Jamie and lay his rifle down on the ground.

"I got her," Jamie said quietly.

The snow fell harder now, covering everything in a smooth white blanket. Jamie tipped his face to the sky and let the cold flakes gather on his eyelashes. He loved it here, too, even though he hadn't said it.

When Jamie looked at his brother, he saw tears streaming down Eric's ruddy cheeks.

"You did it," Eric said, his voice quavering.

He gave Eric a small smile. "Sometimes it has to be done," he said. And for once, he didn't feel like crying.

THE NEVER-FAILING VICE OF FOOLS

James Kearney

Y'know, one thing I've always believed in is not letting your-self get played for a sucker. I don't mean clownin' around like when one of the guys plays a practical joke on you or sumpin'. What I mean is by some girl. I've believed in this since I got into high school three years ago as a freshman. Now that I'm a senior, I believe even more firmly in it.

So far, I gotta admit, I've been doin' all right. I've always had the upper hand. No chick has ever suckered me and, like I said, none ever will if I can help it.

Now I'll admit, I've gone back on my ideas in the last three years. One thing I always said was that I'd never go steady senior year. I did that but y'gotta understand a couple of things before you go jumpin' to any hasty conclusions about what kind of a guy I am for goin' back on my word. It was like this, see, all the girls in my class were already going steady, all the ones I wanted to take out anyway. There was nothin' I could do. Oh, I monkeyed around for a while, took out a couple of girls from Grand Rapids—that's a town about five or six miles from where I live—but they didn't do too much of anything to me. It's not that I thought I was too good for them, y'understand; it's just that I didn't think I could fall for them in a big way. You know how it is.

Anyway, there was this one sophomore in school who wasn't bad. In fact, she was pretty nice looking. I had never seen her be-fore this and I was kind of interested. It started out kind of funny. In the first place, after I found out her name, I forgot it and had to ask this buddy of mine again a couple of days later. Now the thing that was peculiar about that was that it was the first time that that ever happened. Usually I couldn't forget a name for nothin'. I don't know how in the heck I forgot hers, being interested like I was and all. Well, anyhow, the second time I remembered it.

I saw her at a dance one weekend after school started and I danced with her one set, a fast one. Anyway, right in the middle of this song the power went off and the whole place blacked out. All the girls were screamin' and the guys were whistlin' and ma-kin' wolf calls like they were really movers, you know, like they were gonna take advantage of the fact that it was dark when they knew damn well that they weren't. I guess one thing that really made an impression on me right there was that she didn't scream or act scared or anything in spite of the fact she was only a sophomore and kind of immature as sophomores are prone to be, not that it's their fault or anything. She just took it right in stride.

I didn't dance with her again that night but I saw her in school that week and said "hi" and all that jazz but I never did talk to her. That probably would have got her thinkin' I was really goin' wild over her and I didn't want that to happen.

The next Friday night at the dance I saw her again and decided to ask her home. That's considered all right around here and everybody does it. If y'ask me, it's a lot less expensive and a lot less trouble than bringing 'em to the dance, you know, as a date. At least that way y'aren't stuck with one all night. Anyway, as I was about to say, I asked her home and she seemed kind of apprehensive. That got me wonderin' but she finally said all right so I decided not to sweat the small stuff. I found out later that her apprehension was caused by the fact that she was going with this guy. When I found that out, I kind of had to laugh, although I gotta admit, it was a dirty thing to do but I didn't know so it wasn't my fault.

I got her home later than I should have that night. I didn't use my head on that one because I had been takin' out older girls. In fact, she was the first girl I ever took out that was two years younger'n myself. It never occurred to me that she'd have to get home earlier. I called up the next night to find out if everything was all right and I guess it was.

That week in school the guys started givin' me a bad time— like always happens when you go after sumpin' new—and I started to find out a few things about her.

I found out her dad was dead and she was the youngest of seven children. Like I said, she was pretty nice lookin' and had had her way with guys she'd gone with so the guy she was goin' with then didn't say much. She broke up with him pretty quick anyhow. Anyway, like I'm trying to get across, she was pretty spoiled. That didn't sound too good and if I was going to take her out much, she'd have to shape up because, like I said, I'm gettin' suckered by nobody.

Well, I found out that she was lettin' it get around that she had me right about where she wanted me. Now this and the fact that she went out with a kid I didn't much care for, whose primary motive for takin' her out was that he thought he was knifin' me out, got me to the point where I decided to forget about her and I let it get around. Now, y'gotta understand, as far as I was concerned, I was through with her. I wasn't about to let any girl, let alone a sophomore, shove this kid around.

Anyway, she started talkin' it up to one of my buddies whose sister she ran around with. She was trying to get him to fix it up with me, you know how that goes, and he told her it didn't look too good but he'd try. Of course, first thing the next mornin' in school he told me all 'bout it. I decided that maybe I was sittin' pretty good right then and could do about what I wanted without lookin' bad. I started playin' the ol' cool role in school when she was around, you know, pretending I didn't see her and crap like that when I knew damn well she was lookin' right at me. This usually works like a charm and I played it to its fullest capacity.

A couple of nights later after football practice, I was standin' watchin' a JV game and she was about twenty feet away watchin' too—a bunch of sophomores played on the JV? I just pretended like I was really interested in the game and like I didn't even notice her there although I didn't much give a damn one way or the other who won the game. Pretty soon I saw her comin' over to where I was standing and all of a sudden my interest in the game increased about three hundred percent. When she got a little ways away, she said, "Y'know, for a good kid you really are stuck up."

I pretended like I didn't hear her and like I was really surprised to see her there. Anyway, I said, "What?" and she smiled and repeated it. I gotta admit that really faked me out. Most girls would've let it go but she really had guts. She didn't get much embarrassed either. I guess that kind of impressed me.

I talked to her for a while, making sure there were frequent interruptions in the conversation while I paid close attention to the game to see some play that was bein' run, although, like I said, I didn't much give a damn, just part of the role, you see.

We got along pretty good after that. We started going out quite regularly; in fact, it got to the point where she was the only one I was taking out. Now this and the fact that nobody else I wanted to take out was available were the main reasons for my askin' her to go steady. It was just because I might as well have been anyway, you see. Of course, I made it sound like it didn't make much difference to me one way or the other whether she said "yes" or not but she did, just like I figured. I never would have asked her if I hadn't been pretty sure of myself. That'd be givin' her the upper hand and that's one thing you don't want to do—ever.

Now I gotta admit, I was goin' pretty wild over her. She didn't know it, of course. I kept monkin' around with other girls and she didn't say anything in spite of the fact that it bothered her. That jealousy bit is no good and I told her how I felt about it quite a few times so I guess she didn't want to cause any trouble.

Well, about a month and a half ago she went to this one dance that I couldn't make and the next day some kid told me I'd better watch her, that she was goofin' around with some guy at that dance. I started asking around and a couple of other people told me the same thing. This really teed me off because it made me look like a jerk. This I did not like.

I talked to her first thing Monday morning in school and told her that I wanted to hang the whole thing. She knew what I was talking about and kept insisting it was nothing. I figured it had to be something because people were harping on it all day. I mean remarks like, "I'm glad he found out because I don't like to see that happen to anybody," and "I wasn't going to say anything but as long as you already know," that kind of gets you thinking about just exactly what kind of sap you really are. I decided to hang it and I did. Aw, she cried in school and didn't eat for a week and all that jazz but that was prob'ly an act anyhow.

Like I said, that was a month and a half ago and seein' as how I hadn't taken her out, I decided to be a nice guy and forget that she ever did anything. I don't usually do this, y'understand, but I decided to anyway, for her, mainly I guess. She was still feelin' pretty bad. Anyway, she decided to play the role and turn me down. If that wasn't sumpin' else. I imagine she thinks I'll try again but I'll fix her. We're through for good now. I don't much give a damn anyway. I mean, what the hell—graduation is next week and I'm gettin' out of here this summer and goin' to college next year so I won't see her much anymore anyway so I guess it's the best thing. At least I didn't get played for a sucker; that's the important thing. She found out pretty fast that I don't bluff and, as far as I'm concerned, it's her tough luck. No one suckers this kid, especially not a damn little sophomore.

MODEL A

James Kearney

When his chin bumped his chest, he snapped to the chug-chugging hum-humming of the 1929 Model A, the lyrics of the Buddy Holly 45 that he had bought just days before echoing from his dream:

Oh that'll be the day, when you make me cry;
Yes, that'll be the day when you say goodbye;
Yes, that'll be the day; you know it's a lie;
Well, that'll be the day-ay-ay when I die.

He looked over at his grandfather who was driving, a bit embarrassed to have fallen asleep again. It happened every time he rode in this car.

"I don't know how you can sleep in this old rattletrap," his grandfather said again. The boy looked at the old man's sky-blue eyes, magnified by the wire-rimmed glasses that bridged the hawk nose, and even under the brown fedora in the waning November afternoon light he could see that the old man was amused. The aroma of cigar smoke and Copenhagen that emanated from the old man's clothing made him feel warm.

"I don't know either, Pop," he said, smiling. "It just knocks me out. It's the rhythm, I guess."

"Rhythm, my ass," said the old man, as he lifted the large, empty coffee can from the driveshaft hump between the seats, laid it under his lower lip, spat snuff juice into it and carefully set it back on the hump.

The boy suspected that the exhaust fumes seeping into the cab through the rusted floor had more than a little to do with his stupor but he would not say that because the man—the man that he at age sixteen still kissed on the lips when they parted company and would for another two years until one day they (though they expressed no apparent communication whatsoever) spontaneously and conjointly offered to shake hands—was very proud of the old car.

He had been looking forward to this day for almost a year—their annual trip to the grandfather's forty acres in the big woods north of Hibbing. The deer season would open at dawn the next day, Saturday, but he had left school at noon, knowing that he would serve nine hours detention—three for each hour missed—for skipping school to hunt deer because the grandfather had wanted to get an early start. He had no regrets.

He had boarded the Greyhound at the Shell Station at the junction of 169 and Roosevelt Avenue—he had no clue which Roosevelt gave his name to the street—which served as Main Street of Fernwood, the whole six block stretch, and had taken a window seat up near the driver, laying his gear on the aisle seat next to him. The bus wound northeast along 169 past lakes and ponds, woods and fields, and the ubiquitous red, iron ore dumps, now growing over with brush and softwood trees, through small town after smaller town, stopping for a few minutes in each. At one of these stops a dressed-up girl his age had gotten on and, without looking up, had moved toward the seat upon which sat his jacket and bag. He had snatched his gear and put it on his lap but when she did look up at him, she became embarrassed and walked further back. He had been both disappointed and relieved.

Shortly thereafter he returned to dreaming about the buck that had leaped into the road ahead of them as they walked to their stands the year before. It had been a cold morning and he was wearing cotton gloves and had balled his fist inside the gloves because his fingers hurt. When he saw the buck with its wide-spread antlers, he could not find the glove fingers so the animal was almost into the woods on the other side of the road before he located the trigger—he shot high. His grandfather had missed as well. He had vowed over and over again throughout that year that forever after he would bear the cold.

When the bus arrived in Hibbing, his grandfather had collected him at the old Greyhound Depot, the first of its kind in the world, built originally to shuttle the men who worked the iron mines, and they headed north.

He turned behind him in the Model A to look once again at the cased rifles lying across the seat—both Model 1894 Winchesters, his grandfather's .30-.30 and the 1903 vintage .32 Special that he used and would inherit ten years later when his grandfather suffered a fatal stroke as he was kneeling, saying his prayers on a Christmas morning. His grandfather looked at him again, smiling, picked up the coffee-can spittoon, spat into it again then turned back to the darkening road in front of him.

"We're going to find out what kind of a job we did with that tar paper when we came up a few weeks back; it's going to snow tonight, y'know; I hope we don't get wet," he said, smiling.

"Yeah. Me too," the boy replied.

He looked past his grandfather at the sun that was about to be snuffed out by a rising shield of gray on the horizon.

Skeletal trees—birch, poplar, maple and spindly jack pine— lined both sides of the trunk highway. Now and again they passed swamps and iced-over ponds bedecked with lonely, reedy musk-rat lodges and, on some of the ridges, stands of white and red pine that whatever fire had scorched the rest of the country had spared for whatever reason. The boy took note of the clumsy wads of dead leaves near the tops of the deciduous trees and wondered again how squirrels could stay warm in them.

"We're crossing the Gunflint Trail here, you know," said his grandfather, though the boy could see no trail.

"I know," he said.

"It runs all the way to Lake Sup—You know? How do you know?"

"You tell me every time we cross it."

"I do, do I? Well, I'll be damned. I must be getting old."

"You must," said the boy. They both smiled.

Just past the town of Acheron the old man turned the car west—turned as he always did by sliding the steering wheel with his one hand, gripping it with the other, sliding it a few more degrees and gripping until the turn was negotiated—onto a gravel road and the hum of tires was supplanted by the crunch of gravel and the ping-pinging of small stones pocking the undercarriage of the car. The sky was now dark and gray, horizon to horizon, and it began spewing snow, large white flakes.

"Good tracking tomorrow," said the grandfather.

They crossed a rickety wooden bridge over a ribbony ice-bound stream. Suddenly a large specter swooped down into and quickly up out of the narrow beam of the headlights.

"Whoa! Cool!" said the boy. "What the hell was that?"

"Owl," said his grandfather. "A Great Gray."

"I've never seen one before," said the boy.

"But you've heard them" said the old man, "big booming voices they've got."

"Yeah, I've heard them," he said. "They sound like ghosts."

"That they do," said his grandfather.

A few minutes later they passed a driveway on the left of the car.

"Goddamn Gundrums," said the grandfather.

"What?"

"The Goddamn Gundrums. They own the place down that road," the grandfather answered. "You've heard me talk about them before, haven't you?"

"I don't think so," said the boy.

"The Goddamn Gundrums."

"What's the problem with the Gundrums?"

"The problem is that they come up here every year the week

before the season opens and poach and by the time we get here the deer are all spooked and we have to work that much harder for our venison."

"They do?"

"You bet your ass they do. The Goddamn Gundrums. Four or five years ago, before you started coming up here, I was driving in on opening day, about nine in the morning, y'know, and I passed that bunch of Swedes driving out with a trailer full of deer. Tell me they filled out between sunrise and nine in the morning. Goddamn Gundrums. Hell, we didn't see a deer the whole weekend that year."

A few minutes later they turned into their own road, a two-tire track separated by a low ridge of dead grass. The trees and brush on either side closed in tightly now and formed a vault over the road. The darkness became more profound. Soon a clearing opened up before them in the center of which sat the small black shack that they had repaired two weeks before. The grandfather parked the Model A near the steps to the small porch.

"Conal," he said, "you start unloading the gear and carrying it in while I get the shack unlocked and the lamps lit." The old man retrieved a flashlight from under the front seat and climbed the steps to the door, searching his coat pocket for the key to the large brass padlock that secured the hasp. The boy opened the passenger side back door, slid the rifles off the seat, cradled them across the crook of his arm and climbed the steps. First things first.

As he entered the shack, he heard the first sputtering of the first kerosene lamp his grandfather had lit, the one that hung from the rafter just inside the door. As the old man replaced the chimney on the lamp, he said, "We've got to clean these tomorrow. The light's a little dim." He then lit two more lamps—one on the old wooden kitchen table that sat in the middle of the one room and the other that hung on the joist in the corner of the far wall opposite the double bed with its sagging mattress and patchwork cover. The boy propped the rifles in the corner behind the bed under the plank shelf upon which sat two yellowing piles of crisp *Life* magazines from the Forties. He returned to the car and retrieved a cardboard box which contained their food for the weekend—canned beans, pasties wrapped in foil, a can of coffee, milk in a glass bottle with a cardboard cap, a carton of eggs, sausage wrapped in butcher's paper, ground beef wrapped in butcher's paper, a box of cereal, a small bag of sugar, a loaf of white bread, a pound of butter, a small can of Crisco, a few potatoes and onions, bacon and canned stew, two gallon milk bottles full of water. On his final trip he unloaded the two khaki duffel bags—World War II surplus—that contained their extra clothing and two boxes of ammunition. By the time he had deposited these at the foot of the bed, his grandfather had lit the kindling in the new stove that he had had made in the shop at the mine which he had superintended for many years and from which he had recently retired. The stove was simply a metal drum, painted silver, laid on its side with legs welded on the bottom, a grated door hinged on the front and a hole cut in the top at the back into which they had inserted a stove pipe that ran up the wall until it conjoined with the sheet metal chimney in the ceiling.

"It'll be warm in here soon," his grandfather said as he latched the stove door and turned toward the table. "Shit! Look what the packrats have done to the place!"

The boy looked around the cabin. Evidence of a mouse invasion was everywhere. Shredded bits of paper and cotton littered the chipped linoleum floor; a raggedy hole was torn out of one corner of the mattress; little black turds fouled the floor, the table, the three kitchen chairs.

"I'll find the traps," said the old man. "We'll show the little bastards who's boss."

He produced three mousetraps from the cupboard behind the table. "Here," he said. "Put a little butter on the pans and put them up on the rafters near the corners. I'll sweep the place up. Goddamn packrats! The little buggers make one hell of a mess."

By the time the boy had set the traps, his grandfather had cleaned the table and chairs and swept the floor and thrown the refuse into the front yard next to the car. He then laid the pasties in the stove to cook.

By this time the cabin was warming and crystalline spires of frost were forming on the inside of the windows.

Later, as they sat at the table eating, his grandfather said, "Look up there," jerking his chin up to where one of the traps sat on a rafter. A kangaroo mouse had smelt the butter and was nervously approaching the trap. Skitter, stop, sniff. Skitter, stop, sniff. Retreat. Repeat. The two sat motionless at the table watching the execution unfold. Finally the mouse approached the trap, sniffed again, and began licking the butter. The boy felt butterflies in his stomach. Lick, lick, lick, lick, retreat.

"What the hell?" said the boy.

"Just wait," said his grandfather. "He's not done yet."

He was right. The mouse returned to the trap and began licking again until the butter was gone. He continued to scour the stain. Suddenly, the trap snapped—so violently that the boy jumped—and turned over, pinning the mouse by the neck. As it struggled to free itself, the mouse' hindquarters slipped off the rafter and it kicked the air, first rapidly—then slowly—then spasmodically—then not at all.

"Get rid of the little bastard," said the grandfather, "then reset the trap. We'll catch his whole goddamn family."

Holding the trap between forefinger and thumb, the boy carried it out to the front porch. As he pried up the spring with one hand, he grabbed the mouse's tail with the other and when the carcass came free, he tossed it underhand into the snowy darkness beyond the clearing.

As he replaced the rebuttered trap on the rafter, his grandfather said, "Time was we had ways of dealing with gobshites like those Goddamn Gundrums."

"Oh yeah?" said the boy as he sat on the bed. He sensed a story was imminent.

"Oh yeah," said the old man. "Did I ever tell you about the two Finlander rock farmers that lived on that place down at the end of the road past the bend out there? You know, the old Sorenson place?"

The boy had heard many of his grandfather's stories—so many times, in fact, that he could repeat most of them verbatim. The retelling had never dulled his enjoyment of them, however, and he had grown wise to the old man's art. In the stories that the man embellished, the details were mercurial. In the stories that were gospel, the details were constant. He had heard nothing about the two Finnish farmers down the road, however.

"I don't believe you did," he said.

"Well, this was back in the old days," his grandfather began, "when I used to hunt up here with my cronies—Sandy Macgregor, Billy Olson, Mike Hayes—that bunch."

"You've talked about them," said Conal, stretching out on his side on the bed, his elbow on a pillow, his head on his hand.

"I have," said the old man. "Well, we got up here one deer season and for the second year in a row there was sign everywhere but no deer. We weren't used to that, y'know. We liked to hunt and have fun—not just hunt and hunt. We would normally fill out on that first weekend and raise hell the rest of the week. Well, we had a pretty good idea what the problem was. At the time two Finlanders had just begun squatting on that place at the end of the road—an old man and his son—and we figured that they had been living off of venison which was the reason the deer were so gun shy. Well, Sandy was a bit of a hothead, y'know, and he decided to have a word with them. He was a tough bastard, he was, and he was fed up. So we all went down there and Sandy told the old man that he had had enough and that if we ever came up again and the deer were spooked, he would report the two of them to the game warden. Now that was pretty much bluff but the old Finlander got pretty hot himself. He told Sandy to go to hell and that he'd better watch himself. Well, we left, figuring there wasn't much we could do but that night we got to talking about those two Finlanders again and Sandy got more and more pissed off because he felt he'd been threatened. And he had, y'know. By the tone of his voice, we all felt that old Finlander had made himself pretty clear.

Well, the next morning we were walking down to the road, about to drive that swampy stretch on the west side there to see if we could scare something up, when we heard an engine coming from down around the bend. Damned if it wasn't the two Finlanders in their Model T truck. Sandy said, 'Watch this' and he pulled his .30-.30 up" — at this the old man raised both his hands one in front of the other, as if he were holding a rifle, and sighted down the imaginary barrel— "and waited until the truck was just going past us. He squeezed off a shot and the truck piled up in the ditch. Well, we couldn't believe what he'd done but we went running over to the truck and there were the two of them, out cold, the backs of both their necks creased."

"Man! That was a hell of a shot," said Conal.

The old man looked him in the eye. "Almost," he said.

"I see," said the boy.

"Yes, well, Sandy was all for finishing them off but we wouldn't let him. But we had the problem of what we were going to do with the two Finlanders but while we were talking about it, old Arnie Swenson drove up from Hibbing. He'd been drinking all night, y'know, and he was pretty tight. So we told him there'd been an accident and put the two guys into his car and told him to take them to Hibbing to the hospital. Fortunately he was too drunk to remember where he'd got them—or pretended he was, anyway—anyway, he apparently convinced the police. Not that we would have had a lot of trouble with them anyway. The commissioner at that time was a pretty good friend of all of ours."

"So, were they all right?"

"Who? Oh, the Finlanders? Hell, no, they weren't all right. The old man died that night and the son the next day. No one of us ever talked about it so eventually it went away but we didn't have any more trouble with poaching around these parts until those Goddamn Gundrums moved in up the road and if Sandy were here, I don't think we'd have any trouble with *them* either.

"Well, time to hit the sack. We've got to be up before dawn tomorrow. I suppose you're going to read for a while?" He gestured at the piles of *Life*.

The boy, staring at nothing, was lost in his grandfather's story. Suddenly he realized that the old man had asked him a question.

"Yeah," said Conal, glancing behind him at the magazines. "But first I've got to go to the can." He swung his legs off the bed, stood up, and walked to the door while his grandfather began unbuttoning his flannel shirt.

"Close the door behind you, and when you decide to go to sleep, leave that one lamp by the door burning. I expect I'll be getting up at least once," he said.

"I will," replied the boy.

As he closed the door behind him, his nostrils contracted with his first breath of the night air. "Damn," he thought, "it's gotten cold—and it's stopped snowing." Descending the steps, he heard the wind rattling the dead leaves in the lone oak on the edge of the clearing. As he looked up at its dark, looming magnificence, he saw that the sky had cleared. Out of habit he searched the constellations. He quickly found The Big Bear, The Hunter, and the six of The Seven Sisters that were visible and thought that they had moved in the sky since he had last found them two nights before but that thought was put to rout by the shades of his grandfather's story—the shades of Sandy Macgregor, the two Finnish farmers, and his grandfather as a younger man. As he urinated in the snow at the edge of the clearing, he stared up at the deep black sky beyond the stars and shuddered.

WHAT HAPPENED TO MRS. ELEONORA VALDEMAR

Carmelo Rafala

*E*xcerpts from the remaining pages of this diary have been collected here for the purposes of the Court, and are established to have been written between the months of August and October in 1871. The crime scene is twenty miles from Poplar Bluff, Missouri.

August 19th

—seclusion on our remote woodland estate may have taken its toll on me, I duly admit. But I was hardly alone at the time. The boy you hired comes faithfully twice a week to cut wood for the stove or drop off his delivery of vegetables and meats and goes his way without uttering a sound.

Due to your continued lack of response I no longer see the point in sending you my letters, though I continue to write them nonetheless. They sit in the drawer of your desk, waiting. Like me. So I have taken to scribbling in this diary in an attempt to find a home for my many wayward thoughts.

And then there is Amity.

My younger cousin keeps me company, though we do not speak as freely to each other as we once did. Being in the family way does not sit well with her. Since the day my cousin knew she was with child her health took a turn for the worse, and these days she is wracked by a fever that clings to her body. Sometimes I find her lying on the sofa or sitting alone in the kitchen, speaking strange utterances to the air.

I wish I possessed knowledge of the summoning arts and herbal remedies known by the women on her side of the family, stretching down the line and into the past. Women of the dark forest. And maybe if I knew such arts I could help her, because at one point I feared her condition had worsened, so much so that I almost sent for a doctor.

Almost.

Such recklessness would be unacceptable. The comforts you bestow upon me, dear husband, are more than a woman of my low social standing could have dreamed of, and the education you paid for does not go without appreciation. Therefore, it has always been in my interest to protect your good name. Your ruin is our ruin.

So what troubles my heart, you may ask, and presses me to continue writing to you with such urgency? Your latest departure for St. Louis, my husband. That is when my fear truly took root.

The strange and unnatural visitor I warned you of? His presence on this haunted land continues to taunt me like a spectral thing born out of some darker realm of existence.

I often see him in the distance, moving between the tangled trees at dusk with surprising agility. I cannot determine any distinguishable features, and if there is a moon her radiance is not overly revealing.

But he is there, I tell you. Every night. Walking our property. Watching. Maybe even waiting. For what, I do not know. I hardly go outside anymore, and at night I shut and lock every window, every door.

I have taken your Colt repeating handgun out from the closet under the grand staircase and I have loaded it. I now carry the gun with me wherever I go.

Remember, dear husband, I know how to use it. And as the daughter of a backwoodsman of the Ozarks, bred to the dangers of an ancient and unknowable country, I feel safer with it in my hands—

August 30th

—in a rare but welcomed excursion from the house I went out front yesterday to pick lavender that grows by the side of the drive. I find its aroma soothes any troubles the house might hold, softens its darker edges. It was three o'clock in the afternoon.

The delivery wagon pulled up and in his usual fashion the urchin boy bid me a silent hello with the tipping of his ragged hat. He dropped off the food parcel, then handed me your letter which announced your return in two months' time. My initial relief was tinged with cold anticipation.

How long will you stay? Three or four days is usually all you can burden yourself with. You forgot to ask about Amity, about her delicate condition, and not a word was addressed to my welfare. You mentioned nothing of my concern for my unnatural visitor. The grand halls and theatres of St. Louis, and your life there, were all you seem occupied with.

On those rare occasions when you are at home with me, I

always receive the same reply to my queries about the purposes of your trips: business.

Business, you say.

The wind in my ears sounds more like honesty than your excuses. And your apologies, like ghosts, lack substance.

I realized I was alone. The boy and the wagon had gone. I stood with your letter in my closed fist, staring at the bend in the road where the urchin and his wagon must have vanished. The light had long since drained from the sky, leaving me surrounded by cool twilight. Though there was no wind, the tall trees bent at fantastic angles against the sky. The forest undulated, as if it were breathing, and the long grasses parted here and there with the movement of some unseen body.

Shaken with the knowledge that I was being watched, I turned to the house to see that all the curtains had been pushed aside and every window was opened. The front door was a gaping maw, exposing the house's murky innards—

September 5th

—though I am at a loss to understand how the house became so opened to the elements that day, I cannot blame Amity. Despite her occasional labored night walks about the house she rarely leaves her room these days, and I keep the door keys with me at all times. As for unlatching a window, she has never gone against my wishes before, and as she finds it difficult to muster the strength to climb stairs and reach the bedroom windows, I am satisfied she has played no part in this—

September 17th

—there is a drumming at the window behind me.

I sit at the writing desk in your library, pen in hand, steel nib scratching away. Though the sound at the window is persistent an overwhelming sense of dread prevents me from turning around. I fear that to face the one who walks these ancient forests would be to awaken unto myself, to feel the pull of an inhabited reality invisible to our eyes only because we are taught not to recognize its existence.

But what of my visitor's motives? Why does he not burst through a door or smash a window and climb through? And with the house recently found exposed to the elements, God knows he has had his chances to rush inside.

Perhaps he despises ceilings and walls. Perhaps he fears enclosures. If so, is he attempting to lure me out to strike a fatal blow? In my carelessness a few weeks back, while out picking lavender, did I almost fall victim to his dark purpose?

Maybe he is simply trying to drive me mad.

Amity does not react when I announce his presence. She cannot be wholly unaware of the nocturnal mysteries that conspire to torture me, of this I am certain.

The clock strikes nine.

In a moment I will put the pen down, rise from this chair and walk away, keeping my back to the glass and the primeval face I know lingers there—

September 23rd

—it was ten o'clock at night when it happened.

Sleep had not come easily, so I decided to walk the house, checking windows were shut and doors bolted. I was not surprised to find the window at the top of the grand staircase opened. I closed it, though I was certain I had done so previously.

Lamp held high I made my way to the kitchen. Amity stood at the table, and her eyes were glazed over with fever. She was washing her sweating face in the bucket of well water I had brought in earlier.

I took her arm in an attempt to guide her back to her bedroom, a small pantry just off the kitchen, when I was stopped by the skittering of feet outside. It was not unusual for some animal to rummage around the back porch at night.

Thrusting the lamp forward I moved to the window by the back door to see if I could spy the little creature. There was some moonlight. As I approached a loud bang came from the door and I jumped back, knocking into the table.

Amity stared at the door and mumbled something obscure.

I was overcome with dread. It was a sinking feeling that, if you failed to return soon, dear husband, we would both die of madness inside these suffocating walls.

Just as I started breathing normally again a succession of brutal thumps shook the door, one after another, increasing in intensity until I screamed at the vile noise to be gone.

The door shuddered and creaked on its hinges. My cousin moved toward the door. As it did not sit flush with the frame, I could see the door was not locked. I grabbed her arms and pulled her back. With a free hand I reached through the side seams of my petticoat, into the pocket, and pulled out the gun.

Silence filled the room.

I waited, holding her and the gun, for how long I cannot tell. She did not try and break free, and I doubt she had the strength to do so if she tried.

I gathered my wits about me enough to let her go. As I did so I rushed to the door and turned the key. I threw the top bolt across for good measure. As I threw that bolt, I sensed there was a hand pressed against the other side, just inches from my face. Then came a chafing sound: that hand sliding down the outside face of the door. I took a step back. More silence.

Satisfied he was gone, I guided my cousin back to her bed.

Why did Amity reach for the door? Was her intention to stand exposed so he could rip her and her child from the threshold? Or was Amity simply trying to lock the door, as I had done? I asked her these questions and many more, but she only looked at me strangely, as if I were but a wisp of smoke. I wanted to shake her violently for answers, but I lacked the strength.

What good would it have done? Amity has remained tight-lipped for months, speaking only when some need demanded it. Why should I have expected her to converse with me now? She would no more talk to me than you would come home to be with your wife—

September 25th

—my strange ramblings must provoke you to question my sanity. Sometimes I cannot quite convince myself of what is happening.

Believe me, dear husband, I am well enough in body and mind to know that I am lucid and rational and in control of my faculties.

Is it possible that in her present condition Amity could be affecting me? I accept that it is, indeed, possible. Those struck with fever have been known to walk about, to carry on conversations with the invisible, to react to ethereal oddities not seen by ordinary human eyes.

And if the visitor is just some abhorrent nightmare on the part of my ailing cousin, then it is conceivable I have been sharing in her reverie through something similar to hysteria, like those poor souls afflicted by *St. Vitus' Dance*, the thousands flailing about in their madness through the streets of Aachen.

Conceivable. But unlikely. For she makes no sound or movement that would induce me into her supposed mania.

So I must continue to believe the visitor is real, that he is here, and that he is drawn to me.

Or maybe I am, somehow, drawn to him—

October 3rd

—I found myself at the foot of my cousin's bed, gun in hand. She did nothing to indicate she was aware of my presence. She simply lay there, unmoving.

Like me, she is a poor child of this Earth and all its deeper aspects, and that there is some connection between her and my anguish seems reasonable. Would her demise, and that of the child, be the end of my torment? Would my visitor and all the spectral elements of earth and mind, finally, leave me?

It was a strange turn of fate. Strange that I would stop her from allowing a nameless threat to stand in an opened doorway and yet there I stood, just as much a menace as the thing beyond the door.

Though her delicate condition frustrates me, and her silences irritate, my heart has always felt affection for my long-suffering cousin.

I lowered the gun.

I was about to leave when she uttered a single word across the darkness between us.

Rawhead.

October 9th

—I remember the story Amity's mother once told us when we were children, before her untimely death. It was a piece of folklore passed on from her own mother, and from her mother's mother. Of the specter of a beast, born of blood and suffering, evoked from the sodden earth to feed upon the flesh and bone of the living.

And of Old Betty, the witch of the Ozarks who lived in the dark forest—

October 15th

—every day Amity is closer to delivery.

I was eleven when I helped Mother give birth to my dead brother in our cabin. As usual, Father had gone off on another fur-trapping expedition and would not be back for weeks. When he did return, I took the brunt of his despair for my mother's sake. My dear cousin Amity, his own brother's daughter, was not spared. She was only six years old at the time.

Before he departed on another trip, I made sure he would never harm us again, and the official story is that he disappeared in the forests of Arkansas.

I never told you this because my mother, cousin and I agreed to never speak of it —

— I tell you now, as the day draws ever nearer, that Amity has stopped acknowledging my presence. I would like to believe it is the lingering illness and raging fever that makes her eyes brush past me. But I know there is more to it than that.

And you accepted me as your wife. Was it wrong to expect to be treated as such? Have I displeased you so that you would punish me in such a manner by staying away?

And Amity. My cousin. The young woman who bears *your* child. What will become of her?

What will become of us all?

October 19th

— inspecting the house last night, I went into the sitting room to close the curtains. Before I could pull them against the moonlight, I caught sight of my thin reflection in the glass.

I tell you truthfully, the face there resembled mine in every detail, except the eyes, dear husband, the eyes. They did not stare back at me but considered me with deep interest, and with a look I knew contained an infallible truth: that an ancient and familiar hand had laid itself upon me and was somehow calling to me.

Chilled by such a garish idea I turned away from my ghostly double. When I looked back to the window he was out there, my mysterious visitor, standing at the edge of the shadowed tree line several yards away in the grass. How long had he been there looking at me I do not know.

In a fit of madness, I unlatched and threw up the window. I called to him, shouted at him, implored him to be gone, to return to where he came from. I felt my skirts part and the gun was in my hand. I fired into the night. Two shots.

A cloud must have passed in front of the moon for the yard was thrown into darkness. When the light returned my visitor was gone.

I scurried through the house, double-checking the locks on the windows and doors —

October 23rd

—now I remember the creature Rawhead was once a razor-back boar and companion to Old Betty. When she had heard the boar had been killed by a brazen hunter, a man whose blood was full of arrogance and pride, the old woman went mad with grief and summoned more than just the animal's spirit to seek vengeance and placate her anguished heart.

What returned was a form that walked upright, somewhat like a man, and whose head was a boar's skull, stripped of its skin and bathed in blood.

The beast stalked the night lands in want of the man's conceited flesh—

October 27th

—I awoke with a convulsion of arms and legs. It were as if something called to me while I slumbered.

Overwhelmed with a terror I could not explain, I fumbled in the dark until I found the bedside table. Striking a match, I lit the oil lamp and plunged down the corridor, down the back staircase to the kitchen and Amity's room. I threw open the door and stumbled in, holding the lamp out ahead of me, its yellow light reaching into the dark.

The bed was empty.

At the front of the house I found the great oak door thrown open. Outside was a full moon, and its radiance spilled through the corridor, stretching shadows to dark corners.

And silhouetted against the moonlight was Amity. One hand lay against the doorframe, the other arm was wrapped across her swollen stomach.

I put the lamp down and leapt to her side. She turned to look at me. The white nightdress was wet between her thighs, and a glistening liquid covered the floorboards beneath her.

The time had come.

She slid down the doorframe and lay across the threshold, the lower half of her body outside on the cold stones. As much as I tried, I could not lift her and drag her back into the house. Throughout her labor Amity never looked at me but gritted her teeth and fixed her dark eyes upon the sky in silent anger.

There was blood everywhere, on her nightdress, on the stones between her legs, and on the step beneath us. As I got down on my knees to receive the child, hands drenched in gore, my poor cousin let out her first and only cry, a tormented sound imbued with loathing and malice, then fell back upon the stones and died.

And in my arms I held the newborn. Your daughter.

I did not need to turn my head to know my visitor was there, standing at my shoulder. Rawhead. He smelled of damp earth and his queer utterances were deep whispers from the back of a cave.

Oddly my heart did not leap in distress. The fear that had once burdened me did not manifest itself. Maybe the beast had picked up a scent of familiarity upon my skin or in my blood. A scent that tied me to my cousin, the great-great granddaughter of his master. Old Betty of the dark forest.

Still on my knees, I wiped the screaming child clean with my nightdress.

Rawhead's arms stretched out toward me, large fingers splayed.

I quickly glanced at him. Shimmering yellow eyes in a razorback's bloodied hogshead blinked at me. Hair rose from his back and shoulders, glistening in the moonlight.

I gazed hard at my cousin's corpse, growing cold upon the stones. I looked at the squirming infant. The child was the seed of your contemptuous conduct. Amity's dead flesh was the outcome.

So I asked myself: Would you mourn my cousin? And when you returned would you look upon the child, cherish her, and claim her as your own? Would you teach her your manners and customs, as you had done for me?

And if so tell me, husband, would you deem the child acceptable to present to the members of your polite society? Or will she also come to know the pain and humiliation of your long absences?

On these questions I did not linger.

I gave the beast Rawhead the howling child.

Holding your daughter close he made for the wilderness, disappearing as though slipping behind a black curtain.

It started to rain—

October 29th

—the darkness is deep and the stars are gone.

Your house lies open, windows, doors, all thrown wide. I no longer wish to seal myself inside. And I now know that I never wanted to.

Leaves float in and settle on the furniture and the floors, and the scent of damp earth fills the house. Small woodland animals skitter in the kitchen, wrestling for what food is left. At my request the boy you hired no longer comes. Crows perch on windowsills, silent, watching.

What of my cousin? I buried her at the edge of the forest. You will see a wooden marker there.

And I have not seen the beast Rawhead again.

So, unrestricted by time or our misplaced lives, I sit here at your desk waiting for the hour when your carriage will stop outside the front door, as it has always done. You will disembark, walk carefully across the pebbles to the stone step. You will come through the front door and into your once warm and comfortable home. You will find me in the library.

And when that moment comes, I will stop scratching away in this diary, put down the pen and turn to you, fingers clasping the handgun you once kept in the closet under the stairs.

I feel safer with it in my hands—

THE CUSTODIAN

John W. MacIlroy

He thinks about this often now—the flag and the custodian and the sounds of a radio broadcast of a baseball game on a cloudless day in April when he was not yet twelve. Or maybe it was May. His memories fray like the old cotton oxford shirts he still wears.

But when he sees the flag high atop a flagstaff, the sun catching its colors early in the morning, or later in the day when he hears the sharp crack as a gust of wind catches it just right, it all comes back in sharp focus.

And he is sure that innocence is a glorious illusion, on loan only, and just to the young.

* * *

His grade school was a simple red brick building, with white window and door trim and an oversize white cupola crowning the roof. He would someday tell his son it looked like the plastic schoolhouse building on his old Lionel train set up in the basement of his home—only it was two stories tall, had a covered shed for bikes, didn't sport a plastic nail-polish-red shine, and wasn't half-eaten by a rusty-brown spaniel left home alone on a rainy day.

But the real deal, dead center on the front lawn of his school, was the flagpole.

That's just where he now stood, so vividly in his mind, ready to raise the flag at precisely 8:00 in the morning. It was 1957, and a Monday. He's quite sure of that.

Flag Duty was an honorable calling entrusted to the fifth graders. The sixth graders, having clawed their way to the top of the grade school food chain, were coasting, and everyone knew that the fourth graders were mostly morons, and it only got worse as you moved down into the lower minor leagues of his grade school. There really wasn't any training, just a quick tutorial by the custodian about half an hour before the flag-raising. It usually went well, the physics of the whole thing logical, the mechanics fairly simple, the instructions well-rehearsed.

"See?" The custodian looked at the boy. "It's easy."

"Sure." The boy wasn't, of course.

"Just don't screw it up."

"I won't, Jimmy."

The custodian seemed to like it when the kids called him by his nickname, although he was *James* at his second job at a local market, a small mom-and-pop operation where he worked three evenings a week stocking produce and most Saturdays delivering groceries, back when stores did that. The boy had seen Jimmy a couple times in the store, decked out in a snappy light-blue collared shirt, long sleeves rolled up with *Sal's Market* in a dark blue brush-script over the left pocket and *James* over the right.

"All right, then." He handed the flag to the boy. "Just one more thing. *Don't let it touch the ground. No matter what.*"

With a satisfied nod, the custodian slapped the flagpole, smiled, then headed back into the school. Jimmy walked with a slight limp, something the boy had not noticed before.

Now alone, the boy studied the grommets, feeling along the hard white canvas border, stroking the soft cotton fabric. *Yeah, this really is something*.

* * *

The boy took his post beside the flagpole at 7:55, fidgeted for a minute, then started to unhitch the hoisting line to begin the simple process of attaching the flag. But a breeze suddenly kicked up and the line started banging against the pole, softly at first, then more loudly, the sound magnified by the hollow flagpole and the metal clasps.

The custodian's tutorial had not included sound effects, and this was a bit unnerving. He backed off, hoping things would settle down.

They didn't.

Soon, he couldn't tame the beast, his left hand trying to steady the line, his right holding the flag which now threatened to fall to the ground.

"Don't let it touch the ground."

The boy, now thoroughly rattled, managed to force one clasp into a grommet and snap it shut. He was working on the second clasp when the line went totally nuts, the flag flying out of his hand and beginning to stream horizontally like an airport's orange windsock, except this one was red, white and blue.

"No matter what."

Things were soon unraveling at a dizzying speed as he grabbed wildly at the hoisting line, hoping to feed another clasp into an empty grommet, his face flushing with the kind of acute embarrassment only almost-twelve-year-old boys know. Just as he feared the worst—a kind of *runaway flag* breaking away entirely and drifting its way over to the next county, a breezy frolic unimagined by the custodian, or anybody else—he snapped shut the second clasp. The breeze seemed to calm down as he quickly raised the flag up the pole, just a minute or two past 8:00...

The flag was upside-down.

The boy remembered someone telling him that this was the international signal for distress, appropriate had the school come under siege—which, as far as the custodian was concerned, it was. With arms flailing, Jimmy charged out of the school, his limp quite pronounced.

The boy was staring at the upside-down flag, and shaking. "I'm really sorry."

The custodian worked quickly and in silence to undo the damage, righting Old Glory as the boy just looked on. Turning to go back into the school, the custodian just shook his head. The boy, roundly humiliated, slinked off to class in the opposite direction. There were few tender mercies among the many humiliations visited upon the boy in his grade school that year, but this was one: almost no one had actually seen the disaster. Of course, as these things go, the story would soon get around.

* * *

When school let out that afternoon, the boy stopped by Jimmy's basement office to offer another apology. Everyone liked the custodian, and the boy thought it the right thing to do. The door was slightly open, and he knocked on the frosted window which had a wire mesh insert and neat block letters which said, simply, *Custodian.*

"Jimmy?"

The custodian looked up, then waved him in. He didn't get many visitors. The basement, by an unspoken understanding, was mostly off-limits to the kids.

He was sitting at his desk, a battered wooden monster which had likely entered service at the principal's office, then cycled through a couple classrooms until landing in the custodian's office a little worse for wear. The office, the boy saw, was really not an office at all, just an alcove in the surprisingly high-ceilinged basement, the whole space crowded by a monster boiler and several catwalks, one leading to a rear exit door.

There were two windows, opened and high up the wall. They caught the afternoon sun, along with the sounds of boys—his pals, mostly—noisily choosing up sides on the scruffy baseball field in the back of the school. Had anyone pressed him, he would have bet that his best friend—a lanky, slick-fielding kid nick-named Stretch—had been picked first, and the noise as always was about who would take the hapless Bauer twins, even though they claimed their third cousin was the very Hank Bauer playing for the Yankees. A long worktable opposite the boiler was clut-tered with stuff, mostly tools and gadgets and cleaning rags, as well as a brushed-brass work light and a small radio. A calen-dar—courtesy of the local Ford dealership, and featuring a well-painted picture of a handsome couple standing next to a two-tone Fairlane V-8 Sunliner convertible—hung on the wall, next to a Brooklyn Dodgers pennant. An afternoon baseball game was playing on the radio, the Dodgers hosting the Phillies. Vin Scully was doing the play-by-play.

"Bottom of the third, no score. Cimoli, Snider and Furillo com-ing to the plate. Nice breeze blowing in from behind right field. Good crowd today..."

"You like baseball?"

The boy nodded, and stammered. "Yeah, sure, but I just want-ed to—"

"You a Dodgers guy?"

"You bet." The boy really wasn't, his 1956 Topps Willie Mays card stuffed into the brim of his baseball cap pledging his loyalty to the Giants. This was very tricky territory since Bobby Thomson took the pennant from the Dodgers in the bottom of the ninth just a few years before, but he figured a little good will would be in order, what with the thin ice he was on.

The custodian smiled. "Dodgers got a two-run lead heading into the third. Roger Craig's pitching strong today." The boy, oddly, would always remember that detail, along with the hum of the Vin Scully play-by-play.

"The F. & M. Schaefer Brewing Company delighted to bring you the game today. Schaefer Beer, the one beer to have when you're having more than one..."

The custodian's desk was neat, empty but for a few technical manuals, a stack of orange invoices, and a crumpled bag of po-tato chips. A framed black and white photograph sat at the edge, almost precisely in the center of the desk: three soldiers—all un-shaven, their eyes hollow, a heavy bandage around the forehead of the guy on the right, who was smoking a cigarette—were sit-ting on a tank, its treads caked in mud, the gun turret smashed. They were holding an American flag.

"Breeze still blowing in from right, picking up a bit..."

The custodian saw the boy looking at the photo. "That was towards the end of the war, in a little town somewhere in France."

"*Snider takes one on the inside corner. Bill Jackowski calling them behind the plate today. Don't forget to get those Lucky Strikes...*"

"That's me in the middle, the others my best buddies in the platoon." He paused. "I was the oldest, and they called me Pops." He smiled. "I was twenty-four."

"*Hearn, joining 'em this year, on the mound for the Phillies. Touches the brim of his cap, shakes off a call...*"

"The guy on the left—just a kid from some small town in Iowa—played ball at Carolina. Talked about going back to his high school and coaching after the war."

"*Here's the fastball, Snider leaning in. Strike two called. You Dodger fans may remember that Hearn pitched a few years for the Giants, the tall right-hander handing us a 3-1 defeat in game one of that 1951 pennant play-off series...*"

The custodian smiled. "We talked baseball all the time you know, over there."

"*Couple big doubleheaders coming up at Ebbets...*"

The custodian reached over and moved the picture a few inches.

"But he never made it home, blown up a couple weeks after this photo was taken." The custodian paused. "I took some shrapnel in the leg, just below the knee, the same day." He reached over to the radio and turned the volume down, his hand moving the dial slowly, carefully, then looked at the boy.

"The flag tells his story, and it tells my story, and it tells the stories of millions of other guys, guys just like us."

It was very quiet, the boy remembers.

"You see, son, that's the thing." The custodian paused again. "That's... that's the thing about our flag."

The custodian looked away, but just for a moment, then turned and smiled, although it was a sad one, that's what the boy thought.

"But you didn't let it touch the ground, did you?"

* * *

The boy rode his bike to school early the next morning, taking the longer route—the one with a tempting down-hill run, just past the old railroad coal siding. He could take both hands off the handlebars for almost half a minute, and listen to the *ratta-tatta-tatta* sounds of a baseball card flapping against the spokes of his back wheel, rigged with a clothespin like all the boys did. When he got to school and parked his bike he pretended to fuss with the clothespin, but really he just wanted to watch another fifth grader handle the flag duty. A pretty red-head in a bright green dress with yellow flowers—sunflowers, he guessed—was listening to the custodian's tutorial, just as he had done the day before.

He liked her. She had moved into town in the beginning of the year, and sat two rows ahead of him—and she seemed to like him, at least sometimes. He watched the custodian finish his tutorial, slapping the flagpole as he left the redhead to her duties. Within minutes she had raised the flag smartly, even in the breeze, and that made him happy. In class that morning he told her what a nice job she had done. She said thank you, with a look that was curious but not unkind.

* * *

Every so often that spring the boy stopped by the custodian's office to talk baseball, and again the next fall, and on into the next spring—his last before graduating from sixth grade and heading off to middle school. The boy made his last visit to the basement on a muggy day in early June. Goodbyes were something new for the boy, and change was everywhere that spring of 1958: the redhead told him she was moving again, to Texas, but would write; his dog took off one day never to return; his dad lost his job… and both the Giants and Dodgers left them all, moving to their new homes on the West Coast.

Summers would never be the same.

As the boy looked around the basement for the last time, he noticed that the custodian's radio was playing music, and the Dodgers pennant was nowhere to be seen.

SEPARATION

Steven B. Rosenfeld

I.

On a dusty road somewhere in the South Texas scrub, Maria eyes the Border Patrol agent's raised gun, pressing her four-year-old daughter against her hip. Rosalita clutches her toy bunny into the bright flowers embroidered on her shirt. Along the road stand their traveling companions of the past month, clusters of mothers, fathers and children large and small, each group in an agent's gunsight. A small boy glares at the agents, hands thrust into his jeans; his white sweatshirt flaunts the stars and stripes and proclaims "**AMERICA.** LOVE IT OR LEAVE IT."

The silence of the windswept plain is pierced every few seconds by staccato commands: "Don't move!" "Drop that backpack!" "Hands up!" An old yellow school bus comes over a rise, kicking up dust, and stops.

Maria looks up from her daughter and regards the agent. Her long brown hair is disheveled and matted from the month-long trek, her jeans splotched with dried mud. Her dark eyes are soft and moist. Through her faded red t-shirt, she caresses the amulet that hangs on a string around her neck. "*Por favor, señor,*" Maria pleads, "no take *mi Rosalita* from me. *No me quite mi niña.*"

* * *

Maria and Rosalita fled San Salvador the night after Carlos got roaring drunk at his sister's wedding and pointed his pistol at her.

Guns were no strangers to Maria—Carlos and his Barrio 18 gang all carried them. Violence was their creed, machismo their deity and guns their best *amigos*. Three years before, a rival gang had killed Manuel, Rosalita's father, a peace-loving musician and the only man Maria had ever loved. After that, Maria knew she had to seek refuge in Zacamil, the San Salvador neighborhood where Barrio 18 held sway, and take up with a gang member.

Since she'd been with Carlos, Maria had come to expect a slap or two, even a punch, when Carlos drank too much. She'd suffered bloody noses, black eyes, even a broken jaw. Until now, after one of his rum-fueled binges, Maria had managed to put his gun safely away while he slept it off. But this time, waving the weapon in her face, Carlos called her *una puta*—a whore. *"Yo te mataré,"* he snarled, *"a ti y a tu Rosalita también."* I will kill you — you and your Rosalita, too.

Carlos slowly lowered the gun, but the burning dread surged through Maria's body. Recently, her friends Juana and Francesca, also gang members' women, had suddenly gone missing along with their children. Maria told herself they'd managed to escape, but she feared, or maybe she knew, that's not what happened. She wasn't going to wait to see if she and Rosalita would be next. Her 30th birthday was coming up in June, and she wanted to be alive to celebrate it with her daughter.

Maria had a secret bank account, money left to her by her grandmother, Abuela Rosa, for whom Rosalita was named. So the next day, she withdrew it all and delivered most of it to one of the *coyotes* who advertised they could get people safely through Guatemala and Mexico and across the U.S. border. Before she paid the man, she told him why they were running. She wanted to believe his assurances that they would be granted asylum in the United States; what else could she do?

Maria wrote down where to show up that night to join a caravan heading north and later, as Carlos snored heavily, she slipped out of bed, took the household cash from the jam jar in the back of the kitchen cupboard and stuffed her backpack with her and Rosalita's underwear, socks and shirts. In the back of her drawer, Maria found the brightly-painted La Palma amulet Abuela Rosa had given her: *El Cadejo,* the white dog with glowing red eyes from the folk tale Maria had learned as a child and told to Rosalita countless times, who offers protection to its followers. Maria hadn't worn the *cadejo* charm since Rosa died, but that night she pulled it from the drawer and slipped it around her neck. Then she woke Rosalita and they were gone.

Thank God Rosalita had been asleep when Carlos snarled his death-threat. Maria couldn't bear for her to be in fear for her life. So she told her daughter they were going to visit an uncle who lived in San Antonio, Texas, although she had no uncle in San Antonio, nor any other relatives in the U.S. She'd heard awful rumors about parents and children being separated by the American border police. Maria was certain she would never allow that but, deep down, she had no idea what would happen if they made it across the border. She only knew she had to try.

The next thirty days and nights on the road were sweaty and unwashed, often thirsty and hungry, and always scary. At night, in empty warehouses or backrooms, Maria told Rosalita new versions of her favorite stories: the one about *El Tabudo*, the fisherman with big knees who got turned into a fish, the one about *El Cipitío*, the pot-bellied boy cursed to wander the earth forever with his feet pointing backward, and of course many different tales Maria made up about the white dog *El Cadejo* saving children from his arch foe, the black dog with eyes like burning coals. Or they sang together the songs Rosalita loved: *"Las Estrellitas* (The Little Stars)", or *"Tortuguita Concha* (Little Turtle Concha)" or Rosalita's very favorite, *"Tengo una Muñequita* (I Have a Little Doll)." *"No, Mama,"* Rosalita always insisted with a teasing smile, *"Tengo una Conejito"* (I Have a Little *Bunny*).

Once Rosalita was finally asleep, Maria sat up protecting her, guarding the small bit of money she had left for junk food and bottled water, and fending off men who offered their protection but expected favors in return. What sleep Maria got was during the days on rickety buses, or packed into the backs of battered old trucks—when she wasn't trudging on foot, sometimes carrying Rosalita as well as her backpack.

* * *

Now, exhausted but finally in Texas, Maria faces the agent's gun with her hands raised and Rosalita clinging to her side. The agent looms over her as his scorpion-tattooed arms grip his weapon and keep it trained on Maria. In the distance, she can see the live oaks waving in the breeze, but she hears nothing. She feels heavy as a boulder, unable to move, yet she can tell that she is trembling.

"Por favor, señor," she says again, extending her hands, *"mi Rosalita tiene sólo cuatro años, ella solamente me tiene a mi."* My Rosalita is only four, she has only me. *"Volveremos ahora, OK?"* We will go back home now.

Rosalita looks up in fright at her mother. *"No, mamá, no,"* she cries, bursting into tears, *"¡Carlos nos va a matar si volvemos!"* Carlos will kill us if we go back. In that instant, Maria realizes Rosalita wasn't asleep that night. Maria should have known her daughter was too smart to believe they had relatives in Texas. Rosalita has known all along they are running for their lives. Now Maria also knows that returning home is unthinkable.

"I said *hands up!*" the agent growls, gesturing with his weapon, "I won't say it again."

Suddenly, Rosalita breaks away. Before Maria can grab her, Rosalita hurls her bunny at the startled agent and rushes headlong toward him. Her flowered shirt paints a sudden flash of color against the gray scrub. Maria shrieks. She hadn't left Carlos, hadn't trekked 1400 miles, only to have Rosalita shot dead after all.

Maria snatches her backpack from the ground and heaves it at the raised gun barrel, but misses. "¡No!" she screams, "¡No dispares!" Don't shoot! And she launches herself after Rosalita. But her cry is lost in the dry wind rustling through the brush. As she lies at the agent's feet, her head buried in her arms, she notices how the Texas dust smells the same as the dust back home. She closes her eyes and waits for the blast. But the man lowers his gun, bends down and hugs Rosalita.

"Okay, get up and come with me," the agent says, and hands the bunny back to Rosalita. Holding it tight, she gives him a shy smile. He helps Maria to her feet and motions for them to follow him to his car. As they climb in, Maria looks back and sees their companions being herded onto the yellow school bus.

Settling back and closing her eyes, Maria nestles close to Rosalita, running her free hand across the smooth surface of the cushioned seat as she inhales the smell of new leather and the cool air blowing deliciously over her. Yes, she thinks, this is America. We have made it. We will tell them all about Carlos and his beatings, his gang and his death threat. Then, as the *coyotes* promised, we'll be granted asylum and become Americans. *El Cadejo* has protected us.

Suddenly, the car stops. When Maria sits up, she is baffled by what she sees—chain-link fencing surrounding more Texas dust, and two separate gates leading to two barren enclosures. In one of them are hundreds of adults, some talking in small groups, some walking around aimlessly, some rattling the chain-links. The other pen contains only children like Rosalita, some with tears running down their dirty faces, others peering forlornly through the fence into the adult enclosure, still others just sitting on the ground, their dark eyes staring into space.

"Right," says the agent, "here we are." He jumps out of the car and opens the rear door.

Another agent appears from nowhere, grabs Rosalita and pulls her toward the gate to the childrens' pen. "¡No!" Maria screams, and tries to run after her. But her arms are pinned behind her and she is pushed against the car. She turns her head in time to see Rosalita, howling and holding tight to her bunny, disappear behind the fence. Rage storms inside her. The pain she feels is intense, physical. Just then, the yellow school bus pulls up to the gates. Through the bus window, Maria glimpses the boy's sweatshirt: "**AMERICA.** LOVE IT OR LEAVE IT."

II.

Six weeks later, Maria sits alone on a bench in the baking afternoon sun, outside the rundown bus station in downtown McAllen, Texas. She is wearing a gray t-shirt, the same pair of jeans, and flip-flops, but no hat. Around her neck is the *cadejo* amulet. Next to her on the bench is a white cloth bag emblazoned with the red, white and blue insignia of the Border Patrol, containing the few things she has been allowed to keep from her confiscated backpack, as well as the charger for the black GPS monitor strapped to her right ankle.

She wipes the sweat from her forehead and for the hundredth time squints through the glare across the platform, beyond a row of orange traffic cones, at the line that has been inching along all day toward the ticket office inside the bus station. Standing in the line are men and women, some alone but some—the lucky ones, Maria knows—with children again by their sides. All of them carry the same white bags, all have the same black devices strapped to their legs. Those at the rear have just come off the last government bus from La Hielera—the Icebox—the converted warehouse on Ursula Avenue that is the Border Patrol's processing center. Maria came from La Hielera at 10:30 that morning, and has been sitting there ever since.

On the line, Maria sees several women she knows from La Hielera, where they were confined together in metal enclosures, ate meager meals together, showered together and slept next to one another on mattresses on the concrete floors, under thin Mylar blankets barely warm enough in the center's frigid air. She knows their stories—where they came from, why they left, how they made it across, whether they, too, had children taken from them at the border; none of their stories are much different from Maria's. She also knows she will never see them again, because the line they are waiting on is for bus tickets out of McAllen, to California, Chicago, Pennsylvania, New Jersey, to join sisters, uncles, cousins or boyfriends who will take them in as they await their asylum hearings.

Maria has not been given a date for an asylum hearing, and she is not waiting to get on a bus, since she has nowhere to go. So she sits on the bench in the sun. Sweat has soaked through her shirt. She has eaten nothing since oatmeal and weak coffee at the center; she is thirsty, but the bottle of water they gave her is empty. Still, with every hour she has been sitting on the bench, her excitement has grown. For she is waiting not for a departing bus, but for one arriving today from Michigan. On that bus, she has been told, will be Rosalita.

Maria has not seen her daughter since they were pulled from the agent's car six weeks ago. But she has spoken with her—twice. A social worker at La Hielera was able to locate Rosalita. She was in a migrant children's center in some place called Kalamazoo, Michigan. The social worker could not explain why Rosalita was in Kalamazoo; nor could she bring Rosalita to Maria. But she did arrange for them to speak on the phone. Each time, they were allowed just two minutes. Each time, Maria could hear Rosalita crying—as if she hadn't stopped since the day they were separated. Between sobs, Maria could make out *"Mama, dónde estás?"* Mama, where are you? *"¿Por qué te fuiste ?"* Why did you go away? *"¿Cuándo vienes paratras?"* When are you coming back? She told Rosalita she loved her and would see her soon, but it didn't stop the sobbing. Maria felt feeble—even more helpless than when she stood staring at the agent's gun.

At La Hielera, Maria has received all kinds of advice from more people than she can remember: people from the government, some in uniforms, some wearing suits; social workers who said they were there to help her, but couldn't bring Rosalita back; and so many different lawyers she can't keep them straight. One lawyer, an old Chicano with a gray moustache and a rumpled suit, said he was defending her in her "criminal case" (what criminal case? she wasn't a criminal!). He said he had arranged for her to be released on parole, so long as she wore the GPS monitor. He gave her his card, also rumpled, and said she should call him if anything went wrong. Another lawyer, a young woman from a New York law firm who had flown down for a week, said Maria could apply for asylum, but was unlikely to get it. Why? Because even the most credible fear of injury or even death at the hands of a husband or boyfriend ("mere domestic violence," the lawyer called it) was no longer being accepted as grounds for asylum. She felt betrayed—those *coyotes* had lied to her after all. If she couldn't get asylum, why had she come here? Maria told all these people the same thing: all she wanted was to be with her daughter.

The lawyers all told her not to sign anything. But when someone from the government gave her a form and said if she signed it, she would be allowed to see her daughter again, she hesitated. The form was mostly in English, but she saw a line in Spanish that read *"Estoy solicitando reunirme con mi hijo"*—I am requesting to reunite with my child—and the box next to it had already been checked. That was exactly what she wanted, so Maria signed the form.

She must have signed the right form, because last week, she

got a telephone call at La Hielera from a woman named Sandra in Kalamazoo, who spoke to her in Spanish. Sandra said she was Rosalita's lawyer. She explained that a judge in California had ordered the government to reunite children like Rosalita with their parents, so now that she'd located Maria, she would "start the process" and "complete the paperwork." For the first time in weeks, Maria allowed herself to smile, but only a little. She'd learned to be distrustful.

How long? Maria asked. Sandra didn't know, but said she'd get to work on it. When she hung up, Maria could feel her heart beating as the excitement rose inside her. But she was also bewildered. Why did Rosalita need a lawyer? What could she have done wrong? She was only four.

A week went by. Then, last evening, a social worker told her to go downtown the next day and wait for the bus from Michigan. Rosalita would be on it.

At the bus station, the sun has turned from blazing yellow to deep red. Maria's bench is now in shadow, and still she sits and waits. Again and again, she caresses the *cadejo* on the string around her neck, willing the red-eyed dog to bring Rosalita to her soon. Maria has spent the past six weeks dreaming up new stories to tell her at bedtime, humming the songs they will sing, and thinking how Rosalita will gleefully change the Little Doll to Little Bunny. Maria's 30th birthday had passed with no celebration, but now she and Rosalita would have a birthday party.

Maria's lips are dry with the dust of the prairie. The exhaust from buses entering and leaving the station has made her dizzy, but no bus has brought Rosalita. Hunger gnaws at her, but she will not get up even to get a candy bar, afraid that in those few minutes, she will miss the bus from Michigan. Maria knows she must be back at La Hielera by 7 p.m. or she will have broken her parole. So, as the shadows lengthen, she stands each time a new bus pulls into the arrival platform, hurries across and watches as the passengers get off. Still, no Rosalita.

Then, just before 7, a new bus arrives. On the front she reads "DETROIT-DALLAS-S.ANTONIO-McALLEN." Detroit! Maria knows this is the one and her heart leaps. She runs to the bus door, but is pushed back to make room for disembarking passengers with suitcases and packages. Finally, she sees a slim, well-dressed young woman with neatly pinned back blond hair descend the steps, a small traveling case on her shoulder. The woman turns to help a child off the bus. The child is wearing new red leggings and a blue and red Detroit Pistons t-shirt. Her hair is cut short – and she has no toy bunny. But yes! The child is Rosalita.

"¡Gracias a Dios!" Maria screams, *"Rosalita, mi ángel."* She opens her arms and springs forward to hug her daughter.

But Rosalita does not run to her arms. She stares at Maria for an instant, expressionless, then clutches the blond woman's arm and turns away. Nor does the woman look at Maria. Instead, she leads Rosalita into the bus station, leaving Maria standing on the empty platform.

Staggered, Maria tries to understand what has just happened. Then she turns and hurries inside after them. The terminal is crowded and Maria doesn't know which way to go. Finally, she sees a door marked "EXIT-TAXIS," and runs toward it. She emerges just in time to see the blond woman and Rosalita get into a car marked "Immigration and Customs Enforcement" — and drive away.

III.

Two days later, Maria is still in McAllen, not at La Hielera, but in a windowless cinderblock building that used to be a CVS drugstore, but is now a detention facility for reunited families. Rosalita is there too; the blond woman brought her there to join Maria yesterday morning. The blond woman, Maria discovered, is Sandra, Rosalita's lawyer from Kalamazoo. She apologized for what happened at the bus station: no one told her Maria would be there to meet the bus and she had no way of knowing who she was. As for Rosalita, well… this wasn't the first time Sandra had seen a separated child shun her own parent. She had become used to it.

Sandra said she was leaving Rosalita at the family detention center so they could "get reacquainted," but she would be back the next day to "discuss the situation." What situation? Maria had asked, but Sandra just said they'd talk about it tomorrow.

Now, Maria and Rosalita have been together for nearly two days. But the two days have been like a nightmare Maria cannot wake from. For the child who has shared her meals and slept, fitfully, in the next cot is not her Rosalita. She is *una extraña* — a stranger. She has followed Maria everywhere — to meals, to the bathroom, to the tiny fenced-in yard in the back, where she does not play with the other children, but just stands by the fence looking out at the brush. Nor has Rosalita spoken a single word, and when she even looks at Maria, it is with the same empty stare Maria saw back at the bus platform. Most agonizing of all, whenever Maria has tried to hug her daughter, Rosalita has pulled away and refused to be touched. At bedtime, she doesn't listen to the new stories, and won't sing the old songs. There has been no birthday party.

Maria tries not to think about what could have happened to Rosalita in Kalamazoo. She tries to force from her mind the stories she'd heard at La Hielera from the women who'd been able to speak on the phone with their separated children. How shelter workers were forbidden to hug or even touch them. How they were lined up like prison inmates to receive vaccinations. How favorite clothes, dolls and toys had been taken away. Nor can Maria erase the image of the five-year-old boy she'd heard about, who had finally been released to an aunt in Philadelphia, but wouldn't talk to anyone, not even his young cousins, slept constantly or sat crouching in closets or behind sofas, and refused to eat, except for drinking warm milk from a baby bottle. Still, Maria can't believe that her own lively Rosalita, the brave girl who'd charged the border agent just a few weeks ago, could now have become *una extraña*. She waits fretfully for Sandra to return and answer these questions.

Sandra finally appears that evening, after Rosalita is asleep despite the bright fluorescent lights, remnants of the CVS, that will glare until 11 p.m. With Sandra is the government social worker from La Hielera—the one who found Rosalita in Kalamazoo. They motion Maria to a sitting area beyond the long rows of cots, where several women and children are watching TV. There is no privacy, but they aren't there to answer Maria's questions anyway. They have brought some papers with them, and that is the "situation" they need to discuss. Maria has a decision to make.

One of the papers is the form Maria signed weeks ago. She sees her signature and remembers why she signed it—to get Rosalita back. She reads what it says next to the box that was checked before she signed it: "*Estoy solicitando reunirme con mi hijo para el propósito de la repatriación a mi país de ciudadanía.*" I am requesting to be reunited with my child **for the purpose of repatriation to the country of my citizenship**. Maria shivers. She looks at the two women, perplexed.

Yes, Sandra explains, you agreed to be reunited with Rosalita so both of you could be deported together back to El Salvador.

"*¡Dios mío, no!*" Maria says, "*Vamos a morir allí.*" We will die there. She remembers what Rosalita had said back at the border: "*Carlos nos matar si volvemos!*" Carlos will kill us if we go back. She breaks into tears.

"*Espera, María,*" Sandra says, touching her arm. Wait. There's some good news: the judge in California has ruled that the form

Maria signed, with the line pre-checked, wasn't valid. There is a new form, and they have it with them.

"*Gracias, gracias,*" Maria says. She dries her tears and reaches out for the new form.

But the "good news" isn't all that good — in fact, for Maria, it's awful. Sandra has determined that Maria has not yet applied for asylum, perhaps because she was caught trying to sneak across the border. "I only did what those *coyotes* told me," Maria wants to say, but Sandra is not finished. Maria can still seek asylum, but she is likely to be found guilty of illegal entry and deported before her asylum hearing or, in the best case, her asylum claim will be rejected at her deportation hearing. As the lawyer from New York had said, "mere fear of domestic violence" is no longer grounds for asylum. "*Mere* fear?" Maria remembers Carlos's beatings, his gun and his death threat. Her fear is intense, the opposite of mere.

Sandra drones on about needing to show "a well-founded fear of being persecuted on account of race, religion, nationality, membership in a particular social group, or political opinion." But Maria gets it: she will be deported back to El Salvador and, if Rosalita is still with her, she will be deported too. "*Muy bien,*" Maria thinks, as a deep sigh escapes. We will find a way to survive there.

But Maria has another "option," Sandra tells her. Rosalita — and Rosalita alone — has a chance. That's why Sandra has come to Texas with her young client. She has done two things back in Kalamazoo. First, she has filed a separate asylum case for Rosalita. Because Rosalita didn't intentionally enter the country illegally, but was brought in "involuntarily" by Maria, Sandra thinks there's a good chance Rosalita will be granted asylum. "Carlos will kill me if I go back" will be powerful testimony before the right immigration judge — one in Michigan, not Texas. Second, Sandra has found a wonderful family in Michigan who will give Rosalita a foster home and, if she gets asylum, may be willing to adopt her if Maria will relinquish her parental rights.

What? Maria is being asked to let Rosalita go back to Kalamazoo with Sandra? To live with a strange American family Maria has never met while she waits to see if Rosalita will get asylum? And then, worst of all, to give up her rights to her daughter so she can be adopted?

Yes, Sandra says, Maria has understood it exactly. The social worker, who has said nothing yet, now chimes in. "*Sí, María, es el mejor para Rosalita.*" It is the best thing for Rosalita.

Again Maria's tears flow. Her determination melts toward despair. She remembers the old Chicano lawyer in the rumpled suit who said she could call him. Can't she wait until tomorrow to try to talk to her own lawyer, she asks? Not really, they tell her. Sandra must return to Michigan in the morning and has a return ticket for Rosalita. But if she leaves her with Maria, well... as she said, when Maria is deported, Rosalita will go with her.

Sandra gives Maria the new form and shows her two lines, with the boxes still unchecked. The first one is exactly the same as the line that was checked on the old form. The second one says this:

"Estoy afirmativamente, con conocimiento y voluntariamente pidiéndome que regrese a mi país de ciudadanía sin mis hijo menor (s) que yo entienda permanezca en los Estados Unidos para perseguir reclamaciones de socorro disponibles." (I am affirmatively, knowingly and voluntarily requesting to return to my country of citizenship without my minor child(ren) who I understand will remain in the United States to pursue available claims of relief.)

Sandra indicates the second box. *"Marque eso,"* she says. That's the one Maria must check if she wants Rosalita to have a chance. Otherwise...

Maria pushes the form away. She will not do this. Not after all they have gone through, after all they risked on the trek north, after she was sure they were going to be shot by the Border Patrol agent. No, she and Rosalita will go back home and find a way to stay alive.

But then, Maria looks across the room, where Rosalita lies asleep under the fluorescent glare. She thinks about *la extraña* who has been with her the past two days. Not her Rosalita at all, but a strange child who wouldn't smile, wouldn't talk to her and wouldn't hug her. It is that child, not her Rosalita, who is being offered a chance for a new life. It is in her power to give her that chance. How could she not? Isn't that what a mother should do? What Abuela Rosa would have done?

Maria takes the form back. She grabs the pen from the social worker, checks the second box and signs her name. Her tears turn to heavy sobs. She sees the TV watchers turn and stare, but only for an instant; Maria knows they are used to tears.

Still sobbing, Maria lowers her head into her arms. The *cadejo* amulet swings away from her neck. She takes it in her hand, twisting it around so its red eyes look up at her. The folktale says that the white *cadejo* keeps its evil counterpart from stealing the souls of its believers, especially children. Maria takes off the charm, walks quickly over to Rosalita's cot and gently slips it around the sleeping child's neck. Then she turns and rushes from the room, shaking uncontrollably.

PERCH

James D. Balestrieri

He sat on the porch of the cabin beside the lake. For many years now—through springs, summers, falls—he had not even wanted to fish in the lake. He was reading Dante. Rereading. He was spending more time, this time, on the ending. The mug of coffee on the red cedar end table was half gone but still warm.

He looked up and out through the pines and birches at the sparkling light on the never still water.

He was waiting for her, thinking of her, finding her in Beatrice's smile in Dante's words, finding the light in her eyes in the lights that danced on the surface of the never still water.

The phone in the kitchen rang. He set the book aside and stood. He glanced at the coffee. It would need warming. He opened the screen door that led into the kitchen. The spring, a little rusty, screamed as he opened it.

The phone hung on the wall. He let it ring once more, thinking about ignoring it, then thought it might be her, stranded somewhere, at some filling station, with a flat tire or an overheated radiator, in need of rescue.

Thinking about rescuing her brought a small smile to his lips.

He answered the phone.

It was a male voice, subordinate, apologetic, fawning.

"Leave it," he answered.

The voice spoke.

"Leave it until Monday. If he says he can't source the ink for the bottle bonds then he can't source the ink for the bottle bonds."

The voice spoke.

"No. I'll see him Monday."

The voice spoke.

"And if you hurt him, or, God forbid, kill him, then what?"

He didn't wait for an answer. These guys were liable to answer a rhetorical question with an unauthorized action. Rhetoric was not their strong suit. Strength was their only suit.

"Then you've killed our best man," he went on. "And then where are we?"

The voice spoke.

"I know what the word is. But they haven't moved on us yet, have they? So it's just word."

The voice spoke once more.

"Monday," he ordered. "Go home, or go wherever it is you go."

The line went dead.

Far cry from the old days, he thought, when you could bottle caramel-colored rubbing alcohol and make good money, if you could stay alive. These days, since the war, you had to have men who knew their stuff. And you had to operate on both sides of the border. The risk was lower but so was the payoff. And the work was harder. The pie they fought over was shrinking.

As he hung the receiver on its cradle, he heard a car on the gravel drive.

They kissed without saying a word, made love without saying a word.

Beside the car, he had heard the breeze toying with her silk scarf. In the bedroom, he heard waves of wind breaking on the boughs and branches.

After, he made a new pot of coffee. They sat on the porch, listening to the rising wind, watching it scallop the lake.

"He know?" he asked.

"He knows," she replied.

Only once had it ever come up with his business partner, oblique at first, almost out of nowhere, as such things do.

"It isn't the business," his partner had said. "It isn't even that you and I go way back to when we were kids."

He wanted to say nothing, be nothing, and if he had to be anything, he wanted it to be elsewhere. But his feet were rooted to the spot and his back was bent over a wooden case of bottles of the good stuff, the best stuff, their own private stuff, and he knew he couldn't stay silent.

"What then?" he asked, feeling his partner's eyes on him, in him, in his head and running down his spine and in his blood and heart.

"It's that I love you both more than I mind."

He forced his eyes up. He willed his eyes to meet his partner's eyes.

He knew then that she would never come between them. He knew then that he could go on cherishing these rare weekends.

"We've never gone fishing," she said. "I want to go fishing."

"Alright," he said. "This wind will die down at dusk. I'll get the gear ready and we'll go then."

"What will we fish for?"

"What would you like to fish for?"

"Something delicious."

"Perch, then, I think. See that rocky point that juts in across the bay."

She nodded.

"There are lily pads there. And other weeds. There used to be shoals of perch there."

She held her coffee mug with two hands and two pinkies in the air and sipped the steaming brew with a satisfied, endearing slurp.

"Perch, eh?" She arched her eyebrows. "We'll dip them in flour and egg, and finish them with parslied breadcrumbs."

"You know perch?" he said.

"On a plate. On Friday nights at Turner Hall. With schooners of beer, coleslaw, and warm potato salad with bacon."

"You do know perch," he said.

They read then, he with his Dante, she with one of her door-stop Thomas Wolfe novels. Coffee turned to coffee with brandy; coffee with brandy became brandy alone.

The wind died down with the day.

He unearthed two light rods, rigged them with long basswood bobbers about six feet from the gold English bait hooks he tied at the ends of the lines. He realized he had all but forgotten how to tie a clinch knot: thread the line through the eye of the hook, wrap the free end round the running line six or seven times, run it back through the first loop and once more through the large loop you've just made, then pull taut. It wasn't quite a noose, but close enough. He wondered what else he had all but forgotten, things and ways of doing things that had once been second nature. Between the hooks and the bobbers, he pinched three small sinkers onto the line. He hooked the hooks onto the first eyes of the rods and reeled them up until the lines ran smartly along the rods.

He found a small coffee can and turned a spadeful of soft earth in the flower bed he'd made and tended for her. Summer was ceding to fall, so the garden's only colors were the yolk yellow of the Ox-Eye Sunflowers and the pale purple of the Joe-Pye Weed. The worms were plentiful in the dirt and he quickly filled the can.

He slung a wicker creel over his shoulder, picked up the can and rods and called to her.

"Ready?"

"Champing at the bit."

Rowing across the pale orange, pink, and blue mirror, the ripples the oars and boat made were like fingers dragging across and making folds of drapery in smooth satin.

After a few minutes with nothing but the oars marring the silence, he shipped them and looked at her.

"Here," he said. "You want me to put a worm on for you?"

"No, thank you. I'll do it myself."

He grinned at her. He handed her one of the rods and the coffee can. She fished out a worm and threaded it, wriggling and thrashing, on the hook.

"You need a casting lesson?"

"I'll watch you."

He baited his hook. He held the line with the forefinger of his right hand. He grabbed the bail on the spinning reel and flipped it over the spool until it clicked. Then he cast, straightening his forefinger out as he did to let the line peel out. The bobber landed with a plop beside a lilypad. The sinkers took the worm down beneath the surface.

"The lotus flowers are closing up shop for the night," she said, repeating his steps and casting her rig with a swoosh in a flat arc that ended with the bobber righting itself beside a thin bed of pencil weed.

"That they are," he said.

Both bobbers began to dance almost immediately.

"When it goes under and stays, strike," he advised her, though she had already done it and was playing a perch.

"That's a fine perch," he said, lifting his own rod and setting the hook.

"Yours, too?" she said.

"Not as fine as yours, but still an eater."

The perch darted then glided like barred gold in the green water, catching the evening light. They held the spines of their dorsal fins high, and he thought of the fins of the long-extinct Dimetrodons at the Natural History Museum they had seen together when the two of them had managed to meet in the city, and he thought of the fins of dragons that had never existed at all outside of romance and art.

She lifted her perch from the lake.

"Swing it here," he said, and she did.

He swept the dorsal fin down from the fish's head to its tail so it wouldn't stick him, took the hook from its mouth and slipped it into the creel. Then he did the same with his fish.

"That's two," he said.

This time, she let him thread a new worm onto the hook.

Again, they cast.

The bobbers sat there, then began to bip-bip-bip.

"Reel in," he said.

"Why?"

"The breeze has moved us into the shallows where the little fish are. Bluegill and pumpkinseeds. All they do is steal worms. I'll move us a bit."

He rowed them out into the lake, away from the lilypads and pencil weed, and turned the boat so the breeze would rock them gently back towards the beds.

The perch were eager.

"Look over the side," he said, letting a small one go.

"It's so clear you can see the rocks at the bottom."

"Cast away."

She flung the rig long, out into deeper water.

The bobber went under instantly, and stayed under.

She lifted the rod. It bent into a deep arc.

"Not a perch," he said.

"What then?"

"A bass, I think."

The fish ran, zizzing the drag on the reel. Then the fish shot quivering out of the water, went rigid in the air, and fell back with a smack into the lake.

She yelled.

"Smallmouth bass," he said, laughing as the bass leapt and leapt again.

When it tired, she led the bass to his hand. He grabbed it by the lower lip and lifted it from the lake.

"Shall we keep it?" he asked.

"Let it go," she said.

"Good," he said, unhooking the fish and holding it in water, rocking it gently back and forth so the water would fill its gills and refresh it. The smallmouth darted from his hand and angled down into the dark water.

A thin moon rose through gathering clouds. Ululations of loon echoed and reechoed.

She whispered,

> "When the moon was overhead
> Came two young lovers lately wed;
> 'I am half sick of shadows,' said
> The Lady of Shalott."

He wasn't sure whether she'd wanted him to hear her.

He looked into the creel.

"That's plenty," he said. "Reel up."

They stowed the gear, then drifted in silence. Something heavy entered the water from the woods down the shore from the cabin. A shadow began to move across the lake.

"I've never seen a bear here before," he said.

"Did we spook him?"

"Nothing spooks him."

They watched the bear swim with courtly grace across the

lake. They watched him walk out onto the shore, watched him shudder the water off his thick, glistening coat.

The bear turned to look at them, and disappeared into the trees.

He rowed them back to the cabin.

She let her finger trace a track in the mirror of the lake.

"Leave the gear in the boat," she said. "Maybe we'll go out again tomorrow."

In the piney light of the kitchen, he poured her a bourbon and ginger on the rocks, then made a second one for himself.

He filleted the perch while she prepared bowls of flour, beaten egg, and breadcrumbs. He poured olive oil into a pan and lit the flame on the stove.

"I'll dip," she said. "You be the fry cook."

When she handed him the first fillet, she said, "Batter up!"

He smiled. "If we have leftovers, we'll save them for breakfast. Perch and scrambled eggs is nothing to sneeze at."

They ate, cleaned up, chatted. They shared a small sherry as a nightcap. They undressed for bed and shivered into cold sheets.

She kissed him lightly.

"I'm going to sleep like a stone," she said.

"Fresh fish and fresh air."

"Hmmm," she said, "Sweet dreams, Lancelot," already almost asleep.

He wanted to stay awake, to watch her sleep, but his eyes soon shut, then opened, then shut.

He heard the creak of a car door hinge before he was fully awake. Not the slam of a car door nor the squeal of brakes bringing a car to a stop. Nor had he heard tires on gravel and dirt so he knew the car must have pulled over on the paved road, outside and away from the turn in to the cabin.

The hinge. Whoever they were, they hadn't planned for a hinge in need of oil.

He lay still, slowed his breathing to a stop, then listened into the darkness.

A low whistle came from the trees.

"Wake up!" he whispered. "Get up!"

"Stop!" she groaned.

"Someone's here," he said, rousting her.

She was wide awake now, dressing even as he dressed.

"Slip out the back," he told her. "Go down to the pier. Get in the boat and untie it. Let the wind take you. If you have to row, row quietly. And wait there until dawn."

"What are you going to do?"

"Draw them into the woods."

"But..."

"I'll be fine. I know where I am. They don't."

Then she was gone.

He gathered up an old 20-gauge with a shoulder strap that he used to hunt grouse and the .45 that had brought him luck from Omaha to Berlin. He filled the pockets of his hunting jacket— shotgun shells on the left, .45 rounds on the right.

He eased out the front door, crashed deliberately through the dried plants in the garden, and angled into the thickest part of the woods. When he got to the edge, he fired the shotgun back up the gravel drive towards the road. The sound roared the sleeping forest awake. It seemed to cry out as if it had been roused from sound slumber into nightmare. As he moved from tree to tree, he fired again, hoping they would think the two of them were running.

He reloaded the shotgun, slung it over his shoulder, and drew the .45.

Shots rang out. Muzzle flash. Three at least combed the woods, fanned out to push and encircle him. He moved toward the road, thinking he could pick them off where the woods thinned. He saw another flash and heard the bullet rip through leaves and branches to his right. He took aim at the flash and fired. He heard a groan and the sound of a body toppling into the underbrush. He slung the shotgun back until it bit into his shoulder. He fired both barrels. The other two fired at the sound while he ran toward the one he'd hit.

He turned the body over. He didn't know him but he recognized him. Crosstown muscle.

He stood, listened.

The woods quieted.

He heard the hinge. The engine gunned. The car speeding off. Leaving.

He ran then, sliding and all but falling down the slope to the lake.

His feet rattled on the worn, gray boards. The guns clattered. He found her in the boat, still tied to the pier.

She might have been asleep but for the fishing line wrapped around and biting into the skin on her long throat.

They were after her all along. To drive a wedge that would dissolve everything. They had watched them fish. They had made the bear move.

For a fleeting moment he wondered if she'd been in on it, betrayed him and then been betrayed.

The cloud cover broke open, divulging the moon. The shadow

of a branch fell across her face. He touched her as if to brush the shadow aside.

"The web was woven... The charm is broken... " came dimly and corrupt from her poem to his mind. He did not recite the ruined lines aloud.

He thought about untying the boat and letting her drift. He thought about Canada. He thought he owed it to his partner, his friend, to bring her back.

He unwound the fishing line, carried her to his car, lifted her into the back seat, covered her with a plaid car blanket.

He intended to go back down to the pier to retrieve the shotgun and the .45. Instead, his trembling hands emptied his pockets. Shells and cartridges littered the gravel.

He turned to look over his shoulder at the cabin and the lake.

He stood there and shuddered until the ache in his ribs made it hard to breathe.

PAROLE
Mathieu Cailler

(originally appeared in *The Blue Mountain Review*)

After an hour bus ride from the halfway house to West Des Moines, I unload from the back, shuffle by other passengers who have no idea where I've been and what I've done. There's even this little girl, maybe nine, with bright teeth that reminds me of my little sister around that age. The girl smiles at me as I pass through the aisle carrying nothing but gloves and a little spending cash for the ride back "home" in a few hours. I'm encouraged by the girl's grin, like maybe I got a shot at being free—and not just in the literal sense.

According to my calculations, he lives about a mile into town, which is a lot for me, a seventy-one-year-old man with a weak heart, but it's been decades since I've been able to walk in any direction I choose for more than a minute, so I don't mind. One foot in front of the other. One plodding step at a time.

What's the next step here? Do I try and find myself a little job? Something easy? If there are any spots that are hiring an elderly convict, I'm not so sure I want to work there. I mean if *I'm* a catch—how bad are the other applicants?

I don't want to upset him with this drop-in. Hell, even in my free days, I hated the drop-in. People at the door, ringing the bell, and all of sudden, you're fetching cake and pulling out chairs and brewing pots of coffee. I always thought of my welcome mat as sarcastic.

No, all I want to do is look at him. I went to prison when I was thirty-one, and my then girlfriend, Carrie, was pregnant with him. I never got to meet my boy. I never got to hold or smell him. He never visited, and that made sense—a boy should worry about girls and motorcycles, not have to visit his old man in a building meshed of concrete and steel.

I plan to ring his doorbell and ask to see Mr. Larin. (That was the name of my woodshop teacher in high school, and I like the sound of it.) I hope my boy will answer the door, but if he doesn't, maybe his wife will and, while she's explaining that I'm not at the right residence, he'll come up and see what's going on. I'll try to keep the conversation going for a bit, say things like, "Do you know where Mr. Larin lives?" and "Did he *used* to live here?"

With all my questions, I could possibly keep them on the stoop for a couple minutes. They might—*my boy* might—be very friendly, too. He might invite me in to use the phone and get out some pie and Sanka. Do people still drink Sanka? I hope the apple falls far from the tree, though, and when I pass by, he's out with his family on the porch, running a paring knife though a pumpkin's toothy smile, doing whatever it takes to make his kids laugh.

I wrote him letters when I was away. Always a nickname guy, I called him Baby Lou in every one. He never responded, though. In fact, I bet Carrie intercepted my notes, and I don't blame her. I've let it all pass, forgiven everyone, with the hope that they would forgive me. Carrie wrote me a few times, mostly to tell me to leave her and Louis alone—that I was a sperm donor, never his pop, and that his new dad was putting in the hard miles: taking him to school, packing his lunch, and teaching him how to change tires. She was right. I was a man far away, in Fort Dodge, who took Bible class twice a week just so God wouldn't shut the door on me. Sometimes, too, on Tuesdays, I'd take a crafts class. There, we build things out of papier-mâché, little sculptures, and all I could think of was how my life was like a wet strip that had never had the time to harden.

When I reach Beechtree Drive, the street's not quiet and domestic the way I thought it'd be on a Saturday morning. It's humming with cars and passersby, carrying brown boxes and t-shirts and bowls and picture frames. I grab my scrap of paper and check the address. It's the correct house.

A sign that reads ESTATE SALE hangs from the roofline near the front door. The house is big, two-stories tall, painted a creamy white with olive-drenched shutters. There are six blue-spruce trees in the front yard, all the same distance from each other.

Even though it's chilly out, the front door is wide open and a man, a worker in a red vest, nods as I pass the threshold. All these people are stomping along the hardwood floors, unsure of what they're searching for, hoping that a mug and a throw rug will make their Saturday better.

The house has a warm smell to it, like someone has boiled cinnamon sticks. In the foyer, the scent is strong, but it dissipates as I wind towards the living room and stare at a painting over the fireplace of a boat tracing across the sea, its sail full. "A beauty, right?" a woman with a tight face and loose curls says. She also has on a red vest and appears to be working the sale.

"Yes," I say. "Who painted it?"

"It's a Winslow Homer print."

"Nice," I say. "You can almost feel the wind and the ocean's spray, right?"

"I know."

"Where's the owner of the home?" I ask. "Is he moving or something?"

"I think he passed away."

"What?" I say.

The woman taps a co-worker who happens to pass by, carrying a stack of dishes. "The man who owned this home is dead, right?" she says.

The man nods. "Yeah, a couple weeks ago. A heart attack at forty."

I rub my face and feel as though a crack has split around my chest, allowing cold air to seep through and burn the sides of my heart and lungs. This day has kept me going for so long, and I made it, finally, to his home, my shoes aligned on the carpeting where his feet very well could have stood weeks prior. A flare of pain shoots across my rib cage. I clutch my chest, grab hold of the mantle, and count backwards from ten.

"Sir? Sir? Are you okay?" the man says.

I gather myself and assure them I'm all right. "And his family?" I say.

"Think he was a lone wolf," the man says. "This whole thing was all set up by his accountant. He did well for himself, though. I mean this is one nice place, right?"

"Yeah," I say. "It's something." I move about the floor plan. One of the rooms is getting little attention as most of the goodies have been cleared out, so I tuck inside what seems to be my boy's old office. There's wood paneling on the walls, a large bureau in the center, and a closet off to the side stuffed with bowling trophies that signify a perfect game, first prize in a league tournament, and another for third place in a county championship. I never cared much for bowling—any activity you can manage with a cigarette in your mouth hardly seems like a sport—and I know his mother hated it—she often said it ruined her manicures—so I wonder where the love came from, and I wonder how many other loves I missed out on.

A turquoise ball covered with purple swirls rests on the floor, glittering in the soft light that wends through the far window. I brush the ball's smooth surface with my palm.

I was lying earlier when I mentioned the Mr. Larin story. Sure, that was the plan, but if things went to plan, I never would have been incarcerated. I was really hoping that when I rang the bell, Baby Lou would recognize me in some capacity. I wanted something gooey, you know? When you share a cell for forty years, a man finds himself in need of something like that.

I head into the backyard where a group of people are examining a barbeque. One man lifts the lid, pretends to flip burgers and laughs, while his what-seems-to-be wife howls with laughter, then lets out, "Oh, Leroy! You're a hoot."

I take a seat in an outdoor chair on the deck, and when a worker—the guy who confirmed Lou's passing—comes by and asks me if I need help, I tell him that I'm testing out the chair. That seems to appease him and he leaves me alone and files to the far end of the backyard, positioning himself in front of a detached garage, where the door has been lifted and showcases a car that's tucked under a brown cover. He stands near the vehicle, smoking a cigar in perfect rhythm—a puff, an exhale, a flick; a puff, an exhale, a flick. After the man finishes his stogie, he scans the area and tosses the butt far behind the garage.

A short customer approaches the estate-sale worker and speaks in a loud voice, "So I'll do what I can to convince my wife and hopefully be back here in a few hours with my good ol' checkbook."

The worker nods, chuckles, extends his hand, and the two men shake on it. "You got it. I'll take the cover off now, and store it and the other necessary materials in the trunk," the worker says.

"All right. I like your style," the man says. "Positive thinking." The man turns away and the worker begins peeling the car cover off the vehicle. As he works, it becomes clear that the car is facing forward, pointing directly out into the long, flat driveway. I can't help but wonder if the estate-sale crew did that, or if Lou was skilled enough to back his ride up all that way and tuck his expensive car into the tiny garage, but I'm impressed nonetheless.

The worker plucks the cover off the front bumper, giving way to a shimmering, silver Porsche convertible with a black, cloth top. It's not the car that gets my attention—sure, it's beautiful, in seemingly immaculate condition, and picturing my boy driving around his manicured neighborhood in this drop-top is an image I'll love as long I can—no, what grabs hold of me and won't let go, is the white license plate that dangles from the front bumper, like a loose buck tooth. I am far enough away that I need to squint, but with my eyes narrowed, it's clear: My boy had elected to buy a vanity plate which allowed seven characters that he'd used to spell out BABYLOU.

I push myself off the rickety chair and shuffle across the grass to the garage, feeling a tingle in my spine and sharp heat in the corners of my eyes. The worker nods as I approach, and I smile back. "A beauty, right? Only 13,000 miles, too," he says. "I thought we'd sold it the other day, so I had her resting under the cover, but the buyer just called a little while ago and said he didn't want it, so it's back!"

I crouch to my knees and run my hand over the raised lettering on the front license plate, tracing the voluptuous curves of the *B* and the sharp lines of the *L*. "Baby Lou," I say.

"Weird, right?" the worker says. "The new owner—whoever it is—will have to get 'em changed anyway, so it doesn't matter..."

"I hear ya."

"Are you in the market?"

"Maybe."

"It's a stunning car. A five-speed, inline six, good amount of horses and new tires."

"You don't know a thing about cars, do you?" I say.

"Is it that obvious?" the worker says, biting his bottom lip.

"*Good amount of horses* gave you away. Can I take it for a spin?"

"Sure, I just need your driver's license. I'm not allowed to go with you, because my boss won't let us leave the grounds, but you can take it around the block and stuff."

"Oh, I see. Well, I don't have a license."

"Really?"

"Yeah."

"Don't drive anymore?"

"No, I shot a store clerk at a liquor store forty years ago. Never got around to renewing it."

The worker's eyes open wide and he inspects my lips, cheeks, and nose, as though he is going to bring out a pad and sketch me. Then he grabs his fish-bowl belly and laughs. "Good one," he says. "I shot a man in Reno once—just to watch him die."

"Looks like we're one and the same then," I say.

The worker sucks his teeth then says, "But, yeah, if you don't have a license, I can't let you take the car."

"Fair enough. Can I at least sit in it?"

"Of course. Your shoes clean?"

I nod, open the driver's-side door, and plop into the leather bucket seat that wraps my thighs and supports my spine in a simultaneously firm-and-soft way. A warm combination of coffee, maybe some cinnamon, stays with me in the cabin, and with each inhale, I suck the bitter scent into my nostrils, savoring the flavor, almost tasting it as it collides with my tongue.

I depress the clutch and slide the shifter from first to second, then from third to fourth, and up into fifth.

The worker bends down to the level of the open passenger-side window. "Looks good on you," he says. "Like you've been here before."

The world is thick with quiet, like I'm deep underwater; young, free. In this moment, I hadn't gotten drunk on March 1st, 1983; I hadn't had a fight with Carrie about the rent and how I couldn't pull my weight; I hadn't wandered down the road and brought my pistol. I hadn't gotten scared and fired a round into the chest of the young clerk behind the counter for a measly forty-six dollars.

At the end of your life if you've had a total of ten hours of sheer, unbridled joy then you've done something right. All I want now is to collect some hours, so that when the lights go black, I'll know I've kissed a woman, hummed some tunes, and spent some time in whatever way possible with my son.

With the car key glinting on the dashboard, I take hold of my chest and begin to gasp, shake, and flicker my eyes. "Help," I whisper.

The worker peeks back inside, and when I see I have him, I crank up the intensity: I let my eyes roll back and rip open my shirt, causing a button to pop off and tap against the windshield. "Go get my wife," I say. "She has what I need! Please! Hurry! Her name is Barbara."

The worker says a few jumbled words and darts from the garage, his feet banging on the polished asphalt floor, then the gravel, and then the grass. I sit up, straighten my shirt, grab the key with the rabbit's-foot chain from the dash, and jam it into the ignition.

A roar comes up and surrounds the car, echoing in the tiny one-car garage. The attendees of the estate sale all turn around in unison, their eyes lining up on the silver Porsche that rattles in its cage with plumes of exhaust pushing from its pipes and coiling around its frame.

I tear out of the driveway, let first gear redline around six-thousand, and am swinging into the road by the time I pull the shifter into second. My back's alive with cylindrical reverberations, and I can't hear anything but the push of the engine. Alongside the car, hedges, mailboxes, and picket fences blur into one gorgeous swath. I keep my feet hard on the pedals and my hands tight on the steering wheel, where me and my boy's fingerprints get to live with each other for at least a half a tank.

A BURDEN OF TRUTH

Tim M. Ruth

James Robert Whitmore stared up at the clock on the gray stone wall in the tiny room. Eleven-thirty, only thirty minutes left and then they would come to get him. He prayed the priest would get there soon. Whitmore rose up and began to pace from one of the drab stone walls to the other. His stomach started to gurgle, and he wished he hadn't eaten the meal they had brought for him. A knock on the door caused him to freeze. He glanced again at the clock. *It can't be time. Please let it be the priest.* His voice faltered as he called out, "Come in."

The heavy wooden door swung open, and Father Thomas McCarthy walked in. Whitmore rushed to meet him, grasping the old man's hand. He said, "Thank God you're here, Father. I don't think I can go through with this." The priest freed his hand from Whitmore's death grip. Wrapping his arm around Whitmore's shoulder, he said "Well, my son, I'm afraid at this point you don't have much choice. Come now, why don't we use this time wisely. You asked me to hear your confession, and that's what I'm here to do."

The old priest guided Whitmore to a rough wooden bench that sat against one of the bleak walls of the room, and helped him sit down. "Now James, I'm ready to listen."

With wild eyes, Whitmore looked at the priest and said: "It shouldn't be me, Father. I don't deserve this."

"Well lad, the truth is many people feel that you do. We don't have much time. Why don't you share your confession with me? Free your soul, James. Now is the time."

Whitmore had wrapped his arms around himself and was staring at the stone floor. "I'm sorry Father. I haven't been to confession in over twenty-five years. I don't even know how to start."

"All you have to do is tell the truth, son. It's the truth that will set you free."

Whitmore lifted his gaze up from the floor and said, "The problem with Emily was that she couldn't keep a secret, and that's why she had to die."

A look of shock registered on the priest's face, but he remained silent.

Whitmore continued: "Besides, the whole damned thing was her fault anyway. If Emily would have just thrown the invitation away like I had done to all the others, she'd still be alive today. But, oh no, she couldn't leave it alone. She wrote a reply accepting the invitation on my behalf. Can you believe that, Father? The bitch didn't even tell me what she'd done." Whitmore looked into the priest's eyes, expecting to see empathy, but instead, the old man looked like he had just drunk a glass of curdled milk.

He ignored the sour expression on the priest's face and went on. "I found out what she'd done one night when I was sitting in my study reading the New York Times. I came across this article titled 'Whitmore to Speak Publicly, the First Time in Twenty Years.' Of course I'm stunned by the headline, so I start reading." 'James Whitmore, author of the exceptional short story *The Winter's Harvest* and several lesser known works, will be this year's keynote speaker at Bishop Walsh High School in Rochester NY.' The article went on, but I didn't need to read anymore. I knew what happened; my alma mater had sent their favorite son another request to speak at the school. Emily knew I would never accept, no matter how much she badgered me, so she accepted for me.

"Well, I grabbed that paper and marched my ass right out into the kitchen where she was doing dishes, and I introduced the back of my hand to the side of her face. She drops like I hit her with an ax handle. She starts blubbering. 'I did it for you, I did it for you.' I'm about to cram that article down her throat when my cell phone rings. I compose myself a little and answer the call. It turns out to be my old agent, who I had not spoken with in years. He tells me he saw that I was going to speak at Bishop Walsh and he says there is renewed interest in the story. He said he was even getting feelers from Hollywood about a remake of the original film. Well, Father, I start to think maybe it's time to get back out there. Money was getting tight, and I didn't have a lot going on. I hung up the phone and realized that what Emily had done was a good thing. I went over and tried to apologize to her, but she didn't want to hear it. Just stormed off and locked herself in the bedroom. I knew it would take some time, but she'd come around. She always did."

The more Whitmore talked, the more he relaxed. *The priest was right; confession is good for the soul.* He checked the time again and saw that it was eleven-forty-five. Only fifteen minutes left. The priest saw Whitmore look at the clock, and he tried to interject, but Whitmore stopped him. "I'm sorry, Father, but I only have fifteen minutes left, and I want to finish with the confession."

The priest nodded his head and said, "Go on."

"Well, the next morning I amble out into the kitchen, and I

see that Emily had placed the invitation to speak at Bishop Walsh on the kitchen table. At first, it was an ego rush to see it there. After all these years I was going back, and I was going back because they wanted me. Just like the coaches wanted me when I was their star quarterback." A smirk came to his face. "Just like all the girls wanted me when they were in the back seat of my car."

Whitmore stood up from the bench and started to pace the room again. "The problem was she left that goddamn invitation on the table. Sorry about the profanity, Father. I know that's wrong, especially at a time like this."

The priest waved his hand to continue. "Well, day after day I see that invitation sitting there, mocking me. That's when it dawned on me. I don't know how she found out, but somehow she knows the story that made me famous wasn't mine. Every morning the smug bitch sits across from me drinking her morning coffee, pretending to read the paper, but I know what she's doing. She's trying to break me. She wants me to admit that I took that story from Timmy Wills, and then killed him to cover it up. That wasn't going to happen, though, Father McCarthy, and I'll tell you why. Unlike Emily, I can keep a secret. Twenty-five years have gone by, Father, and I never breathed a word about what I did to Timmy. Not a *word* until this very moment."

He smiled an ingratiating smile and said: "I know you can keep a secret too, but I guess that comes with your line of work, doesn't it, Father?" The priest's eyes were wide, and locked onto Whitmore. The old man's face was ashen.

"Anyway, no one should feel sorry for Timmy. The little dweeb was lucky to have me as a friend. God knows he didn't have anyone else. Seriously, the only thing the kid had going for him was that he could write. I saw the way the whole damned English class would hang on his every word when that five foot nothing twerp stood in front of the class and read one of his stories. Instinctively, I knew that he had something I needed. And I was right. When he read me his story *The Winter's Harvest* I knew that was it. I asked him if he had shared the story with anyone else yet, he said no, that I was his best friend, he wanted me to hear it first.

"Well, that was all I needed to hear. I asked Timmy if he wanted to go fishing on my dad's boat that night. I still can't believe how excited the moron got when I asked him that. He accepted on the spot, and I knew that I was going to get what I needed. I told him that I would get in trouble if my dad knew I took anyone on the boat so he shouldn't tell anyone he was meeting me. Just before he left, I told him to bring the story with him because I wanted to hear it again that night. You should have seen the look on his face; you would have thought the prom queen had just asked him on a date."

The priest's cell phone buzzed. He said "excuse me" and answered the call. "Yes, I understand. I'll wait for you here."

Ending the call, the priest looked to Whitmore and said: "They're on their way."

The panic that had been in Whitmore's eyes when the priest first entered the room was gone. He was ready.

Whitmore looked to the priest and said: "I'm almost finished, and I need to get this out before I walk out that door." Without waiting for a reply from the priest, he continued. "You probably can imagine what happened to Timmy when we got out on that boat, but I still feel I need to say it. We had a few beers as we headed out onto Ontario. I even let Tim drive the boat for a while. When we got about twelve miles out, I killed the motor, and we just sat there and watched the moonlight sparkle on top of the water. For a minute I thought about not doing it, but that's exactly what a loser like Timmy would do. I came up behind him and cracked his skull with a propeller wrench. He crumpled to the deck. Out cold.

"Then I wrapped an old anchor chain around his legs and tossed him over the side. He came to when he hit the water, and for a moment he floated there at the surface and stared at me. He never said a word; it was as if he knew this was what life had in store for him. The image of that pale white face in the middle of that cold black water was hard to look at, but it didn't last long. The weight of the anchor chain pulled him under, and he was gone."

Whitmore analyzed the priest's face for a reaction. The old man was shaken and pale. "Now you know what became of Timmy Wills. A lot of people thought the little freak ran off and joined the circus or something just to get away from life on his father's farm, but I knew better... and now you do too.

"Some people would have been dumb and tried to do something with Timmy's story right away, but not me. I waited two years before I took it to a publisher. The rest, as they say, is history."

Whitmore heard them coming down the hall, and he looked up to check the clock one last time. Twelve on the dot. Time was up. He turned back to the priest. "Emily put me in this position, and now she's at the bottom of Ontario with Tim. Now I have to deal with what she got me into. Thank you for listening to my confession, Father. It has made all the difference in the world."

Just then the door opened, and Monsignor Carl Rickman

walked in with three members of his staff. He looked at Whitmore and said, "I hope our prayer room here at the monastery wasn't too spartan for you, sir."

James Whitmore smiled, "Not at all. It was just what I needed. I have to tell you, Father McCarthy was a godsend. As you're well aware, I haven't spoken in public in over twenty years. I had a terrible bout of stage fright before Father McCarthy arrived, but he helped me get through it. I don't think I could give today's commencement speech without the steadying hand the Father provided."

The monsignor nodded and smiled at the priest, then said "Thomas, perhaps you should sit the commencement out. You don't look well. The old man raised his eyes up to the monsignor, and feebly nodded his agreement.

Whitmore drew in a deep breath, "You know I told Father McCarthy that I didn't think I deserved this, but through the power of prayer and confession I see now that indeed I am the person that should be speaking to these young people today."

Clapping his hands together, Whitmore said, "All right then. Let's go inspire the newest graduates of Bishop Walsh." Smiling one last time at the old priest, he turned and headed out to greet the adoring assembly.

A DAY ON THE CREEK

Vernie Singleton

Some people around here think Grandpa is a mean man. I've seen him gentle as a kitten then turn like a bulldog. But as far as I'm concerned, even as a child growing up, I always saw he had good reason to defend what was his. So far, I've learned to stay in a safe place with Grandpa. I'm lucky. It's a natural thing—bloodline, I guess. But some people rub him the wrong way like I saw some years ago when I was in training to be a man.

Seven years ago, when the tide was about to turn and the air was calm, I watched through our fine-mesh screened window as Grandpa carefully lowered the seasoned crabbing gear into a patched-up burlap croaker sack.

"Grandpa—how many sandwiches you want?" I yelled to him as he worked in the yard.

"One'll do me fine, Henry. Take time and clean up your mess in there."

"Yessir, I will." I packed one extra for Grandpa and me to share.

As Grandpa tied the sack closed with an old shoelace, a brown wood-paneled station wagon cruised into our yard and parked under the shade of a pecan tree by the shed. A small stranger jumped out of the car like a jack-in-the-box. He wore tangerine and yellow striped shorts that stopped abruptly at his knees, and a tank top the color of the Caribbean seas. Maybe he had just gotten off a cruise ship. He was no taller than I was at eleven, even with his baseball cap on, but he was a man—as I would later know for sure—a different breed from Grandpa, but still a man.

I knew this man was a stranger because Grandpa made no effort to approach him as he came forward, appearing to know Grandpa well.

"How do you do, Mr. Holmes?" began the man, reaching out both hands, then fanning away a flock of swarming gnats.

Grandpa returned the greeting, right away slipping both of his calloused hands deep in his overall pockets, as if trying to protect something.

"This is a lovely place you have here," said the man, gazing at the red brick porched house and surrounding grounds with bursting blue hydrangeas, oleanders, and fruit and pecan trees. Bobbing his head up and down in definite approval, he smiled real hard.

"Pardon my manners, Mr. Holmes, but my name is Spencer Wilson. Miss Ruby Simmons on the usher board at Mount Zion told me about you, that you might be interested in selling some land," he said with a big grin, like he had already gotten what he came for.

"Ruby?" Grandpa paused. "Simmons?" He hesitated again, and then released a nagging cough as though he found the name hard to swallow.

"Live up there at the head of the road, yessir." the man continued, as if missing Grandpa's discomfort with Miss Ruby's name.

"I know Ruby, but I ain't never tell her no such lie as that. Where in Hell's Nation she get that from?"

"We-e-e-l-l-l," stammered the man. "I might have asked her who had an acre or a lot or something to sell. I don't exactly recall how I put it."

"Either way you put it, it ain't me you lookin' for. I ain't got nothin' to sell," Grandpa said, taking his eyes off the man, turning to the screened window where I stood packing tomato sandwiches for our lunch. The air was still and I could hear everything.

"C'mon, son, 'fore we miss our tide," Grandpa yelled to me. He brushed away some gnats, and spat. Then he covered up the frothy, moist spot on the ground and faced the man again.

"They say these gnats bring good fishing—find that true down here?" the man asked, fanning the pests from his face. I knew he was in a tight spot with Grandpa, and trying to make conversation.

"Never mind that. Just look here, Mister. I don't know where you get your information from, but there ain't none of my land for sale, never was, and never will be. Understand? Now you can take another slow gazin' drive back out here 'cause me and my grandson is fixin' to go in the creek." Easing a hand out of his pocket, Grandpa demonstrated how the man could make his way back down the dry, unpaved road.

"Mister Holmes, I didn't mean you any harm," said the man, reaching out to Grandpa.

"Any harm?" Grandpa mocked him, stepping back, his face twisted and unnatural. "You got no callin' down here in the first place. A person can't breathe in peace these days. Day in, day out, coming and going, people of every make and model after the same thing. Come to steal a poor man's last breath. That's what it is."

"I'm not like that, Mr. Holmes," said the man, his chest thrust forward like his free-flowing words.

"You here, ain't you?"

"Like I said, Mr. Holmes, Miss Ruby sent me. She's about to lose her property up there."

"I don't know nothin' 'bout that woman," said Grandpa. "Tell me she's shrewd as they come."

"I can tell you, Mr. Holmes, I rent from her. All us renters have to move, even Miss Ruby. She can't even live out the rest of her days on her birthright." His voice raised with excitement and disbelief.

"Her daddy, Old Man Cecil, must be turnin' over in his grave 'bout now. People lived like people on that Simmons land, raised chickens and grew first one thing and then another before I had sense, and I turn seventy-five in November. Why they got to move?"

"They want to put a road through her property. The town's behind it, but the county and state are tied up with it, too, pushing out people to make things better for developers. Something about eminent domain or something. I don't know, Mr. Holmes. Nobody to fight for her. Even Miss Ruby said she can't go up against Wall Street with no money, and especially at her age. But I thought I could buy a piece from you and put up a double-wide for my wife and two boys. I married late."

Grandpa spat again. "Let me tell you, son. You barkin' up the wrong tree. Wall Street gonna lay down the law. This here is a different breed of people you dealin' with now. Twenty years ago, maybe, but these ones don't care a bit about age or how long you been here. And I can tell you, they gonna outlaw trailers on this island altogether, sure as the day I born. Watch what I tell you."

"But why, Mr. Holmes?"

"They think trailers not in keepin' with the high-priced spreads they got squeezed in every corner of this little island. See, some of the trailers is right next to some of them fine homes. But we been here first. These well-off folk don't want to be lookin' down from their second-story balcony onto some fabricated box. They scared it's gonna bring down their personal property value. You know how it is. Then we got some of our own saditty black folks sayin' 'why don't you build a nice house on that valuable land you got?' like they so well off they don't know 'bout makin' minimum wage, scrapin' to pay land tax, or mixed up with family land tangled in heirs property and such. But time's gonna bring a change. The bottom's gonna rise to the top. Watch what I tell you."

Grandpa tested the weight of the croaker sack, then set it a few feet in front of him like he was ready to make a move.

"Well, maybe me and my family could stay here until that time comes?" said the man.

"I don't think you understand, Mister. You know how much chillun and grands I got? What I look like sellin' to you or the next man that comes along when I don't know what's down the road for me? My family need a place to stay too. We ain't got money to go buyin' land someplace else. All I got is these ten acres. Some people think land don't run out. What you say on that?"

"All I need is—"

By this time I had reached Grandpa and the man.

"C'mon, son, let's go catch us some blue crabs 'fore they take a notion."

Grandpa didn't even give me a chance to say a formal hello. He grabbed the sack and the bucket, handing me the dip net to carry. As we headed toward the creek, I heard a faint voice behind us on the trail.

"Can I come?"

We stopped and so did the gnats, as if to hear Grandpa's response. Grandpa turned around and faced the man, confused as to whether those feeble words had come from a blind old man or a lost child. Grandpa's eyes and lips twitched in surprise. He looked like he hurt for the man. Like he would've looked at me if I wanted something and there was no way he could get it for me and didn't know how to tell me. No matter what he was thinking, the words came out through clenched teeth. "I ain't gonna sell you no land, but come on."

The sun was hot and bright at two o'clock in a clear blue sky, but there was a stirring breeze ruffling the bushes along the shore. The man trailed behind Grandpa and me down a narrow footpath, through summer vines growing wildly on both sides. The bateau was tied to the dock, like a vibrant green leaf floating on the outgoing tide.

"This it?" asked the man. He pulled the boat closer to the dock with the attached rope so we could all get in.

"You familiar with this sort of thing?" asked Grandpa, surprised by him.

"Familiar? I grew up on the creek," he said, sticking out his shallow chest, so glad to be part of Grandpa's and my team.

"No kiddin'," said Grandpa.

"As a matter of fact I grew up over there on the muddy shore where we used to bog for crabs." He pointed to where Grande Marsh Mall loomed on the far side of the creek. "You know Sally Wilson?"

Grandpa nodded, smiling for the first time.

"Well, I'm her son. I grew up in what they used to call Cornpatch."

"Yeah, I know the Wilsons, Sadie Mae and Bessie and all them. It's still Cornpatch to me. Your family sold some land years ago, when development first started. Y'all followed the old north star—right?"

"Yessir. Now those stars are leading some of us back south. I may have left the land, but the land never left me."

"How 'bout that." responded Grandpa, pushing off the dock with the grey splintered oars.

"Yep. I grew up on the creek, and hunted raccoons and rabbits, sparrows and deer, like the rest of the boys. Now I paint those critters for a living."

"What you mean, you paint them?" Grandpa asked with wonderment.

"I'm an artist. I sell paintings and drawings of wild animals, landscapes and some portraits of people, but mostly animals. I'm surprised you never heard of me, Mr. Holmes. My paintings are in some of the local restaurants and public buildings throughout the county."

"Don't get out to such places, Mr. Spencer."

All I could think about was Mr. Spencer must be pretty good to sell pictures of animals that can't even pay him to paint them. I said, "That's so cool. Can I see one?"

"Mind your manners, Henry," Grandpa snapped, handing me the plastic bag of chicken backs for bait. He rested the oars, giving me a stern look. "Watch how you get in grown people's conversations. I told you about that."

I held my head down, but my ears were wide open.

"Tell me this, Mr. Spencer," Grandpa continued. "How can you buy waterfront property here on Indigo Island and can't even make a decent livin'? You hustling pictures? You from here. You know land ain't cheap no more."

"I do make a decent living, Mr. Holmes. I've taught in public and private schools up north and down here. I give private art lessons, I have illustrated two children's books and my original paintings sell for quite a bit, plus I sell prints. That old car I drive may not look like much, but my family is well provided for. I'm just trying to get a footing on some property here back home."

"Look here, son. Don't get me wrong. I'm sure you take good care of your family, but I can't sell you no land. And if I did, which I ain't, you'd have to give me a cashier's check, 'cause I won't finance nobody. And that's that."

"Then lease it to me until I find something I can afford."

"You don't give up, do you, Mr. Spencer?"

"Can't afford to, Mr. Holmes."

151

"In your line of work, you deals with a lot of white folk, don't you?"

Mr. Spencer folded his arms and gazed out at the open creek, his head tilted away to block the sun from his peaceful dark eyes. He stayed silent.

Grandpa followed up. "And you probably married to a white woman, ain't you?"

Was Grandpa picking a fight? He seemed to be getting on Mr. Spencer's nerves. The man looked straight at Grandpa and lowered his voice, as though trying to hide his words from me.

"Mr. Holmes, I'm sorry you had to take our conversation to such a level. But, yes, I deal with a lot of white folk in my line of work—white and black and everything in between and all around. And, no, I am not married to a white woman. I'm married to a yam. You know what that is?" he asked, as he tied the chicken back so tight onto the crab basket that I thought the string would cut the bait in half.

"You surprise me, Mr. Spencer. Just the other day I had to explain to my grandson what a 'yam' was, and I told him never to call a light-skinned black woman a yam to her face because it might get him in trouble." Grandpa looked at me and winked, then back at Mr. Spencer. "But, boy—you all right!"

"You ought to see some of my work, Mr. Holmes," now a little bit more at ease that Grandpa had loosened up to him.

"No, I don't need to do that. I ain't gonna buy nothin'."

"Come on, Mr. Holmes. Some of my paintings are in galleries all over the country just for people like you to look at. Don't have to buy a thing."

"Must be ain't no good then." They both laughed.

We drifted into the mouth of our favorite crabbing hole, a flooded inlet where oyster beds stand at attention at low tide, but we still had some time to get back to the dock. You could tell that the creek water had started to head back out to the ocean because the wet waterline on the dock pilings had crawled down the thick weathered wood. We stayed on the creek for nearly two hours, catching near a bucket of crabs that went to Mr. Spencer, since they were mostly caught on his line.

Our new friend praised me for my tomato sandwiches, asking me lots of questions about school and what I planned to do with my life. He and Grandpa hit it off like reunited old-time buddies, talking about people I had never heard of or who had died or moved away. Mr. Spencer even shared stories about his own family.

"When the war broke out," he said, "the Civil War, that is, and

Southerners fled the Sea Islands for their lives, the Confederate plantation master over there at Cornpatch took the best plantation mule and the best slave man, set them up under an old oak tree where he had buried the family's treasures, and shot them both dead. Folks believed that both of these strong and loyal spirits would protect the valuables from looters until the family returned to claim their belongings. If anybody tried to dig up the treasure before they returned for it, the two spirits combined would conjure a terrible storm, scattering and killing the thieves."

Mr. Spencer's grandmother told him that that slave who guarded the treasure under the draping oak was his great-great-grandfather Bachuss, and that his descendants who stayed on the island after freedom came pooled their money and bought a hundred acres in Cornpatch—part of the land the Union had set aside on Indigo for newly-freed slaves.

"Did anybody ever find the treasure, Mr. Spencer?" I asked.

"We're living it now, Henry. We're living it now. The beauty and bounty of the land is all the treasure we really need."

It was a good day on the creek. The rocking of the bateau on the outgoing tide helped to soothe Grandpa's spirit so that he could enjoy Mr. Spencer and his stories. But I knew the talk of buying and selling land would come up again and I prayed they would remain friends, no matter what.

When we returned to shore, I transferred the crabs to a croaker sack and walked Mr. Spencer to his car. As we stood there he told me that, when he was a boy, he and his friends were eager to be men, so they hunted like grownups. One day, they found a raccoon trap in the woods with just the animal's foot in it. The coon had bitten off his foot to free himself. That made him realize how much animals loved life and freedom too, and he never hunted again. He was fourteen years old.

Mr. Spencer opened the back of his station wagon to a treasure box of prints—raccoons, leaping and grazing deer, and the most realistic birds of every color, some standing on the creek edges and some perching on pine and oak limbs, as though waiting to fly away. He gave me a notecard in pen-and-ink of a raccoon looking like it had a story to tell. Then he reached into a shallow flat box and took out a large color print of a man who sat knitting a cast net.

"Who is this?" I asked.

"An old friend," said Mr. Spencer. He rolled up the paper like you'd roll up a document of graduation and walked with it over to Grandpa, who was sitting on the porch step.

"See if you know this man."

Grandpa arose with one hand balancing on his knee to help him rise up. He took his time, examining every inch of the painting, but lost his smile in serious anticipation as he studied each stroke of the painting.

"This here James Miller 'self," exclaimed Grandpa. "Well, I'll be doggone if this ain't my old creek partner. How you know 'bout us?"

"I didn't know anything for sure except that you were both old-timers who might have known each other. I painted this a couple years after Mr. Miller died. I got permission from his daughter, Miss Alice, to use some old photographs."

"You sure done somethin' this time, Mr. Spencer. I tell you. Yessir, this is the man hisself." A smile overcame Grandpa's face. Then he ran his calloused fingertips across the surface of the print as if he could feel the beaded knots in the net hanging from the knitting pole. Grandpa studied the picture some more, turning his face to the sky as if he could hear Mr. Miller saying "no more pain, no more sorrow. I am free." The details of the painted net glistened in the soft afternoon sunlight. Grandpa's friend's face looked satisfied, like he had nothing else to do but finish the net.

* * *

Later that night, Grandpa told me something that caused him to cry when he thought about his friend. He said some years ago, a young realtor came to Mr. Miller for help. The man had bought land next door to Mr. Miller's property to build housing that poor working people could afford. But he was landlocked and needed someone to sell him a right of way. Grandpa said Mr. Miller prayed for the man to be successful with his business because he thought housing was a good idea and that the man had a good heart. So, he sold him the right of way across his property so that the man could make a road to his seven acres.

Come to find out, the man was fronting for some white people. He sold his property and Mr. Miller's right of way to a big-time developer who built and sold expensive homes. This broke old man Miller's heart and two weeks later he fell out with a stroke. Grandpa said that was a hard lesson to learn for both of them. He said he could hardly take a chance with anybody now because you can't tell these days who's scheming and who's for real.

* * *

Grandpa snapped out of a trance. "Okay, Mr. Spencer. I ain't buyin' this picture and I ain't sellin' you no land. C'mon, Son, get in the house." Grandpa ushered me up the steps onto the porch.

I had listened to the hard and soft exchange between Grandpa and Mr. Spencer all afternoon, but had lost track of who had outshined the other. I followed my instructions, waving goodbye to Mr. Spencer, confused as to what else to do. But I was sure to take my place back at the kitchen window.

A calm came over Mr. Spencer's face, as if all the fight had left him. He took off his cap and held it low with both hands in front of him, real solemn, like he was about to pray.

"Mr. Holmes, it's been a pleasure to spend time with you and your grandson today. I enjoyed myself and I appreciate the crabs. I hadn't been on the creek like that in over thirty-five years. It does something to you. You brought back some good memories for me today." Mr. Spencer walked over and rested a hand on Grandpa's shoulder. "I won't bother you anymore about your land, because I know you have to look out for your grandson and the rest of the family. I know how that is." He looked toward me, still at the window. "But I'm not too young to remember either, when all of us on this island were one—men, women, and children," he emphasized by pounding one fist into an open palm, then holding it to signify unity. "You know what I mean? We have both been there, when people could count on one another to help each other through tough times. I'm fifty-five years old, but I remember those times too."

Grandpa dropped real hard onto the top step of the back porch as if he had lost his balance and his breath, but still had a grip on the picture.

"I want you to have that picture, Mr. Holmes."

"No, no!" objected Grandpa, struggling to give it back.

"It's a gift from me, like you gave me gifts today. You didn't have to let me be a part of Henry's and your day on the creek."

"Thank you, Mr. Spencer, for your many gifts as well. I appreciate your stick-to-it-ness for your family. It's good to see that in a young man. God bless you for that. I know my grandson picked up some pointers too." Both of them looked up at the kitchen window, where I stood. "If you ain't got nothin' in a year, come back to see me. But—if you got a taste for some more blue crabs— come back anytime. They'll be bitin' for another couple months." Grandpa reached out to Mr. Spencer, and shook his hand.

* * *

We never saw him again, and that's been seven years, because I'm a senior now in high school. Never heard anything of him, either. He appeared and disappeared. I couldn't imagine him a hunter, or even someone who bogged in the mud for crabs. There was something about him, though, that reminded me of my Grandpa—not the way he looked, but something deep down inside. I could see it, I could feel it when he told his stories, and when he was so generous with his smiles, even when Grandpa called him a boy. But it didn't matter to him. He had come through that same line of upbringing, respect for elders and their insight that made everything all right in the end because we knew they were looking out for our best interests. I could just tell he was a man and was going to make it, whether Grandpa sold him the land or not.

And until this day, as I stand overlooking the creek, with firm footing on God and family soil, I never understood why Grandpa didn't tell Miss Ruby not to send people to him for land. He always turned them down after a talk in the garden as he cut okra, or as he cleaned mullet fish behind the shed, or while he picked up pecans from the pecan orchard grounds. Any time of year, Grandpa always took time to hear their side—white, black, everything in between and all around, as Mr. Spencer would say—as though it all meant something to him.

NEW WORLD

Scott William Woods

I'M ALMOST THIRTEEN, old enough to know what's going on. Like three days ago after Scouts, and the chat with Dad on the way to the car that began 'Did you get your bowline?'

Dad was grilling me about whether I got a requirement signed off for my next rank, grilling me in the parking lot. It's always like that, even though he's just been right there at the meeting scrutinizing me. Or always like that except for when he has to work.

Those days Mr. Woodward takes me. Dad and Mr. Woodward were next-door-neighbors growing up, and he's a fireman too. I like it when Mr. Woodward drives because he has a Corvette, a yellow one, 2014. And he doesn't stay to watch but drops me and picks me up afterwards.

A bowline is one of the knots you use to make a loop. Loop knots are all different—a double half-hitch slides both ways, a taut-line hitch tightens but won't loosen, and a bowline doesn't slip at all. I chilled Dad out by reciting the mnemonic. That's the word that won me this year's spelling bee—I remembered it because it rhymes with 'demonic.'

I think I'm doing pretty good. It's only a year and a half since I crossed over from Cubs, and I've already got my Scout and Tenderfoot ranks and as of tonight the final requirements for Second Class. But Dad is all over me about making First Class by the April Court of Honor. When *he* was a boy they didn't even have that initial rank of Scout. As if getting to Eagle wasn't hard enough already without another step.

My father's name is Duane Sutridge. We live in a burb town on the Connecticut shore, and a lot of my friends' parents work at the university or the drug company and moved here for the job from all over. Not mine, though. Our Sutridge ancestor came on the first ship bringing settlers.

So you might think we'd be rich, but we're not. Dad's a fireman, and Mom's a library assistant. Even though our family name is on stuff all over town, like Sutridge Hill and Sutridge Street. But we don't own any of it and haven't for 300 years, according to Dad, who says our family was never good at business. Not like the other old families. I know a kid whose ancestor came over on the same 1639 boat as mine and shared in the first division of the land same as mine, and his family still owns a big orchard and an upscale specialty market and tons of other properties.

Dad belonged to the same scout troop as me, but he didn't quite get his Eagle. Something to do with the building materials he needed for his project not being delivered on time. You have to make Eagle before you turn eighteen, or they won't give it to you at all. Dad, being Dad, completed the project anyway, of course.

So he's basically living again through me, as if me making Eagle will make up for him not getting his. Like I said, I know what's going on.

But I don't mind. I like Scouts. Some of the kids at school think it's lame, but I just curve them.

There's probably another reason Dad wants me in Scouts. Another reason besides that I'm the only boy in the family. It's just me and my baby sister Teresa, at home now of course with Mom. The other reason is that scouting is kind of a paramilitary organization. The fire department's the same way. Mom says Dad wanted to join the Marines after he graduated high school.

Dad had quit interrogating me, and we'd been quiet for a couple of minutes. But a good quiet, a close quiet. These times when the parental units ferry me around are useful for finding out stuff. The important stuff, the kind of stuff they don't always want to talk about. Now I wished I'd chosen the front seat, so I could see his face.

"Dad?"

"Yes, Son?"

My name is Thomas, but Dad always calls me 'Son' when we're alone. The name's actually Thomas A. for Thomas Aquinas, but no one outside my family knows what the A stands for, and I plan on keeping it that way. I tell my friends it stands for 'a' Sutridge.

"Why did you want to join the Marines?"

Dad took some time to answer, so he needed to think about what to tell me.

"The Marines are the best," he said. " 'The few, the proud.' I guess I thought if they took me I'd become proud of myself."

My father is a very brave man. He's gone into burning buildings lots of times to rescue people. And that's not counting the ones he helped get out when the Amtrak train derailed or the times he operated the Jaws of Life on I-95 with gasoline leaking. But he can also be kind of clueless sometimes. "No," I said, "I didn't mean why the *Marines* specifically. Why did you want to join the military?"

"Someone needed to protect the country," he said. "But that was a long time ago."

I knew there was more there, so I waited for it. Besides, it wasn't all that long ago. Dad and Mom got married right after high school and had me within a year. Dad's only thirty-two.

Sure enough, in another minute he went on. "I was young— barely 18. I wanted the adventure. To see the world. Christ, I'd never even been out of the state."

Dad hardly ever swears. Of course he wouldn't when Mom's around because she's so religious. She has a brother who's a priest, and when she was little she wanted to be a nun. But Dad hardly ever swears even when it's just the two of us. So I knew that back then he wanted to see the world like mondo strongo. "Wouldn't the Marines take you?"

"No, they wanted me." Dad stopped again, and this time I couldn't bear to keep quiet.

"Then why didn't you join up?"

He took a long time to answer, and we were almost in the driveway before he did.

"I guess you could say it was love."

"Love?"

"Love," Dad said. "Love always wins out, in the end."

Dad and Mom must've really been in love, for him to give up his dream for her.

Two days ago Dad had one of his every third day 24-hour shifts at the firehouse, and Mom went to PTA after dinner. Sometimes she leaves Teresa with Mrs. Woodward, but that didn't work because of parent duty for Sacha Woodward's choir rehearsal. So I got stuck watching the baby for a few hours.

The mystery about Mrs. Woodward is maybe the one thing I haven't figured out at all. When her family moved here from wherever they lived before, her father didn't already have a job and they didn't know a soul. When I ask the units all they say is 'They heard the schools were good here.'

But as for watching my sister, I was okay with that. I knew what my parents were thinking. We live in an expensive town, and we can't afford to waste money on a babysitter, not when we have a free one living right with us. And maybe if they can save a little I might just get that iPhone for Christmas.

Besides, Teresa was asleep, and both units being away offered the perfect opportunity to play Call of Duty with my best friend Mike on Xbox. Mom doesn't approve of first person shooter games, and Dad always backs her up. Even when she isn't there, since that time she laid into him. But I think Dad is conflicted because in the game the shooter's a Marine.

After an hour Mike IM'd me that his mom was making him

finish his homework. Which was okay because Teresa had just woken up and started crying.

Her diaper was all swollen and heavy like it was full of pee. I hoped it was just pee.

I picked her up and carried her over to the changing table. When I laid her down there she stopped crying. Smart girl. Teresa could tell what was coming. I know it was gross, but I bent down and gave the diaper a sniff. Yep, just pee.

The two little tape tabs came loose easily, and I picked up both her ankles in one hand and used a wipe to clean her privates. Then I scooted the diaper out from under her, and rolled it and the wipes up into a ball, reattaching the tape. It was the size of a softball, but twice as heavy, like one that got hit over the fence and laid out all winter at the edge of a marsh. I stepped on the diaper pail pedal to raise the lid and finger-rolled it in. Two points! And the foul.

The next step was to whoosh her bottom with talcum and put on a fresh diaper. When I reached for the powder and stepped on the pedal I kept a hand on her just like Mom said. Teresa could roll over now, and we didn't want her rolling off the changing table. Too bad there's no merit badge for this.

Teresa knew we were done and started smiling and goo-gooing and reached out her arms to be picked up. Mom thinks she'll start to crawl soon.

I picked her up under the arms and held her up high. That wasn't so easy to do any more. Then I dropped her down and blew a raspberry onto her tummy. Teresa laughed—she loves that. So we did it some more: raise, raspberry, repeat. After a few of those I set her on my hip and gave her a whirley-bouncey ride. "*Who's* the best big brother? *Who's* the best big brother?"

'Who's the best big brother.' I was glad no one who could talk was there to hear me. During the whirley ride I noticed again that Teresa has Mom's eyes. They taught us in health this year about the egg and the sperm and how every kid is a 50:50 mix of both parents. But it must be 50:50 on average, not exactly 50:50 on everything. For some things you get all or nothing from one parent—like my eyes are brown like Dad's.

Yesterday at school I got an A on another science quiz. Mom and Dad are always amazed by my grades. They say maybe I'll even get a scholarship for college, the first Sutridge to go, after almost 400 years in America. I know Mom would have liked to go though, if she could have afforded it. You should see the books she brings home. *I and Thou* by Martin Buber. Immanuel Kant's *The Critique of Pure Reason*. Mom says without books you live a life devoid of meaning. Dad keeps saying that after I make Eagle maybe I could even get an appointment to Annapolis. In case you didn't know, that's where you go to college if you want to be an officer in the Navy or Marine Corps. Notice I mentioned the Marine Corps. My dad can be pretty transparent.

Dad's interest in the Marines extends even to his hobby. Miniature wargaming, if you can believe anyone could do something so boring. He sets up these complicated battle scenes in our basement. Right now he's working on Drewry's Bluff from the Civil War, where the United States Marines engaged the Confederate States Marines. Mr. Woodward's hobby of course is repairing and restoring cars, like the yellow Corvette he rebuilt after the original owner totaled it.

Dad couldn't take me to basketball yesterday evening because of bowling night. I was hoping Mr. Woodward would do it, and not just because of the Corvette. Mr. Woodward is very funny—Dad says he's the life of the party. Mom especially laughs at his dumb jokes like the one about the Swede who was so dumb he stared at an orange juice carton for twenty minutes because it said 'Concentrate.' He gets away with it because his grandparents immigrated from Sweden. But the Corvette and Mr. Woodward were on fire duty that evening, so Mom had to take me and bring Teresa with us. Mom said she might as well stay and watch.

Basketball isn't as much fun as it used to be. A lot of the other guys in seventh grade are getting their growth. Mike was my height last year, and now he's almost six feet and has to shave, his chin anyway. I don't get to play in the games as much as I did. Next year we start having a school team and if I don't grow I might not even make it.

I looked up puberty on you-tube. Don't tell anyone, but I'm still Tanner stage two. My balls are a little bigger, but my dick isn't, although I am getting boners more often. The video said both the timing and the tempo of puberty are unpredictable. Tempo means how fast it goes once it starts, so there's still hope I'll be as tall as Mike in time for the 8th grade team.

There's some hope, anyway. Like I said, I know what's going on.

* * *

Tonight it's just me and Mom and Teresa for dinner, because Dad and Mr. Woodward are at their Odd Fellows meeting. That's a really jank name, Odd Fellows, and when I ask Dad why they're called that he says nobody knows for sure. The origin is lost in history.

After dinner I'm alone in my room playing Minecraft with Mike on the iPad I earned selling popcorn for the Cubs when Mom walks in. I keep asking her to knock but she never does. She claims I don't hear her with the earbuds, which is not true.

"Thomas?" she says.

I know that tone of voice. The one where she goes up too high at the end and holds it too long for an ordinary question. The one that means she wants me to do something she knows I won't want to.

"Mom! You're interrupting the game!" It's worth a try, but it hardly ever works when she uses that tone.

She ignores my objection like I thought she would. "Mrs. Woodward just texted. She says Sacha is having trouble with her math homework again and asks if you could go over and help her. Since Mr. Woodward can't."

This is the downside to being a whiz at math.

Maybe whining will work. "Aw, Mom!" I drag out the O in Mom and put a quiver in my voice when I do it.

"Don't 'Aw, Mom' me. The Woodwards are our good friends."

Mom and Mrs. Woodward have been best friends since Mrs. Woodward moved to town so mysteriously the middle of their sophomore year of high school. I guess the friendship took because they were both Catholics. There's not as many Catholics in my town. A lot of people are still Congregationalists like my dad, but he's only a Christmas and Easter kind of guy. Mom and Mrs. Woodward still go to Mass together every Sunday, just the two of them.

Sacha Woodward is in my grade but two or three months older than me. She's going to be thirteen in February. I've known her since we were babies. Mom has all kinds of pictures of the two of us—lying on blankets, being pushed around in strollers, taking baths together. Our families have been close like forever. We've even gone on joint vacations a couple of times.

And Sacha's not bad for a girl, I guess. We went out some when we were in the first grade, but after that it wasn't cool to admit liking girls. I used to be taller than her, but not since the school year started.

"And it's the least you can do," Mom finishes.

Once someone says 'the least you can do' the argument is over. So a few minutes later there I am, heading over Woodward-ward. Mom never thinks that's funny. I can take my bike because we haven't got any snow yet that stuck. Which is good because our driveway snakes all the way behind our house and is a bitch to shovel.

There's lots of different kinds of houses in my town. The university and drug company people have built loads of new Mc-Mansions on cul-de-sacs. Our family can't afford one of those. There are a few houses from the colonial days close to the town green, a couple of them going back to the 1600s even. We can't afford one of those either, and definitely not one of the upgraded capes from a hundred years ago close to the water. But back in the Fifties they built lots of small ranch-style homes on the main roads further inland, and that's where we live. Mom wishes we had a bigger one. The back door opens right into the kitchen, and everyone's always tracking in mud. Dad says we're lucky the university and drug company haven't priced us out of the market altogether. The Woodwards' house is a ranch too, down the street two or three minutes by bike, depending on how fast you pedal.

When I get there Sacha lets me in because Mrs. Woodward is nursing Robby. His real name is Walter, but they call him Robby, why I don't know, maybe because Walter sounds so dorky, but then why name him that at all? The Woodwards had him not long after Teresa was born—I guess my mom and Mrs. Woodward like being preggo together. It's going to be great watching Robby grow up.

I'm kind of disappointed I didn't see Mrs. Woodward. There's the mystery, and then she's always been really nice to me. Her job is interesting, too—counselor for a crisis hotline. Some of the people that call are suicidal. You must need wicked empathy to help someone like that.

Sacha's house has a dormer built into the finished attic, and that's where her bedroom is. She takes me up and we do her homework at her desk. There isn't much left, just the last little bit that was kind of tricky.

Then I start to look around like my work here is done, but Sacha asks if I want to chillax with some tunes and I say sure. She knows all the lit new bands, and I get to sound sophisticated when I say their names. She plugs her iPod into some speakers, picks something she says is by French Truncheon Soup, and lies down on her bed. I slouch in her bean bag chair between the head of the bed and her genuine retro lava lamp from the sixties. She told me she bought it from a place in New Haven called The Group W Bench.

After maybe twenty minutes she rolls over onto her stomach to look at me and asks how I like the music. I'm not a fan—I get it that the Truncheons're on trend now but their songs are kind of... mournful and full of words like 'Destiny' and 'Fate' and I don't think the members are even French—but I don't want her to know I think any of that, so I say it's sick.

She looks at me some more, and then she says, "Want to hook up?"

I've never hooked up with anyone before, and my heart starts slamming out of my chest and you could water the garden from my palms.

Sacha must have guessed, because she says, "Hey, it's natural. You'll be a star horndog before you know it." She invites me up onto the bed.

Some other group starts up from the speakers, but I barely notice. Sacha is considered hot by almost everyone. A little Goth but hot. She bleaches her dirty hair blonde like her mom, but Sacha's has blue streaking and it's long on the right side and buzzed on the left. In the last few months she's started to grow some tits. I overheard Mom talking on the phone with Mrs. Woodward about going out to buy Sacha's first bras.

She lies on her side, so I lie on mine too, facing her but as far away as I can get without falling off, until she pulls me closer by my shirt. I don't know what to do with the arm I'm lying on, whether I should let it trail out behind or hold my hand out forward or keep it under me. I do know I have a ferocious boner.

Sacha leans in and kisses me. I'm embarrassed about my braces, but she has them too and so in a moment I start kissing back. Sacha keeps her lips all soft and wet and I copy her that way. I'm really glad I agreed to help with her math homework.

After a few minutes her tongue comes out and tries to part my lips. I'm startled and pull away, but she says, "It's called tonsil hockey," and so I lean in again and let her. Then I make my tongue slither all around hers for a while, and when she pulls hers back into her mouth I go in after it.

She leans her head back and says, "See? You're a natural."

"Sacha, you're beautiful!" I say.

She dimples and says, "Do you want to see my boobs?"

I can't even croak an answer, but Sacha understands and unbuttons her shirt. She has a black bra on, and I can't believe I'm actually hooking up.

"Do you like the bra?" she asks.

"It's swag," I breathe.

Then she asks if I want to touch her boobs, and now I'm like ecstatic I kept both hands in front. The bra material is shiny and smooth, satin, I don't know, or silk, and when I squeeze it her tits are soft underneath, giving and then recovering, pliant maybe, like a moist sponge only slower to rebound and not wet.

"Sacha! *What* is going on here?"

Over my shoulder is Mrs. Woodward standing in the middle of the room, feet apart, hands on hips. I guess she doesn't knock either.

I levitate off the bed and streak for the door, holding my hands over my crotch to hide my boner. I don't even notice the stairs, but I do notice Mrs. Woodward screaming after me to stop. I don't though.

Once I'm mounted on my bike and in motion, I glance back and see Mrs. Woodward in the doorway talking on the phone. I can't tell if she looks more angry or more worried.

* * *

I don't think I ever pedaled faster. We don't have any streetlamps in my town this far from the green, but I don't care if I can't see a pothole at this speed with just the moonlight. I need to get away from there.

When I reach the house next to ours, though, I slow. And pull off the road into the moon shadow under the big red cedar. What am I going to do when I get home? Mrs. Woodward called Mom. Mom already knows all about it. What am I going to say?

Mom will be just as mad as Mrs. Woodward. She'll tell Dad. He'll be mad too. It's goodbye Scouts, goodbye screen, and good-bye basketball. They'll probably ground me for half a millennium.

Just a few minutes ago I was so high. When I kissed Sacha it was like I'd never actually lived in my body before. And I was good at it, without even trying. And touching her tits through her bra—I was on my way to the secrets of the world.

But then Mrs. Woodward found us. God, I've never been so scared. Skewered in my soul. What seemed so good and pure was *bad*. Evil. I will never live the evil down. And I'll never hook up with anyone ever again.

Out of the corner of my eye I dimly see something yellow moving. A car, pulling out of my driveway.

A yellow Corvette.

* * *

Mr. Woodward's supposed to be at the Odd Fellows meeting with Dad. What's he doing at my house?

Probably Mrs. Woodward called him, too. Maybe he's going to murder me for taking advantage of Sacha.

But there's no way he had time to get here from there.

So he must have left the Odd Fellows before Mrs. Woodward found us. Mom must've called Dad—maybe Teresa has a fever or something—and Dad asked Mr. Woodward to check on them. Everything is fine and so he's leaving.

See, he's turning left, away from his house, back in the direction of the Odd Fellows. I watch as he drives another half block. Then his headlights come on, and I can't even.

Why was he driving with his lights off? It's night time. If this was a routine visit he would have them *on*. If Mrs. Woodward called him because of Sacha and even if he had time to get here and he was looking for me, to kick my ass, he would definitely have them on. And he would have turned the other way, toward his house.

The truth knocks me off my bike into the grass. One minute I'm leaning on my right leg, and then the leg gives way and I start to fall toward it and the bike starts to fall the other way but gets pulled back, and before I know it I'm on the grass with the bike on top of me.

Mr. Woodward was trying to sneak away from my house before I got there. Mrs. Woodward called Mom to complain about me, and Mr. Woodward was already there with Mom, and he tried to sneak away before I found out.

Mr. Woodward was already there because he was hooking up. With my mother.

It's all too much to take, and I just lie there in the damp grass in the dark under the bike. The handle bar gouges me in the side but I don't care.

It's not even an option to slink home and hide out with my family. It will never be the same. My family is destroyed. Mom and Dad will get divorced, and Mom'll probably take Teresa with her, and it will be just me and my dad. He will never speak to Mr. Woodward again, and we'll never see them. My life is basically over. At twelve.

For sure I can't call Mrs. Woodward's hotline. I'm going to have to like hang myself. Or what do people do, run a bath and slit their wrists. And not just cut the vein, which is stupid because it never works, but the artery. That's going to hurt, warm bath or no warm bath. And hanging will be worse, choking and not being able to breathe. Like the feeling you get when you can't hold your breath anymore but forever instead.

If I'm going to kill myself at least I don't have to put up with this handle bar gouging me until I do. I throw the bike up and off me, and I realize I'm mad.

Sacha and I didn't do anything wrong, not really. We were just kids, doing what kids do. What kids have always done, for millions of years.

Mr. Woodward on the other hand was hooking up with the wife of his best friend. You don't do that to someone you're supposed to care about.

And Mom is cheating on Dad. She's cheating on me, too. On our family. On Dad, and on me, and on my baby sister. She's a traitor to our whole family.

Suddenly I don't care anymore whether Mom is mad at me about Sacha. I'm mad at her. I'm just going to march in there with my head held high and wait for Dad. And tell him. And watch Mom get what she has coming.

To my surprise, Mom doesn't start with Sacha, or anything about hooking up. "Hello Dear," she says. "Everything go okay at the Woodwards'?"

But she knows. She's sitting at the kitchen table like she was waiting for me and looking nervous. The twirls in her hair give her away.

'Dear.' I like that one. Not only is she cheating on our family, she's lying through her teeth.

"Sure," I say. "Why wouldn't it?"

"Mrs. Woodward called to say you left in a hurry."

So she's going to pretend Mrs. Woodward didn't tell her about Sacha. She's offering a deal. I don't tell Dad about Mr. Woodward, and she won't tell Dad about Sacha. Well, it isn't going to work. I don't say anything and after a little while she goes on.

"But you seemed to get back home in the usual time. Even a little late."

Fishing. She's fishing. To see if I'd say I saw Mr. Woodward or explain why I didn't seem to rush home. But I'm not going to relieve any stress for *her*, that's for sure. Not after what she did.

"Yeah," I say.

Dad's car pulls into our driveway. He's home early from the Odd Fellows. Mom must have called him.

He comes in the back door, and his eyes meet with Mom's, and she leaves without a word for the front of the house. That's where their bedroom is.

Dad goes over and sits at the kitchen table. I'm still standing, and he pulls out a chair and says, "Have a seat."

I sit. I wanted to talk to him so bad, but now that he's here I'm scared to start. So much has happened tonight. The only thing I have left is the hope that Dad will make things right, and I don't want to lose that too. What lie did Mom tell him?

"I hear you and Sacha were kissing."

"Yeah."

He doesn't seem mad about it, which is one good thing, anyway.

"I take it she was a willing participant?"

"She seemed to be."

There was a note of defiance in my voice that I couldn't keep out.

"The guy always needs to make sure about that."

I nod. Also I notice he said 'the guy' instead of 'the boy.'

"Was that your first time?"

Something in me wants to deny it, to pretend that I've already had loads of experience, but this is my dad, so I say, "Yeah."

He gets that faraway look in his eyes and the little closed-lipped smile like he's reminiscing. "I remember my first time. Very well. It was like I'd died and gone to heaven."

I take a deep breath and let it out. I'm smiling the same smile. "Yeah."

"Of course I was almost fifteen, but I guess kids grow up faster these days."

I don't answer that, and Dad lets the silence lengthen. I study the chandelier over the kitchen table that Mom wants to replace so bad. Then Dad breaks the silence with a question. "Son, is there anything you want to tell me?"

Mom would never have told him I might have seen Mr. Woodward leaving, so I wonder why Dad thinks there might be something else. But maybe he can just tell. And he knows not to ask directly, that I won't say more unless I want to.

Part of me doesn't want to tell him about Mr. Woodward anymore and instead to pretend nothing has changed and just go on with our lives the way they've always been.

But Dad asked the question to me the same way Dumbledore asked it to Harry Potter, and Harry never told and it always caused big trouble. And I don't think I can really pretend anyway. I'm so mad at Mom.

So I tell him.

"When I got home from Sacha's I saw Mr. Woodward's car leaving our driveway. With his lights off."

I stare him straight in the face as I say this. I want to look away, but I can't. I'm desperate for any clue from his expression that will signal how everything will change.

And what I see is not what I expected. It isn't shock. It isn't rage. It isn't despair.

It's relief.

He tilts his head back slightly, sucks in a short breath, holds it for a moment, and flutters his eyelids a couple times before releasing in a whoosh.

"And what did you make of Mr. Woodward doing that?"

Now I'm mad at Dad. He's not supposed to react like this. I stand up and start yelling.

"What I *make* of it is that he was trying to *sneak off*. That he'd been doing something he didn't want me to *know* about. Something *wrong*. That he was *hooking up* with *Mom*."

All this time his expression of relief keeps getting stronger and stronger. I can see it in the half-smile and the turned-down outer eyebrows.

"I know," he says.

He couldn't have surprised me more if he'd bitten a rattlesnake sunning itself on High Head. "You know?"

I'm not mad anymore. No point being angry in the last instant of your childhood.

"Yes," he says, and I can't help but marvel at the kindness in his voice. "Sit down again."

I take the seat, because I don't think I can go on standing.

"Your mother is in love with Mr. Woodward. Has been for a long time."

"And you didn't do anything about it?" I splutter.

Dad shakes his head 'No,' and I can tell he feels sorry for me.

"No, because *I'm* in love with *his* wife. For even longer."

I mean to say "What!?" but I don't know what actually comes out.

"That first kiss I told you about was not with your mother. It was with Mrs. Woodward."

Dad pauses, maybe to let me ask a question, but I can't speak.

"But at the end of high school," he continues, "we had a fight and broke up. It was so stupid of me."

I can't feel anything at all now, but I can read the look on Dad's face. It's the saddest face I've ever seen.

"I wanted to go into the Marines, as you know, and I wanted her to follow me, and she said she needed to stay here. It took me a few days to realize I could never leave her, but by then she'd gone to Mr. Woodward for consolation, and teenage hormones being what they are, one thing led to another. It was only one time, but Sacha was on her way."

Mom comes out from the hallway. She never went to the bedroom. She's been listening. And she's smiling.

Dad turns to her, and she just smiles wider and nods. Dad gives his attention back to me.

"They asked the priest, and he said the only option was for them to get married. Your mother and I were both heartbroken, and I guess we had that in common, and we decided we might as well get married too."

There's no stopping Dad now, even if I could try.

"At first we all just suffered, and then we started using birth control, and then a couple of years ago we just decided to stop."

He must need to get it all out, but I need to take it one thing at a time. I blurt out, "So why did you have me?"

Mom answers. "At the time we thought we had no choice but to make the best of the situation."

A *bad* situation. That's me, the best of a bad situation.

Mom must be able to read my mind because she says, "And we both think making you was the best thing we've ever done."

Which isn't saying much.

But it does seem at least like I was wanted.

And although my parents had been deceiving me, at least they hadn't been deceiving me about who my parents are.

My brain shifts as smoothly and automatically as the yellow Corvette's 6-speed transmission.

They say that no matter how bad things are they can always get worse. I need to check on something that's niggling at me. "So Sacha is definitely Mr. Woodward's daughter?"

Dad handles this one, nodding gravely. "You and Sacha are not related."

If there's anything good about all this, it's that my first hook-up wasn't incest.

I paid attention in seventh grade health, and I know what the birth control thing means. It explains why I didn't get a little brother or sister for so long until Teresa. I wonder if Mom told the priest and if she got absolution.

And then they stopped the birth control. "So Teresa... is not my sister?"

Dad looks at Mom, and she fields this one. "She's your half-sister. I'm her mother, but her father is Mr. Woodward."

They don't make me ask the next question. "And Robby is your half-brother," Dad says.

My parents both take deep breaths and let them out slowly in unison. They seem to be at the end of what they want to say tonight. But I'm not done yet.

"Why didn't you tell me before?"

Dad says, "We were waiting till you were ready."

But I'm not ready. I had no time to *get* ready.

"Waiting more than ten years," Mom says.

Dad tries to guess what I'm thinking. Maybe he can tell I'm having trouble doing that for myself. "You must feel we betrayed you," he says. "That we were lying to you all this time."

I do feel mad about that, so I say, "It's worse than when I had to learn on the school bus that the Easter Bunny wasn't real."

"I remember you were really upset with us over that," Mom says.

And maybe I'm really upset again now. There must be so many things they lied about.

"Do you even go to the Odd Fellows?"

Dad's face blushes. Unbelievable that *this* is what embarrasses him.

"Mr. Woodward and I are both members," he says, a request for forgiveness clear in his voice. "But we hardly ever go at the same time."

"PTA?" I ask Mom. "Bowling?" I demand of Dad.

They both hang their heads. These were all just cover stories for hooking up. Last night Dad was with Mrs. Woodward instead of bowling. Two nights ago Mom didn't go to PTA but over to Mr. Woodward's house.

No, I'm definitely really upset. How really upset exactly I won't know until we talk about the most important thing.

Like, what is going to happen now. How life is going to be different. So I ask them.

"We're getting divorces and remarrying," Mom says. "You children will stay with your mothers in the same house and the fathers will switch places."

"You can't do that!" I yell. "Remarriage is against the Pope!"

Dad and Mom look at each other, and both of their faces are stricken. I guess I shouldn't shout, but I don't care. I'm losing my dad. No matter how bad things are they can always get worse.

"You'd still see your father all the time," Mom says. Then she acknowledges, "You'd see Mr. Woodward more than you used to, of course."

I'd get to ride in the Corvette more. I know this is stupid as soon as I think it, but my brain isn't exactly working right.

"We'll ask the priest to get us annulments," Mom says.

Dad looks at Mom and shakes his head, but she's already continuing. "If he won't do it Mrs. Woodward and I are going to become Episcopalians."

"Son," Dad cuts in, "what your mother means is—don't worry about it. We don't have to do this right now if you're not ready."

Mom must realize she got a little side-tracked. She nods in confirmation. "There's no rush. We've waited ten years. We can wait awhile longer."

She's willing to convert for Mr. Woodward.

"I don't know," I say.

I really don't. At this exact moment I'm thinking Dad will probably push Robby for Eagle and Annapolis too.

Dad's face has the kindness expression again. "More information than you need right now?

Part of me wants even more information, like why Mrs. Woodward's family really moved here, which now I'm sure Dad knows all about. But only part of me. The best the whole of me can do is shrug.

"Well, don't worry about it," he says again. "Things are going to be fine."

Grown-ups are so lame when they try to reassure kids.

I'm definitely old enough to know that.

THE TOKEN COLLECTOR
Jayne Adams

Jimmy Rourke ate the last of his mother's cookies from lunch, snapped his lunchpail shut, turned down the tollbooth's heater and clocked out as the evening shift guy came in. The receipts from his shift had been a few dollars short when he'd tallied. His attention had been focused on the Herald sports page when some guy'd handed him a bill and he'd mistaken a fin for a sawbuck, returning too much change with the token. Mother MBTA would get hers, though, out of his next paycheck. Jimmy was still beaming a smile as broad as Revere Beach.

"Hey, Mickey!" he called to his relief, "Got the seat all wahmed up for ya. It's gonna be wicked cold tonight. Have fun, you poor divvil!"

Mickey clicked the booth's door lock in reply, punctuating the air with a rude gesture.

"Jimmy, ya got somewhere to go or somethin'? Ya look like a guy about to have his first date yaw're grinnin' so hahd."

Jimmy flashed a smile but ignored him and let himself through the Employee-Only gate. Waiting on the inbound side of the elevated platform for the next train, he whistled *Jingle Bell Rock*. He was in such a good mood Christmas *could* have been next week. He had a great story to bring to the bar at last.

The Orange line train rattled into Mass. Ave. Station, swirling papers and trash before it on the tracks, as the sloping winter sun painted its last gold touches on the aging brownstones and slushy streets below. Jimmy stuffed the Herald into the trashcan and boarded the last car, his mind made up to call his brother with an excuse. He could always see his nephew play basketball. Don Bosco High wasn't that great anyway. What couldn't wait was the crowd at Sully's.

* * *

He burst off the train one stop down, took the flights of iron stairs two at a time, hustled up Berkeley Street and yanked the tavern door open. The combined smell of industrial-strength disinfectant, tobacco smoke, stale beer, and roach-killer hit him all at once.

Ahhhhh, he thought. *The smell of a bah always brings me back to the glory days.* He glanced up at the TV as he took the first seat at the bar and remembered the Celts were playing the Sixers later. This new kid Larry Bird had Boston delirious about B-ball again. *Even better,* he chuckled to himself. *I'll have a good audience before tipoff.*

He ordered a draft and checked his view of the door in the mirrored back bar. Satisfied that he could see everyone arrive from this vantage point, he grabbed his change off the bar and sauntered down the back hallway to the pay phone.

When his brother's wife answered, Jimmy used the "strep-throat" voice he used for sick calls to work. The less said, the better. "Mah-gret, tell Denny I'm too sick to meet him for Mikey's game, okay? Headin' home. I'll call him tomorrah. Thanks, Hon, I will. Yep, hot tea."

That piece of business concluded, he returned to the front bar and swung back up on his barstool, ready to greet the regulars as they filed in. He employed his most jovial call-outs and friendly patter to assemble the guys he wanted in front of his spot at the bar, holding them in place by calling out their brand of beer as they arrived. The bartender found this method an effective distribution system and went along, handing bottles one by one to Jimmy, who delivered them into the correct hands, then relayed their money back over the bar. He soon had a happy, warmed-up crowd gathered around: some other MBTA guys from further down the line, the day counter-guy from the Deli on the other corner, a couple of firemen from the local firehouse, and Butch, an off-duty cop from Precinct 4 up the street. The place filled up. Beers and shots lined the length of the dark wood bar. On his third beer, Jimmy stood up by his stool, legs wide apart, and found his opening in the conversation.

"Yeah? That's a good one, Hannon! Well I was pickin' my winners in the booth ta-day when I hear a buncha guy's yellin' somethin', then a broad screamin' her head off."

"Whaddja do, Jimmy? Duck down in the booth?" Jerry from Dudley Station guffawed.

"No, wise guy. I seen a buncha teenagers come off the train. They musta been cuttin' school—but I never seen no broad. So I figured she was comin' *up* the stairs to catch the next one. The noise was comin' from about halfway up."

"Couldja see'em, man?" *Saulie from the deli.*

"Nope." Jimmy turned to him, warming to this tale. He'd always liked Saulie. "I thought I bettah check it out, so I locked my cashbox and came outa the booth. Locked it behind me," he said with a sidelong glance at Dudley-Station-Jerry.

Ya couldn't just signal the Transit cops?" called out Tommy Hannon. *Those fire boys*, Jimmy noted. *Always team-thinkers.*

"What, and wait fawr her to get killed or somethin'?" He paused to let that sink in. "So I go to the top of the stairs and, shuah enough, there's this blonde girl layin' on the landin' and there's these six goons circlin' her.

"How big ah they?"

"*Big*. And they looked up at me. I could almost hear 'em think, 'He ain't gonna stop us.' I don't know what happened to me, but I jus' saw red. I mean *RED*."

"I'da called the Transit cops," Saulie offered, using his huskiest voice.

"No time. I came down those stairs like a ton o' bricks, screamin' like a hellcat. Hit two a'them and we fell forward, ass over teakettle. Fell into the next two, rollin'. The last two jus' turned and ran. They *all* jus' got scared and ran like rabbits," finished Jimmy with a flourish as he drained his pint. He paused again. "I got her number."

They burst into applause and whistles.

* * *

The rest of the night was a blur, a shot-and-beer haze that hoisted him on its shoulders at closing, carried him back up the iron stairs, put him on the last night train, and deposited him at Bunker Hill Station. Jimmy stumbled into his old bedroom and fell on the bed, his last thought as he smiled a dreamy smile and slipped into a contented snore, *Bettah than I even hoped. Free drinks faw days* and *I'm the talk of Sully's.*

As he rode "the rattler" between Bunker Hill and Massachusetts Avenue on Monday, Jimmy realized how much he was looking forward to work. As Dudley-Station-Jerry once put it, "These jobs suck the brain right out of yaw head." *Not that Jerry's brain would put up much of a fight*, Jimmy chuckled to himself, *but he's right. Havin' somethin' sensational to talk about was cause for celebration around the "T".* Jimmy sat up a little straighter in his seat. *Why, what I did was practically a public service!* He hopped off the train at his station and clocked in with unusual enthusiasm.

As he had anticipated, the guy from the MBTA barn was making his rounds, collecting tokens from the turnstyles. He'd already heard about Jimmy's heroics and clapped him on the back saying, "Way to go, Jimmy! Buy ya a drink next time I see ya at Sully's!"

Jimmy enjoyed shrugging it off. Ah, it was nuthin' really. You'da done the same."

Mickey showed up thirty minutes early for the next shift later on that day. He put his face right up to the booth's barred window, grinning so hard Jimmy thought his face might crack in the cold January air. "You!" he shouted. "Why didn't ya tell me? Ya nevah said a word. And ya got her numbah? No wonder ya had that shit-eatin' grin on your face Friday!"

Jimmy let him go on, shrugging his most nonchalant shrug and smiling out through the bars. "How about stop embarrassin' me and just let me outa this cage a little early?"

"If ya have my seat all wahmed up, I'll even clock out faw ya," Mickey laughed. "But really, Jimmy, I never knew ya had it in ya."

* * *

The following day, Saulie from the deli showed up at the "T" station with a huge bag. In it, Jimmy found his favorite: a Reuben and some half-sours, a bag of chips, a soda, and an extra large slice of cheesecake wrapped in wax paper.

"Saulie, wow! Ya should'na. I'm almost embarrassed, but thanks, man. It's my favorite lunch."

"Aw, you deserve it, Jimmy." Saulie looked like he wanted to say something more. "I'm, uh... I'm proud you faced those goons. Good to know there are still stand-up guys around."

Jimmy looked down at his shoes. He felt a blush start to bloom from his neck to his forehead.

* * *

Butch, the cop from Precinct 4, sat at the bar when Jimmy got to Sully's after work late Wednesday. Butch always looked disgusted and always spoke in questions. Jimmy had imitated him once for a few laughs at the bar. *Like he's interrogatin' ya.*

"Jimmy, got a minute?"

All this adulation was starting to get on his nerves, but Jimmy pasted on a jovial face and ambled over to Butch's stool. "Faw you, Butch? A'course."

"Maybe you heard awready? They read us a complaint at shift change today? How we gotta watch out for six punks, descriptions, and what-not? A blonde girl came in and made a complaint. Said they attacked her at Mass. Ave. Station last week? Said lucky she still had a body cast on from a back surgery a coupla months ago. Saved her when they dragged her down. Said lucky she was wearin' big heavy lace-up boots. Kicked two of her attackahs down the stairs, and the rest fled. And know what, Jimmy?"

"Nope, can't imagine."

"She said she kept hopin' the token collectah guy would come to her rescue, y'know? And, Jimmy, know the paht I just can't get ovah? He *nevah* did. Ya believe that, Jimmy?"

THE TELEPHONE CALL

Skip Robinson

Won't be long now. I can feel it. He'll call, just like she said; I know it. Like my old man says, "treat rich people right and they'll take care a yah, cuz they got the money." Then he'd smile his crooked smile and swallow more beer.

Course my mother wasn't any too pleased when a couple a months ago right after I turned sixteen—didn't have to waste time going to school no more, or worry about the draft, cuz Nixon, that dick as my old man called him, had ended the Vietnam War—I got this job, the one I have now, mating on a charter boat. Same one's tied up at the end of the dock. The big white motor yacht. You can see her from here. Name's SEA DUCER.

I didn't do it just for the paycheck, though. Like my old man used to say, when he was sober enough for me to understand him, "if yah want to be rich, you gotta hang with rich people. Money likes money," is what he always said.

So I figured what better place for me to meet rich people than working on a charter boat. You gotta be rich to pay thirty thousand dollars a week to go for a boat ride.

Like I said, won't be long now. I can feel it.

Tell yah how it all started. It was our second charter; the first had been a stinker. Group of rich kids down from college on Spring Break. All they did was drink beer and raise hell. When they left the boat, they didn't even thank us, never mind a tip. But the second, oh boy was it different.

I'm putting fender boards away when the limousine pulls up for our second trip. I close the top on the storage box and lean against the bow rail to watch Mr. and Mrs. Panaro, the couple who are to spend ten days with us, step from the black stretch Mercedes. Five hours late, yet they're moving like time is something that belongs to them—only them. At over three thousand dollars a day I figure the clock has already burned a grand but doesn't appear they care.

He's tall and slender with silver gray hair and dark complexion—looks Italian to me. His wife's younger. I guess she's maybe twenty-five; so maybe thirty years younger. She's wearing a beige jersey pantsuit of some kind that matches the color of her shoulder length, blond hair and clings to what looks to me, even from where I'm standing, like the body of a centerfold—more of that later.

I'm helping the chauffeur with their luggage when I get a good look at her, I mean up close. I'm crossing the aft deck with the final load and stop to listen to Captain Bud telling the charterers not to hurry, since he's decided he ain't gonna leave until tomorrow.

"Why is that, Captain?" From his tone, the well-tanned Panaro doesn't sound like he's asking a question. Kinda put you in mind of a Cary Grant character, you know, cocky.

"Wind's up. Liable to be pretty rough." Captain gives him back. "We'll get off early tomorrow, like we was supposed to today, afore it picks up again, we might—"

Panaro cuts right in—didn't let old Captain Bud finish. "Nonsense, this is nothing, Captain." Just like Grant would've said.

"Not what we're gettin' here I'm talkin' 'bout. Be different offshore."

"Mrs. P and I aren't paying to sit here at a dock in Fort Lauderdale, Captain." His hooded eyes sink deep into his face when he notices me standing behind his wife. "Just have the kid there finish getting our clothes aboard, and we'll get underway."

Mrs. Panaro's standing at her husband's elbow, shifting her weight from one foot to the other. She turns, looks at me and smiles. Her face is real soft, none of the telltale crow's feet at the eyes like her husband. Right away I have the feeling she's sorry her husband's called me kid, but we'll get to that later. I'm guessing she's maybe seven or eight years older than me—you know, gettin' to middle age, but not old yet.

Captain Bud's sun cracked lips curl back in a half smile, wide enough so's you could see his tobacco stained teeth. "Whatever you say, Mr. Panaro."

About an hour later we're standing in the pilot house—me gazing out at the waves. The short, wiry, bow-legged Captain Bud Parent holding SEA DUCER, our sixty-six-foot, custom motor yacht, on a southerly course. Already the gentle up and down motion is making me sleepy. I'm trying to figure out what Captain Bud was saying about crossing the Gulf today: that a wind, blowing opposite to the way the Stream flows creates waves twenty feet high. Didn't seem possible—so comfortable right now.

When the Panaros come on deck she's changed into a pink turtleneck, fits her real good, and matching slacks. She hikes herself up on the high bench seat just to port of the steering console and looks out the windshield. Her husband stands next to her and right away he begins teasing her.

"See, Pamela, I told you. There's nothing to be concerned about." She didn't say anything—just swayed gently with the motion of the boat. I make a conscious effort not to watch her sweater tighten against her breasts—I don't let myself even think the word tits—as she moves back and forth. Like I said, she had quite a shape, even at her age.

When we turn ninety degrees to port and head offshore the boat's motion isn't so smooth no more. We're running more into the sea, and the waves are banging against us pretty hard. Spray's flying overhead, some landing on the windshield—enough so the captain has to turn on the wipers.

That's when I see them. She must have too, cause a moment later Mrs. Panaro slides forward on her seat and leans closer to the windshield to get a better look—like she couldn't believe what she's seeing—staring directly ahead to where her husband had told her Bimini would be. I can tell she's trying to figure it out. She touches his arm.

"Peter," she says, without taking her eyes off the sight that appears each time the windshield wiper blade sweeps past, "I thought the Bahamas were low, flat islands."

"They are, Pam."

"What's that?" She points. "Should it look like that?"

"No ma'am," Captain answered first.

"Peter, it looks like a mountain."

"Nope, not mountains, ma'am, and the Island's is too far away to see from here," Captain says. "That ain't Bimini, ma'am. What you're seein is the ocean." He spins the wheel a quarter turn to keep her head into the seaway. "Them's waves, not mountains ma'am. Looks like mountains, though, don't they?" He sniggers.

"They're too big to be waves, Captain." Sounds more like a question the way she says it, her voice rising. When she speaks again her voice sounds small, you know, like a kid asking a question she's afraid she knows the answer to and don't want to hear. Reminded me of my kid sister when she used to ask my mother if she could do a sleep-over at her friend's house.

"Is that where we have to go?"

"Yep."

"Is it okay?" She pauses, "I mean," she turns to look directly at him, "Is it safe?"

"Nonsense, Pamela," Panaro chimes in. "The ocean looks like that sometimes. It's nothing to worry about. Right Captain?"

Captain Bud never takes his eyes off the waves. "Don' know. Looks pretty nasty to me."

"Mr. Parent are you trying to frighten my wife?"

"Nope, wasn't tryin' to. Just answerin' her question, is all."

"Tell her the truth." Panaro looks from Captain Bud to his wife. "Pam, honey, from this distance waves look bigger than they are."

"What I was tellin' her is the truth." Captain's voice more clipped than usual. "Looks pretty rough to me. Like I said when we was still at the dock, that maybe we should wait to see what tomorrow brings."

The tall man's deep tan shades to red, his voice clipped—determined, you know, like Gary Cooper in High Noon. Spittle escapes his lips when he says the Captain's name. "Parent, we've been through that."

From where I'm standing, doesn't look like Captain Bud hears him—keeps looking straight out the windshield at the waves, spinning the wheel each time we crest one and fall into the trough behind it.

You can tell from Parent's tone he's strainin' to sound more encouraging "If the breeze lets up, sea might moderate. Hope so, but with a nor'easter it can run like this for a couple a days." He squints into the horizon where Mrs. Panaro saw what she'd thought were mountains. "Once we get into that," he points with his left hand, "might be too late to turn her in the sea."

"What exactly do you mean, Captain?" she asks.

"If it's as rough as it looks, I'll be wantin' to keep her nosed into it so's to keep from broachin' her. We'll be in for a long, rough ride if that's the case."

The two big diesels are making so much noise and she's talking so soft, I barely hear her ask, "What does broach mean, Captain?" The way she looks at him, like an animal, ears flat, about to be punished, I have a hunch she knows but is hoping she's wrong.

"Can't hear you ma'am. What'd you say?"

"You use the word, broach, Captain. What does that mean?"

"Broachin'? It's when you get broadside in a sea that's so big the boat founders." She looks questioningly at him. "Take on so much water she either sinks or rolls over, ma'am." He says it without any emotion, his voice flat.

I didn't much care so much about Mrs. Panaro anymore. Captain's scaring the bejesus out of me. I hope he's kidding. In the weeks I'd been mating for him, I'd learned he liked to tease people, specially me, but I have a feeling this time he's serious. Mr. Panaro keeps his eyes straight ahead, appearing not to hear the captain.

"Oh God, Peter. What if he's right?" She fingers a jeweled crossed, hanging just below the roll of her turtleneck. "Should we turn around?"

This time Panaro's voice comes out of the side of his mouth. "Stop it, Parent, damnit. You're scaring the hell out of my wife. Tell her we're not going to roll this baby over."

"No, don't believe we will. Just explainin' to her what it means is all."

"Well, that's enough explaining." He put's his hand on her shoulder. "Pamela, why don't you go below where you won't see the waves? I'll stay here with the crew."

"Go ahead Mrs. Panaro. Husband's right." The crash of the spray against the windshield is so loud, Parent almost shouting now to be beard. "Always looks worse than it feels, or for that matter, than it is. The lower you are in the boat, less you'll feel her rock and roll."

Not a half hour later SEA DUCER is punching forward into waves ten to twelve feet. Each one crashing over the port bow so hard the Captain throttles the engines back to just above idle speed. I wedge myself into the opening of the doorway down into the salon to keep my balance—wouldn't look good for the mate to be thrown to the deck. Every fifth or sixth wave I crouch down to look through the hatch and check on Mrs. Panaro. She's lying on her side on the salon couch, her face buried into the back, her feet pressed against one end, with her arms pushing over her head against the other—reminds me of the exercise we did in gym about dynamic tension.

We're being slammed so hard I grit my teeth to keep from biting my tongue. Captain Parent's standing next to me looking at the ocean trying to guess which way SEA DUCER is gonna be tossed, so's he can anticipate and steer against the wave. His gnarled little hands spin the big mahogany spokes full left, in the next moment, full right, to keep the bow pointed into the sea. As we lurch back and forth I remember Mrs. Panaro's question— about getting turned sideways.

* * *

None of us see it coming, not even the Captain. Just as SEA DUCER regains her balance at the top of one wave she plunges off the crest and slams into the trough, but the next one's a rogue compared to the others: so tall when it starts coming at us I can't see the top of it out of the windshield; so steep that when we climb the front of it I think we'll fall over backwards. Then SEA DUCER's bow breaks through the curl at the top and keeps right on going, past the steep back side of the monster that drops away like a mountain chute—over fifty tons of boat is now airborne.

Near the entire length hangs in mid-air until we topple over and fall, careening into the watery ravine with such force that SEA DUCER slithers over onto her side and keeps rolling, picking up speed until we lay completely flat on the starboard side. The port propeller surging and shuddering as it breaks free of the ocean. I hold my breath, waiting to hear the other prop come to the surface. If it does, we're on the way over — upside down. Water sweeps over the deck house. Both Parent and Panaro crumple to the floor. I'm pitched through the companionway hatch into the salon.

I close my eyes, still straining to hear the vibration of the second propeller. Nothing. Just the high-speed whir of the port engine windmilling in free air. Then the noise is swallowed by the ocean. Time stops. I feel the hull shudder. The acrid smell of raw diesel oil from the two mains below fills the salon. The floor below me tilts. We're rolling back upright. My eyes snap open. The leather couch with Mrs. Panaro struggling to hold on is rushing at me. It's like she's riding the biggest, fastest side-sliding sand crab in the world. I tumble clear and watch it crash against the salon paneling.

SEA DUCER is now rolling from gunnel to gunnel, tossing the furniture from side to side like ice cubes in a cocktail shaker. With each roll I dodge the oncoming couch and try to slow it down. But it continues to slam against the inside of the salon wall paneling, finally tearing it open all the way to the hull planking. How many more times before it breaks through and slides out into the ocean — with her on it? The next time it skitters past I follow the heavy piece of furniture across the floor, grab a metal-framed coffee table and wedge it between the couch and a built-in cabinet. It holds.

Meanwhile the Captain must have climbed back to the wheel. I hear him rev one engine full ahead and one full astern to get her around before the next wave grabs us, maybe roll us this time. When we stop banging and twisting I realize he's made it. We're turned and heading in the same direction as the waves now. Feels like we're riding on a hobbyhorse, climbing slowly up the back of each wave and then falling smoothly into the trough of the next.

Mrs. Panaro releases her grip on the couch, sits up, puts her feet on the floor and looks around. Her eyes are tear-filled and glassy like a fawn's in a headlight.

"Jason." Just the way she says it, really soft like, I can tell she needs me to hold her. I put my arms around her. Her wet face presses against my shirt. I can smell her perfume over the diesel exhaust fumes rolling up over the transom in the following sea and spilling into the cabin. My hands are stroking the silky, soft hair that two hours earlier I'd only dreamed about touching. Her body's trembling. I flex my arms, so she can feel how strong I am, increasing the pressure to pull her against me.

That's when I see his white boat shoes, then the cuff of his slacks, in the doorway. Panaro's taking the three steps down from the pilothouse into the salon. I try to edge away from the Misses, but too late. His head clears the hatchway. He looks around at the wreckage. His gaze stops. His face darkens.

"Pam, you all right? What happened here?" Now he's looking directly at me. "Hey, you, what are you doing with my wife?"

She pulls away. "Peter, it's okay," she says in a soft, even voice and slides away from me on the couch. "He saved my life, Peter."

Panaro must have hit his head on something when he fell; there's blood on his forehead, just over his right eye.

She jumps from the couch, runs to his side. "Oh, Peter, you're hurt."

I'm so impressed how she handles him. He's completely flustered, I can tell, and forgets what he's probably thinking when he saw us together.

"It's nothing. Must have hit the edge of the seat when I was thrown onto the deck."

She pats his head with a hanky she pulls from somewhere and says something to him I can't make out. The boat lurches. The two of them stumble, turn and climb the three steps to rejoin the Captain. I stay below to finish putting things in order, as much as I can—you know, one hand for the boat and one for me. Mostly I want to avoid contact with both the Panaros. Give her a chance to smooth things over. When I climb the steps to the pilot house about half hour later I don't look at either of them.

Two hours later we're back in our slip. I drag out the hose and fall to washing the salt off the cabin sides. That evening when the Panaros leave SEA DUCER I still haven't spoken to them.

Once they're off the dock and into a waiting limousine Captain Bud walks up behind me and taps me on the shoulder. "Hey kid, what happened down there?"

"Nothin'."

"Oh yeah. Somethin' must have happened. Nobody said a word all the way back."

"I'm tellin' yah, nothin' happened."

His weathered face cracks a crooked smile, "Her old man catch you tryin' to jump her bones?"

"No, wasn't like that." I shrug and walk away to stow the hose in the deck box forward.

* * *

Three days later we've made temporary repairs to the salon, bought replacement furniture, and are ready for the crossing at dawn. The wind's blown out and the Gulf Stream's like a river of gentle rollers. The Panaros had chartered a plane the night they left the boat and flew across. They meet us at the dock when we arrive in Nassau.

Soon as we're tied up she takes me aside. Tells me how grateful her and her husband are for what I'd done and want to do something real nice for me.

"Peter will get in touch," she says real soft, like that other actor in High Noon—actress actually, Grace Kelly. I can tell she really likes me and will make certain that Mr. Panaro won't forget.

* * *

Like I said, I'm expecting a call from him any day.

THE TANNER GRAVES

Douglas Campbell

When Kristen and I bought our West Virginia property, a hundred and seventy acres with an old farmhouse at the head of a hollow, we knew it included a small ridge-top cemetery, a plot reserved in the deed by former owners of the land, a family named Tanner. The lawyer who helped us with the transaction assured us that was a common practice, and from then on we hardly gave it a thought. During the growing season we'd sometimes hear the faint sound of a mower coming from that distant ridge, and whenever one of our hikes took us up to the Tanner graves we always found the plot neatly trimmed. It was a charming spot, flat and grassy, a sunny clearing with a big arc of open sky, a respite from the steep slopes and deeply shadowed, sometimes gloomy light of the surrounding Appalachian forest. On our first hike there, shortly after we moved in, the four wooden grave markers were badly deteriorated, the boards rotted and soft, all of them leaning, two poised to topple. The names and dates of the deceased, painted on the boards long ago, had faded to illegibility. A month or so later, when we passed that way again, the markers had all been replaced, four fresh oak boards firmly rooted and standing straight. And this time someone had painstakingly burned the names and dates into the wood, giving us our introduction to Guthrie, Sarah, Terence, and Beatrice Tanner.

Sixteen years later, one year after Kristen had left me, a tall, wiry man knocked on my door one Saturday afternoon in late July and introduced himself as Will Tanner, and the young boy with him as his son, Davy. They'd come, Will said, to remove the remains from the four graves on the ridge and take them to another piece of Tanner land near Glenville.

"We're aimin' to move as many Tanners as we can into one spot."

"Makes sense," I said, "but I hope you have four-wheel drive."

"Yes sir, we do." Will took a step back and pointed toward the driveway beside the house. "That there's our Wagoneer."

I stepped out on the porch and looked at the Jeep, its two-tone green paint faded and scratched, but with an orange left front fender that looked glossy and new.

"Don't look like much, but she runs good," Will said.

He had a quick, engaging smile and stood half a head taller

than me, and I'm six-two. His face was narrow and bony, with a thin nose bent slightly to the right, and he wore a plain white t-shirt drastically too large for him. It billowed in the breeze like a sail.

"That's good," I said. "The only way to reach that ridge is the old logging road you probably saw when you drove up the hollow. And it's rough."

"Oh, I know, I been up that track many a time," Will said. "Some of us takes turns doing the mowin' up there. We won't have no trouble. We'll take her nice and slow."

"Can I give you a hand?"

"That's good of you, sir, but we'll be alright. Them graves was hand dug, they ain't deep. And them coffins'll be rotted. All of 'em in the ground forty years or more. I figure we'll dig down to where we can pry the lids off and lift the bones out. Leave them coffins right where they set. Don't you worry, we pull up any wood, we'll bury it back. We won't leave you no mess."

He nodded toward Davy, who kept rocking from foot to foot or clomping around the porch in brand new work boots clearly purchased with growth in mind, as oversized on his young feet as the white t-shirt was on his father's lean torso. "I expect Davy here'll be all the help I need. He's a hell of a pick and shovel man."

Davy flushed and rocked when he heard that, embarrassed and delighted. He was built differently than his father, thick in the chest and broad in the face, his plump cheeks pink as chunks of ham. But he was still a boy, no taller than Will's chest, arms and legs more baby fat than muscle, to my eye a year or so short of adolescence and undersized for pick and shovel work. But his restlessness and the smile on his face told me he was thrilled to be on this mission with his father. Enthusiasm is a well of strength, and Davy certainly had that.

"We don't want to bother you none," Will said. "You never give us no trouble about havin' them graves up there. We sure do appreciate that."

"Well, they've never given me any trouble," I said.

Will laughed. "Yes sir, they's mighty quiet folks, ain't they?"

* * *

Several hours later, I pulled my boots on and headed out to see how Will and Davy were coming along. I needed to get out of a house that without Kristen too often felt like a grave itself. I still hadn't quite come to terms with living in a house that didn't also shelter her. We'd been happily married for twenty-five years,

long enough for the contours of our lives, our routines and pref-
erences, to blend seamlessly and comfortably. I'd wanted it to go
on forever, and had never doubted that it would.

Strangely, it's not the sight of her I miss, or her touch. Those
are the obvious things you're forced to give up on right away
when someone slips out of your life. What I miss are little things,
things you hardly notice day to day. What gets to me now is the
quiet. The silence in this isolated house can be so ruthless and
unyielding it begins to have its own weight and presence, a palpable force that holds me in a tension difficult to break. Sometimes, listening for any noise at all, I hear soft static with a barely
perceptible whine in it. It's nothing more, I've come to think, than
the sound of my own ears straining at the task of listening. I've
caught myself standing motionless and expectant, listening for
the sounds Kristen made: the soft thumps and creaking wood
when she came down the stairs, the pouring rain of Kristen in
the shower, her voice singing along with Aretha Franklin in the
kitchen while the house filled with the aroma of her homemade
pizza or lamb curry. You grow accustomed to such things, and
it's all too easy to lose sight of how precious and comforting they
are, the countless sensory reminders that someone you love, and
who loves you, is nearby. But with a year of solitude behind me I
don't listen like that very often now. Not like I did in the months
immediately after she left. I'm a slow learner, but futility is a per-
suasive teacher.

Throughout her career as a high school art teacher Kristen
had kept her own creativity alive and vital, painting landscapes
and still lifes in oils and watercolors. Our farmhouse had four
bedrooms, three more than we needed, so she had her own sunny
studio to work in. And she worked fiercely, often all day long
on weekends, sometimes pushing herself to the point that come
evening I'd find her on our bed, sprawled out on her back. She
didn't mind if I interrupted her now and then to see how her latest work was progressing, and it was always a pleasure to go into
her studio and find her sitting or standing at her easel over by the
window, catching the daylight. Kristen had amazing long, thick
black hair that she tied back in a broad, sloppy ponytail when she
painted, and the first thing I'd do was go behind her and take that
ponytail in my hands and hold it, squeeze it, and stroke it, loving
the bulky softness of it.

"This is by far your biggest paintbrush," I said one day when
I was playing with it.

Kristen laughed and her hand jerked, leaving a swipe of blue
paint where even I could see it didn't belong. "Look what you

did," she said. "You just ruined an immortal work of art." She swung around with a narrow-eyed, murderous face.

"It's not really ruined, is it?"

"I'll fix it," she said. "Then I'll fix you."

"Uh-oh. That's how my mother described a dog with its testicles removed. 'He's been fixed,' " she'd say.

Kristen nodded a little too enthusiastically. "Exactly what I had in mind," she said, but before she finished saying it she broke into a smile, green eyes bright with a manic, unabashed joy. I saw that look many times on days when her work was going well and she was soaring on currents of confidence and inspiration, like the hawks that often circled above our hollow. I loved seeing that euphoria take hold of her, and sometimes envied it, though I'd stumbled close to it myself, even in my far more prosaic role as handyman in residence. I'd felt genuine elation looking at the jungle of bountiful garden I grew each summer, the sandstone patio I'd laid behind the house, and my masterpiece, the decorative post and rail fence I built to border our front lawn. I'd cut all the wood out of own forest, locust for the posts, oak for the rails. I'd shaved the bark, drilled the holes in the posts, dug the postholes, and put it all together, each post and rail unique and pleasing to the eye.

Things weren't perfect, of course. We lived through many of the disappointments and frustrations common to the human lot. But those rarely involved our relationship. In our private life, I dare say we were unusually stable and happy.

* * *

The ridge where Will and Davy were working was a long way from the house, about as far as you could walk and still be on my land. The graves sat on the crest of the ridge, the property line maybe thirty yards beyond them. On my way there I veered off the most direct route to visit a spot that became a favorite for Kristen and me the moment we discovered it. Halfway or so up the hillside in back of the house, it was an area strewn with a jumble of boulders, some as small as a bowling ball, some the size of a pickup truck. They'd prevented tree growth and created a clearing that allowed a panoramic view of the house, the garden, and our three old Stayman apple trees that shaded the back yard. Many of the boulders were cushioned with bright green moss, offering comfortable places to sit and enjoy the view. It was a place to linger and take heart, to feel the exultation that always seems to accompany a view from on high. What spreads above and ahead of you draws the eye higher and farther. Down below you the everyday world, so exhausting when you're running circles in the thick of it, looks pleasingly diminished, humbled, far less daunting.

I hadn't visited that spot for months, and was glad to be headed there, but troubled to find myself unusually leg-weary and short of breath as I made my way up the hill, so much so I considered stopping for a breather. I refused to let myself do that, but I did slow my pace, something I'd never had to do before. Kristen and I had hiked all over the surrounding hills without ever needing to rest, despite the steep hillsides, the treacherous footing in the loose leaf mold, and the usual forest obstacles of boulders, fallen trees, and downed branches.

When at last I reached my favorite mossy boulder, I sat down with a long, audible groan of relief, wondering if I'd be able to stand up again. Melodramatic, of course, and I laughed at myself, but not a comfortable laugh. What was wrong with me? We used to hike at least once a week, but in the year without Kristen I'd only hiked two or three times. So I certainly wasn't as fit as I'd been. Was it just that? Or glistening snakes of yellow fat growing thick in my arteries, the gush of my blood choked to a trickle? Or prostate cancer, spreading with its slow stealth into my bones? I knew men my age who'd been knocked down by such things. But if something like that were happening, I reasoned, wouldn't I feel much worse?

You couldn't sit in that spot for long, however, feeling troubled. My anxiety lifted as I took in the view of the little patch of earth where I'd made my happiest home: massive, pure white clouds adrift in the blue overhead, the familiar contours of the hills that sheltered the house, the forest in deep summer green stretching as far as I could see, the supple sway of wild rye, Queen Anne's lace, and ironweed down along the creek. Using sketches and photos, Kristen had painted that view in all four seasons. The sun-washed summer version, the very view I was looking at, was still with me, hanging on the wall above the fireplace.

* * *

On the whole, Kristen enjoyed her teaching career and worked hard to kindle a flicker of creativity in the spirits of the adolescents who passed through her classroom. But that work could be discouraging, and over the years she told me many times how much she was looking forward to retirement, how it was her dream to have all the time she could possibly want to devote herself to her painting. Frugal by nature, and smart with her money, she was able to retire at fifty-six, and at first she seemed thrilled. In the first two weeks of her new freedom she completed half a dozen paintings.

Then something changed. I was still working at my job as regional operations manager for a supermarket chain, and came home one evening to find her slumped in a chair in front of the television. Unlike her, but I let it pass. The following evening, however, when I found her stretched out and half-asleep on the couch, I knew something was wrong.

"Did you paint today?" I asked.

"I did not," she said. "I've stagnated."

"Stagnated? That seems sudden. What brought this on?"

She ran a hand straight back through her hair and let out a sigh. "I've been stagnant for a long time actually."

Kristen's bouts of discouragement were rare, but when they occurred the ditch could be deep. A troubling stillness settled into her face and eyes, and she became listless and pale, as if she'd been drained of blood.

"Scoot over," I said. She slid her butt toward the back of the couch and I sat down on the edge. "Tell me what you mean. You've been so productive lately. You don't seem stagnant."

"Productive maybe, but uninspired. I keep doing what I already know how to do. And I'm not sure how to break out of it. All I know is I don't want to be just another little old lady painting still lifes."

I laid my hand on her belly, wanting the warmth. "That's not the worst fate I can think of."

"I'm tired of painting apples and barns. I want to paint feelings. And ideas."

"Apples and barns sound a lot easier."

Her head was propped on an arm of the couch and she rolled it from side to side. "It has nothing to do with what's easy. If your art is easy you're just killing time."

"Well, that's true," I said. "Doing the easy thing doesn't usually produce your best work."

"Exactly. Like your fence out there." She managed a hint of a smile and brought a hand to rest on top of mine. "You could have built it in half the time if you'd gone and bought all the parts at Home Depot. And we'd have a run-of-the-mill fence. But you challenged yourself. You took all the time you needed and made something beautiful."

"Thank you."

"There's so much for me to explore, Patrick. I've been hiding in my comfort zone way too long. I need to change that. I need to grow."

"Then do it, sweetheart," I said. "Do whatever it takes."

Poking around on the internet, she got wind of an advanced painting class in Charleston, and signed up for it. She forged into new territory, and as often happens when a person does that it brought the unexpected into our lives. The unexpected in this case came in the form of Marcus Rollins, the instructor of the class. A surrealist, according to Kristen, with a modest reputation.

After the first class Kristen was giddy, wired with new energy. She went to her studio before I left in the morning and was still there ten hours later when I got back home. Her paintings took a strange turn: an angry mob with huge, deformed noses brandishing pitchforks and axes; a train made of giant bullets running on tracks made of crushed human beings. I was enthralled and delighted for her. Marcus, she said, was a wonderful teacher, patient, articulate, encouraging.

Shortly after the class ended, she joined a three-week group tour of Italy's art treasures, with Marcus as tour guide. The trip had been a revelation, she said when she returned. She'd learned so much, and Marcus had amazed them all with the depth and breadth of his knowledge. The lavish praise for Marcus began to worry me, but I tamped it down, scolded myself, in fact, for allowing any suspicion to come between us. I wanted to trust her and had no reason not to. In all our years together, Kristen had never given me the slightest reason to question her love.

She arranged for private lessons with Marcus, twice a week. A month went by, at which point it seemed all I heard from Kristen was "Marcus says this, Marcus thinks that," a running feed of his maxims and opinions. Like I said, I'm a slow learner, but that's when I understood where things were headed.

Still I hesitated, searching for the right approach, the right words, the right moment to bring it up. Kristen and I had always communicated calmly and openly, but we'd never come up against anything as delicate and dangerous as the subject of Marcus. Fear, however, has a life of its own, and mine finally surfaced one night during another of Kristen's recitations of things Marcus had said, things Marcus believed.

I held up both arms as she was talking. "Kristen, stop. Stop, stop, please." She looked at me, surprised. "Look, I don't want to hear any more of the wit and wisdom of Marcus Rollins, okay? I'm glad you're getting along so well with him. But I've heard enough."

I'd never spoken to her that way, with that kind of insistence and exasperation. I hadn't shouted, had taken pains to speak softly, but you can put a sharp knife in a quiet voice. When I hear myself in memory I know that's what I did. In any case, it brought about the breakthrough we needed, the reckoning that had become inevitable.

I asked her what was going on with Marcus, and whether she'd slept with him.

"Absolutely not," she said. "But he's been incredibly generous and kind with me. If you're asking me if we've grown close, yes, we have."

"What does 'grown close' mean?"

She sighed and shook her head. "I'm not sure, Patrick. I honestly don't know."

I waited, gave her a chance to say what I hoped she'd say, what I needed to hear. She gazed out the window at the darkness. "Is that all you have to say?" I finally asked.

"What do you want me to say?"

"I don't want you to say anything in particular. It just seems to me that at a time like this there are things you might want to say. Or do."

She shrugged, looked out the window again, said predictable things about being confused, needing some space and time. No reassuring embrace. Not a word about our lengthy history, her ongoing love and commitment.

We muddled on, as people do, but not for long. I felt betrayed and self-righteous; Kristen seemed to feel shackled and resentful. A pattern of touchiness and bickering took hold between us that we couldn't break. I wish it had ended more gently than it did, but overall we managed to keep things reasonably civil. We fought through scenes painful to remember, but we cried and held each other too when it all felt unbearable.

Sometimes a cold wind blows through me and I harden, thinking how I didn't deserve to be treated that way, how wrong of her it was to do what she did. But that's predictable too, a self-serving plunge into the blind thoughtlessness of looking at things solely from my point of view, through a dark lens of grievance. Doing that dishonors both of us and obscures a larger, truer view of our story, in particular the fact that Kristen and I gave each other twenty-five years of loving, fulfilling companionship. And I remind myself that Kristen wasn't born into the world to be my possession or the source of my lifelong contentment, and that in the course of simply living her life she met someone more in tune with the future she envisioned for herself. That wasn't her fault. It wasn't my fault. It was just a fact, something that happened entirely by chance.

Every so often I get an e-mail from Livorno, on the west coast of Italy, where Kristen and Marcus now live. Scraps of information about her new paintings and her new life so far away. She sounds upbeat, and I always send an upbeat reply. People think age strips you of hope and desire, and in some cases that's true. But sometimes, even late in life, a dream can blossom into an imperative, and in my best moments, despite the hurt, I try to remember that and wish Kristen well.

* * *

The afternoon had turned sultry and I'd worked up a good sweat by the time I climbed to the ridge top where the graves were. Will and Davy had sweat streaming down their faces, their clothes soaked, streaked and blotched with dirt. Will's t-shirt, flapping in the breeze earlier, was pasted to his ribs by sweat. Four large cardboard boxes stood off to the side, lined with black plastic trash bags and labeled with the names of the deceased. The Jeep was parked nearby, rear tailgate open. When I arrived, Will and Davy had just unearthed the last of the four coffins.

"You darn near have it whipped," I said.

"We been hard at it," Will said. "I always did hate diggin'. Nothin' but plain hard work."

"That's the truth," I said. "I learned that when I built the fence in front of the house."

Will pulled his t-shirt up and tried to find a dry spot to wipe his face. "Yes sir, postholes'll make a strong man cry for mercy."

I asked Will how the four people buried in the plot were related to him.

"Guthrie and Sarah was my grandparents on my father's side," Will said, pointing to the boxes that held their bones. "Good hardworkin' folks. Kept a store near Ivydale for near fifty years. Right there's my Uncle Terence. Drinkin' man. Layabout. Worked some on the barges outta Wheeling. Killed there in a knife fight."

"Tanner seems to be a common name around here," I said.

"Oh Lord, yes. Tanners ever-where. We got it all wrote down, family book goes back five generations. Workin' on number six."

He pointed to the last, unopened coffin in front of us. "This here's Beatrice Tanner, my first cousin. I was eleven years old when she died. She was just nine. Me and her, we got into all manner of mischief. Story I always tell about her is how she saved my ass from a whippin'. I tell it, but I ain't proud of it, not one bit. I stole a bag of ginger cookies one time, you see, from Holton's bakery in Glenville. But now I didn't steal 'em for myself. I give that whole bag to Beatrice, 'cause I knew ginger cookies was her favorite. Only she got caught eatin' 'em out behind the chicken shed. Her daddy asked her where she got 'em, and she told him she was the one that stole 'em. He whipped her so bad she couldn't hardly walk." He extended his shovel and laid the steel tip softly on the lid of Beatrice's coffin. "Ain't that somethin'?"

"It certainly is," I said. "She sacrificed herself."

"Yes, she did. I never have felt right about it. Never had a chance to make it up to her, neither. The influenza killed her not long after. Tell you what, I cried for a week. I loved that little slip. Puppy love, you know?" He cleared his throat. "Cutest thing you ever seen," he said, so softly I barely heard him.

We all went quiet, Davy studying his father with a mix of bewilderment and apprehension, as if he were looking at a mysterious and untrustworthy stranger. Will pulled his shovel back and jabbed the tip in and out of the dirt again and again, his eyes on Beatrice's coffin. The jaw muscles down the side of his lean face tensed and relaxed. Finally, he shook his head and drove the shovel in deep with his foot, so it stood up by itself. "Alright then," he said, "time to git her outta there."

He and Davy pried off the rotted coffin lid. A foul stench rose, which the breeze, thankfully, quickly dispersed. Inside were scraps of clothing and hair and two disintegrated leather shoes, all clustered around Beatrice's bones.

"I'll git her in the box," Will told Davy. "You load them other boxes in the Jeep."

Poor Davy. He was staggering in his big clumsy boots, the pink ham of his cheeks burning fiery red. The thrill of the day had evaporated. He managed to wrestle the box labeled "Terence" into the Jeep, but when he tried to lift the "Guthrie" box he lost his grip, dropped it, and lurched forward onto his knees. "Fuck!" he said. He stood up and lashed a booted kick into the side of the "Beatrice" box where his father had begun placing the bones of the little cousin he'd loved.

With one quick, long-legged stride that looked almost like a leap, Will closed in on Davy and with a roundabout swing of his right arm smashed the side of Davy's head with his open hand. Davy never saw it coming. He screamed and spun as he fell, and landed hard, flat on his back. "Goddamn it, you show some respect," Will shouted. "Them's your people."

"They're not people," Davy shouted back, tears and sweat glistening on his cheeks. "They're just stinkin' bones!"

"Don't you smartmouth me, son!" Will went after him again,

looking as if he wanted to kick him. Davy rolled away, then scrabbled and clawed through the dirt on all fours, trying to escape.

"Will, no, no, no!" I shouted, running to overtake him. I grabbed him by the arm and stopped him. "Easy now. No harm done." I pointed at Davy, who'd given up and flopped down motionless on his stomach. "Look at him. He's exhausted."

"You got a lot to learn, son," Will said. But he wasn't shouting, and he backed off. I went and helped Davy sit up and get to his feet. "Come on, I'll give you a hand," I said. He wiped his wet face with his filthy shirttail, leaving slashes of dirt on his cheeks. Then together we carried the "Guthrie" and "Sarah" boxes to the Jeep.

* * *

When they had Beatrice loaded we said our goodbyes, and Will and Davy four-wheeled down the hill with their cargo. I stayed there at the gravesite, the disturbed earth lying in random heaps and swirls, here and there a dark scrap of coffin wood they hadn't reburied. Then I spotted what looked like a bone where Beatrice's grave had been. I bent over for a closer look—sure enough, a little finger bone.

I picked it up and held it flat on my palm. From the hand of a little girl, but it made me think of Kristen's hands. They were one of her nicest features, large hands, palms softly padded and warm, fingers long and slim. Holding hands was something we'd loved doing, anytime, anywhere, out for one of our anniversary dinners or simply negotiating the aisles at the supermarket. We'd slide and rub our finger joints together in a way that felt good, and in playful moods we'd intensify that friction until it started to hurt. One day when we did that—in Home Depot, I think—Kristen swung her lips and warm breath close to my ear and whispered, "Fun pain," a meaty oxymoron that still makes me laugh when I think of it. And I'd loved the way she moved her hands, precisely and efficiently, in smooth, flowing arcs that mirrored the grace and thoughtfulness she brought to everything she did.

"Not people," Davy had said. "Just stinkin' bones." I understood him, of course, the core truth discerned by the child's eye. But in another sense, I thought, Davy couldn't have been more wrong. Standing there in the muggy breeze and the evening light, I envied the Tanners for that family book of theirs, those generations of bones to care about, and the prospect of the years that remained to me touched me, for the first time, with a profound unease. I'd been so tied to the past, so bound by what I'd lost, that I'd given only the haziest thought to what lay ahead. I'd reached the homestretch of my walk in the sun, with time poised to do its merciless work on me. No Kristen. No siblings, no children. No one's bones to care about and no one to care about mine.

I knelt down, plunged my hands into the churned up dirt of Beatrice's gravesite, and scooped out a shallow hole. I placed her finger bone in it and covered it. Then I stood and pressed the soil down with my boot, leaving one more waffled footprint among the hundreds we'd left there that afternoon, every step of our hectic presence stamped in the soft earth, visible there until the next hard rain.

FOG

Jean Rover

Clement Diddle used to have a job in a book bindery. That was before the fog came and he quit, or maybe he was asked to leave. He couldn't remember which. Just that he wasn't able to concentrate and went out on disability. That's where the checks came from.

At the book bindery, all those clunking machines talked to him at once. It was better now because he only had Izzy. Those little blue pills helped, too. People didn't understand. He had this gift. He could hear voices that they couldn't. At first he thought the voices were from his neighbor's TV coming through their shared wall, kind of like a swarm of bees nesting in the plaster, but then the pulsing water in the shower talked to him, too. People were so one dimensional.

Clement lived in an efficiency unit on the second story of *The Beverly*, an older brick apartment building off Cliff Street. His place was at the very end, next to the stairs, so he could come and go without running into other tenants. Those people that always smiled and said, "How ya doin'?" They didn't care and he didn't know.

His little space was his world, and it had everything he need-ed—a tiny bathroom, a couch that opened to a bed, one brown Naugahyde recliner, a refrigerator, kitchen sink, a two-plate stove, and a table for his computer and precious printer. Clem-ent had always lived alone, but not lately because Izzy, his ink-jet printer talked to him: "Go there. Go there. Do it. Do it."

Having a printer was expensive because it required reams of paper to keep it talking, and it couldn't be any ol' paper. It had to be smooth, bright white, and just the right weight. Clement liked to rub the paper against his cheek before he loaded the tray. He always typed in the same thing— *Talk to me. Talk to me, Talk to me*—in fourteen point Times Roman. No printer would take his message seriously if he used say, Comic Sans or BaaBookHmk. And why were there so many fonts anyway? It was confusing and the world didn't need them.

Once he hit file, print, he'd close his eyes and listen to the chugging sound. It was like music. The printer fired up and calm swept over him. "Good job. Good job," Izzy said.

Having a printer was a job-and-a-half because once Izzy

spoke, Clement had to shred all that paper. He couldn't dump Izzy's droppings—they might contain a secret message or could bring him bad luck. Fortunately, his shredder didn't talk, it just murmured *whirrrrrrrrr* as it chewed the sheets and spit out strips.

* * *

Clement used to belong to an online chat group before his fog worsened. He'd struck up a conversation with a woman named Butterfly who suggested they meet for coffee since they both liked the same things: corn curls and Snickers bars.

Clement opted out because he knew she wouldn't be interested in him as a person. No woman ever was. And the picture he'd posted online wasn't really him. Clement was a big, overweight middle-aged man with reddish, balding hair, freckles, and beefy arms. A pair of vertical lines ran up his forehead almost to his receding hairline. His gray, dead eyes stared out over a button nose and knob-like chin. He always wore black slacks and a black T-shirt. Colors didn't do anything for him, and besides, too much color made him anxious.

Butterfly devoured romance novels and chatted about them nonstop, which baffled Clement. Why would anybody read those things? He never read books. Whenever he did, the print ran together making him reach for another pill. His favorite reads were those chocolate candies that had little messages inside their wrappers which he saved and comic books, especially ones about Batman or monsters from outer space. Those things were straight forward, easy to follow, and made sense. The world needed sense.

Besides he never trusted women. Not really. When he asked Izzy if he should hook up with Butterfly, she said, "Don't go. Don't go." Computers, especially ones with printers, were like windows—you could see the world, but you didn't have to go out into it. He liked it that way.

Clement Diddle. Clammy Clem. Fiddle Diddle. None of it was his fault. When he was in grade school, the kids used to tease him about his name. Gray mixed with rocks in the head, like a big cement mixer they said, taunting him. What kind of a chance did he have with a name like that? Shiddie Diddie, Shidiot, Piddle Diddle, they called him. His mother said to pay them no mind. He was different, special even. And that's all he can remember of his childhood. The rest of it was haze.

* * *

Clement always parked his blue Toyota pickup in a particular spot even though parking places at his apartment weren't reserved. He had to have that same spot, the one over by the oak tree with its thick trunk and sprawling branches that seemed to reach for him. He loved that tree, and it helped him remember where he left his vehicle. Anxiety kicked in whenever he had to park anywhere else, leaving large wet spots under his armpits.

Emery, that skinny, snot-nosed thirteen-year old, never failed to park his mountain bike in Clement's spot. The little dipstick left it there while he ran up to his apartment somewhere in the complex, never in a hurry to move it. That meant Clement had to get out of his pickup and shove the blasted thing aside before he could drive in.

The damn brat. He does that on purpose. And who names a kid Emery? What do the kids call him? Em? Emmy? A friggin' sissy name. Besides that, the little weasel had zits all over his pinched face and dark-framed know-it-all glasses. Clement never much trusted kids—especially not ones with pimples and egghead glasses.

One day, after returning from the drugstore, Clement had had it. He refused to jump out and move the bike. Instead, he blasted his pickup right into it, crushing the front wheel and its fender. Once parked, Clement tossed the bike as hard as he could onto the sidewalk. *That'll teach the little shit.* There was no one around to see what he'd done, so he clumped up to his apartment and typed as fast as he could. *Talk to me. Talk to me.* He ordered ten copies and clicked file, print. The printer cranked up, chuntering, "Deny it. Deny it."

Clement spent the rest of the morning filing candy wrapper messages. What else was there to do? Finally, he decided to go to the grocery store, although he hated going there. Too many people, and all those squawking brats with their dirty shoes and diapered butts riding in the carts like monkeys. That's why, for the most part, he went late at night. Unfortunately, he was all out of apricots and almonds, another of his favorite things next to corn curls and candy bars. Just the thought of pressing an almond into a soft apricot and slowly chewing was orgasmic.

He put on his black hat and hopped into his pickup. He had to laugh. The bike was gone, except for one bolt lying there on the asphalt. Too bad. So sad. He would've loved to see Emery's face when he discovered his precious bike was a heap of metal. Twit, twit, twit.

Satisfied, Clement gunned his engine and drove off to Big Mike's Market down the street. He went there because he loved looking at the bulk food bins all lined up in neat, gleaming rows: beans, spices, rice, cereal, flour, all kinds of noodles, tea, piles of candy, and things he never heard of like quinoa and anise seed. He could find almost anything he wanted in the bins. It was like Christmas all year.

* * *

Clement grabbed a cart. He picked out a gallon of milk and a couple loaves of bread before hurrying toward the bins. Wheeee. He filled a bag with almonds, listening to the whooshing sound they made as they filled his plastic bag. He tied it off and wrote down the bin number. Now, onto the apricots.

A small boy, with dirty blond hair, opened the lids of various fruit bins with his chubby hand and watched them slam shut. Every time a dropping lid made a bang, he'd giggle. "Ricky, come here," his mother called. Ricky didn't listen. "Rickeee don't do that," she said again, her voice rising. The boy ignored her.

Clement towered over the boy and watched the little chub wipe his nose on the back of his hand. In his other one, the kid carried a small, red toy car. "Whroom, Whroom," he said, as he drove it on top of a bin lid.

"Get away, listen to your ol' lady," Clement said in a gruff voice. Ricky paid him no heed. He lifted the lid of the apricot bin and let it fall. That infuriated Clement. Apricots were sacred. When the kid's mother went around the corner to look at cereal, the little snot stuck his tongue out at Clement. Then he opened the bin and reached in with his hand. The same one he's used to wipe his snotty nose.

Oh, dear God. Who'd want to eat those apricots now? How dare that little shit defile his precious apricots. Then, the darn kid did the unthinkable. He dropped his toy car inside and looked up at Clement with a wide grin. "Car gone," he said.

That did it. Clement grabbed the kid by the arm and smacked him hard on the bottom.

Ricky wailed and took off in the direction of his mom. "That bad man hit me," he yelled, sobbing.

"What man?" He heard the woman say.

Run! Clement disappeared through the work area where the staff unpacked boxes and headed out fast to the dock. *Phew no one was there.* He jumped down and huffed and puffed his way back to his apartment. He didn't even stop to get his pickup. Even Clement knew you never touched somebody else's kid. The police would be after him.

His heart beat was chaotic like that last time he'd had a panic attack. Oh, God, he needed Izzy. Once home, he turned on his computer and with shaky hands typed, *Please Izzy. Talk to me. Talk to me. Talk to me.* File. Print. He waited. Izzy said, "Bad move. Bad move. Hide out. Hide out."

Clement hunkered down in his apartment. He couldn't sleep. What if the store had cameras? There were cameras all over these days. He tossed. He turned. He didn't have a TV. Watching things moving on screens freaked him. And how did he know that the TV wasn't watching him?

The next morning, Clement snuck out and swiped the landlord's newspaper from his door step. Back in his apartment, he flipped through the pages. *Oh, no! There it was.* A small story. Police were looking for or seeking information on a man who assaulted a four-year old child at Big Mike's Market. No description. The little boy said the man was "big and mean looking." His mother claimed "the brute" left a handprint on little Ricky's bottom.

The article warned the public to be on the lookout. What was worse, it said what the penalty was for assault. Relieved they had no description of him, Clement tossed down the paper and pulled the drapes.

Mid-morning there was a knock on the door. *Who could that be?* Clement peeked through the drape covering his side window. Yikes. He spotted a police cruiser parked on his street.

His shirt stuck to his back. He could feel his face flush. *What to do? What to do?* He rushed to his computer and sent a document to his Izzy. The paper jammed. "Shit. Please Izzy, please."

The knocking got louder. Clement tugged at the jammed paper, clearing the roller. He tried again. Finally, the printer kicked in, "Don't talk. Don't talk."

Clement wiped perspiration from his forehead with his sleeve, took a deep breath, and opened the door. "Yes," he said, in his most innocent voice.

The officer looked him over. "You Clem Diddle?"

"That's Clement Diddle. Nobody calls me Clem."

"Clement then. Folks at the Big Mike's found a vehicle left in the parking lot. It's registered to you."

Oh, no. My pickup. Clement scratched his head. He remembered what Izzy had said, "Don't talk. Don't Talk."

Think. "I, uh, I'm diabetic and got shaky, so I didn't feel like driving. Afraid I'd pass out. Low blood sugar makes you crazy. So I wandered a bit. Sat down, ate a candy bar, came home, crashed. Wanted to get the pickup, but haven't been feeling well. Still feel weak."

"I see," said the officer.

"Heh, heh," said Clement. "Thought I was dying."

"Did you go into the store, Clem?"

"That's Clement."

"Uh-huh. So did you? Go into the store?"

Is he trying to trip me up? "Nah, nah. Wanted to, but I was wobbly. Just sat there. Didn't want to chance drivin'."

The officer's eyes narrowed. "So, you were in the parking lot?"

"Yeah, sure."

"You see anyone running from the store?"

Clement swallowed hard. "Nah. I always park in the back. Less hassle and I was pretty lightheaded." His legs trembled like Jell-O. "Why? Was there a robbery?"

The officer crossed his arms and stared. Finally, he said, "Well, you better get the vehicle. The store manager is complaining about it."

"Sure," Clement said, "Sure. I'll get on it." He watched the officer leave. *Phew. That was close.*

He hugged Izzy. "Good job. Good job," she said.

A watermelon smile covered his face. "I pulled it off," he shouted. Now, all he had to do was go and get the pickup, but first, he'd check his mail. *Who knows? Might be another disability check.* He could never remember when they were supposed to come, just that they did.

He looked for his number—195—in the row of black metal mailboxes hanging on the brick wall. There were no envelopes or advertisements in his box—only a note pinned to the magazine holder with a clothespin. Clement unfolded the note and read: *I saw what you did. Wait for further instructions,* printed with a blunt, lead pencil.

Clement's whole body shook. He needed water for his suddenly dry throat. *Jesus, a witness.* Back upstairs Izzy said, "Oh no. Oh no."

While walking to Big Mike's, Clement belched up stomach acid. Without warning, he heaved his breakfast onto the asphalt, took a deep breath, and wiped his mouth on his sleeve. When he reached the parking lot, he looked over his shoulder. Nothing. He drove back home and parked his vehicle in the spot under the oak tree. At least he didn't have to mess with that damn bike.

Up in his apartment, he fumbled with the computer keyboard. After several typos, he finally wrote: *Talk to me. Talk to me.* This time in sixteen-point bold. "I'm desperate, Izzy."

He clicked on file, print, and held his breath. The printer made its initial chugging sounds before spewing, "Check again. Check again. Watch it. Watch it."

* * *

He spent another sleepless night. He didn't bother to pull open the bed, just laid on the couch with a blanket and a pillow. The next morning, his neck hurt and his back ached. He dragged himself up and splashed cold water on his face before sneaking out his door and down the stairs. Careful to look both ways, he crept along the brick apartment walls and lifted the landlord's newspaper.

Safe in his apartment again, he brewed himself a cup of instant coffee by boiling water in a saucepan. He no longer used the coffeemaker because the grounds looked like dirt, and its gurgling and popping sounded like a drowning man gasping for air. *What was it saying?* It scared the bejesus out of him.

He blew on his coffee and took a long drink before thumbing through the news. Nothing. What did that mean? Was he being set up? Was that note on his box some kind of sting operation? He'd seen shows like that on TV. Well, when he had one. He couldn't remember when that was. Did he ever own a TV? Or, was it someone else's? The fog. That goddamned fog.

The blue pills. He went into the bathroom and swallowed one. Afterward, he retreated to his recliner and thumbed through a comic book, waiting for the medicine to kick in. *Was there another note waiting for him outside?* He didn't want to seem overly anxious, in case someone was watching his moves.

Ah, 10:00 a.m. The mail would be there. He lumbered down the stairs and over to the mailboxes—only one envelope, his electric bill. Sure enough there was a note fastened with a clothespin. It said, *I'll be in McVeety Park tomorrow at 1:00 p.m. Bring cash. Go to the garbage can by the men's john. Wait there.*

Blackmail! It didn't say how much money. It probably would be a lot, but it was better than prison. He couldn't have Izzy in the slammer. He'd be locked in there with all those dirt bags. Bad people. People that would glare at him and God knows what. What would he do without Izzy? Who would talk to him and tell him what to do? Izzy was all he had. He didn't have a family, did he? If he did, he couldn't remember them. But sometimes when he was sleeping, he thought he felt his mother's hand covering him, like that big oak tree in the parking lot reaching for him. Maybe Mom would come tonight. Dr. Morrison said his mother wasn't really there, that he was hallucinating, but Clement knew it was her.

He lay awake all night listening to the clock ticking and the traffic moving. *Was there someone on the stairs? Maybe I should hide Izzy.* He heard the roar of the big metal dinosaur that came every Wednesday morning. It lifted the garbage bin outside and swallowed its contents, its two eyes gleaming in the darkness. He pulled the blankets over his head whenever that monster came, growling.

Bleary eyed, Clement forced himself to get out of bed. "Get it. Get it," Izzy said. Mid-morning, he put on a fresh black T-shirt, drove to the bank, and withdrew $5,000 from his account, leaving a zero balance. It was better than jail.

"Are you sure?" asked Chelsea, the short, chubby teller. "Are you closing your account?" Her black, curly hair and one squinty eye reminded him of his mother. Whenever Clement went to the bank, he searched out Chelsea because she was patient and helpful. Besides, you could trust a person who seemed like your mother.

"No," he said in a quiet voice.

Chelsea gave him a long look.

"Somethin's come up. I mean, you can't leave a printer all on its own," he said.

She cocked her head. "What's that? Are you okay? You want me to call someone?"

"No. No." He looked over his shoulder to see if anyone was watching.

"You seem nervous."

"Don't be hassling me. It's my money."

"Yes, it is," she said. "Just wanted to make sure you weren't being scammed or something. There are a lot of bad people out there."

"No. No scam."

She counted out the bills and put them in an envelope. "You take care," she said and gave him that sweet Chelsea smile. "Don't be flashing your money around. Hear me?"

Clement turned and left. He'd have to wait for his next disability check to live on. He drove his pickup back to the apartment planning to walk to McVeety Park. Before heading out, he put the money envelope in a plastic Big Mike's bag.

* * *

There was only one set of toilets at the park. Ah, there it is the garbage can by the men's john. That must be the one. He checked his watch—12:55 p.m. He waited.

Nothing.

What was that? Ah, a flushing toilet. Soon, an older man, wearing a blue sweater and slacks, came out. Tall and thin with a serious Clint Eastwood face, he loomed over Clement as he approached.

Clement shivered, feeling his damp skin under his T-shirt. Maybe the guy was an undercover cop. Maybe he should all out confess. "I didn't mean to," he blurted. His ears were pulsing. "The kid was ruining the apricots."

The man paused and peered at him. "Mean to do what?" He gave Clement a "go ahead and make my day" look.

"The bins. I was at the bins," Clement said.

"I don't know what you're talking about," the man said. "You homeless?"

"No," Clement said. "I came to pay up."

The man's eyes narrowed, his frown deepened. "Damn druggies," he muttered as he hurried away. "They're all over. Can't even stop to take a piss."

False alarm. Clement wanted to cry. He needed Izzy. *What to do? What to do?* He sat down on the ground and held his head. Minutes passed, but they seemed like hours. He opened his eyes and two feet planted themselves in front of him. He followed the feet up the pants legs, the chest, and finally the face.

Emery.

"It was you that broke my bike," Emery blurted. "You pay up or else, I'm reporting you. You can't trash someone's property and get away with it." He took a breath. "And I saw you steal the landlord's newspaper. For sure, he'll put you out."

The little sniveling pissant. Clement wanted to pinch his head. "Idiot. You don't leave a bike in a parking space."

Emery didn't budge. He balled his fists, his skinny body standing firm. "People say you're a real nut job, but you don't scare me. Pay up or else I'm telling."

"A nut job? Why you little pock-faced bastard." Clement leapt to his feet. He wanted to jerk those smart-ass glasses off Emery's face and stomp them into pieces—well, after he strangled him.

Emery's hands made fists. He hopped around in his tight jeans like a boxer. "Go ahead," he shouted. "They'll lock you up."

The word *lock* hit Clement like a wave. He stopped, fumbled with his plastic Big Mike's bag, until he found the envelope and pulled open the flap. He held out two $100 bills. "That enough?"

"That's more like it." Emery grabbed for the money and stuffed the bills in the pocket of his hoodie. "See ya around." His mouth made a smirk before he scuffled off.

Drained, Clement watched him leave. He couldn't help it. He burst out laughing. He wasn't going to jail. No, he'd be able to see his Izzy again. Feed her. Listen to her. God, he needed Izzy. And now he knew. You don't harm kids. Izzy had been clear about that, "Bad thing. Bad thing. Never touch. Never touch."

"That little earwig didn't even say thank you," Clement said, talking to himself as he trundled homeward with $4,800 in his pocket. "The bike. It was all over that goddamned bike. Ha." People on the street stared at the orange-haired hulk walking along, babbling to himself.

Home. Such a precious word. Such a special, safe place. When he reached the parking lot, he threw his arms around the big oak trunk and rubbed his cheek against the rough bark. "Thank you, Mother." He chugged up the apartment stairs, unlocked the door, and hung his hat on the coat rack. "Izzy, sweetheart." He gently caressed and kissed a stack of twenty-four pound bright-white paper and lovingly fed her. Once he typed in his message and hit file, print, Izzy hummed and slipped into her tender rhythm. "Sleep now. Sleep now. Sleep now."

OF HALF-HOUSES, WITH VERNON

Gregg Cusick

Ontario County, Upstate NY
March 1971

Vernon paused over the broom and leaned his weight off the long-ago injured ankle, thinking *the boy will come today.* He gazed around the modular housing factory, a hangar really, where the half-houses were assembled, and pictured the boy, Walt, riding his knobby-wheeled bike along the cow paths and across the cornfield, just stubble now in late winter. Vernon waited, amazed as ever at the two rows of half-houses, the production line where what began as a plywood platform over 2"x10" joists gradually grew a frame and walls and windows, wires and pink insulation and even a roof, where at the end of the assembly line rested a completed half-a-house, its open side where it would meet up with its partner now covered in heavy plastic.

Vernon loved this place, and each of the nine renditions inside. The first half-house, barely a platform, meant potential to him, what can be accomplished. And each successive stage meant something in some development—the framing and drywall and sheathing, not quite like a being in a womb, that grows from cells inside to out, but not unlike it either, he thought. Stages changing, maturing until the final completion, at least half-completion, when the semi-house is ready to be trucked to the site and joined with its matching other.

He loved the smells—sawdust and pine lumber, steel and sweat—and its sounds—hammers and power saws whirring, shouts and laughter from men grateful to have jobs and happy to work on a crew like he recalled his teams in high school—they all played football and basketball and many a third sport. Times they still reveled in. Causing Vernon to remember his passion, his basketball days just down the Thruway, his records for points in a game and in a season. And also then: the big farm kid from Sanford who came down on Vernon's ankle and the sound, the awful crack that everyone in the stifling gym heard. But still, that time was when he'd felt most alive, and even hopeful, to be together with a group of young men and a common purpose. He'd had a best friend on the team then, who'd been killed in faraway Korea soon after graduation. Vernon still missed Jeremy.

He looked toward the hangar's small steel door that sat beside the enormous garage doors that let the half-houses out, and in the small square window he saw for a split second the boy's face as he jumped from outside to see in. Then, again, like he was on a pogo stick. Vernon moved toward the door, but the boy was already using his key.

* * *

Little Walt—what the family called him but Vernon never did—had first met Vernon when his father, Big Walter, brought him on a summer Saturday to the big hangar where the team of workmen like Vernon would construct the half houses, assembling them like oversized popsicle-stick structures, their sticks 2x4s, their Elmer's Glue 16d framing nails. Walt had put out his hand and shaken with the six-foot-nine Vernon, a man so thin he was something of a 2x4 himself. His long fingers that could surround a basketball made Walt's hand disappear up to the wrist. Still there was firmness and kindness to the grip.

That was the summer when Walt went to Cleveland to stay with his grandparents, a long three weeks of living quietly in a small old house that smelled of overripe fruit and pipe smoke. With sometimes loving, sometimes grumbling people Walt was told were old and sick. Who loved him but hated noise and mess and everything that went with an eleven-year-old boy: the muddy sneakers and broken dishes and running in the house *didn't I just tell you NO RUNNING IN THE HOUSE!* But Walt was there because his parents needed time to talk things out, is what his mother told him. Yet when he came home they were only quieter, as if they had talked for three weeks and had nothing left to say.

It was then that Walt had borrowed his father's key to the hangar one Saturday morning and rode his bike to the Sanford Hardware. Where old Mr. Bailey, who'd lost three fingers on his left hand to a hay baler, cut him a duplicate. So that Walt could escape his quiet house and play among the developing half-houses. And when he let himself in that first time, Vernon was waiting. Saying nothing at the start, he moved to the first half-house, little more than a platform, a stage. Where then he asked Walt for the first time, what do you see, what's different? And in this way Walt's instruction began.

Albany, NY
March 1995

On late winter days now I sometimes look out my window at the pigeons and the pigeon-colored sky and below it the dirty snow that melts some then and refreezes each night, and I think of Vernon and the hangar and my father, too, who tried to keep the company going through the long Rochester winters, when the ground was concrete and foundations couldn't be dug, but the half-houses had to be shipped—no storage room in the hangar. So then they'd sit on their lots like kids without mittens and get pummeled by the weather, their plastic covering no match for the winds, the snows. While at the factory the new halves kept rolling out, the assembly line and the assemblers a busy team, still laughing mostly up until paychecks began bouncing.

I look out of my office—I'm an architect, not starving, not a name you'd know—and think of my partner at home and our new, thirteen-year-old son. And I miss Vernon's soft calm voice, his kind words, his understanding. I know our boy, Justin's his name—I might have chosen Jeremy, but he came to us with one and it suits him—faces challenges at school and in the neighborhood. Quiet, smart, adopted. Anything different, kids pick up on. Like noticing something that isn't gray, I think, as a light snow begins outside.

Ontario County, 1971

Vernon and Walt nod to one another, and Vernon shuffles across the smooth concrete floor down the wide corridor between the two rows of half-houses to number five. Where they'd left off last time. Walt is near bounding while Vernon limps slightly, his face showing a near smile.

At the fifth half-house, changes are visible from the fourth, and Walt steps into the framed front doorway. Vernon stands before him, his six-foot-seven coming near up to Walt's four-foot-something, nearly eye to eye.

What do you see, Walt?

And Walt is full of answers: First, the doorway and windows are framed, he says.

And they weren't in number four?

No, um, yes, he looks over to the previous model. Yes, he says. The electrical is in.

All the studs are up, and the wiring is into the kitchen and around the living room.

What are you standing on?

Floor joists, Walt says. And floor sheathing on top of them. Plywood, ¾″. No drywall yet. Some insulation started around bedroom, bathroom. Kitchen and bathroom not yet plumbed. That'll be number 6 or 7, I think, he says, looking at the next two units. With the wiring I can't walk through walls anymore, he tells Vernon, who gives him an odd smile.

Other days they play hide and seek or just sit in the break room and talk. Vernon smokes and drinks RC—*Royal Crown Cola*, Vernon says with a little reverence—while he allows Walt one choice from the snack machine, for which he has a key. Usually Walt points to a Planter's Peanut Bar.

Sometimes Vernon tells Walt of the men who work on the crew there in the hangar, the frame carpenters and finish carpenters and tradesmen who complete these half-houses from nothing but their sweat and effort in ten steps and in just two months. Walt listens rapt, as amazed as his tall friend. Vernon clearly loves these men, has laughed with them on the good days and commiserated, too, when a stop at the horse track on payday left them short, left them on the couch at home.

And sometimes Vernon tells Walt stories of his high school days, of basketball and his teammates, especially his friend Jeremy who joined the Army soon after graduation and hadn't come back from Korea. And years later his friend on the crew in the hangar whose name he's never told the boy but who reminds the boy of Jeremy, the way Vernon describes him.

Did you have lots of girlfriends back then, when you were a basketball star? Walt asks once. Were they always shorter than you?

Walt has a crush on a girl who is taller than he is, the daughter of a woman who works in the office of the housing company. The office is a finished model so people can see how spacious and comfortable their new home will be if they buy one. Melanie's mother works "at reception," she's told Walt. That's the living room really, with a desk and couch and coffee table. One night when Walt was visiting Vernon—entering with his own key, his secret copy—Walt looked out from the hangar and saw his father entering the model house with Melanie's mother. They were laughing and his father, Big Walter, stumbled on the steps and she helped steady him, laughing harder. Walt had told only Vernon of this—no one else ever knew. And Vernon puffed on his Pall Mall in the break room and had a sad look on his face.

Your father is a good man, Walt. He gave me my job here. Inhale, exhale. I could tell the boy now, he thinks. Instead, he says, Sometimes even good people make poor choices.

Albany, 1995

I can still recall Vernon's use of the word "poor." At that time I could only think of those with little money. Like Vernon often said, Sanford is a small town, and the differences between folks is there for all to see. Our school bus was a forty-minute ride around cornfields and wheat fields and hayfields and grazing fields, past huge old farmhouses and sagging shacks and new developments with small affordable houses like my father's company built. And everything in between, where most of us were.

The bus driver, Mrs. Worthingham, was called Wart-in-ham or just "Wart," because she had one on her face, and we thoughtless kids wouldn't miss such a difference in a person. She'd stop at the ends of long dirt driveways and mile-apart houses, and sometimes the kids in threadbare clothes would come racing out, while from the bus windows we watched and waited. Like the Beckers and the Claytons, their many kids tearing toward us as their sagging mother, like that woman who lived in a shoe, watched from the porch. In a soiled apron, looking decades older than my own mother, who rarely left the bed at that time, sometimes Mrs. Becker might offer a wave or even a tepid smile.

Ontario County, 1971

Walt never told his father what he did in the hangar or about his talks with Vernon. And Big Walter never asked. But as Vernon and the boy progressed through the half-houses—the boy analyzing the features and development at each stage of the assembly line—their conversations developed, too.

If it was by the 5th half-house that Walt told Vernon of seeing his father stumbling into the model home with the mother of his classmate Melanie. By the 6th or 7th, Walt told Vernon of his own mother. That past year, within months of each other, both her parents, Walt's grandparents, had died. Her father first, a term Walt would learn then, although understanding would come later: by his own hand. A vet of both big wars who'd made the world safe for democracy, he couldn't make his wife well of the cancer, couldn't bear to be a burden to his family, Walt would learn. Then Walt's grandmother passed, silent and painfully, medicated.

She maybe never knew, Walt tells Vernon, meaning maybe she never realized that her husband had preceded her.

Maybe she did, too, Vernon puffs and thinks aloud. I picture them together again, reunited as soon as she left this earth.

Vernon thinks of his old friend Jeremy then, of course, and smiles sadly to Walt. But knowing the boy will understand soon.

So what's different, he pauses, then asks.

Insulation, he says. All over. Remember when I could walk through the walls?

What else?

Walt gets serious-faced. My mom. My mom's different.

And so he tells Vernon about what his father has called "the sadness," how his mother spends her days in bed, how she cries often and hugs Walt and listens to AM radio, a transistor that sits on her bed beside her and gives off tinny music and commentary, news of the war in far-east Asia, Neil Diamond with "Cracklin' Rosie" and Carole King's *Tapestry*. How his father is always working or says he is—Walt doesn't mention Melanie's mother, but they both think it. And how his father is different, too.

You have to be there for your mother, Vernon says. She needs you. Just let her hug you.

And when Walt looks reassured and confused both, Vernon tells him it's very hard to understand death. Especially for your mother about her father. And about the way he chose. He pauses to light a Pall Mall, and his face is dark, grayish, almost translucent in the boy's eyes. His neck red and abrazed, like he's shaved with a dull razor. It's hard to understand, but don't worry, because you will. Inhale, exhale. I did. Again he almost tells the boy.

Albany, 1995

The snow is gaining density if not speed outside my office window. Clean, white, unlike the old leftovers on the ground. I've got a design for a small-house addition spread before me. I think of my wife, Ash—sorry, not Melanie, although we still keep in touch and exchange cards at the holidays. I think of my thirteen-year-old son, adopted just a year ago, Justin, who says he likes boys more than girls. This could mean several things, at his age, of course, but I embrace this news, and his honesty. And I worry.

As for the clients, I need to design something feasible and creative both, and I've been putting them off. It's a 1910 farmhouse and they've got more kids on the way. I don't know how they vote, or how open they are to something a little different.

I look back now near twenty-five years and I wonder why I didn't wonder what Vernon did when I wasn't at the hangar, what he did all day, what he ate and where he showered or shaved or even slept. I guess I just pictured him in the break room drinking RC Cola and putting the bottles into the plastic racks for the credit, puffing Pall Malls—I can smell them now, still indulge a smoke myself now and then, though haven't seen a Planter's bar in years. And then I'd see him returning to the broad push-broom that he'd slowly slide up and down the smooth cool concrete between the half-houses. Endlessly, like my father said painters worked the Golden Gate Bridge, finally finishing only to start again at the beginning the next morning. Did they feel a sense of victory, of closure at least, upon completion, if all the time they knew they'd just be starting over the next shift? Did Vernon find closure, find peace? I didn't wonder then that Vernon seemed to exist just for me.

Ontario County, 1971

Vernon leaned on the wide broom and thought, I will tell the boy today. But even then he was not sure he could. Not sure he was willing to, either, because it would mean an end to something.

The boy let himself quietly in. Vernon looked up and toward the door. The boy smiled, flushed from cold and effort, exhaled once inside as if: made it. Vernon returned the smile, feeling a bit of his resolve seep away.

Without words, the two moved to the 9th house, Walt again near bounding, Vernon slightly limping, using the broomstick like a ski pole.

In the nearly a year that he'd been visiting Vernon at the housing factory, Walt had talked of everything. He'd addressed his father's infidelities and his mother's sadness, his own school battles with bullies and insecurities within himself. His interests, of course in housing and construction and design, and his yearnings and doubts.

What's different? Vernon delays his own reveal. What do you smell? He asks then as Walt stands in the half-house's front doorway, looking slightly down now on the six-foot-seven Vernon.

Not so much of the nails-smell, or the sweat of the framers. Still the cut pine, boards and studs, the wood stain, a little of the construction adhesive. Looks to #10. Next with the carpet, the smell like Dad's new El Camino.

What else is different?

The doors are in. He touches the front one where he stands, looks at the hole where the knob will be but isn't. No hardware yet.

They trade observations for a few moments then—the windows, but those had been in since #7; the carpet, visible next door in #10—when Walt tells him: You know what's different? I am.

Vernon doesn't know if the boy means some specific thing, or everything. Or that he's just realized it or always had, but it is now okay somehow. He knows now he should tell him.

Walt looks around the vast hangar and seems somehow so confident. If the boy had said the same thing months back, when they'd been playing or analyzing the first few half-houses, Vernon can't imagine Walt's voice would've had the same quality. Vernon has to tell him now. He inhales.

Come on to the break room, Walt. I'll buy you a Royal Crown Cola, and a peanut bar.

You see, Walt, I'm different, too, Vernon begins once they're settled.

Albany, 1995

The flurries have become a wet heavy big-flake late-March thing, a mess tomorrow or worse if it freezes overnight, which it will. But we're late winter and can see the end. Sure, we'll get a foot sometimes even in May, but there's hope now at least. I look down at the plans and proposal for the farmhouse addition, and try to focus on what more I could offer. I check messages on the machine and hear my mother's voice, cheerful and earnest, wanting to schedule "an outing, a, what do the kids say, 'hookup'? with Justin, just the two of us if he's willing to be seen with an old lady." I smile and think of how Justin will respond to this, what, date, that his grandmother is inviting. He's much more poised and more thoughtful than I was at his age. I wish my father could've met him.

But after the divorce, my father quickly drank and smoked and overworked and remarried. Not quite in that order. And then three years ago now, his heart gave. While my mother found a person she loves, turns out it was the person inside her. And if you'd seen her then and saw her now you'd swear she'd awakened from a coma. She's like thirteen in a way, like Justin turning to herself, with a family and grandson to live for, but still discovering the person she is. And person she was, even then, inside my father's house. In the upstairs bedroom listening to Jack Slattery on the AM radio or something from Carly Simon, or crying with Carole King that "It's too late."

Vernon and I both probably knew somehow that when we

reached the tenth and last of the half-houses—the one with the roof shingled and the plastic-wrapped open end, and the new-El-Camino smell in the carpeted living room—that we'd reached some kind of end. Vernon of course always had, although I was then, as now, a bit of a slow learner. But that was why I couldn't be there for the last.

It had nothing to do with what he'd revealed at #9. Neither of which was so surprising. Both sad and courageous, and more than thoughtful. But I shouldn't have been surprised.

Ontario County, 1971

Something I didn't tell you, Walt. Not the difference, now. He drags off the Pall Mall, and even pauses for a sip of RC.

The boy sits, munching the Planter's bar, thinking what an eleven-year-old boy in his situation might think. Thoughts like fireflies in July: so valuable, but too many to individually appreciate, blasting off there, then there, and what about those way over there. The boy is a good listener, and patient. Listens, waits.

In this town, and upstate, in these times, my friend, it's tough to be different. You know this.

He watches Walt intently, his face for changes and recognition, understanding.

Here in Sanford, at least, in this time, he tells Walt, a man can't be with another man. That's just too different. Even a grown man, living alone as I did, caused people to watch from a distance and point and talk into their palms as if they were sneezing, to their friends at church or the bank or the IGA. Bless you, I'd sometimes holler.

I've told you of my old friend Jeremy, who died in a war way back. My teammate in high school and closest one, but he didn't understand what we could be together. The times just didn't allow it. And then there was my friend on the construction crew here in the hangar, I've never told you his name and I won't. We were together, and satisfied. But the world today can't handle that, is suspicious. Especially of *satisfied*, do you know what I mean? Didn't you tell me your friend Melanie got asked what are you so happy about? It's like that.

So someone on the crew—again, I won't give a name—complained. And then when called into the factory office, my friend, he told them that my attention was unwanted, inappropriate even. He'd never said so before, but he was afraid for his job. Your father was the one who was assigned to tell me. To terminate me.

I felt betrayed by all sides. I took my last paycheck from him and shook his hand, though I wished I hadn't. Cashed my pay and headed to the track. Drank and bet and won, doubled my check, and then lost it all. I drove home drunk and returned to the apartment, what had been our place, mine and his, until just weeks before.

Ontario County, 1971

The boy sits as ordered, panting from the exertion, his face puffy red. The boy's father, the bigger Walt, studies his son in the kitchen of March lighted by the moon reflecting off snow. Ghostly light, the boy thinks.

His father sips from a glass of syrup-colored liquid, lights a cigarette. Sips again, then asks again *where the hell were you, were you at the factory, how'd you get in?* The boy thinks: he couldn't call it the hangar, that's what Vernon and I call it; he wouldn't know that.

Big Walter sips again and sways against the butcher block, and the boy thinks of seeing him that night with Melanie's mother, stumbling up the steps into the office, the model home.

Then his father says a strange thing, something the boy has no idea where it came from. He asks his son, remember the tall man you met at the plant one Saturday, the old basketball star?

At this little Walt looks up.

Remember when you were in Cleveland with the Grans?

Walt registers then, nearly meets his father's eyes.

Well, I'm sorry to be the one to tell you—he says somehow formally, not fatherly at all. But your tall friend got fired from the company, and after that he went home and he killed himself. Your mother didn't want me to tell you because it might upset you, but I said you were man enough to understand. Like I see you're man enough to be out at all hours on a school night now, aren't you?

* * *

Vernon is thinking he's laid it all out, and has revealed too much at once, has blasted his young friend. Not according to plan, he thinks.

Then Walt's turn to inhale, taking a second to process. Then the boy has a question.

Do they got RC where you're at?

You're talking about *Royal Crown Cola*? Well, yes, Walt. All I could ever want to drink, if I can get to it.

Is Jeremy there?

God I hope so, friend. I'll try and let you know when I get there.

Albany, 1995

Out the office windows, the snow harder, heavier. These big flakes won't last long, can be endured, and maybe there won't be teens tonight as called for. I phone back my mother, thanks, and message that we'll work with the calendar and make the date with Justin happen. Call Ash, tell her I'm on the way. I'd love to get some plan for the clients' addition before I head out, but I know the rural roads are getting worse. I picture the city roads giving way to the country, and while I work in a city I feel like I'm still up there, in the county where I came from.

At thirteen, after the 9th half-house visit with Vernon, I might've somehow known I'd be a no-show for our final meeting. I remember I thought of Puff, and Jackie Paper, and still now I'm near tears. But that missed connection, I tell myself, had nothing to do with what he'd told me at #9, what he'd revealed to me.

On the plan in front of me, I add the modular units I'd been thinking of, the cubes that were so 1970s and so practical and affordable. And handsome, next to an early-20th C. farmhouse. Different.

Deeper snow outside, maybe four inches already, but still, somehow like distant, like in genes, I know this one is not the big, deciding blow. It'll be okay on work and home fronts, and even with Vernon. I lean back and channel him, daydreaming really, and ask him again if they've got RC where he is. If they have Pall Malls. If they have Jeremies. I tell him I need him, that I always did. But more than ever before because of my Justin.

I know, I know, he says in my dream. And yes. They even got Planter's Peanut bars, when did you last see one of them?

I've missed you, I say.

I know, same back.

And I've been thinking about Justin, how you could help if you were willing.

Oh, Justin, yeah. We've met, don't you worry.

And I can see him dragging thoughtfully on his Pall Mall, a little smile not even visible at the left side of his mouth. But he means it.

The plans for the farmhouse addition, the ones I've proposed at least, involve a few small, inexpensive, pre-fab cubes. My father's factory could've rolled them out of their assembly line in days, fully formed. Their foundations of poured concrete, no need to wait for the ground to, if ever, thaw. The units would connect naturally—and as incongruously—as a basket to a backboard. The whole plan is a little bit of embracing tolerance, appreciating the farmhouse of the past and the progressive designs that came after. Put them together, allow them to stand next to each other, and to work with each other. That's my hope.

WHAT THE
SEASONS BRING
Heather Luby

John Marshall, sixty-six and staring down the last corridor of
life, leaned on the dusty tailgate of his pickup. He studied the
FOR SALE sign freshly stabbed into the soil of his property.
His wife Vida placed it in the yard the day before, but he hadn't
agreed to any of it. The fact his grown kids were in Texas didn't
change a thing. A daughter married to a man as bland as khaki
pants. A son he'd stopped caring to understand twenty years ago.
He'd never considered the clay soil and white oaks of his Missouri home would cease to be the landscape of his life and he
wasn't going to consider it now.

And yet, when his mind wrote out the list of reasons to stay, he
knew Vida would find a way to cross off each one. She might have
reasons to stay too, but she only needed one reason to go—grand-
babies. Deep down he knew the only real thing holding him back
was Walt. But what kind of man picks a stranger over his wife and
family? And wasn't that what Walt had become, a stranger?

There was no light yet from his kitchen window and the dirt
of his driveway and the road beyond lay settled. He watched as
the sun painted the land with amber light where it rose from the
ridgeline. He pulled a handkerchief from the pocket of his blue
jeans and wiped his forehead, damp in the heavy summer air.
He pushed himself from the tailgate and walked till he was close
enough to give the sign a good, swift kick from his boot. It fell
forward from the split earth. John flung the sign into the bed of
his pickup, already practicing the words in his head that might
buy him a bit more time.

* * *

John sat at his linoleum kitchen table, a full cup of coffee in
front of him, and his toast turning cold. Vida wiped crumbs from
the kitchen counter and chatted absently of the upcoming Fourth
of July holiday, cataloging which children and grandchildren
would be visiting up from Texas. She sighed in a pretend display
of frustration as she listed all the food she would have to prepare
to satisfy them.

"Johnny always insists I make my chuckwagon beans, but Amanda only likes the macaroni salad, so—"

"Vida," John said. She continued, now pacing with a pen in hand, scribbling in the air as she searched for scratch paper. "Vida," he said again.

"More coffee?"

John shook his head, but she was already bringing the pot.

"Want a bowl of cereal," she asked, nodding to his toast, now soggy with butter. She stood perched and waiting.

"How about you sit down."

She placed the coffee pot on the table and smoothed out her dress before sitting down in the vinyl-covered seats. The deep breath forced through her nose sounding like a complaint. John considered the tired look in her eyes, the hurried way her gray hair was pulled back and nestled in a loose bun. It wasn't hard for him to remember taking thick handfuls of her chestnut hair in his hands, kissing her, right in this very kitchen.

"Well, I'm sittin'," she said.

His practiced words failed him. "We're not selling."

"Now, who said you decide." Vida shot up from her seat.

John held up his hand to her, as if it could halt not just her words, but everything.

"Don't put your hand up to me, mister," she fired back. "I've already listened to all your nonsense."

"You don't have to like my reasons. I've got them and we're not going to discuss it further." John pushed himself up from his own chair and dusted imaginary crumbs from his jeans. He hitched up his belt and arranged himself with an authority he didn't feel, hoping she wouldn't test. "Maybe in a year or two—"

"And then what?" Her voice softened. She stood and walked the coffee pot back to its warmer. She spoke with her back turned, her words preceded with a sigh. "I know he's your friend, but Walt has care now." She turned to face him. "We're your real family."

"Now that ain't fair and you know it." John could feel his color. He hadn't given Walt as a reason to her or anyone, not once, and living in a *rest home* hardly counted as care. "I'm needed here. Maybe not by you, but *you're* not my only obligation."

He knew it was the wrong thing to say, but he turned and walked the worn path down the hallway just the same. The hardwood sloping with age, exhaling with familiar groans under his weight. He grabbed his hat and his keys from their hook. He called back over this shoulder. "I've got to open the store."

His truck kicked a cloud of white dust as it turned onto the highway toward town. He wondered if Vida was watching, standing at the window over the kitchen sink like so many years, but he couldn't risk looking back.

* * *

John parked his red '92 Ford pickup in his usual spot behind the hardware store. It was early yet, but he expected to see a few of his regulars soon, before the heat of the day settled in and made work slow and tiresome. He unlocked the back door and took in the sharp smell of pine and metal. The gritty sound of his footsteps carried through the aisles. He switched on the overhead lights and walked to the front to unlock the door. He almost called out to Walt in the back, like he had for over forty years, but instead he whispered his name.

He wasn't coming back. Everybody knew when you start needing someone to keep tabs so you don't wander off, that's pretty much the end of things. John pictured Walt growing deep lined in the face, sitting in front of a silent TV down at the old folk's home. The damn Old Timers whittling away what was left of his mind. A fate John knew plenty of folks would say was too kind for a man like Walt, as if kindness was something best rationed by the righteous.

For decades Walt occupied the small aluminum desk at the back of John's store, but also a seat at his dinner table and in his john boat. Even now, Walt's office smelled sweet of tobacco and John lingered in the doorway before he sat down in Walt's chair. It was the type of chair that rolled around on casters, and didn't really do much to support your back, but Walt never would replace it. Either the man was too stubborn or too grateful, it was often hard to tell.

He'd kept things how Walt liked them. A Styrofoam cup nearby for spitting, the day's paper folded just right for reading the sports section. The bourbon in the bottom drawer. John pulled it open and let a near full bottle roll into his hand. He held it careful in his lap. He wondered if Walt could still remember why he kept that bottle, if he would remember all the blurry years before he beat the stuff, or any the rest of it. John suspected if a person had to forget the good along with the bad, then it was too high a price to pay for a cheap kind of peace. Hadn't losing his only child been payment enough?

It occurred to him taking the bourbon to Walt might be a way to know how much of his friend's mind remained. If Walt would feel betrayed if he left for Texas, and left him behind. Only way to know was for him and the bottle to pay Walt a visit. The few phone calls he'd made to Wedgewood Gardens to check on Walt's state of mind never garnered him much information, seeing he wasn't family by blood. Nobody seemed to care he was footing the bill.

He locked the store and flipped the dusty sign over to CLOSED. He placed the bottle in the passenger seat next to him and pulled onto Main Street. He tipped his hat toward the sheriff, who was parked as usual at the edge of town hoping to catch an outsider rolling through a stop sign.

* * *

Dressed in his usual jeans and worn western shirt, Walt was sitting in a floral armchair at the window just inside glass front doors. John thought it seemed reckless, putting a man in Walt's condition so close to an exit. He stood in the doorway, holding the bottle of bourbon folded inside a newspaper under his arm. The front desk had one nurse, talking on her cell phone, who waved him in.

He walked past her and sat down across from Walt. He slid the bottle out from the paper and placed it on the small table between them. Walt eyed the settling waves of dark liquid, then looked up at John.

"You're here a bit early today." Walt said.

John wondered if he should play along. If Walt believed he'd been here before, who did he think John was? He was ashamed it'd taken him so long to come, but he'd feared seeing Walt the way he was before, the night he'd brought him to this place. Angry, spit gathering at the corners of his mouth, sure his wife was off with another man and they'd stolen his TV, replacing it with *some Chinese piece of shit* to hide her *goddamn deception.*

It was true Belinda was off with another man, only she'd been married to him for near twenty years, living out in California. John tried to reason with him, but Walt started ripping out his own hair, clawing at his head. When John grabbed him, he realized he was scaring Walt even worse. John was downright terrified himself. The sheriff found them in the bathroom, Walt crying into a wet rag and John gray in the face, trying to doctor the raw spots on Walt's head with shaking hands.

"I's just out and thought I would come sit a spell. You had breakfast?" John asked.

It'd only been a few weeks, but John thought Walt looked thinner. His hair grown shaggy around his ears.

"I did. Biscuits, I think. They do 'em up good here with the sausage gravy I like." Walt cocked his chin and scratched at his days-old whiskers.

"How they been treatin' you here? You like it?" John couldn't help but question a place that didn't give a man the dignity of a proper shave.

Walt raised an eyebrow in suspicion. "How come you ask so many questions? Are you a government man?"

"It's John. John Marshall."

Walt didn't look comforted. "Marshall? I thought I'd warned you to stay away from my Jenny." Walt leaned forward, eyes sparking.

"It's John from the store, where you work." He paused. "We fish together. Every Sunday."

Walt sat back in his chair, but still didn't say a word. John continued, "I brought you some whiskey."

"None of that piss from Tennessee, is it?"

"Wouldn't let it cross my lips. No Sir. Kentucky true here."

* * *

John wanted to see if he would drink the bourbon. He knew it was a cruel thing to do to a sober man, but maybe it would tell him what he needed to know. If the taste of whiskey on Walt's lips didn't bring back what'd he done to his own child, then those memories were gone forever. If they were gone, surely everything else that mattered was gone too. John just wasn't sure which he needed to be true.

"Well, whatdaya waiting for?" Walt's voice was almost too loud. "Ask Jenny in the kitchen if she'll pour it up for us."

"I'll do that. You just sit tight." John stood.

Forgetting things, appointments, names and such, was to be expected. But forgetting his own daughter was dead, forgetting his part in it? John picked up the bottle and placed it under his arm. He left the paper on the table, folded to the sports page.

"Tell Jenny to bring us some of those cookies I like too, she'll know what kind."

John paused, speaking to Walt or maybe himself. "The wafers. You like those little crème wafers. Orange the best."

Outside at his truck, he looked back one last time. Walt, framed in the windows, waiting.

* * *

The house was hot and noisy, full of bodies and laugher or arguments; it was hard to tell. Children ran underfoot hollering after each other, and four dogs were ready to claim even the small-est scrap of food. John was tired. He knew he should be thankful the kids and grandkids came up from Dallas for the fourth of July, but none of it pleased him.

John watched Vida in the kitchen. Her face was a little damp from the heat coming off the stove, but he liked the way it made her cheeks flush. She wiped her hands on her apron and started pulling silverware out of the drawer, calling over her shoulder, "Somebody come make drinks."

The smell of beans and smoked meat was already drawing the voices and bodies closer to the kitchen.

"John, honey," Vida called into the living room. "Can you run out to the garage and get me a bag of ice from the deep freeze?"

John looked around wondering if he should ask one of the younger men to do it. The garage was an old shed his father built when he was just a boy and it sat halfway across their large yard. He could ask John Jr., but Johnny was too busy telling Amanda about some stock purchase he'd made. It galled John to see the man his son had become; a man who always stunk of the booze that drove his wife away. And God knows John didn't feel like asking his son-in-law. Michael might help, but then he would have to talk to him, and that just didn't seem worth the trouble.

Vida poked her head around the corner just as he was about to walk out the back door. "Hurry now, supper's almost up."

In the garage, John pulled the ice from the freezer. When he turned around Amanda was standing in the doorway, her curly hair pulled into a ponytail with a pink ribbon, as if she wasn't a woman of forty.

"Hey Dad, need a hand?"

"Nah, I got this, pumpkin. Ain't too old just yet."

Amanda stepped aside and held the door. She looked like Vida, only her hair was still dark instead of gray. She had always been John's favorite; though it was getting harder over the years to keep up the bond they once had.

"Momma says you're worried about leaving Walt."

"Did she now?" John walked back toward the house. He knew Amanda wanted him to say more, but he wasn't in the mood to argue.

The sun was pulling low and the sound of cicadas was ris-ing in a shrill chorus somewhere in the distance. John could feel the sweat from his forehead slide down into his eyes. Blinking through the sting, John realized he didn't have an appetite. He was too hot to listen to Johnny complain about his ex-wife, too hot to tolerate Michael's regurgitation of the *New York Times*, and too hot to ignore Vida's attempts to deploy the bunch of them against him.

"Why don't you take this on inside. I'll be along in a minute." John handed off the bag of ice to Amanda and turned back toward the garage.

Amanda spoke after him. "Momma said he doesn't remember. Maybe it's the Lord's way of finally giving him some peace after what happened."

John considered his response. What a man can rightly say to his own daughter and still maintain family relations. It occurred to him the whole bunch had been praying for Walt to disappear from their lives for some time. Now it was happening, they each wanted to disguise their impatience as righteous or worse yet, divine intention.

"Won't you get that ice to your momma before it melts."

* * *

John knew where Walt kept his extra house key—under a frog statue, just to the side of the cement porch steps. The damn thing was left by the lady who lived there before. It was frightful in a way, a frog wearing lipstick standing on hind legs, holding a polka dot umbrella.

It didn't feel right being in Walt's place uninvited, but never coming back again didn't feel any better. The air was dead and hung about the room. He caught whiff of something between wet animal and wasted milk and decided to avoid the kitchen, picking a loveseat on the far end of the room instead. He sat down and listened to the clock tick, wondering how Walt had slept with the damn thing making an announcement of every spent second.

The place was a shrine to Jenny. Photos dug out of old shoeboxes and photo albums and then framed with no purpose or plan, arranged in no particular order. It was a wonder his ex-wife Belinda let him keep a single one, but then again, she didn't exactly hang around long. John couldn't recall if she even stepped foot in the place after the funeral.

Headlights fanned their white light across the room. John could hear heavy boot steps coming down the walk. There was a rap at the door before the sheriff pushed it open. John knew Barry was a grown man, but he could only see Barry as the kid Vida caught looking at nudie magazines out in their garage, their own son Johnny denying he had any part in it.

"Out for a drive?" Barry took off his hat in the doorway.

"Something like that." John didn't get up from his seat. "Vida call you?"

"Just to ask if I'd seen you around." Barry said. "Everything alright?"

"How's those kids of yours?" John asked. "Heard Daniel's gonna play varsity next year."

"Kid's built like a damn tank." Barry laughed and then poked his head out the door long enough to spit.

John wanted to like Barry. He'd been a decent enough kid. He kept on with his family and did his part, unlike his own son. But the badge made him a little too self-satisfied for John's liking. Barry stepped in and took a turn about the room picking up odds and ends, fishing trophies and framed pictures, turning them over in his hands and then putting them back, not quite the way they were before.

"You been over to see Walt?" Barry asked.

"I have." John didn't want to offer up more than Barry deserved.

"Don't suppose he'll be coming back here." Barry glanced toward the kitchen and sniffed the sour air. "Might be he could sell this place, if it's cleaned up a bit. Might help pay his way."

"Might could. 'Course he don't own this place. Belinda does."

"No shit." Barry slurped up the juice from his chew. "Somebody call her?"

"Not me."

The sheriff walked a last loop around the room, stopping in front of a picture of Jenny in her cheerleading uniform. "I don't guess I ever understood why he stayed *after*."

"I don't guess you would."

"You always did have a soft spot for that old drunk."

John didn't have a response. There was nothing he could say to this generation of men who didn't understand the definition of loyalty, of sharing the weight of another man's burden.

The sheriff walked back to the door. "I've always wondered how you forgave him." Barry turned his hat over in his hands before putting it back on. "I know Johnny never did."

John stood up, the room suddenly too hot. "I don't reckon Walt ever did anything that needed Johnny's forgiveness and certainly not mine."

"Must be I listen to too much gossip then." The sheriff tipped his hat at the door. "I'll tell Vida you'll be home soon."

* * *

The house was dark when John pulled into the drive. A figure sat on the squat front steps of his house. The sight of his son made a lump of anger rise up in him he didn't know how to beat down. Vida loved their boy deep, right down into her bones, but John didn't know how to grow that sort of love for him. His heart felt starved by his son's inability to take responsibility for his life.

John sat collecting his words before walking across the yard. He saw the glowing tip of a cigarette and smelled the cheap menthol smoke in the air. The tree frogs gave a shrill call.

"You know your momma hates you smoking under her roof." John stopped at the steps.

"Good thing I'm out here then." Johnny drew a long pull from his cigarette.

Neither man made room for the other to pass.

"That was pretty shitty of you today, driving off, leaving momma and us wondering where the hell you went."

"Sometimes a man has responsibilities, but I don't guess you know too much about that."

Johnny stood up. He was a big-shouldered sort of man, passed down from Vida's stock, but still freckled like a boy.

"Jesus, it's always the same with you." Johnny said, mashing his cigarette under his boot. "Whenever you're finished being a self-righteous asshole, you have a dinner plate in the microwave." Johnny turned and walked up the steps.

"Why'd you never tell me you were foolin' with Jenny?" John heard his own voice ask the question—the one he'd been turning in his mind the whole way home—even if he already suspected the answer. "Folks talked then, *after*, but you never said nothing," John said.

It was dark, but John could see his son reach for the door handle, grasp it, then let it go. Johnny turned around to face his father. "I was a kid."

"You were a twenty-year-old man," John said.

"Sure, but I was also a kid who didn't want to give his dad another reason to think he was a fuck-up," Johnny said. "Look how that turned out."

"You don't think telling your part was the right thing? Folks mighta thought differently if they knew what happened."

The porch vibrated with the baritone of boot steps as Johnny crossed back to face his father. He spoke barely above a whisper, but with a tone full of fury.

"Knew what, exactly? That the love of my life had a raging drunk for a father? That he said I wouldn't ever be good enough? That he wasn't going to let me ruin her? That she was sneaking back in her window with my ring on her finger when he shot her?" Johnny's voice trembled. "What exactly would've made folks think differently about ol' Walt? That maybe it *wasn't* an accident or it was supposed to be me?"

"You watch your mouth." John said.

"Or maybe," Johnny said, leaning in, "When it comes to Walt, folks have always known what you refuse to see."

Johnny turned away from him to go inside. In all his years John never raised a finger to wife or child. He knew plenty of times that warranted cause for it, but he liked to think himself better tempered than his own old man. But in the moment, John's hands weren't connected to reason. He took the steps between them in a blink and felt his fist connect with Johnny's back. His son pitched forward, crashing into the front door.

Johnny whipped around, but John was already stumbling backward down the steps and into the yard.

"Jesus Christ!" Johnny came down the steps rough, towering over his father. "Have you lost your damn mind?"

"You never told me!" He tried to stand up, but the pain in his ankle screamed fire up his leg.

"Get the hell up before momma comes out here and finds you like this." Johnny reached a hand out for his father, but John slapped it away.

John felt like his heart was a stabbed balloon. Snot and tears ran into his mouth. "He meant to shoot *you?*" It wasn't a question. John felt the shock of his own words because he faced the truth of them.

"And I bet you wished he had." Johnny whispered.

John felt the cold guilt of not knowing if it was a lie.

The porch light burst on.

"What in the Lord's name is going on out here?" Vida pulled her robe tight over her chest and stepped outside. "One of you'd better answer me."

"Why don't you go make some coffee, Momma."

"Don't you order me around. What's happened here?" Vida gathered her long gray hair in one hand and twisted, still holding her robe closed with the other.

"Nothing," Johnny said.

Johnny reached down and grabbed his father under his arms and hoisted him up. John sank into his son's grip. The bugs were already gathering toward the lights. The sound of their bodies beating against the glass, the hurling force of their destructive desire, was the only sound John could hear.

* * *

The late August sun came up hot. The bleached grass crackled underfoot. John hadn't been able to sleep and left before dawn. It was now past noon. He'd managed to pack up what was left of Walt's belongings from the store and Walt's home, and delivered them to the storage unit he'd rented. All that was left was one more delivery.

John carried a small box out to his truck. He walked with the deliberate steps of a man assembling a map in his mind should he ever need to find his way back. As he drove through town he saw Barry standing outside the grocery, drinking a coke and talking to a woman with copper hair and a tattoo from knee to ankle. The sheriff tipped his hat at John, and he enjoyed ignoring it.

* * *

"Good morning Mr. Marshall."

John nodded hello to the nurse, Delmer Teague's niece if he correctly recalled, and continued down the hallway until he came to the right door. He shifted the box to his hip and gave a little knock. The door was already open.

"Walt, it's John," he called out as he entered.

Walt was sitting in a chair by his only window. John placed the box on a table near the bed. The room was tiny, the bed taking up most of the space, reminding John of the hospital room where his mother died.

"I brought you a few things."

"You did?"

"Thought we might sit a spell and go through them."

"I guess I could tolerate a little company."

John brought the box over and placed it at his feet. He sat down in the only other chair. It seemed inconceivable to him a person's mind could wipe itself clean of so much muck. It seemed as illogical as being washed clean in the blood of Jesus. But maybe it wasn't like that at all. Maybe it was more like the mind just locked up a room and misplaced the key.

"Thought you might like a few pictures of Jenny."

"Did you know she's planning on applying for college? Smart as a tack, my girl. She's gonna get out this here town." Walt slapped his knee as he spoke, as if it was the damndest thing he'd ever heard.

"She sure is something, isn't she?" John gave himself permission to pretend. He pulled a picture of Jenny from the box. She was maybe ten in the photo, a fishing rod in one hand and the other on her hip. He held it up for Walt so they could both look at her, all sunshine and promise.

"Remember the time we took her over to Bull Creek?" Walt began, never taking his eyes from the photo. "We fished all day. Her and Amanda both got some of those Kentucky bass, then she fell right out of that johnboat, takin' the cooler and all." They both chuckled at the memory. "Boy, she was madder than a hornet."

John waited, no longer sure he could play along. Maybe Walt would never have to remember. But now John was left alone with the truth. *It was supposed to be Johnny.*

Walt pulled pictures into his lap, surveying each one with the kind of arrogant nostalgia that comes from being the parent of living child. The two of them sat quiet for a bit. John watched the parking lot, his eyes sparking stars from looking at the reflection of sunlight off the windshields. It was hard to look at Walt now.

"We should go fishing sometime," John lied.

"You think you can get us some of those night crawlers I like?"

"Never did know why you liked them so much."

"They last longer. A bucket of those and you don't have to go home for quite a good while."

Walt's gray hair seemed to sprout from his ears, instead of his head. Someone would need to cut it. He was about to say so when he noticed the pictures slip from Walt's lap onto the floor. There weren't many lucid times left, but John already recognized the change in Walt's expression when they arrived.

"They won't let me go to her grave. They won't take me. They won't let me go." Walt voice was suddenly angry, and his eyes disappeared behind a rush of tears. John wondered if he should get someone, but he was afraid they'd make him leave without getting to say his goodbyes.

"I'll take you," John said. "We'll go right now."

* * *

The only bench in the overgrown cemetery faced a pond skimmed over with algae. Beyond the pond were rows of tract homes. John picked up the bench, one side at a time, and turned it to face the view beside them: a landscape dotted with cylinders of hay. Thunderheads crowded together in the distance. They sat down shoulder to shoulder.

"You'll keep up the flowers for me?" Walt asked.

"New ones every month." John answered, knowing he'd already made the arrangements weeks ago.

"You figure you'll get in much trouble?"

"Nah. I may not be your next of kin, but ain't no judge in these parts gonna hassle me for taking you for a little drive."

"It feels good to be here," Walt said. "Even if it's just for now."

Then, without pause or deliberation, John pulled Walt into his arms and hugged him to his chest. John gripped his best friend beyond the awkwardness, willing himself to make a memory of the moment. Walt hugged him back, but his hold felt slight and wavering, as if he were clutching a stranger in a moment of catastrophe. And maybe he was.

He let Walt go.

They sat and watched the baler in the distance, moving down another row, trying to beat the rain. John took it all in, one the last time. He knew the seasons and what came with them.

THE SEARCH FOR ST. FRANCIS

Lawrence Buentello

Flora woke that morning knowing she was going to die.

She felt strange to know the certainty of death's coming as she lay in the light of the rising sun falling through the cloudy window glass.

Though she was old, old enough to fall under life's shadow even in the vernal months, the intuition was so sudden it seemed more of a warm revelation, and so she wasn't chilled. She felt a subtle exhilaration to know that she would finally be able to lay her mortal burdens down and join the Holy Spirit; perhaps this was a selfish reaction, but she had lived a long, labored life.

She moved to sit on the edge of the bed, setting her feet on the floor, prepared to rise as she had so many times before, on sunny mornings and rainy mornings; but today she knew she was going to die, and it was not enough to greet the morning in an ordinary way.

She breathed deeply as she tried to reconcile her thoughts with the scent of kitchen grease and old perfumes. She combed her dense, gray hair with her fingers while her eyes searched for a tangible artifact to verify her revelation—an angel in the shadows, or a glimpse of the Savior. She waited for a sign of ill health, a cough or pain in her chest more suited to a dying woman.

She did not feel particularly ill, which seemed unnatural to her, but she did not question God's will.

She studied the pine furniture, the bureau and the mirror reflecting her own aged body dressed in an old nightgown, photographs set in tarnished silver frames, and the sullied wallpaper illustrated with Golden Retrievers and fleeing quail. She sensed her mind wandering, as it often did these days; memories as briefly seen as moonlight flashing on fields of corn, or horses grazing in a pasture, or the faces of relatives laughing through scenes of life played long ago. Somehow she could not merge the two in her mind—her great collection of memories, and the supernatural presence of her own death.

Then she realized she was staring at the dogs in the wallpaper, as ageless as they had been forty years before when the room had been redecorated. They stood poised in small patches of grass, their muzzles lifted to the birds in the sky. And then she thought absently, as her fingers ceased their gentle grooming of her hair — *the dogs.*

The unspoken question lingered as she walked to the bathroom to clean her face and change her clothes. Her face asked the question again as she studied herself in the mirror. *Flora*, she thought, *you are alone, and no one will help you with your responsibilities.* Her dentures lay waiting in a glass on the basin, but she left them in the glass, intending to have a soft breakfast. Her wrinkled brown skin and shining white hair seemed all too ready for everlasting sleep, but she knew she wouldn't be able to rest before finalizing her affairs. Not that she had much to consider — she only wished her son would cease his drifter's life and come to her now. But he wouldn't come; she had no idea where he was in the world. He was her only child.

She walked in bare feet to the small kitchen and opened the back door. The warm morning greeted her with bright light, the scent of grass, and the flowers growing below the kitchen window. She stood a moment observing the world beyond her door, a beautiful morning of sunlight and silent trees by the hills beyond the field. She'd lived in the Texas farm country for seventy-five years but still found the dry fields and bent mesquite trees as comforting as she had as a child. Then she found two old pots and swung them together like a poor man's bell, filling the air with the flat sound of ringing metal. She struck the pots together several times, because she knew the older dog was nearly deaf.

As she scrounged the dog food in the cupboard the two dogs ambled up the steps of the back door and entered the kitchen. She turned and smiled. The younger dog, Buster, an off-brown German shepherd with floppy ears, yawned as it stretched, exposing its teeth as its mouth opened and closed. The older dog, Buddy-Boy, a dun-colored mutt with short legs, waddled slowly to her side, its tongue lolling from its muzzle. She'd kept dogs throughout her life, from the time she was a little girl. They were always her best friends and companions. Her husband had died long ago. She lived alone, with only her dogs to keep her company.

"Ándele," she said as she bent to shake the food into the metal dishes by the door. "Eat your breakfast while I'm still alive to give it to you."

She rose, her body protesting the strain of the heavy bag, and returned the bag to the cupboard as the dogs sniffed their bowls and began eating the food. A boy delivered groceries to her every week, paid for by her husband's pension money. She hadn't left the house for months.

She sat at the table, thinking of what she might eat for her own breakfast, but the thought of dying left her without an appetite. When she was dead she would have no more need for earthly things, the taste of food or drink; what would she have for sustenance, if not the blessing of the Lord? But though *she* would have no more need of food or water, what about her dogs? They would still be alive after she was gone from the earth. She wouldn't be alive to strike the pots together any longer to call them to their meals.

"What's to become of you, my beautiful boys," she said, "when I'm taken up? Who will feed you? Who will give you water?"

There was no one else living in the house to feed the dogs, or give them water, or care for them. They had been good dogs, standing by her in the mornings as she cut down the corn, or watching her protectively as she washed her clothes under the summer sun—they deserved to be fed and nurtured, as much as any children left behind. What could she do? She felt as if the shadow of death was moving over her to take her away, but how could she leave her dogs to the harsh countryside?

"I can't die until I find another home for you," she said as she watched the dogs at their bowls. "That would be my only prayer to God. I must find you a new home before He comes to claim my life."

When the dogs were fed, she dressed herself and found an old umbrella to shelter her body from the sun. Several houses stood along the road on which cars seldom passed, some nearer, and some very far away. She didn't know her neighbors well—she'd always kept to herself and her own ways. But now that she was dying she would have to amend her social failings by seeking out her neighbors to see if they would keep her dogs when she was gone. It would be a long walk to the first house, longer to the second, and much further to the next. She wondered if her legs would carry her that far, but she had no other choice.

Before she left the house she searched through the drawers of the bureau and found an old, faded print of St. Francis of Assisi. Vivid colors illustrated the peaceful face of the robed saint as he ministered to birds and beasts. She thought that if he traveled with her some divinity might bless her mission, so she slipped the picture into the pocket of her dress and gathered the umbrella.

* * *

The road beyond the dirt pathway to the house was old and dusty, with wide shoulders overrun by patchy weeds and stones. She moved down the shoulder patiently, held closely in the circular shade of the umbrella, her feet slowly searching for safe passage through the debris. The dogs followed, sometimes venturing toward an interesting scent, before returning dutifully to her side. They raised their heads to her from time to time, perhaps wondering in their own way why their old caretaker was traveling so far from home. The sunlight around her glared brightly from the ground, but it was still cool enough to walk. She didn't know how far she might have to go before finding a home for the dogs.

As she walked along she whispered her rosary, her eyes to the ground, praying for God to give her body enough strength to keep walking down the road.

Presently she raised her head and saw the little house standing on a gray-green rise. She knew a man lived there, but didn't know anything about him. He seemed the kind of man who didn't like strangers, but she couldn't let the fear of being turned away keep her from her mission.

"It's a long way up the hill," she told the dogs. She laughed, and smiled. "Keep me going a little longer, and maybe you'll find a new home."

Already her feet ached, but she kept walking, certain that the pain meant little in the face of impending death.

She walked slowly up the hill, encouraging the dogs to follow, and then paced stiffly from the road to the front door of the small, ill-kept house. She moved up the steps and knocked on the door.

For a moment she thought no one was home, but then she heard footsteps from within, and the door opened onto shadows. An older man stood in the doorway, his bald head catching reflections of the sun, his small, blue eyes staring on her without expression. Dressed in coveralls and a white t-shirt, he straightened as he studied her, his chin tilting slightly.

"What do you want?" he said, his voice heavy with age.

She ignored the fear she felt in her heart and said, "My name is Flora. I live down the road from you."

"Yes," he said, his eyes watching her as a hawk watches a small animal from high in the air. "I know you live down the road. You're the old Mexican woman. What do you want?"

"Death is waiting for me," she said. "But I have two good dogs that still need care. I must find a home for them before I die."

He seemed to absorb this information without understanding it. But then his eyes narrowed, and he shook his head.

"How do you know you're dying?" he asked.

"I know," she replied.

"You're a foolish old woman."

"God told me that He's coming for me."

"You're superstitious. Did your doctor say you were dying?"

"I haven't seen the doctor in years." She glanced upward, as if acknowledging the God he too easily dismissed. "God told me in a dream that I was dying. Now I must find a home for my dogs."

The man stared at her for a moment, then past her to the two dogs lying panting on the dirt in front of the house. His mouth pressed into a tight line, and then he moved past her and walked down the steps of the porch. He stood over the dogs shaking his head. Now fully exposed to the sun, the pale skin of his head gleamed brightly. He turned to the woman again.

"These aren't good dogs," he said. "They're mongrels. Just turn them loose and they'll find their way."

Flora regarded the dogs, then said to the man, "They're not mongrels. They're beautiful dogs. Don't you like dogs?"

"These aren't good dogs. They're no better than strays."

"They need a home."

The man turned away from the dogs and walked back up the steps. He turned from the doorway.

"I don't want your dogs. If you wanted to give away worthless dogs you should have stayed in Mexico."

The old woman straightened against the man's words. "My family is here, in this country," she said. "My home is here, too."

"Well, this is *my* property," the man said. "Take your dogs and leave. You have no business here."

"I'm searching for a home for my dogs. It is a Godly thing that you would do for me."

"You talk about God, but you don't know God. He does for those who do for themselves."

"God wants us to be charitable."

"You're ignorant. I'll bet you couldn't even read the Bible. How could you possibly know God?"

"I know God because He lives in my heart."

The man shook his head. "You're a superstitious Catholic," he said. "You don't know God."

"Please, I need to find a home for my dogs."

"Go away," he said. "Go and die, if you're so certain of it. Go find God that way."

"You're afraid of God," she said. "You're afraid of beautiful things."

"You're a foolish old woman."

"Why do you hate people for who they are? What have I done to you to make you hate me?"

The man said nothing. But she knew what he would say, if he chose to say it.

She stood staring at the man standing in the doorway of the sad, lonely house and then nodded, more to herself than to him.

"May God bless you," she said, "and give you peace."

Again, the man said nothing, but his expression told her of a philosophy free of God's love. This man would never keep her dogs, or care for them as she did. This man was not inspired by any saint. Perhaps he had lived too long in the difficult countryside and had misplaced God's affection. She turned away from the house and began walking toward the road. The dogs rose from their rest and walked alongside her, their tongues lolling in the rising heat.

She walked down the hill and along the road, the shadow of the umbrella's bell doing little to keep the heat away. She wouldn't think of returning home, though, until she found a new home for her dogs.

* * *

After a half hour she raised her head and saw another house standing in a beautiful green swath of grass. She believed a couple lived there, but she couldn't remember for certain. Perhaps they had children who would like to keep her dogs.

"Ándele," she told the two dogs at her feet as she waved her hand. "We still have far to go before we find your new home."

By God's grace, she managed to walk down the long path from the road to the house past several brooding oak trees. The house itself was cheerier, brightly painted, and large, a good house to keep dogs. She stood for a moment before the steps of the porch and removed the picture of St. Francis from her dress. *Please let these be good people,* she thought as she stared at the beatific face. Then she replaced the picture and knocked on the door.

The woman who answered gazed on her as if seeing an apparition. Certainly few strangers arrived at the doors of the houses along the empty road, but perhaps the appearance of an old woman was even more peculiar. Flora stepped back on the porch as the woman moved through the door wiping her small, dark hands on a dish towel meditatively. Her dark eyes were kind, though, her short, curly black hair glistening with the sweat of chores. She seemed nice to Flora, perhaps nice enough to take the dogs.

"Can I help you?" the woman asked.

"I'm Flora," she said, "and I live down the road from you. Death is coming for me, but I have two dogs that still need care. I have to find a home for them before I die."

The woman's hands fell still in the towel. She glanced down the road, perhaps to see from where Flora had come, before regarding the old woman again.

"I'm Marlene," the woman said. "How far did you walk?" "About two miles or so. But it's not a long walk to find a home for my beautiful dogs."

The woman stared past Flora to where Buddy-Boy and Buster lay panting on the grass.

"These are your dogs?"

"Yes."

The woman nodded then and said, "Yes, I remember that an old woman—that you lived down the road. I don't believe we've ever met."

"No, I'm afraid I don't get around much these days. I'm afraid I've been a bad neighbor."

"No, that's all right, it's perfectly understandable. Do you live with someone?"

"No, I live alone." She laughed beneath the umbrella. "If I lived with someone I wouldn't have to find a home for my dogs."

"Are you ill?"

"I'm dying."

"I see." The woman's eyes seemed filled with concern, but she shouldn't have been concerned. "Flora, that was a long way to walk. You must be thirsty. Let me get you some water."

"I'm fine," she said.

"Let me get you some water."

The woman stepped back into the house.

Flora turned to the dogs.

"This may be a good home for you," she said. "This woman seems like a very good woman to me."

When the woman returned she handed the glass of water to Flora, who drank despite saying she wasn't thirsty. She was glad for the water, too. Soon a tall, dark man appeared through the door, very thin, dressed in a blue cotton shirt, jeans, and boots. He stood beside the woman, glanced at the dogs, then stared at Flora.

"Hello," he said. "I'm William. My wife told me one of our neighbors was visiting."

"I'm not really visiting," Flora said as she handed the empty glass to the woman. "I'm on a mission. I must find a home for my dogs."

"If you're not feeling well we should drive you to a doctor."

"I don't need a doctor. A doctor can't keep me from dying, if God has already decided it."

The man and woman glanced at each other, and Flora could see the concern on their faces. She was afraid they were concerned for the wrong reasons; death is frightening to those who are far away from it, at least in their minds. Young people didn't feel death in the air in the same way as the elderly. This was her impression of things, but they needn't be afraid of death, since death was inevitable. This was God's contract with the living, that all things met with life were also met with death.

"You don't have to be worried for me," she said, patting the man's arm. "I'm not afraid of dying. I'm only afraid of leaving my dogs alone."

"Why don't you come inside the house," the woman said, "and we'll talk about it. Maybe we could call someone for you."

Flora thought of her son, so far away and unavailable to her. Still, it was nice of the woman to invite her in. But she wouldn't be distracted from her purpose.

"Will you take my dogs?" she asked the couple. "Will you let them live with you?"

"The dogs aren't my concern," the man said. "You need to think of yourself. You need proper care."

"I've cared for myself all my life. And for these dogs. I only need to see to their future. The Bible says that we should care for those who need our care."

"The Bible says to care for *people*," the woman said, almost meekly. "You need care, not your dogs. We could call someone to come get the dogs for you—"

"No!" Flora drew away from her. "You'll call no one for my dogs! They're my dogs and you have no right!"

"I'm sorry!" the woman said, staring desperately at her husband. "I didn't mean to upset you."

Flora calmed herself, but knew the couple would not give a home to her dogs. They didn't see her beautiful dogs in the same way as she did. They wouldn't be able to offer them the same love as she provided. This realization saddened her, because she thought the man and woman were decent people, but they simply didn't understand her need.

"We must care for the least of us," the old woman said. "I'm sorry, but I must find someone who will love my dogs as I love them. Thank you, anyway."

She turned to leave.

"Let us help you," the woman said, but her husband touched her arm and she fell silent.

"You're not in your right mind," he said, but not angrily. "You can't go wandering all over the countryside because you think you're going to die. It makes no sense. Let me drive you back to your house."

Flora turned. The dogs were already on their feet, staring at her expectantly. "God bless you, both," she said. "I know you mean well, but I don't need you to call anyone for me. I could never take the chance that you wouldn't call someone to take my dogs away. I'll find them a home, a good home."

The man said something more, but the old woman didn't hear his words. He may have been a kind man, but his words had frightened her, and she knew she couldn't stay. She was afraid he might call the county sheriff to take her away. She and the dogs passed the oak trees along the path until they were on the shoulder of the road again. She gazed up at the sky from under the umbrella. The sun shone brightly among the clouds. She stared down the long, dusty road and began walking again.

* * *

She and the dogs traveled a long way without seeing another house. She knew they had walked for miles, but there seemed no promise of meeting anyone else before she grew too tired to continue. She stopped several times for rest and prayer, thinking about her life during these times, and about the dogs. She had always lived a decent life, but knew that even Job had suffered under God and so she didn't expect God's favor. The angry man had been correct when he said that God would grace those who worked for their own blessings. She wouldn't tempt God's grace by succumbing to her weariness.

She walked on, her dogs following loyally beside her, until she raised her head from the sunlight and saw a house in the distance.

She sighed and whistled to the dogs.

"Let's go, my boys," she said. "This may be a home for you."

She walked along the road until she stood beside the mailbox standing by the path to the large frame house, which was painted yellow with white trim; then she turned and moved stalwartly toward it, the dogs matching her pace.

She knocked on the door of the house and after a moment a middle-aged woman opened the door. Her hair was laced with fine silver strands, her dress was modest, but comfortable. Strangely, her expression offered Flora no hint of emotion. Her skin was fair, and the old woman felt as if she were addressing a marble statue.

"Yes?" the woman asked.

"My name is Flora," the old woman said, "and I live down the road a very long way from you. Death is going to take me soon, but I have two dogs that need a home if I'm to die. Do you think you could give them a home?"

"I'm Arlene," the woman said. Her expression remained unchanged. "What are you dying of?"

"I don't know," the old woman answered truthfully. "But I know I'm dying."

"How do you know?"

"God told me so in a dream."

Only now did the woman's expression change—she smiled, but humorlessly. "It was only a dream," she said. "If you haven't been diagnosed by a doctor then you couldn't possibly know you were dying."

"If it was revealed by God's word, then why should I need a doctor to confirm it?"

"Flora, I'm sure it was only a dream."

"Just as I'm sure it was God's word."

"I won't argue with you. I see that it would do no good. But I don't think you're going to die."

Flora wondered why she felt strange in the woman's presence. She didn't understand the feeling, but continued her plea.

"Do you like dogs?" she asked.

The woman, still standing firmly in the doorway, said, "Yes, I do like dogs. Sometimes I like dogs better than people."

"Do you think you could give these dogs a home?"

The woman stared past Flora, glancing only briefly at Buddy-Boy and Buster. She shook her head. "I'm afraid not. I already have a dog."

"They could be company for your dog."

"No, I'm sorry."

Flora had come a long, long way, and was very tired. She knew to turn away from the woman's house meant that she would have to walk even further, or surrender her search altogether. But this woman didn't want her dogs.

"I'm sorry, too," she said sadly. She turned to walk down the steps.

"Flora?"

She turned again. "Yes?"

"You're not dying," the woman said. "You should go home now."

"God has spoken to me. I'm going to die, it doesn't matter what you say."

"It does matter, because God didn't speak to you. It was only a dream you had, not a vision."

"How could you know? Don't you believe in God?"

"No, I don't," the woman said, very calmly, very surely. "I don't believe in God because there *is* no God."

"There *is* a God," Flora said, just as surely. "I'm sorry you don't see Him."

"I'm not sorry, because I'm happy without Him. What good is a God who only tells you that you're dying? And to give up what you love?"

"The will of God is His own. Why should I question it?"

"Because it makes you do foolish things. It makes you believe you're dying. It makes you walk a long way down the road to look for someone to take your dogs because you believe what you perceived in a dream. Don't you see that's true?"

"It's not true," Flora said. "God was kind enough to let me know I was dying so I would have the time to find a home for the dogs I love so much. Why is it so difficult for you to believe that?"

"You're not looking for God's grace," the woman said. "You're looking for the grace of someone who would be kind enough to take your dogs. You should believe in people, not God."

"I'm looking for the God in people. It's God's grace that allows us to do good for one another. And to love dogs no one else would love."

"But you're not asking God to take your dogs. You're asking a person. Don't you see the difference?"

"I'm sorry you don't have God in your life. But please don't try to take God away from me, too."

"I can't take something from you that you never possessed."

"I'm sorry for you," Flora said. "You're a beautiful woman, but you would be more beautiful if you accepted the God inside of you."

"You're asking for *my* grace, not God's."

"But if I have neither, why should it matter if I prefer to feel the loss of God's grace over yours?"

The woman said nothing. Perhaps she was too young to know the determination of an old woman who had nothing but her faith; long ago, when her husband died, she questioned God's decisions to do the things He chose to do, and she lost her faith for many months. But it was only grief that had blinded her to a love that was always present. She soon decided that she would rather believe in God than know there was nothing but indifference in the world, despite all the grief she had experienced in her seventy-five years of life.

Flora turned away from the woman again, and this time the woman failed to call her back with another argument.

* * *

She led the dogs away from the house and onto the road again, but she was so tired, so weary. She didn't understand why God would send her so far from home only to be turned away, time and again. She stood by the road in the blossoming heat, hiding beneath the umbrella's shade, and removed the picture of St. Francis from the pocket of her dress. *I guess this woman may be right*, she thought, *I haven't found God's grace, though I'm far from home.*

The dogs stood by her legs, panting. She stared at them and realized that the three couldn't keep walking indefinitely. They would have to turn back home.

She wanted to cry, but found no tears. She felt forsaken, but knew she couldn't blame God. She would have to believe the same as the woman, that people held no grace above their own human desires. *What should I do?* she asked the image of St. Francis, but, of course, he couldn't reply.

"I don't know what to do," she told the dogs. "God sent me on this mission for you, but I haven't been able to find anyone to take you."

The dogs wagged their tails, listening.

Or perhaps, she thought, staring once again at the picture of the saint, *God sent me on this mission to discover something more.* Death was too much of a luxury—she had found too much comfort in the promise of eternal rest to realize the depth of her responsibilities. These people she had spoken to were telling her as much, whether or not they knew they were speaking for God. She'd been sent on a mission to discover the right person to care for her beautiful dogs, and now she knew who that person must be, and what grace she must sacrifice.

"The world is a hard place," she said to the dogs. "So if no one will care for you, my children, then I will have to stay alive to care for you myself."

In her heart, she knew this was the truth.

She replaced the picture of the beloved St. Francis and turned to face the way from where they'd come.

"Ándele," she said, finding a little more strength in her body. "We have a long way to go."

She passed all the houses again, slowly, heartened by the loveliness of the stark countryside, before finally returning to her own house. She thanked God for the strength to walk all the way back again, and then rested after watering and feeding the dogs. Weary, the dogs lay on the floor of the kitchen and slept.

When night came, and she was dressed again for sleep, she sat on the edge of her bed staring at the Golden Retrievers on the faded wallpaper, afraid of what might await her in the night. But God was good, she was certain; He would call her when the time was right, but only after her beautiful dogs no longer needed her care.

That night she slept with the picture of St. Francis beneath her pillow, and it was a long night, but a good one.

A PRACTICAL WOMAN

Ginny Hall-Apicella

On April 9, 1866 one year to the day since Lee's surrender at Appomattox Courthouse, Margaret Foster, hearing the cow's bellowing and the horse's frantic neighing, hurried to the barn, slid the heavy door open, and saw Abel, her favorite son, dead, and hanging from a joist. She collapsed to her knees.

"Lord God Jesus, no, no!" She screamed and clapped her hands over her ears to ward off the wail of her despair.

Could it have been just months ago that she had glimpsed her boy's slow-footed trudge up the road, past the pasture, and the red-leafed sugar maple? He was not marching but placing one boot grudgingly in front of the next at a reluctant pace. There were no crowds shouting hurrahs, only Margaret, who dropped her pail and splashed through the creek, never-minding the bridge a few yards beyond.

She crushed him to her in an embrace that only a mother, or a lover, was allowed. Pushing him to arms' length, she gave him her full regard. She examined his gaunt face, his full beard. She knew that when he left, a razor had never touched him. His eyes were as empty as his sleeve pinned up to the shoulder of a faded, patched Union jacket. This was not the vigorous, fanciful boy she had hesitantly permitted to leave her for the Second Vermont Volunteers. Margaret had thought it was not their fight but Henry, her husband and the boys' father, had insisted. He banged his fist on the worn, pine table. Both his sons, Isaac and Abel, would fight to keep the Union intact. Yes, indeed, they would rid the country of the abomination of slavery. God would once more hold the union in his sacred palm when the black man was free.

Henry Foster was an abolitionist like his Vermont Congregational neighbors. When Garrett Smith or William Lloyd Garrison came to speak nearby, they jostled to hear him and shout assent. The truth was, most of those farmers had little knowledge of slavery and had scarce seen an African man, woman or child unless they had travelled to Brattleboro or Boston for a new plow or a broadcloth church suit.

While Henry was an abolitionist, Margaret was a practical woman. Who would help Henry with the spring planting if his sons were gone? Who would guide the plow through the hard-scrabble fields? Who would fell the red oaks at Dead Horse Creek?

She and her daughter Lettie might help, but though willing, they lacked the brawn of Isaac and Abel.

"I'll manage," insisted Henry. He might hire one of the Hitchcock or Stoughton boys. Yet those boys volunteered, too, looking for adventure, bugles and admiring female eyes. Mr. Lincoln had asked for ninety days and his boys were just the ones to do it. By autumn, he pronounced, they would be home and all would be well with a house undivided.

What Henry could not have foreseen was that those ninety days would become a three year enlistment or that he himself would be felled, not by a Minnie ball or a horse's hoof, but by a fall ague. Henry coughed, he sweated, his body shook with the chills. Margaret piled him with quilts and placed a mustard plaster to his chest; she supported his head while she poured willow bark tisane down his throat. The fever didn't break. She and Lettie sat bedside applying cool compresses to his brow. Dr. Melbourne shook his head, clucked his tongue, and remarked, "His lungs are bad. Little to be done but wait."

They waited. They prayed. Two weeks later, Margaret, Lettie and Henrietta Hitchcock laid him out on the bed, bathed him, and dressed him in his Sunday suit. George Hitchcock built a pine box and dug a grave by the Norwegian spruce on the hill near where lay the three Foster babies who never reached their first birthday.

* * *

Beyond her cries, Margaret heard the throaty mewling of Maisey and the frantic neighing of the plow horse. Margaret, a capable woman, needed to stop her lament. She needed to get her boy down and bury him proper. She wasn't a woman given to asking for help. She was efficient and determined; she never shirked a duty. First, she must deal with Maisey, a cow hours beyond her milking.

Margaret grabbed the bucket and straddling the milking stool, pulled teat after teat until the cow's bag was empty. Putting the bucket aside for the barn cats to squabble over, she led Maisey out of the stall and to the pasture. Returning to the barn, she approached Samson, the only remaining horse after Margaret was forced to sell Henry's prized Morgans. Samson, spooked, pawed at the stall's boards. He sensed that all was not well. She sidestepped his agitated hooves, removed the halter from the hook, and placed it over his head. She tied a rag over his eyes so he would not see what she had — Abel's dangling corpse — and led him from the barn into the paddock. She pitched a forkful of hay onto the ground. Later, she could give him a feed sack of oats.

Margaret climbed the steps to the hayloft. From closer up, she glanced at Abel's visage: the bulging eyes, the blackened tongue protruding through purple lips. She felt last night's dinner rising in her craw and retched. She clamped a hand over her mouth. No, she would not regard him again. This was her son, the boy who had given her joy with his tricks, the boy who shared her love of lilacs and fried turnips. She would not behold him at his worst but look only at his boots and consider how she would get him down.

She would not allow his body to fall to the hard-packed dirt floor of the barn.

Descending the steep stairs, Margret spied the farm wagon. Hurriedly, she moved the blocks from behind the rear wheels and pushed them aside. She released the break and, using all her strength, pulled the shafts and pushed from behind until she had lined the wagon bed up directly under Abel's hanging body. She engaged the break. His fall must be as gentle as possible. Retrieving the pitchfork, she ascended the stairs to the hayloft and pitched fork after fork of hay into the wagon below. Again, she avoided looking at the silent flag of her son draped from its horizontal pole. She continued until she determined a comfortable bed was fashioned.

Margaret, a sharp-witted woman, wondered how a one-armed man accomplished his own execution. The grain scythe was on the loft floor. He must have tossed the rope over the joist, used the scythe to retrieve it. Tossed and retrieved, again and again until he thought it secure. She had watched him throw a rope over the split rail fence and thought nothing of it. He might have used his good arm, his teeth, and the strength of his knees to make the knot. Then, he'd have slipped the noose over his head and jumped from the loft into the barn's open air. Once again, she felt the rush of vomit rising and choked it back.

She picked up the scythe and cut at the rope above his head. It only sent his body swinging. Considering again, she eyed the rope looped several times over the joist and commenced sawing at it with the scythe. For the good part of an hour, she sawed and hacked cutting through the rope into the wooden beam. When she reckoned that she was almost through, she made certain that the wagon was directly below her boy. With a final thrust of the curved blade she saw Abel fall, like a bird from a nest, to the hay-cushioned cart below.

Looking down, she was thankful that his head had landed

face to the hay though his limbs were akimbo. She rushed from the loft and clambered into the wagon. Margaret tore off her muslin petticoat and swaddled it around Abel's head. When his head was fully enveloped, she tenderly turned his body over, straightened his arms and legs and cradled his head in her lap. She began to croon a lullaby to him. It was the same song she had sung when she had rocked and suckled him as a newborn, swaddled and snug by the fire. Without removing the protective petticoat from his head, she loosed the noose from his neck and flung it to the ground. She lowly keened for her son, now lost to her forever.

She remembered the day he had returned.

"Mama, your son has come home to you," Abel said wrapping a single arm around her shoulders.

"The Lord has answered every bit of my prayers."

"I heard 'bout father but they would not let me leave."

"I knew it. I wrote a letter to your captain but he says that no ways could you be spared. But don't you fret, you're safe home now. I'm as pleased as any mother could be."

"And Isaac? You heard 'bout him?"

Margaret nodded her head turned her face so Abel would not see that tears had sprung up.

"Isaac got took at the Wilderness. Wished it had been me instead."

"Got a letter." She patted the pocket of her apron. "Died at that prisoner camp. Newspapers said they hardly fed 'em. Let our Union boys rot in their own filth. My poor Isaac."

"Damn rebs. You should have seen him at Fredericksburg. No one braver than Isaac."

"Hush now. The war's good and over and you're home."

"They say the war's over but ain't so here." Abel pointed to his arm. "You and father named me wrong. I'm the unablelest man you ever seen."

"I'm not listening to such foolishness. You're still my boy."

"You tell me what's the good of a one-armed farmer." His brown eyes flashed; he kicked a stone at his feet.

"We'll figure out what you can do but now's not that time. Now's time for celebrating that you come back."

His eyes surveyed the field and the kitchen garden, overgrown despite Margaret's efforts.

"Where's Lettie?"

"Lettie? Two winters ago your sister up and went down by Lowell to work in that woolen mill."

"And left you here by yourself?"

"Well, Abel, we'd no money to speak of. Lettie went down

there working her fingers clear to the bone. Every week she sent me a letter and one dollar so's I could keep up the farm. Regular as rain. Then she took up with a patent medicine man. Lettie said there weren't no young men left for marrying in Vermont. I've not heard from her in 'bout a year." Taking the only hand Abel still had, Margret led him toward the house.

Abel fumed and carried on about Lettie's desertion while Margaret took his tattered haversack from his shoulder and sat him by the fire. Though it was past breakfast time, she cooked him red flannel hash with two fired eggs on top, just the way he liked. She gave him the last of the squash pie with this year's maple syrup drizzled on top.

By and by, they found things that Abel could do by himself. He could milk Maisey, one teat at a time until she could give no more. It took twice the time it would have taken Margaret but she let it be. He could scatter feed for the chickens but, as Abel rightly said, that was women's work. He could pick apples from the orchard, but could not turn the screw on the cider press. After the last frost, he could not guide the plow. He could only follow behind Samson and Margaret, and plant the seed potatoes by hand into the freshly tilled furrow. This he had done as a child, he complained. It was not work for a growed-up man.

That was not the worst of it. Abel chose to sleep on a pallet by the fire instead of the bed he had shared with Isaac. From her bed upstairs, Margaret could hear him shout out in his sleep. Most nights he paced back and forth in the kitchen and sometimes she heard him call out his brother's name. Once, when one of the Hitchcock boys was deer hunting, they heard the crack of a rifle. Abel jumped up, knocking over the chair, and crouched warily by the hearth. Other times, Margaret would come upon him with the Springfield cradled under his remaining arm, gun barrel out the window, staring at the tree line.

When visitors came calling, he disappeared. He refused to go to town with Margaret. If he went to town alone, he returned with a bottle. Henrietta Hitchcock remarked that Abel had grown quieter than a church mouse. Margaret did not answer.

At times Margaret saw glimpses of the son she knew when he regaled her with stories about the soldiers he met from far off states or sang her songs he'd learned by campfires. Most of the time though, he avoided her eyes or flinched if she touched his arm. He seemed like a stranger who just had Abel's face. Margaret, a woman who did not ask for help easily, consulted Dr. Melbourne and the Reverend. Neither elixirs nor prayers did Abel much good.

* * *

Now, Margaret must bury her son. She hastened to the house and pulled the quilt from the bed—the one she and Lettie had pieced together four winters ago—and grabbed her sewing basket. Climbing back into the wagon, she fashioned a shroud for Abel and sewed it tight. There would be no pine box for him. She returned to the paddock and led a now calm Samson to the wagon. She backed him into the shafts and fastened the straps and buckles. She stowed a pick and shovel next to her boy's silent, sewed-up corpse and clambered up into the high wagon seat. Snapping the reins on Samson's back, she drove him up the hill to the spruce where near half of her family lay.

Spring arrived early that year and the unfrozen soil yielded to her spade. It took near two hours for Margaret to dig a hole to satisfy her. Then she carefully lifted and dragged her bundled boy and laid him by his father and infant siblings. Looking far up into the branches of the spruce, she wondered if its roots would possess all the Foster clan. She prayed and sang all the hymns she could remember. There was no need to call the Reverend.

Shoveling the dirt back in place took less time. Margaret mounted the wagon's seat and steered Samson back to the barn, unharnessed him and guided him back to his stall. She returned to her kitchen and glanced at the cold fire. Fanning the few live coals, she tossed in more kindling. When the fire rose, she added a hickory log. She took off her muddied boots and rubbed warmth into her half-froze feet. The fire mesmerized Margaret and she sank heavily in her rocker, her body aching with every kind of exhaustion.

One year since Lee's surrender, she thought, and what good had it done? Who won? Not Abel. Not her. She had lost everyone and everything. All her men were dead and her daughter gone missing. It was more than any mother could take in. Her grief was deep and abiding. Margaret wept. She sobbed. She broke.

She slipped from the chair and lay slack and crumbled on the floor by the struggling fire. Weary with grief, she fell into the sleep of the unconsoled. She was once more awakened by the mewling of the cow, left in the pasture too long and in need of a milking. Margaret, a dutiful woman, arose to find Maisey.

HECTOR RAMIREZ

Sean Winn

Philip Nolan looked out his living room's bay window, beyond the patio and well-trimmed lawn, at a sycamore tree standing in his neighbor's yard. It had flushed a range of yellows and was starting to lose the first of its oversized leaves; they occasionally turned loose and drifted down in a sawing pendulum fashion against a crisp blue sky. In their Plano, Texas subdivision, everyone else had builder-standard oaks and elms... two per lot according to the agreement, usually one in the front yard and one in the back, but occasionally both in the back. Philip wondered how the people across the back fence ended up with a sycamore. It had been twelve years since the houses had come up, and the neighborhood was finally starting to take on a mature look. The Cowboys game was on behind him, the sound off due to it being half time, with the Rams ahead by a field goal. The doorbell rang, interrupting his musings.

"Hey, Hector. Come on in." Philip leaned in and pressed hard when he shook Hector's hand, which was more of a calloused paw. He had learned that if he didn't give him a good squeeze back, that his own hand would get crushed. Hector Ramírez's handshakes weren't like those of the bankers and accountants that Philip dealt with at the office. Hector wasn't that tall, but barrel-chested and thick from regular labor. Although Hector was now running three crews doing renovations, he still worked half a day alongside his men in the afternoons. Philip envied Hector for his entrepreneurial spirit. "Heather isn't here. She and Stephanie are off somewhere. I heard something about a big sale, but didn't catch the details." The Ramírezes had moved into the subdivision about the same time that the Nolans had. They lived three streets over, but Philip and Hector had not met until their daughters became friends in junior high school. Stephanie Nolan and Heather Ramírez were now seniors at Plano West Senior High. Initially, the parents chatted at school functions, but after the daughters began having sleep overs and running around together, the Nolans began inviting Hector and Claudia to social gatherings. Philip and Hector became particularly close when the two families went skiing together a couple of years ago. "Is everything okay?" Hector looked serious, not his usual self.

"Cowboys are on, huh? Not quite the team they used to be, but I still love 'em. Ahead or behind?" Hector asked.

"Behind."

"Figures." Hector took a deep breath. "Listen, I wanted to speak with you about something. Do you have time to talk?"

"Sure. Have a seat. Coffee?" Philip clicked off the television as they eased into the couch in the living room.

"No. Thank you. Actually, it's more a favor I have to ask," started Hector. One hand was clenched around the other. "The girls – they are so close, and …" his hands opened and he leaned forward, but he fumbled for the words. "It's …"

"Spit it out, Hector. What's up?"

"I …" Hector coughed. "Well, I have a deportation hearing coming up, and I might get sent back to Mexico. If I lose the case and have to go, then would it be all right if Heather stayed with you for six months until she graduates high school in May?"

"Wow. I mean, yes. I mean – we're happy to help. Heather is practically family, you know. But, back up a minute … what do you mean deported? Even if there is some kind of mess-up with your paperwork, I wouldn't think that they could do that. You've been here for, must be twenty-over years, right?"

"No papers, man," said Hector. His paws spread open in front of him as if there was nothing else to offer.

Philip ran his hand behind his collar, wincing a little as if he were massaging a sore spot on his neck. Most of his friends favored immediate deportation of anyone caught in the country illegally. Questions were starting to trip over one another to get out, but Philip wanted to make his friend comfortable first. "I'd better get us a couple of beers," he said standing up. "You're really not legal?" Hector shook his head. He was solemn given the implications, but offered no apology.

Philip came back with a Sam Adams and a Dos Equis. Philip usually drank wine, but when he did have a beer, it was a Dos Equis. He passed the Sam Adams to Hector and slumped back into the sofa with a thump. Philip kept a few Sam Adams in the fridge as that was Hector's brand – he was over at the house often enough. The irony had occurred to him before, but now it took on a new proportion. He didn't quite know where to begin, and at his first question surprised himself: "So, no accent?" Hector spoke crisply, with only a faint trace that he was not a native speaker.

Hector grunted, a little of the tension coming out of his shoulders. He eased back on the couch, but not really spreading out his mass. He was familiar enough with Philip's politics to know that he was probably not a fan of people being in the country undocumented. "I did at first. Well, actually, I didn't really speak English at all. Broken English a couple years later, still with a heavy accent."

"And then?"

"Well, I bought some tapes. I listened to the nightly news and tried to sound like those guys. Most newscasters don't seem to come from anywhere ... America, right, but you can't really tell which part. I would switch around to the different channels seeing if I could emulate them. Tom Brokaw was my favorite. I read a lot, literature as well as science and sociology to make up for the schooling I missed. I found that I got along better outside the community when I didn't sound like a *bracero*. I had plans for a future, you know, and thought that if I was going to be marketing to *Anglos*, then I would be better received if I sounded like them."

"An undocumented worker..." Philip smiled and shook his head. The term didn't even fit, he thought, given that Hector wasn't a worker, per se, since he employed others. "I never would have guessed."

"You never asked," Hector shrugged, relaxing more now that he could tell from Philip's body language that his status wasn't going to put a knife in their friendship. "It's not the sort of thing you go around telling people. Cheers." The two men clinked their bottles together. Hector took a swig of his beer. "If they do ship me off, I'll miss these," he said, savoring the rich maltiness as it went down and looking at his bottle as if reading the label for the first time.

"Ok. So how did you get here... overstay a visa or something?"

Hector shook his head. "For all the fancy work that you do, interacting with CFO's and all, you can be a little naïve sometimes. I came like everybody else... I swam across the river." River came out more like '*riiiver*', with Hector laying on a heavy Mexican accent for effect. He seemed more himself now.

"Was it as hard? Coming across, I mean."

"Well, I'm not sure what you've heard," Hector began, "but it was damn hard. Getting across the river is easy—its barely more than a puddle in some places—but the long open stretches where you are less likely to get caught can be brutal." He was reflecting. "I guess we weren't exactly well prepared for what we were getting into. We had a gallon jug of water each and a package of Wonder Bread. It is a long stretch across the desert, though, and disorienting when walking at night to avoid the heat and the patrols. We hadn't eaten in nearly three days when we came upon a nest of piglets. Four of us were travelling together: a distant cousin of mine, and two men we had just met. One of the guys managed to grab a piglet, and the other one started to dance a little jig, singing that it was going to be the best bar-b-que that we had ever eaten. That piglet was squealing something fierce." Hector was gazing out the window, but turned back to Philip, leveling his eyes on him. "Now, a wild momma hog isn't just a fierce defender of her babies; they weigh in at over 500 pounds, and are amazingly fast. I started backing away and telling the guy that he had better let that thing go – I was from the country and knew the danger. Maybe he was a city boy and didn't know any better, or maybe the hunger was getting the better of him, but he wouldn't turn loose and tried to muzzle the piglet instead. That's when I heard something crashing through the scrub not more than 10 yards off to my left. She was on him in a flash, his screams drowning out those of the piglet. That sow chewed his ankle to the point of not being able to put any weight on it; it was probably broken. His hand had also been mauled. One finger was missing, and a chunk of flesh was absent from around his jaw where she sank her teeth in before dashing off with her baby. The whole thing was over in seconds, and was a blur given the dim light of a three-quarters moon. The guy, I forget his name, was unable to walk, and we were nearly out of water with miles and miles ahead of us. I'm not proud of it, but we left him there, his cries growing fainter as we put more distance between us." There was a silence, both men processing and reflecting. "If I'm deported, I guess I could go with the *coyotes* again, but it's more dangerous now. More chance of getting mixed up with *narcos*."

"And what year was that?" asked Philip.

"1999. After tariffs were removed under NAFTA, prices tanked when US corn flooded in. Our family had been maize farmers in Chiapas for generations, but prices slid to the point where there was no money left after selling the crop. All around our village, people were giving up... Ever read *Grapes of Wrath?* The late '90's was our Dust Bowl. Like how the Okies went to California, I was one of the thousands trying my hand north of the border. You guys like to think of it as a pull factor ... people coming to the land of opportunity, right? That's true for some, but at that time, it was mostly NAFTA pushing a wave of us."

The men were quiet for a moment. "Damn," Philip finally said. His brow was furrowed, wrestling with some long-held notions on free trade. Not three days ago, a colleague at the office, Bobby, had gone on a rant about how heavily the government was subsidizing midwestern farmers. The guys had had a good chuckle about it. They considered Bobby a little kooky; he was a heavy tea partyer who was prone to the occasional conspiracy theory, but the figures he gave seemed legit. Philip vaguely recalled hearing about problems in the Mexican farm sector years ago, but hadn't connected the dots with domestic policy, and certainly not to immigration. He still felt that his view on enforcement of immigration laws was correct, but it was different when you knew someone personally. Hector wasn't just a statistic. "Damn," Philip said again, staring at the blank TV screen, which had a ghostly faint reflection of the couch. "I could maybe be a character witness for you at the trial. I *will* be a character witness at your trial." He nodded, as much to himself as to Hector. "If you need one, that is. I don't know anyone in the immigration department, but I'll ask around... and of course be a backstop for Heather if worse comes to worse."

"Thank you, Philip." He exhaled, scooting forward onto the edge of the couch and jutting his hand out to shake Philip's. "I appreciate that; I really do." He was speaking quickly now. "Either the courts or the school might also need you to become legal guardian. We're still checking on the details, so I don't know for sure, but would that also be all right? It would automatically fall away on her next birthday."

"Sure... I mean, I need to run it by Alexa, but I think that would be fine." He wasn't as excited as Hector. Philip rubbed the back of his hand that had just been mashed. He knew that Alexa would be all-in, but worried about what his boss would say if word got around the office that he was helping an illegal immigrant. "Like I said, Heather is already practically family." Their wives, Alexa and Claudia, had not bonded as much as Hector and Philip had. They were friendly with each other, but not as close. Claudia did not seem as comfortable around *Anglos*. Some of it was language. She would chit-chat, but if someone told a joke and everyone got the punch line except her, she would become self-conscious and turn quiet. Alexa also suspected that Claudia didn't entirely approve of her outspoken liberal views. Philip and Alexa, for their part, rarely agreed on such things either, joking that there was no point going to the polls since they would just cancel each other's votes out.

"Claudia is also in the same hearing, I take it?" Philip asked. Hector nodded. "And Heather ... a DREAMer?"

"No, she's a citizen, actually. I met Claudia not long after I had come across the border. She was working in a bakery using someone else's social security number. We fell in love straight away. Six months later she was pregnant. Heather was born here, so she is a citizen. Quite a while back I made sure that she had a passport and all her necessary documents. If Claudia and I do get deported, we're hopeful that Heather can sponsor us back in once she is legally an adult."

Philip shook his head. He tucked one foot under the hook of his knee and adjusted his weight on the couch. The leather creaked faintly. "It's a lot to take in. How about your business; what is going to happen with it?" Philip knew from past conversations that Hector had started as a laborer laying tile, but had learned the trade, then framing, carpentry, and even some masonry. Eventually he went out on his own with small jobs he could do by himself. Over time, he developed a network of subcontractors and began taking on more complex work. Despite an eighth-grade education, Hector was sharp and good with numbers. Philip now wondered how many of Hector's workers were in the country legally, and whether they would all lose their jobs if Hector was deported.

"Man, I don't know." Hector shook his head. "Heather doesn't know it yet, but she is about to get a crash course on the contracting business. She is going to have to toughen-up fast. This, I suppose, will be her version of crossing the desert. Hopefully my guys can estimate the time and materials for her, but she is going to have to be the face to the clients. I don't know... I'll do what I can by phone and e-mail from Mexico, but beyond that, I just don't know. Maybe she can keep it afloat until Claudia and I get back. Would you be willing to be an officer of the company? Keep Heather from getting lost in what the bookkeeper puts together, that sort of thing? I don't really trust getting a nominee from a law firm to stand in as a Director, and she might not be able to sign some things until she turns eighteen."

Philip cleared his throat. "No, not an officer." He wasn't about to have his name on company documents if he wasn't 100% sure that everything was on the up and up. Even then, there might be some sort of liability if a guy were to fall off of a roof or shoot his foot with a nail gun. "But I'll answer any questions that she has, of course. I don't really know anything about construction, so not sure if I could add much, anyway." He hoped that wasn't part of Hector's survival strategy for the company.

"Yeah, no problem. Yeah." Hector was conscious of having overstepped. As grateful as he was for the help with his daughter, he was very worried about his business, and the family's finances collapsing along with it. Both men took a sip of beer, conscious of the ramifications.

"The girls," Philip began. "They are making applications to the same schools and are quite excited about—"

But Hector cut him off, waiving his hands. "No, no, no. There won't be any college if the business falls apart. It's as simple as that. I know she has been dreaming of college, especially ones that have old buildings with statues in front of them, tangle-headed professors in tweed jackets, and all that. But the fact is, the money for all that comes from the business, and if it's gone, then college is gone."

Philip was taken aback. Hector had his arms crossed and his brow furrowed again. He had always been so doting on his little girl. Philip didn't dare suggest that scholarships could bridge the finances and still make the ivy league possible. He cleared his throat again. "Get you another beer?" Philip certainly needed one.

"No. No, if you are okay with the arrangement, I want to start organizing a stack of information for Heather. I won't start the discussion with her until you and Alexa have had a chance to sit together and decide for sure. If you don't mind, though, text or call me once you have talked it over. Heather doesn't know about the arrest yet—or the hearing—I wanted to make sure she had a home before dropping it on her. It might be a long night; she'll have a lot to absorb."

* * *

"Hey, got a minute?" Philip slipped into Gerald's office. It was one of those glass fish tank types that surrounded an open floor plan to let in light and give the illusion of general transparency. Philip had worked for him for three years. Gerald was a rising star in the organization, and had an ego to match. Philip had been hoping to call in sick on the day of Hector's hearing, but that was going to be a problem now. "Look, I'm not going to be able to make that meeting tomorrow," Philip began.

Gerald was gathering up some papers and slipping his phone in his pocket. "Didn't you hear the speech I just gave on the floor? Gotta be there."

"Look, I've got a thing. I just can't make it tomorrow. I'll be in early Thursday and can get up to speed on how it went, and—"

"What could possibly be more important than the shit-show that has blown up with our biggest client?" Gerald looked at his watch. "I have to be on the fourteenth floor, then get downtown. We'll talk tomorrow."

Philip was in the door, blocking Gerald's exit. He didn't move to let him pass, which raised Gerald's eyebrows, but stopped his forward progress. "I'm just letting you know. I have something tomorrow that I can't cancel. I'm sorry, but I'll do what I can to prep the others, then catch up on Thursday."

Gerald squared his hips and leaned forward a little, his lips narrowing into a wry smile. He was not used to being challenged, but relished the occasional chance to make it known that 'mine-is-bigger-than-yours.' "Philip." He paused for effect. "I want you at that meeting. This is an all-hands meeting with our biggest client. That means all-hands. You know the ultimatum that they've given us. We're in crisis mode—got it? Unless it is your mother's funeral, be there." Gerald's smile got bigger, having located his scapegoat. Now he half-hoped that Philip wouldn't show up for the meeting. "If you're not there and they walk, then it's hanging on you." He brushed by Philip out the door. "I'm late."

* * *

A streaked grey sky hovered overhead as they splashed through puddles pulling into the parking lot. Climbing down from the Ford F-150, the wind hit them. Winter had settled in and a front was moving through. "*Estamos aquí?*" asked Claudia.

The location of the trial did not impress Hector either. He assumed the trial would be at the courthouse. As he pictured it, there would be a formal seating gallery with the judge on an elevated mahogany podium behind a carved, hip-high divider that the bailiff would respectfully open when it was his turn to come forward for his case. At least that was how things were on TV. Due to the high volume of removal cases, though, part of the Immigration Court was operating out of an annex building, a nondescript concrete box miles from downtown that revealed no effort at landscaping or design. There were four-foot high address numbers in black affixed to the scruffy white background of the building. It could just as easily have been the offices of a materials supply company or a medical office building past its prime.

Philip's car pulled up behind theirs. Stepping out, his shoes narrowly missed a pool of slushy mud. Stephanie buried her hands in her pockets and dashed over to Heather's side. Philip waved and clicked his key; *boop-boop* went the Mercedes with a blink of the lights before making his way towards the family. He pulled a scarf around his neck and buttoned his suit about him as he approached the truck. Hector had wondered whether Philip testifying would help or hurt his cause, given that Philip more or less helped his clients evade taxes by putting together overly complicated structures that exploited loopholes and grey areas in the tax codes. In a letter-of-the-law sense, Philip simply

helped them to legally 'avoid' taxes, but in a spirit-of-the-law approach, Hector felt that it was pretty clearly 'evading' taxes. As he
understood it, every few years, the tax authorities would cotton
on to a scheme and attack it, at which point the accounting firm
that Philip worked for would get to bill their clients more to help
them defend the structures that they had cooked up for them in
the first place. Hector found that whole corner of the industry
unethical, but he was cutting corners on taxes too, so didn't want
to be a hypocrite. He had decided that the judge was unlikely to
get into the details of Philip's career anyway. More probable was
that the judge would just note that a big shot professional was a
genuine friend, prepared to take in his daughter if need be. Hector didn't judge Philip too much for what he did for a living, but
he did wonder if Philip saw his job for what it really was. Mostly,
though, he was just grateful for him being here.

Other than the small Department of Justice seal affixed as a
plaque next to the door, there would be no way of knowing that
you were in the right place. *Qui pro domina justita sequitur* was
written in Latin along the bottom of the seal. Hector snorted; *that
is just plain pretentious*, he thought. Inside was a long, stark corridor reflecting fluorescent light that came from drop-down ceiling
squares that had noticeable brown patches showing like nicotine
stains. Sound bounced indistinctly off the hard tile floors and
bare walls. It wasn't exactly chaos, but the hallway buzzed with
activity. Lawyers were herding groups of people, mostly of Hector's complexion, with a tense quickness into some rooms, while
other groups exited at intervals. Those exiting moved much more
slowly. Most had long faces, but occasionally there were hoots
of elation as soon as a group came out one of the doors flank-
ing the hallway. Others just confused as more technical explanations were translated into Spanish for cousins and *abuelas*. "But
I thought he said that we could stay," a woman of about sixty
implored in Spanish, her beaming round face lengthening as her
smile melted, her wrinkles changing direction as with a shifting
water current.

"219. This is our chamber. Better get comfortable," said Hector's lawyer. "Could be fifteen minutes, or it could be more than
a couple of hours before they call us." The lawyer was younger
than he was, but was highly regarded, having come up through
MEChA and LULAC before becoming a partner in a private practice. As lawyers charged by the hour, though, Hector hadn't really gotten to know him, preferring not to have chit chat on the
timeclock. Hector tried to look confident. The nicest suits in the
building that he had seen so far were his lawyer's and Philip's. He

hoped that that was an indicator of better odds than the rest of the masses around him. Hector motioned for his wife to take the end of a bench next to another family, while he sighed and sat down on the floor with his back against the wall, arms propped on his knees. A few feet away, Stephanie squeezed Heather's hand and told her that everything was going to work out fine. Heather's head was up, though, and her shoulders square. Heather made a slow turn, surveying the corridor with sharp, dark eyes, arms somewhat akimbo on her hips. *Good,* thought Hector, *she's not cracking. She's forming opinions, weighing things.* Earlier he had noticed her comforting her mom rather than clinging to her. He followed his daughter's eye: the clusters of people outside the various rooms had the look of cattle in holding pens, waiting to be run through the chute to the auctioneer.

Philip pulled over a metal folding chair over beside Hector. "I've been meaning to ask you – so how do you think they caught you?"

Hector picked a piece of lint off of his slacks. "Don't know," he said. "Could have been a competitor. I wouldn't put it past that Eddie Nunez; he made a pass at trying to hire away some of my guys not two weeks after I was served papers. Or it could have just been a misguided Trumpy who can't see that I'm hiring Americans ... not that my *entire* payroll goes to citizens." He looked up and winked. "But still. I'm good for the economy and I've never had so much as a traffic ticket in all these years. It's really good of you to be here, by the way."

"No problem. I didn't have anything that was so important that it couldn't wait."

"Docket numbers 9264-D, 3486-S, next in cue!" It was the mousy haired clerk with the shirt two sizes too large for his Adam's-appled neck who periodically popped out of the room to announce how things were progressing inside. He looked like he wore his father's shirt.

"That's us. Game face, Hector," said the lawyer.

Hector, Claudia, and their lawyer settled in behind a desk facing the judge while Philip, Stephanie, and Heather filed into seats in the front row of chairs directly behind them. Hector turned around and gave a smile to Heather, noting again that she looked particularly strong today, quickly becoming a woman. "Thanks for everything, Philip." He then turned back around, breathed deeply, and patted Claudia on the leg.

"In the removal case of Hector Ramírez, file number 9264-D, and Claudia Ramírez, file number 3486-S," began the judge before reading out the specific charges. She had grey and black streaked hair, pulled back to reveal an olive-toned Italian face. She read from an open manila folder held not quite at arm's length as an adjustment to focus the text for aging eyes. Her glasses were square-ish, and would have been condescendingly too far down her nose if she hadn't still squinted a little. There was no animosity in her voice, which was strong and clear, but which also belied a certain boredom in having read out similar charges for probably the twentieth time that day. Laying down her glasses, she looked at the defense table, business-like, with a slight puckering of her lips as she paused to survey the family. "Mr. Ramírez, you first. How do you plead?"

Hector still couldn't get over how non-binary the situation was. With so many layers of issues, he felt that to frame it as a yes/no question defied logic.

"Not guilty, Your Honor."

THE BABY JESUS IN PHNOM PENH

Nim Stevens

1970
The Mickey Finn

"Ah, bạn của tôi," said the waitress. "Đây không phải là thời điểm tốt để cho bạn uống. Mama-san muốn tất cả tiền của bạn tối nay." *Ah, my friend. This is not a good time for nursing your drink. Mama-san wants all of your money tonight.* The diminutive Asian pitched her voice so only the big-boned American at her side could hear. Her skinny legs hanging from the bar stool looked grubbier than usual tonight.

He spoke back in the same private tone. "We're out of here tomorrow."

The young soldier did not understand Vietnamese and the waitress spoke no English but this did not hamper their conversation. Jake sat on his favorite stool with his favorite gal, not looking too closely at the staff as they scurried in and out. He was the only customer and without a crowd to absorb the light the room seemed brighter, more hectic. Even the vermin were restless; dark corners rustled with activity.

Though the visibility did not flatter the hard-used building, the GI was determined to have a good time. He had to say goodbye and he had to get drunk. That was tradition. He had long known how to sneak back into the barracks so he didn't worry that technically he was considered AWOL. He acknowledged that he was a fully owned component of the US Army and that wither they goeth so goeth he, but not before he said farewell and not before taking enough ethanol to make his teeth numb. He drank with intent.

"I'll miss this place," he said. "Except for the rain. And the bugs. And the smoke and guys shooting at me from hiding." He tipped his waitress and bartender, then raised his bottle. "Here's to Vietnam."

As the air-con struggled to remove the scent of torched foliage the beer began its buzz through Jake's cranium. The waitress spoke.

"Thật không may là bạn đã đến trong đêm nay," she said.

"Việt Cộng đã tăng lên và bị giấu trong các đường hầm. Họ đã không chờ đợi khởi hành của bạn." *It is unfortunate that you came in tonight. The Viet Cong have increased and are hidden in the tunnels. They have not awaited your departure.*

He understood one word only in the spate of melodious sound. Viet Cong. He nodded wisely.

The CO had given specific orders in these last days, forbidding army personnel to leave the base. That worthy had not explained his reasoning to the grunts but the rumor mill filled in the rest. Viet Cong already held the town but would wait patiently and without hostility for the base to dismantle, biding their time until the choppers and tanks moved out before beginning the heavy work of mining the locals for information and supplies. The American troops were happy to play dumb and make nice. The killing would resume soon enough.

Jake, though, had always despised gossip and his comrades respected his sensitivity. No one had explained to him the dangers of the transitional period and this was why he had the bar to himself tonight.

The big farm-boy looked at his little companion fondly. She reminded him of his sister when she was a baby, except, of course, that his sister was a big redhead that could fit four of these Vietnamese girls into her dress. But in spirit. They both had that cynical sparkle covering vigilant concern. He missed his sister.

The waitress let him talk for a while, listening politely until it was her turn, then spilled incomprehensible sounds into the pause.

"Nơi này sẽ không còn nữa. Cô đã không mong đợi kinh doanh nhưng ở đây bạn. Các túi của bạn sẽ trống rỗng khi bạn rời đi." *This place is to be no more. She did not expect business but here you are. Your pockets will be empty when you leave.*

She looked warmly on the big soldier. He reminded her of her little brother. Except for coloring and size, of course, and the fact that her brother was now dead. But still… He had the same foolish honesty and innocence that made her want to defend him. She knew she would fail, though. Again.

"The thing is." Jake had reached that level of inebriation that made repetition seem the very essence of profundity. "The thing is, I've enjoyed getting to know you gals, even Mama-San over there." He turned to face the door where a heavily mascaraed woman regarded the two from her throne. Jake smiled and waved. She showed him her black teeth. He returned his attention to the little girl at his side.

The waitress was not a little girl but a widowed mother who'd sent her children deep into Cambodia to keep them safe. With the farm burned and the men fighting or dead she stayed behind to fool the Viet Cong and make money for her remaining family.

Mama-San made peremptory nods and eye movements. Her patience had reached an end.

The waitress obeyed her employer's cryptic instructions and intruded on the soldier's monologue with a blatant sexual advance, making sure Mama-San could see. She expanded her chest until her nearly flat breasts jutted their nipples at Jake.

"Fucky fucky?" she said loudly. "Thôi cậu bé lớn, chúng ta hãy lấy tiền đó đi bạn." *Come on big boy, let's get that cash off you.*

Jake laughed and patted the top of her head before returning to his beer. He liked girls and he liked sex but he could never put his dick into one of these china dolls. He knew bigger seven-year-olds.

The waitress sighed as Mama-san gave a nod. The bartender doctored a beer with something white from an envelope before sliding it to the gormless private. Jake lifted the cold one in appreciation and looked into his little friend's eyes. They had transformed from glittering, black stars to fatigued, dark pools. He could almost make out her irises.

He emptied the beer in one long pull, suddenly saddened by the company. "You Baby-San sweetie," he said, then threw a salute and about-faced to the door. The spin continued in his brain long after it finished in his body but the waitress was there to help him. She guided him outside before he toppled.

In the dark she helped two men pull him from the path. One of the men wore stolen American boots and kicked Jake viciously in the temple before stripping him of his money and clothes. The waitress watched impassively but in her secret heart she spat in the booted man's face. He was already unconscious! She returned indoors as the men pulled the big blond deeper into the dark.

Behind the Bar

Jake's head hurt and his stomach roiled. Above him light swirled in the blackness, mists in moonlight. The sight made him sick. He rolled to his stomach before spewing green liquid, then turned his head and snuggled to sleep in the warm puddle.

Jake's head hurt and his stomach roiled. There was something wet under his face. It smelt awful. He rose to his hands and knees but the nausea came again and he heaved and heaved but nothing came out. Devastated, tears welling at his inability to vomit properly, a small sob escaped that split his head wide open. He slewed forward. His face hit the dirt with a splash. Fresh jungle dirt. It smelled good.

There was a snail. It warbled and weaved, waving its antennae, green and beige and moist. It looked to be the size of an apple so Jake stretched out to toss it away before it slimed up his face but he could not reach it. Gently, he closed his eyes. He tried to die there, alone, but his usefulness was not at an end. Fierce men argued nearby.

"Anh ấy chết rồi à?" *Is he dead?*

"Anh ta không thể tìm thấy ở đây." *He can't be found here.*

"Bán đứng anh ta. Anh ta biết những thứ quân sự, phải không?" *Sell him. He knows military things, no?*

Children called and he heard the hiss of water on hot metal, then helicopters and the smell of diesel. The Marines? The Army! The soldiers were small and brown but it was an army, there in the jungle, and they took him away and brought him somewhere dry.

To the Brig

The dry place jounced and rattled and Jake concentrated on holding his head together. It was split open, he knew, but if he could keep the pieces. The air, if possible, grew thicker. He awakened from dreams of drowning to find he was not underwater but needed his full attention to draw the wet steam in and out of his lungs. The air was green, he saw it bouncing through a small opening in a canvas flap. When his hunger for air was sated unconsciousness returned; the next time he awoke the air was black and not as wet, though his dry place had become a sodden lump of padding beneath him. Straps held him on a bench as the jeep trounced and hurled deeper into the Cambodian hills.

At last the bumping stopped. Small strong men removed his straps and took him to a new bench. It was dry.

* * *

"Cái gì thế này?" *What is this?*

A hard man with black eyes pointed at Jake with disdain. Jake heard a familiar voice and Mama-San's face rose like a harvest moon over the hard man's shoulder.

"Bạn cung cấp tiền cho người cung cấp thông tin," she said. "Anh ta là quân đội Mỹ. Hãy cho tôi tiền của tôi." *You give money for informants. He is American Army. Give me my money.*

"Tại sao đầu cậu lại băng bó?" *Why is his head bandaged?* The man turned to Jake. "What is your name?" he said in heavily accented English.

Jake stared into the man's eyes and opened his mouth. He wanted to ask the man to repeat what he'd said but could not form words. He and the black-eyed man looked expectantly at each other until Jake, exhausted, closed his eyes.

Jake's new captor turned to Mama-San. "Người đàn ông này có vết thương ở đầu. Anh ấy không thể nói, anh ấy không có ích gì với tôi." *This man has a head wound. He can't talk, he's no use to me.*

"Anh ta chỉ mệt mỏi thôi." she replied. "Hãy cho tôi tiền, bây giờ." *He is tired only. Give me money, now.*

The hard man lifted Jake's head by the hair then dropped it in disgust. The persistent ring of a gong took Jake far from the argument. When he awoke he was alone.

There was food and water and he ate and drank but threw it all up. His only visitor was Mama-San's friend who spoke to him in atrocious English and in Vietnamese but Jake, though his power of speech had returned, did not know the answers to the man's questions. He knew nothing of military plans or deployment of troops.

He slept, and when he woke it was to nauseating agony from his head. Jake worried when he was conscious but that was rare.

"Oh God, get me out of here."

The Visitation

There was no direct connection between the spectral visitors and Jake's ongoing projectile vomiting but thirst had become the center of his being, with a broken skull and abdominal pain as secondary considerations. So, in the dream-like logic of a closed head injury, he hoped the visions meant he would no longer puke everything he swallowed.

The first to arrive, because of geographic nearness (as the others later explained), was The Buddha. Buddha manifested as the handsome young Siddhartha, seated in the lotus position, a water blossom in one graceful hand. He appeared near the wall of the cell, but, receiving no reaction from the wounded man on the cot, floated closer and handed over the flower.

"All things occur and the Buddhahead says: Watch as the wheel rolls," he said.

Jake stared as the blossom fell from his powerless hand. "What happened to the waitress?"

"No one saves us but ourselves." A tiny frown appeared on Siddhartha's tranquil face. "No one can and no one may. We ourselves must walk the path." He cast a covert glance at the gold Rolex on his left wrist, then tried a new tack.

"All wrongdoing arises because of mind. If mind is transformed can wrong-doing remain?"

He spoke English but Jake didn't understand. His broken head must be getting worse.

The Gautama drew breath to produce further gems of understanding but his discourse was interrupted by the arrival of the Prophet Mohammed and the Baby Jesus, wrangling for position in the cramped room. After some elbowing they settled down in metal folding chairs, one on either side of Jake's cot while Buddha floated in the full lotus, his back straight, his face serene.

"The merchant of shoddy product must find an early stall at the market," Mohammed muttered, glancing askance at Siddhartha. The Prophet dressed in snowy robes that accentuated his dark hair and eyes.

"Sorry I'm late," said Baby Jesus. "I was in Italy when I got the call. Took a few minutes."

"And I was in Mecca," said Mohammed.

Jesus took the floor. "I understand you're in a bit of a bind," he said. "You called out to God but you're not registered in any religion so…"

"Buddhism," cut in Siddhartha, "is not a religion, it is a philosophy…"

"Yes, yes," said the Prophet M., "but the boy is eager to barter. If this is not to your liking…" Mohammed indicated the door. Buddha responded with a resplendent halo that illuminated the dark cell.

The Baby Jesus, fresh from a visit with The Pope, appeared as a chubby blond boy of four, eyes of purest blue with golden ringlets of hair tumbling about his head. A good Cuban cigar appeared in his cherubic hand and he puffed it into life. After regarding the burning end he turned his considerable charisma on Jake. "Are you a church-going man?" he asked.

Jake swung his legs out of the bed, causing the celestial presences to scatter. Head down, the young man settled in a sitting position, staring intently at the filthy floor. Knives of pain stabbed his brain. Maybe now I can hold down some water, he thought. With shaking hands he poured and drank thirstily, then stared into a corner, waiting for his gorge to rise. The water stayed down.

The avatars reshuffled in haste to be in Jake's view in the new position. The seated deities pulled their chairs to face the mark but Buddha forced himself between them by the simple expedient of floating in front of them, blocking their view. They moved their chairs to either side.

All of this activity made Jake dizzy. Bracing his hands carefully on his knees, he raised his head and ejected a stream of water. Siddhartha, having seated himself nearly in the boy's lap, received the full load. He purified himself with a pass but not before the Prophet and the Christ Child made suspicious choking noises, their eyes rising into happy curves. It was some moments before gravitas resumed.

Jake sank back on his cot, frustrated. He was, he suspected, actually dying of thirst.

"Why are you here?" he asked.

The Prophet spoke. His hooded black eyes captured Jake's. "You cried out in your pain," he said. "You cried to God that you were ready to take up your spiritual duties, needing only divine guidance to begin."

"I said all that?"

"You paraphrased," admitted Buddha. "We," he gestured with his hand at the three of them, "have come to present the benefits of our faiths."

And so began the lessons, though Jake did not hear much of the discourses that followed. Mohammed pulled at a bubbling hookah, Baby Jesus smoked his cigar and Buddha sullenly cast attar of rose in an attempt to purify the air. As the waters of life deserted the farm-boy the Prophet Mohammed explained the five pillars of Islam, Siddhartha the light in every soul, and Jesus the forgiveness that knows no bounds.

The words washed over the dying man like a purling brook. He remembered the violent silence of the Great Plains buried in blizzard, the razor clarity of being hunted by ruthless enemies through a hundred shades of green. Little beauties and wonders alternated with trials and catastrophes as he lulled his spirit out of the stinking hut. He did not hear when the speaking stopped.

The heavenly visitors gazed down at their non-responsive audience.

"He's really sick," said Jesus.

"You think?" said the Buddha. "He needs medical help."

Jesus rose and grew in stature and soon the strong young carpenter in homespun gown approached the fading boy. Radiance swelled, the room filled with the Light of the World. The Christ reached out his hand...

But was rudely pulled back. The other two deities would have none of it.

"No, no," said Buddha, shaking a finger.

"No fair," said The Prophet.

They laid hands on the Fisher of Men, restraining him from his errand of mercy. Jesus struggled against them and it nearly came to blows but the Great Ones heard the pounding of boots and shrank into invisibility.

"I saw a light," said a voice from without. "Check to see if there's anyone left." They spoke English, better yet, American, and the voices of his countrymen pulled Jake toward consciousness as they battered down the door to his lockup.

The Other Waitress

A year later in an Arkansas diner, Jake sat at the counter, drinking a preliminary coffee. The air was cool and dry. The smells of bacon and fried potato evoked sad remorse in the former soldier. The powerful emotions of head trauma were not yet under Jake's control, though he did manage to adopt a manly grimace which halted the sentimental tears before they spilled down his face. He missed the wet jungle which had been his home for three long years. He missed Vietnam.

When the Diplomatic Services, dressed in khaki and heavily armed, discovered him in the jungle hut, some argued he should be executed forthwith. Those brave men had been rescuing people for months and the continuous demands of triage had left their moral compasses severely battered. Why save a man so near death, a man who may, in the hands of the enemy, have disclosed state secrets? His pitiful condition may have swayed them; at any rate room was found for the kid in the increasingly overloaded helicopters.

The Army found it prudent to hold off on a general court martial until Jake's return to health. By then investigation showed that the clueless soldier wasn't privy to any great secrets nor did he have the acuity to sell them. He had clearly consorted with the Vietnamese, some of whom were probably the enemy, but as this was true of the entire military presence in Asia no man-hours were spared to prepare a case. He was shipped back to the States for his long, slow recovery, grateful to be alive.

He'd been unable to explain why he'd been found deep behind enemy lines at the start of a major military movement. Jake's clearest memory of the period surrounding his skull fracture, excepting the pain and nausea, was of the heavenly visitants in the jungle hut. He spoke of them at great length for a while but was finally convinced by his psychiatric team to shut up on that subject.

* * *

The waitress returned to take his order. His eyes traveled to the girl's neck and she flushed, thinking the pale young man was admiring her modestly draped form. He was not. What caught his attention was a little gold cross hanging in her suprasternal notch. It fascinated him and he couldn't tear his eyes away until a whiff of smoke distracted him.

Sitting in a booth at the window were a strange trio: a huge Oriental, a brooding Arab, and a blond toddler who appeared to be smoking a cigar. Jake knew this was the hallucinations again and guiltily turned his attention to the menu. He gave his order, trying hard not to look at anything.

* * *

"He fancies her," said Siddhartha. Today he appeared as the fat Buddha, laughing and drunk and no respecter of dietary restrictions. At the moment, however, he did not laugh or enjoy his grits and red-eye gravy. His lips made a tight line.

The Prophet turned to Jesus in righteous wrath. "This is not an even playing field."

"Are you calling me a cheater?" The Christ Child narrowed his sky-blue eyes and used his cigar as a pointer. "Let's not forget we found him in a Cambodian POW camp. Who had the home advantage then?"

The two Prophets of the Book looked at The Laughing Buddha. He continued eating ham and eggs, his expression now radiating tranquil blamelessness. Jesus raised his dimpled shoulders in a shrug. "It could have gone either way."

"Peh." Mohammed sat straight and tall, his fervor burning with desert-heat. "Why did I attend this summit? Islam sweeps up nations entire. I have no need of this one confused soul."

Buddha and The Christ gave him a look. The first Muslim had the grace to look abashed but their arguing was attracting attention so the threesome faded into a cobwebbed corner, watching Jake closely as they continued their infinite bickering.

* * *

Jake had recovered from his lapse, helped along by the waitress who began telling him the latest jokes. He didn't understand at first and it took him awhile to smile, let alone laugh, but his face eventually cracked open and he guessed his happiness wasn't too hysterical. She kept swinging by with her coffee pot.

She reminded him of that other waitress in Vietnam although her green irises were clearly distinguishable from her pupils. But the sharp edge and the warm heart and the fierce loyalty were the same. He liked her. He tried to get her phone number. She wouldn't give it but did manage to let him know which church she visited on Sundays and that was good enough. He'd just have to go find her there.

THE NO WAY WAY

Marjorie E. Brody

"No way."

"Way."

"No way."

"Way."

Molly put her hands over her ears. "Stop it, you two."

"But I really did it," Ben said. "I went to McMurdock's backyard and walked in their cemetery."

A slight breeze rustled the leaves on the maple trees bordering the street. The setting sun made the trees' shadows twitch on the sidewalk.

Charlie stopped walking and crossed his arms over his chest. "No. Way. You'd be dead if you *really* did it. Or you'd come away messed up in the head, like that Harris kid or that crazy Kaufman guy."

Ben shrugged. "Believe me or not. I know what I did. I know what I saw."

Charlie stuck out his chin. "Oh yeah. So what did you see, Brave Guy?"

Ben stared directly into Charlie's eyes. "Why, I saw…"

He hesitated a beat. "I saw…"

He hesitated two beats. "*Him*. Dead Mr. McMurdock."

Molly gasped.

"Yup," Ben continued. "Old Murdering Murdy McMurdock himself. Walking around those grave stones like he owned the place. Like he controlled the dead the same way he controlled the living."

"Did he see *you*?" Molly asked.

"Molly!" Charlie pointed to Ben. "You don't believe this faker, do you?"

"I don't know yet," she said in her most adult voice. "Depends on what he tells us."

Ben shrugged. "Why should I tell you guys anything? You aren't going to believe me." He waved to something behind Charlie and Molly. "Would they, Mr. McMurdock?"

Charlie and Molly spun around. Molly threw a hand over her heart.

"Ha," Charlie said. "There's nothing there." He turned back to Ben. "You think you're such hot stuff. Well, we don't believe you for one second."

Molly breathed in quick little breaths. She didn't turn back to the boys.

"Come on, Molly," Charlie said, "there's nothing to see 'cause he's a big liar. Big, fat, humungus—Hue. Mong. Gus.—liar. Wait till the boys at school find out who's trying to be a hot shot by telling freaky, untrue," he rolled his eyes, "Murdering Murdy McMurdock stories."

Molly turned around slowly, almost hypnotically. Her face expressionless.

Ben ignored Charlie. "Did you see him, Molly?"

Molly's bottom lip quivered. "Y-y-yes. I saw him."

Charlie's chin dropped and his mouth dangled open. "What! How could you? There's no one there." He looked over his shoulder and panned the area. He glared at Ben. "You've got to be proud of yourself, scaring a girl with your lies."

Ben's left shoulder yanked back as if shoved and he lifted his head to look up. "What do you want, Mr. McMurdock?" He waited a moment, listening to something, then shook his head. "But he's my friend. In fact, Charlie is my *best* guy friend. I couldn't do that to him. No way."

Charlie looked from Ben to the space that held Ben's attention to Molly who seemed to be watching Ben and McMurdock chatting with each other.

Suddenly, she cried out, "No, you can't make him do that. Ben couldn't hurt a fly. Don't make him—"

She whipped around to Charlie, her wide eyes full of fear.

"Charlie," she whispered, her voice high and breathy. She raised her hand in front of her chest and gave him a private back-off flick.

Charlie took a mini-step backwards. And another.

Just as he raised his leg to sneak a third step, Molly shouted, "Run, Charlie. Run!"

Charlie did a one-eighty and fled down the street, his terrified scream trailing him.

Ben moseyed up to Molly and they silently watched Charlie's escape. The sun had disappeared and only a streak of orange remained in the ink blue sky.

Molly gave Ben a coy smile.

He nodded ever so slightly, took her hand and walked with her to the movies.

ELSIE "PEACHES" BOULWARE, AGE 69

Jon Tuttle

Devoted wife of legendary coach Sonny "Bullwhip" Boulware, who in his 27 years at the helm led the Allenville Armadillos to three lower-state championships and was twice named Class 2A Coach of the Year. Died Tuesday, February 12, at home, of causes unknown.

Born in Esterville on May 1, 1950, to Mr. and Mrs. Archie "Hog Head" Snook and attended the Chains of Faith Christian School for Unruly Girls in Polk County, where she made a good account of herself in knitting and spelling. When she was sixteen she met her beloved husband Sonny Boulware, All-District starting outside linebacker for the Paulding High School Fightin' Catfish and three-time varsity letterman, when they danced together at a dance. She was plump but enthusiastic, and long story short they got married three months later and stayed that way for 53 years for better or worse.

She is survived by her beloved husband, Sonny "Bullwhip" Boulware, who was born in Coweta on December 7, 1945, the day that will live in infamy, and their six daughters, Emmylou, Dolly, Crystal, Loretta, Patsy and Tammy, who if they're reading this should know their mother missed them every day and cried and cried and probably would have forgave them but it's too late now. Also she had two brothers, Baxter and Dexter, who are long haul truckers and they have their own bait shop on Pollard's Pond and also played high school football, though neither one was All-District.

She is predeceased by their first baby boy that died of a miscarriage just two months after they got married, which she also cried and cried. That baby is buried up at Hope Springs Eternal Cemetery and she visited his grave every Sunday until things got so she wouldn't leave the house anymore and where she will soon lay beside him in her eternal repose with her savior Jesus Christ. His name was Lil Bub. Also her parents are dead and her uncle Tommy "Chunk" Snook, a fine fisherman who choked on a sandwich before his time.

Soon after that her beloved husband went to fight the communists in Vietnam, but his tour got cut short when he got injured so bad in the Dak To province they said he'd never have any more children, but he proved them wrong by having six baby girls in a row, who maybe God might forgive but he won't. To this day he cannot mention the horrors of war, like stepping on a bouncing-Betty one night on patrol, surrounded by Charleys in the rain and covered in mud and blood and all around him there was screaming, except at the VFW on Tuesday nights. He got awarded the Purple Heart, which he proudly wears at the VFW on Tuesday nights and on his suitcoat every Sunday to church and shows it to all the Cub Scouts, but which he will pin it on Peaches this Saturday as she lays in her coffin in his favorite yellow dress, because she was so proud that day she drove him to the recruiting office and she got so sad he was gone she just cried and cried and could hardly write him any letters she said.

Most folks think she was called Peaches because she was from Georgia, but she wasn't, she was from Esterville, which is in South Carolina between Pomaria and Whitmire. She was called Peaches because she loved her peach brandy so much, and also peach vodka and peach rum, until her husband had to put an end to it after an incident at the PTA. And her hair was light orange like a peach and her cheeks were round like a peach and her arms were kind of furry so she kind of looked like a peach. He is called Bullwhip.

After the war, Bullwhip took a job coaching the JV team at the General T.A. "Boots" Mauldin Middle School and teaching auto mechanics until he worked his way up to head coach at Allenville, where he won three lower-state 2A championships and coached thirty-seven players who got college scholarships despite playing in the worst cinder block stadium anyone ever saw, including Javier Bustos, a great big Mexican boy who used to come over and mow the lawn every Tuesday night while coach was at the VFW, until he got drafted by the Steelers and played four years defensive end though he wasn't a starter. His number 99 got retired at Allenville and Peaches cried and cried when he went away. He was like the son she never had if you don't count Lil Bub.

Coach still remembers that day he won his first lower state championship and the Armadillos all carried him around on the their shoulders and Javier Bustos squirting his Gatorade all over and the band played "That's The Way Uh Huh Uh Huh," and he looked up in the stands where Peaches always sat way up on the top row, all bundled up and sipping on her Hot Peach Jubilee she called it. And he waved his fist and she waved hers back so hard she almost fell over, it was the best day of her life. So that's how he's going to remember her, sitting up there waving her fist, admiring her husband coaching those young men out there crashing into each other like stock cars filled with pride and love.

She is also survived by her black cat Delilah. She kept lots of black cats, for reasons unknown. Some ran away or got carried off by hawks, but the rest are buried in the back and she visited them a lot too until she stopped going out of the house.

No woman's perfect but she came close as she could and Bullwhip forgave her the rest. She loved little children and tried to run a daycare out of the home but that didn't pan out after the incident at the PTA. And sometimes she'd knit him something but it was way too small. And sometimes she said some things she didn't really mean, like at night, when she and Delilah sat there on her couch with all the lights turned out. But she was a good cook and studied her gospel three times a week with Pastor Ricky Tabor while Coach was out at football practice. When he got home she was always singing the hymns to herself.

The funeral will be this Saturday, February 15, at ten o'clock at Grendel Free Will Baptist Church. Memorials can be donated to the Coach Sonny "Bullwhip" Boulware Stadium Fund at his home at the far end of Dog Leg Road, which is the first left after the old Shell station on Highway 207.

Coach Sonny "Bullwhip" Boulware appreciates the many kindnesses of his friends and neighbors as he gets a grip on this great tragedy but wants everybody to know he's a strong man with a good forgiving heart and he's still in reasonably good shape for a decorated veteran and has a bass boat and respectable retirement account squirreled away and is generally agreeable to eat just about anything and can tolerate a cat.

THIS KIND OF HEARTBREAK

Kathryn Brackett

W hen Debra came out to work Monday morning, she gasped at the dead man slumped over the wheel of her silver, two-door BMW. Small rivulets of sweat ran from his temples to his pallid left cheek, stopping at the thick excess of a splotchy neck squeezed into a tight collar of a coat that looked too small. One freckled hand lay inches from the ignition wires, the other grazing the tip of a crowbar in his lap. Debra stepped back, caught her heel on a buried sprinkler head, called 911, and eight minutes later Officer Jim Caldwell was asking questions on her lawn, ducking his head in and out of the car window.

She gripped the passenger side door for balance, trying to look like she wasn't about to fall to pieces as the officer leaned into the backseat. "What's in these baskets back here?"

Debra's heart was thumping in her ears. She could barely breathe.

Officer Caldwell jerked upright. "Ma'am, are you okay?"

She swallowed. "I feel a little queasy."

"You want some water? I've got some in the car."

"No," she sputtered, "but thank you."

"You cold? I got a blanket in there too."

"No." She hadn't needed a coat this morning. The weather was tricky in South Carolina sometimes, and she'd been walking around coatless in October for the last few days.

Officer Caldwell pulled tissue from his pocket. "You wanna cry?"

She blinked at him.

"I'm sorry," he said gently."You look very emotional, completely normal in a situation like this."

"How long have you been doing this? You know, telling people what they look like, offering water and blankets, and tissue?" Her voice was light, comical in a bizarre way.

"Twenty-three years." Something about his lingering stare made her feel more comfortable. He was about her age, late forties, tall and sinewy, with a trimmed goatee sprinkled black and gray, much like his short hair. Suddenly she realized she was attracted to this man, an awkward moment to make this assessment.

Debra shifted her eyes to the dead body, and that's when her stomach twisted a little more. "What do you think happened to him?"

"Probably a heart attack."

"How long do you think he's been there?"

"Judging from the rigor mortis in his limbs, I'd say three or four hours."

She shivered.

"You always park outside the garage?"

"Yeah. There's a lot of stuff in there."

"You didn't hear your alarm go off?"

"I did, but I thought it was someone else's and the noise only lasted for a few seconds."

"Yeah, because he disabled it." He glanced at the front door of her house. "You live alone?"

"Is there anything else I need to do?" Debra asked quickly.

"I need information off your license."

She hunted in her purse, handing him the card. He glanced at it. "Bradley. Any relationship to Steve Bradley? The defense attorney?"

Debra swiveled her finger around the empty space where her ring finger used to be. "He's my ex-husband. You know him?"

"Not really. I was filling in for a buddy one time at the courthouse during one of your ex-husband's cases. He was intense, really knew how to hustle." Debra didn't respond to this accurate judgment of Steve's character. "One more thing," he added. "Tell me what the baskets are for in the backseat."

"Oh, they're just for work. I own a specialty shop downtown where I arrange cheer packages for people. I was going to deliver them this morning." They were neatly wrapped and stuffed with well-preserved cheese, crackers, candy bars, small toiletries, motivational books, and musical selections. Each one held a strong red bow in its center. Her heart fell. Should she throw them away now? What customer wanted a package when a man had died near it?

Debra rolled her eyes over the scene of the crime again. The smallest details resonated now: the car was a sporty coupe, 6 Series, full package, but there was a triangular dent in the door now and gritty brown mud on her mat. Then, as if suddenly placed there, she saw the gold band on the dead man's pudgy left finger. He had a wife, and now that wife was a widow. Before she could stop it, her morning breakfast rushed up her throat and flew out onto the lawn. Yellow, gooey egg chunks lay inches from her feet. Embarrassed, Debra shielded her face as Officer Caldwell hurried over with a rag. He wrapped an arm around her waist, guided her to the house, up the steps and into the living room, where he assured her, with utmost confidence, that she would feel better.

* * *

But that was a lie, because as the hours ticked on so did the drama in her front yard. More inquisitive policemen and the coroner arrived. They roped off the scene, dusted her car for prints, working around the dead man's body as gently as a newborn's. EMS made lines on her lawn with the wheels of the gurney. A reporter anchored herself in front of the window where Debra had planted herself. She yanked the curtains closed then peeked out the side of them. Later Officer Caldwell knocked on the door with her cheer packages stuffed in his arms. "We need to take these as evidence, and your car."

Debra tightened her hand around the doorknob. "I don't think I want the packages back."

"Are you sure? There's some good stuff in here." He had a cute, goofy grin on his face.

"I just don't know what I want right now. Can I think about it?" And when she considered the car, an anniversary gift from Steve seven years ago, long before the affair, she wondered how she'd ever get behind the wheel again knowing someone had died behind it.

"Tell you what," Officer Caldwell said, "how about I keep these for you until in the morning. You can come down to the station and get them, or I can bring them back."

"Okay," she said, "I'll let you know."

He smiled at her then went back to his duties. A wrecker pulled up and took her car. People slipped away one by one from her yard. After the house was hers again, Debra busied herself by washing dishes and organizing one of her closets. That's where she came across an old sweatshirt of Steve's. Many of his things were abandoned in the house. They'd been divorced for two months, and since the separation, the idea of Steve had hardened in her gut. He'd traded their lavish six bedroom home for a downtown condo with Karla, a gangly bottle-blonde in her early thirties who worked as a stenographer at the courthouse. He told Debra about the affair three months after it started and moved out shortly after. His leaving was a painful stab to the chest and Debra just knew she'd never stop bleeding. She'd seen Karla once, at the courthouse when she was paying taxes. Debra half expected a rueful glance from the woman or even a shameful drop of the head but all she got was smug body language as Karla traipsed off down the hall with her shoulders held high. Debra had driven straight home and burned some of Steve's clothes, and one of his favorite running trophies. It seemed like the safest thing to do since setting him on fire would send her to prison for the rest of her life. As she watched the trophy melt and distort, she wanted to see Karla's face do that; the bitch wasn't even all that pretty, at least not by Debra's standards. Her ass was flat, she didn't have any boobs, and the lower half of her body seemed like it would never see the slightest hump of hips, total opposite features of Debra's curvy figure that still turned heads. People often said how pretty her brown curls were too, how her smile lit up a room, so how had all those admirations stopped resonating with Steve? How had their marriage dried up after twenty years? The questions still plagued her.

Truth be told though, sometimes Debra was glad he was gone, particularly when she sifted through her pantry to see items arranged out of alphabetical order, something that would have driven Steve up the wall, and oh, the dental floss, that damn, damn dental floss that he slid between his teeth after the smallest snack. They never had enough floss in the medicine cabinet. Despite these peculiarities, he had been her husband, and she loved the idea of being married. There was something about that fluid connection with another person that made her feel whole. And now she was half the person she used to be.

Not long after Steve left, Debra picked up a self-help book about grief and learned that many people felt like the end of a relationship was similar to losing a loved one in death, something she knew very well. Steve had been there when her parents passed away; her girlfriends had been there too. Those same girlfriends supported her when she told them about the affair, and Debra knew they'd be there now if she just picked up the phone and called them, but she didn't want to discuss the attempted robbery any more than she'd wanted to talk about the sadness she'd felt when her husband chose another woman over her. The grief was still a hook in her heart that she couldn't get out, and now as she thought about her car and the cheer packages in the backseat, she remembered the one she'd sent Steve and his new girlfriend right after he moved in with her. It was loaded with large jawbreakers, black licorice, sour candy worms, violent horror movies, two pair of brass knuckles, and a whip she found in a novelty shop. Debra had arranged all the items in black shrink wrap, topping it with an eye-popping red bow, her signature style. Then she scribbled a note that read: "May these things comfort you in your time of insanity."

She wept hard after she mailed the package though. She cried for months, in fact, wondering if the faucet inside her would ever twist off to let her breathe again. At times she still felt this way and knew she needed to move on. She missed having a partner, someone to come home to after a tiring day, someone to hold her. True companionship. Natural things.

Debra tucked Steve's sweatshirt back where she found it then picked up her address book, flicking her gaze over customers' names. Her passion for helping others started in college, when she worked as an assistant for Meals on Wheels. Eventually she started her own business, naming it Cheer Packages Galore. That was eighteen years ago. Since then her hard work had expanded beyond South Carolina into Georgia and Tennessee. The best part of her job was watching her clients' moods turn on a dime when she delivered a package. Steve had understood this and used to make deliveries with her until his own career excelled. He made partner in the law firm, and eventually that success led to more stress between them. Some nights he was so ornery that Debra didn't want anything to do with him. She'd lie in bed with sour tears glued to her eyeballs while he grumbled on his side, but how could she be with him when he was so disgruntled all the time? Though they hadn't spoken in months now, part of her wanted to call him. The silence in the house was palpable, crawling up her back like a mysterious insect.

The afternoon and evening dragged on, and Debra watched reruns until she eventually fell asleep on the couch. At 3 a.m., she bolted upright from a noise upstairs. Scrambling off the couch, she clutched a high heel, the only sharp thing nearby, and surreptitiously roamed every room until her paranoia ran out. But she didn't get back to sleep.

* * *

Debra waited for a cab the following morning. She'd called Officer Caldwell to set a time to collect the baskets. He said he could bring them to her, but she needed to get out of the house. Her phone buzzed. She glanced at the text. One of her girlfriends had seen the news that morning and wanted to make sure she was okay. Like she'd done with her other friends, she lied and said she was fine.

Debra scrutinized the perimeter of the house suspiciously, as if waiting for someone or something to jump out at her. Perfect green hedges sat like army officials around a regally built brick home that she and Steve had purchased together shortly after they married. Every room had a theme: a fitness room, a game room, a relaxation room, their bedroom, where Debra remembered making love with Steve countless times. Even now she could feel his fingers on her thighs. She took in a sharp breath, pushed it out, saw it swivel around her mouth. It was cold, very different from yesterday. Autumn leaves swept up in a brisk wind, and Debra huddled into her coat, wondering why she was waiting for this damn cab outside. Nothing she did anymore made any sense.

Finally the car pulled into her driveway with a white-bearded black man behind the wheel. A cautious expression spread through his thick glasses as she slid into the backseat. He adjusted the rearview mirror, finding her eyes then nodded in the direction of her house. "This your place?"

"Yeah," she answered slowly.

"It ain't haunted, is it?"

Something heavy sank low inside her chest.

"I saw what happened here on the news this morning."

"So does that mean you're not going to give me a ride?"

He faltered with a response, and jagged, unrestrained tears attacked Debra's eyes. She tried to wipe them away quickly, but they rushed over her lashes beyond control. The man cursed under his breath, opened the glove compartment, and handed her Kleenex. "I've been driving people around for thirty years and I've never made anyone cry. I'm sorry." When she didn't take it, he added, "It's clean."

More tears leaked through her eyes as she grinned and dabbed at her face. "What's your name?"

"Roku."

"Thanks for the tissue, Roku."

He nodded and backed out of the driveway. Not far from the house, she noticed a photo of a toddler paper-clipped to his sun visor. "Who's that pretty girl?"

Roku's shoulders bounced happily. "My baby, Amelia. Ain't she sweet?"

"She sure is."

He chuckled as he tugged his grey beard. "Amelia was a surprise. Our first and only."

"I know all about surprises," she said sarcastically.

"You got kids?"

Debra shook her head. She couldn't have children and Steve hadn't wanted to adopt so they'd gotten comfortable with the idea of it being just the two of them, but now it was just her. Roku talked about his daughter the entire way to the police station. He seemed like a good-natured soul, and Debra loved the way he spoke about his child.

When he finally stopped talking, she said, "If you'll just wait on me, I won't be long."

"I have to keep the meter running."

"That's fine." Then she thought of something. "Do you own this cab?"

"Yes, ma'am."

"I won't have transportation for a while and I need to make deliveries, run errands this week, maybe longer. Could you drive me around?" She had plenty of people who could deliver her packages; she could even use one of the company vans, but she was a little afraid to drive right now. Her focus was off.

Roku kept a steady grip on the wheel. "If you paying me, ma'am, I'll be wherever you want me to be."

"I'll pay twice what I owe you. Will that help?"

His brow furrowed. "You serious?"

She'd never been more serious in her life. "I need your help."

A huge smile cracked open his face. "Okay, we got a deal then."

She shook his hand then entered the station and found Officer Caldwell hunched over a stack of files at his desk, bearing down hard on a pencil. His head popped up at the sound of her voice, and a gracious smile flushed his cheeks. "Mrs. Bradley. Good morning."

"Please call me Debra."

"Only if you call me Jim." He pulled out a chair for her, stopping inches from his own before sitting down. "Can I get you some coffee?"

"I'm fine, thanks." She looked around the small space, not sure what to say. Finally, he said, "So, the man in your car was named Frank Williams."

"What do you know about him?"

"He worked at a boxing plant in Boiling Springs, spent about eight months in jail last year when he stole a Mercedes in Greenville County. He's also been caught up in a few smash and grabs."

"How did he die?"

"Definitely a heart attack. His wife, Regina, identified his body yesterday." He sighed. "It took a hellava long time to stop her from crying."

Debra's throat tightened. "What does she do?"

Jim leafed through a nearby folder. "She's a waitress at a diner."

"Is she a criminal too?"

"Nope. Clean record. Seemed pretty nice."

"Any children?"

"Twin boys, seniors in high school." He looked at her. "Frank's obviously been doing this for a long time. His luck just ran out on you."

Debra placed a hand over her mouth. Jim instantly held up a dented trashcan. "Are you going to be sick again?"

A laugh rippled up her throat, and the worry in Jim's eyes dissipated. He excused himself and came back with a bottle of water. She unscrewed the top, and a thought ran through her mind as she drank. "Can you give me Regina's number and address so I can pay my condolences?"

Jim stopped short. "Huh?"

"It just seems like the right thing to do."

A crinkle lifted on his brow. "Mr. Williams tried to steal *your* car. You got that, right?"

Oh, she got that, all right, and part of her was furious at being put in this situation. This man had died in a car she loved; what he'd done was gross, unnatural, and terrible; yet, in spite of that, she felt pity for him, and for his family. She couldn't ignore that innate quality of her personality but God knows she wanted to. "I know it's weird," she said, "but comforting people is what I do. I need to speak to his wife. I can relate to her loss, somewhat."

Jim rubbed the back of his neck, his face caught in a decision. "I can't give out his information." His eyes jumped around the room. "But nowadays you can find anything online, and you can look in the *phonebook*, especially for digits that begin with 5-7-8."

Debra reached out and squeezed his hand. It was large and warm, safe. "I appreciate your help."

Dark red circles filled his cheeks as his gaze deepened. "You're welcome."

She glanced at her watch. "I need to go, so do you have my baskets?"

"That depends, are you going to trash them? 'Cus there's some stuff in there I could use."

She chuckled. "No, I decided to keep them. Besides it's not like the man died on them." Her voice trembled.

Jim gave her an understanding nod. "Debra, I know this is a difficult situation, but I get the feeling that you're a very strong woman. You'll get through this. Plus, you've got a nice car. I'm just glad he didn't take it." She almost wished Frank had; maybe he'd still have his life but then she'd have another set of problems on her hands.

"Keep the car as long as you need to," she confessed.

"You can get it back today if you want."

"To be honest, I'm not ready to drive it. Give me a little while, okay?"

Jim arched his brow. "Okay."

He disappeared around the corner, returning with the baskets. He trailed her to the cab and placed them on the backseat as Roku peeped over his shoulder at him. Then he handed her his card. "My cell number's on the back, in case you ever get in a jam."

She told him thank you then got inside the cab and instructed Roku on where to go next.

* * *

There were twelve Frank Williams in the phonebook, but only four began with 5-7-8. The first three calls didn't pan out and the fourth just rang. She tried that one the rest of the week, and even looked for an obituary in the newspaper but didn't find one. Then, on Tuesday, a little after a week since the incident, a young boy answered the phone.

"Is Regina there?" she asked nervously.

"She ain't home."

Debra's heart thudded. "Are you her son?"

"Her nephew. Wanna leave a message?"

Breath skidded into her throat. "I'll just call back." She hung up, stared at the phone then cursed herself. What the hell was wrong with her? All she had to do was leave a message. But why was she even calling this woman in the first place? It was stupid. She fixed a glass of brandy and gulped it down. After three more drinks, a fierce buzz pulled her down to her knees in the middle of the kitchen, and she just started sobbing. Oh, God, she hated alcohol. But it wasn't that. Something in her was shifting, stirring up old memories, forcing her to face demons she'd been running from a long time.

Anxiety haunted her the rest of the week, even as she made her deliveries. On Saturday, Roku took her to Lizzy's house. A longtime customer, Lizzy was a sharp-tongued ninety-year-old lady who lived alone and was proud of it. Debra admired Lizzy's independence, wishing she was as comfortable in her own life, because lately, especially since the botched robbery, her nights were mangled with restless sleep. Sometimes, even after setting the house alarm, she slid furniture in front of the doors. She triple checked the locks and made sure to keep a loaded gun in the nightstand. Before bed each night, she prayed she'd never have to use it because God only knew where those bullets would go.

Debra had a lot of nightmares now too. She'd see Frank's contorted chapped lips hanging over the steering wheel, the wrinkled patch of skin over his eyelids. These awful visions swept into her mind now as Roku parked alongside Lizzy's curb. Debra undid the woman's package and tore into a Snickers bar, munching it like it was popcorn just handed to her. Then she made the package look pretty again, dismissing Roku's curious stare, and slid out of the car as she cradled the basket up the walkway. Lizzy's Victorian house had bright red steps and a wraparound white porch. Debra heard a creaking noise, a familiar sound, up ahead. She followed it to the backyard, finding Lizzy sunk low in a rocking chair, dressed in a down feather coat, green sweats, purple socks, and white tennis shoes. Her legs were skinny and carefully stretched out before her.

She turned her head from the pond. "You're late."

"Sorry. I had a lot of deliveries this morning. Been a little backed up."

"And how is that my problem?"

Debra edged closer, holding her tongue. This woman was a bitch sometimes, and she knew it. Debra forced a smile on her face. The wind whipped it away, and she twisted up her face as the season rolled off her neck.

"You ain't got enough clothes on," Lizzy spat.

"I thought it'd be warmer today." She gave the woman her package. "And I threw in that extra cheese bread you like. Consider it on the house."

Lizzy poked a trembly finger through the items. Tiny blue veins stretched across her face, magnified in wrinkled, translucent skin. She scowled. "There ain't but nineteen candy bars in here."

A sheepish look crossed Debra's face. "I kinda ate one."

"You got as much sense as a bull eating beef!"

Her cantankerous tone flew all over Debra. "Don't yell at me!" she shot back. "I've had a rough week."

The woman glared.

"I bring you exactly what you ask for each month, and I even gave you free bread this time and you're upset about one candy bar?"

"You bring exactly what I *pay* for each month," Lizzy snapped back. "That includes twenty Snickers."

Debra gritted her teeth. She wasn't one to disrespect her elders but she wasn't one to be walked on either. Humility filled her soul, and she said, "Okay, I'm sorry. I'll send you another one."

Lizzy rolled her eyes and muttered, "Ah, hell, it ain't no big deal. This time."

Debra peered at the pond. It looked cold and empty.

"Why you so cranky today anyway?" Lizzy asked.

Debra stared at her. Clearly she hadn't seen the news, and she didn't want to bring it up. "I haven't been sleeping well."

"Jack Daniels is good for that," Lizzy rattled off. "Put a little bit in some hot tea with a squirt of honey and you'll sleep like the dead."

Debra cringed.

"Of course you could always take a sleeping pill or get one of them sound machines. I hear they help." Debra was a little surprised at this suggestion and appreciated the woman's efforts to help her. "Anyway," Lizzy said, "you best get on now. My stories are coming on soon and it'll take me all of ten minutes to get my ass outta this damn chair."

"Want me to help you?" Debra was already leaning in as the question left her mouth, but Lizzy waved her off.

"I got it. You keep going. You got work to do."

Debra took her time leaving the yard. She waited out of sight around the corner of the house until she was sure Lizzy was safe inside then she made her way back to the cab where Roku was waiting patiently.

* * *

Debra tried calling Regina more times over the weekend and into the following week, but all she got was ringing. Maybe this woman didn't have an answering machine? Maybe she'd figured out it was Debra's number and was ignoring her? She flung the phone across the room and ducked her head when batteries ricocheted in all directions. A putrid taste coated her mouth, her insides, and she paced the house like it was on fire, searching for ways to unload the heaviness that was anchoring down her guts. She found more of Steve's things. She flung leftover pieces of his life into boxes, not caring if she broke delicate objects. When she taped the last one, she broke into a loose fit of tears. Why did she have to be so feeble when it came to this man? Why had she had to love him so much? She cradled her stomach, gasping for air as pain drilled holes throughout her entire body. It took a while for her to stop crying, for her to pull herself to her feet and clean her face. Her agony slipped back into its quiet, dark place, leaving her with a feeling of immense relief. That was the beauty of tears, at least you felt better, albeit a little torn up. She took the boxes downstairs to the front door and texted Steve. He responded within the hour, said he'd come get the rest of his things, and then, in a way that felt too official, asked if she was okay "since everything that's happened."

She blinked at the text. Rage tapped around in her chest. Though he hadn't contacted her about the robbery, Debra knew how much Steve kept his nose in the news. What she didn't know was why it had taken him so long to check on her. It had been two and a half weeks since the incident. Even neighbors she didn't talk to often had asked if she was okay. His question bothered her badly and she wanted to rip into him. Did he even care about her anymore? And that's what she texted him back. Within minutes, her phone was ringing in her hand. It was him, his name still programmed on speed dial, a name she'd ached to see flash up on her screen so many times in the past. A tornado of anxiety spun in her chest as she let the call go to voicemail. She listened to his message on speakerphone, sinking into the memory of his voice as it filled the kitchen. "Of course I still care about you, Deb. I wouldn't have asked if I didn't. I saw what happened, and I was gonna call you, I just didn't know what to say. I'm sorry, okay, and I'm glad you're doing alright and that you still have the car. I know how much you love it. I'll come get those boxes on Monday. Just leave them on the porch. Take care."

Take care. That's what people said to survivors after funerals. Since the separation, this incident with Frank had been the hardest thing she'd dealt with and she was getting through it, all on her own. It felt good to feel that kind of strength, and it felt good to delete Steve's message.

She left the boxes on the doorstep the following morning, and they were gone by the time Roku dropped her off for the evening. Later on she sat on the porch with a cup of hot tea with Jack Daniels and honey in it. The sun was gone and darkness swelled around her, setting a morbid mood in the still eyes of a gargoyle statue posing not far from the front door. The thing was creepy, but it looked so composed, so sure of itself. Steve had stuffed its exploding mouth with azaleas in hopes of diminishing its frightening presence, and right now, Debra decided, come morning, she would remove those flowers, let that gargoyle breathe. Brisk air whipped through her lungs as she took in a deep breath. Pine trees rattled everywhere, and shadows crawled in her direction, but she wasn't afraid because something was changing in her spirit, something she liked.

Jim called at the end of the week. She was reading a book in bed and pushed upright nervously against the pillows. He'd been leaving messages about her car for a while, but she hadn't called him back, mostly because she wasn't sure she wanted the car anymore. Plus she'd gotten comfortable with Roku. It was wonderful, actually, sitting in a vehicle without worrying about operating it. She didn't have to think about traffic or turning on signal lights, paying attention to other people; it was just her and the ride, chauffeur style. And to top it off, Roku had become her friend.

"Hi," she said gently.

"Oh, my goodness, is this a real voice?" he said cutely.

"I'm sorry I haven't called you back. I promise I'm coming to get my car."

He half-laughed. "Are you sure? Because I think you've abandoned it."

She chuckled.

"I was really calling to check on you though. How you doing?"

"I'm okay." And then: "Is this part of your job, checking on women after men have died in their cars?"

"Yep, you're the sixth one tonight."

She laughed hard. "Well, I appreciate that. Actually, I appreciate everything you've done, even calling means a lot." Silence crawled awkwardly through the receiver, and Debra bit her bottom lip, wondering if she'd said the wrong thing.

"You know, Debra, I'd really love to take you to dinner sometime."

A warm spot spread in the middle of her throat.

"If it's a bad idea...."

"No, it's not," she finished for him.

"You seem like a wonderful woman. I'd just like to get to know you."

"I'd like that too," she squeaked.

"Good," he said, and she could tell he was smiling. Their conversation went on into the night. Topics about their favorite foods, movies, colors, and music filled the hours. When they finally hung up, she rolled over and closed her eyes. It didn't take long to fall asleep, and she stayed that way the rest of the night.

* * *

After the weekend passed, Roku drove Debra to the police station. Clouds were guarding the sky and a crisp air rustled leaves that had lost their way. She gave Roku his last check, surveying the surprised look on his face as he took in the amount. She would never get tired of seeing that expression on people's faces. It made her feel alive. "This is too much," he gushed, "more than you owe for the last few days."

"You deserve it."

Roku hugged her tightly. "I always say God works in mysterious ways, but Lord knows I never saw you coming. You have no idea how much your money has helped me and my family. God bless you."

She squeezed his shoulder. "Same to you. And tell you what, how 'bout we go to lunch soon. I'll pick you up."

"Not in your car, you won't!"

They roared with laughter, and Debra watched him get in the cab and drive away. Then she found Jim. His face illuminated as she drew closer. She gave him a light hug, then, inches from his face, thought of kissing his cheek but wondered if it was too soon for that. But from the apparent attraction in his eyes, she knew he wanted her to, so she did. A tender grin cut his lips, and she pulled back with a balmy face. Jesus. She really liked this guy.

"So, you got my car ready?"

"No, I decided to sell it." He winked as she playfully rolled her eyes. She signed a release form and followed him outside. The BMW stood out distinctively in a parking lot among other vehicles. Morning sun slid off the windshield in sparkling slants, and the rims shone like silver carets.

"I had it cleaned inside and out," Jim confessed. "Thought it might be easier, and I got that dent in your door fixed."

Debra squeezed his hand, told him thank you. Her heart ticked like a steady machine in her chest as she slid into the driver's seat. A new car scent filled her nose, and she nestled into her familiar spot behind the wheel, the leather interior slippery under her cotton pants. She made quick adjustments to the mirrors, and that's when Frank's face materialized in her head, but the vulgarity was gone. All she saw was a plain face with closed eyes.

Jim watched her closely. "You gonna be okay?"

"Yeah," she replied, and turned the key. The engine revved to life. "I'll call you later, okay?"

He nodded and stepped back as she pulled out of the parking space. The clouds grew heavier as she progressed up the highway, and rain was trickling on the windshield by the time she got to her shop. She grabbed the largest basket she had and filled it with food, candy, toiletries, and books about grief. Then she put the basket in her car and drove to Regina's house.

She'd been there once before, with Roku. It was only a half-hour commute from her place, in an area known for shootings and robberies, but now that Debra considered this conclusion, it didn't make much sense because someone had tried to rob her in a ritzy neighborhood. The day she came with Roku, she ordered him to pull up to the curb and slink down in his seat while she did the same in the back.

"Who we spying on?" he'd asked giddily. "Your ex-husband?"

"Oh, please." Then she explained where they were.

"Ohhh," Roku oozed. "You gone go in and cuss her out?"

She heaved a sigh, rolled her eyes.

"Then why we here?"

"I'm not sure. I think I just wanted to see where she lived."

"Ain't you mad at her?"

"I don't really know. This wasn't her fault, you know. It was Frank's."

"Maybe she put him up to it?"

"Or maybe he was just a criminal." The statement felt like a permanent nail in a cross. At that point, she'd zeroed in on the two-lane road lined with barren trees and houses tacked together by broken shutters and chipped paint. Frank's brick abode had shabby windows, crumbling steps, and a shattered porch light. Cars filled in the perimeter of the driveway, but today all Debra saw was a weather-beaten teal Corolla.

She took a moment to collect her thoughts then surveyed the area for safety and put the car in park. She got out, jerked the front seat up, and grabbed the basket, stepping onto slippery autumn leaves with caution. Halfway up the yard, she snagged her high heel in a hidden broken piece of concrete and went toppling forward, scratching her left hand on a rock as the package faceplanted. She cursed loudly, brushed off the shame, then stood up and bunched the jumbled basket in her arms. It took a few minutes to get to the door, took even longer for someone to come to it after she knocked, but soon a woman called out, "Who is it?"

"I have a package for Regina Williams," Debra announced.

She anchored the basket in front of the peephole, hiding her face, in case Regina recognized her. The door cracked open, and Debra shifted her neck to find one cautionary blue eye staring back at her. "I ain't ordered nothing," the woman piped up. She looked past Debra and her face instantly lost color. It was the car.

Debra moved her face into full view, and Regina stood frozen in the doorway. The lady had volumes of wavy brunette hair piled high on top of her head with piquant, olive cheekbones shaping a resilient face close in age to Debra's.

"Can I come in?" she asked.

The woman hesitated.

"I promise I'm not here to cause trouble. I just want to talk." She lifted her shoulders. "I brought you a cheer package."

The lady took a careful step to the right, and Debra slid past her into the room. She placed the basket on a table as the woman motioned for her to have a seat on one of the recliners. Debra wondered if Frank ever sat there. She caught Regina sinking into a doughy-looking couch. A tiny flat screen TV wailed drama from a daytime court show, and Regina lowered the volume without looking at the button on the remote.

"Is anyone else here?" Debra asked.

"No, my boys are at school."

Family portraits hung on the walls. There was one of Frank with stern, beady eyes, a smile on his face. He looked so human. She peered at a peace lily in the corner. "That's pretty."

"Yeah, got it at the funeral. I hate these things though. They don't never die."

"Everything dies eventually," Debra said in an even-lined tone.

Regina didn't blink. "You want something to drink? I got sweet tea. And I got some sandwich meat if you're hungry. I had more food but it just went to waste. I don't know why people bring so much to eat when people die." She bit her bottom lip, darted her gaze to the floor.

"I think they do it because they don't know what else to do," Debra offered.

"I reckon so." The woman knotted her hands in her lap.

"I tried calling several times but couldn't get through."

"Oh, I turned that ringer off. Got on my nerves, all them people calling." Her voice shook. "I was actually gonna call *you*, but I didn't know what to say. It's been almost a month since everything happened, and I've just been waiting for the right words to come to me." She paused, and Debra watched her take a long, concentrated breath. "I don't want you to have no ugly thoughts about my husband, but I see how you could because of what he was doing to you when he died. He wasn't an ugly person though; he was just trying to provide for us. We all got sides to ourselves that people don't understand."

"Did you know he was going to steal my car?"

"I knew he was going to take somebody's, I just didn't know whose. I'm sorry he did that to you." Her voice trembled badly, and Debra stared down at her stinging hand because it was too painful to give her eye contact. Regina followed her gaze. "You're bleeding, hon."

"It's just a cut. I fell outside."

"Oh, God, I'm so sorry. Let me fix that."

Before Debra could protest, Regina was rushing to the back of the house and returning with a first aid kit. She took Debra's hand, dabbed the wound with alcohol then blew on the cut when

Debra grimaced. That small act of kindness unnerved her, and now she understood how Regina must feel with her being here.

"How long had you and Frank been married?"

"Thirty years."

"Wow, a long time."

"Yeah, I was barely out of high school when we got hitched." She put a band-aid on the cut, and Debra thanked her. Regina nodded at the basket. "Thank you for that. But I can't understand it, after what he did."

"It's like you said, we all have sides to ourselves that people don't understand."

"So you ain't mad?"

"Not at you."

"Please don't be mad at my Frank." And the request was so palpable that Debra felt close to tears.

"I resented him a lot when it first happened," Debra confessed, "and I won't apologize for that because I think it's a very natural thing to feel, but now that I've had time to process everything, I realize this whole situation has brought me to a new place in my life. I'm not saying what Frank did was right but you're the one who has to live with his choice, and I know how hard that is."

Regina began to cry, and Debra sat there, watching her. She didn't touch her, didn't do anything, since she knew this woman had to face this agony alone. Finally, she got up and Regina followed her outside, stopping on the lawn, staring intently at the car with a mixture of sorrow and longing swimming in her eyes. Until then Debra hadn't been entirely sure why she felt compelled to meet this woman, but now she knew.

"My ex-husband bought this car brand new for me years ago and now it has almost 180,000 miles on it. Your husband could have chosen any car in my neighborhood to take, but he chose mine, and I think he did me a favor." She removed the key from her key ring and gave it to Regina. The woman blinked. "It's your car now if you want it."

"Huh?"

"You can sell it if you want and use the money for your family."

"But how can you do this?"

"Because I've been where you are."

Debra opened the driver's side door and motioned for Regina to get inside. A moment of resistance registered across the woman's face until finally she took three steps in the car's direction and bent down to sniff the inside like she was a dog checking out a treat. Then carefully she crawled in, nestled into the seat, and stuck the key in the ignition but didn't turn it. Debra stood by the door, watching. Regina rubbed the contours of the steering wheel with shaky hands. Her head dropped in the exact position as Frank's had been. Jagged breaths coursed up her throat. The sobs were fierce and ugly, and Debra knew how malevolent this kind of heartbreak was, and would continue to be, as long as Regina had this car. For that reason, it seemed wrong to deliver this package to her; on the other hand, it seemed rightly deserved, and that's the part that stayed with Debra the most as this woman she didn't know found her breath and turned the key.

THE WORKSHOP
Martha Weeks

The flick of an eye. That's all it was. And Mattie Dorsey would have missed the look had she not been counting seat numbers to locate hers in the packed plane. Again she glanced at the ticket in her hand. Twenty-four A. Window. The coiffed blonde who already occupied that seat had immediately looked down to her lap after their initial eye contact and continued to do so. The poacher looked vaguely familiar. It was the hair, fluffed and sprayed, big hair they called it in college. Mattie pulled her roller bag, bumped past elbows on arm-rests and smiled at curious children in mothers' laps. Ahead of her, a large woman crept down the aisle in slow-motion and grumbled under her breath until she finally stopped and said, "Hallelujah," loud enough to be heard by all.

The woman's back was broad and creased where her bra and jeans cut into flabby flesh. Her overstuffed bag blocked the aisle. Mattie looked from the bag to the overhead bin. *No way.*

The woman turned toward the side of the plane, leaned over, exposing white cotton Carters, and bent her knees. With a loud grunt, she grabbed her bag's handles and swung upward; the roundhouse momentum carried the bag directly into the lap of the man in the aisle seat.

"What the..." he said. His forearms folded over his head a second too late.

The woman panted, her breath a foul cloud of greasy food odors. Perspiration dripped from her nose. "Ohhhhh... I'm sooo sorry."

Mattie gagged, held her breath, then slipped the shoulder strap of her purse over her head and grabbed the handle of the woman's suitcase and in one movement hoisted the bag into the luggage bin.

The man cursed under his breath. "She's sitting here?" Mattie nodded.

"Yes," the woman said. "I have the window seat, if you'll, uh, get up and let me get to it."

While the two passengers situated themselves, a flight attendant retrieved the boarding pass Mattie dropped during the assist, thanked her, then escorted her to her seat and said to the blonde, "Ma'am, I believe you're in the wrong seat."

The blonde looked up from her magazine. "Oh, really? I actually prefer the window and since I'm already here..."

Mattie studied the blonde's face. The hair clicked. The last time she'd seen Carol Ann Jones she'd hoped it *was* the last. The flight attendant stepped back. Mattie lifted her suitcase to the overhead bin and said, "Sorry. I requested the window seat when I made my reservation."

"Ma'am," the flight attendant said to the blonde, "the flight is full. May I please see your boarding pass?" Carol Ann dug in her purse and produced a pass.

"I'll have to ask you to move to the aisle seat, please."

Carol Ann's frown looked all too familiar to Mattie. *Spoiled, selfish, narcissistic bitch.*

When she was seated and her seatbelt secured, Mattie turned her head slightly toward her seatmate. "It's been a long time, Carol Ann."

After an awkward pause, Carol Ann said, "Yes it has," and a breath later, "I see some things never change."

Mattie frowned. "Oh?"

"Still everybody's friend?" Carol Ann tipped her chin to indicate several rows up.

Mattie looked into Carol Ann's heavily lined and mascaraed eyes. "She needed help."

"Don't they all," Carol Ann muttered as she looked back at the magazine in her lap. "So, what takes you to Philadelphia, of all places?"

Mattie had no desire to chat, didn't want to know how many children she had, if any, or where she lived or whom she'd married. She silently cursed the Delta agent who had seated them side-by-side and wondered at the odds of that happening. She opened her paperback and said, "I'm going for work."

Soon after takeoff, flight attendants rattled by with the drink cart. Atlanta to Philly was a short flight. Mattie asked for Pellegrino; Carol Ann for white wine, but after she poured a cup and sipped, she sent it back. "It's not cold enough. I can't drink that. Bring me a Vodka tonic with a twist of lime instead. I assume you have Vodka."

Mattie glanced at the attendant who maintained a smile and pleasant attitude as she gathered the empty bottle and cup of wine and left. Moments later when the drink arrived, her seatmate had a fit that there were no limes onboard. Mattie focused on her book. For the next thirty minutes, she read and glanced out the window now and then while Carol Ann flipped noisily through her magazine and ordered another drink. When the plane began its descent, Mattie tucked her book into her shoulder bag and looked down at the city of Philadelphia, the waterways, and the flotilla of mothballed battleships at rest alongside docks.

It had been years since she'd been to Philadelphia; the writing workshop was the perfect excuse to return. She'd attended numerous conferences and workshops. This one got her attention because one of the guest agents represented her genre, suspense, and had a soft spot for southern authors. She'd paid for a ten minute critique session with him and was eager to get his take on the ten pages of her manuscript that she'd emailed to him.

As soon as they landed, Carol Ann grabbed her oversized black leather purse and rushed to the door. Mattie got her bag and saw that Carol Ann was first in line to exit. Several minutes later, Mattie chuckled when she entered the terminal and watched Carol Ann's mad-dash to the lady's room. Since she hadn't checked a bag, Mattie headed straight to the cab line though part of her wanted to stick around to watch Carol Ann in her six inch stilettos as she wrestled her bag from the conveyor belt at baggage claim. She'd kicked the shoes off on the plane. They couldn't be comfortable. *Idiot shoes.*

* * *

Late that afternoon, Mattie checked in at the Rittenhouse Square Hotel along with several other workshop attendees. One had researched restaurants for the free Friday evening. They decided to freshen up and meet in the lobby at six o'clock. After a hot shower, Mattie looked over the workshop material she'd printed from the internet to refresh her memory. They'd probably talk over dinner about who was going to what lecture tomorrow. At ten minutes before six, she went down to the lobby. It was a popular bar for the after five crowd. One of the fellows she had met earlier waved her over.

"Mattie, I heard the agents hang out here before they split for dinner."

"Okay." She looked around the bar. "I'd love to meet my critique agent before tomorrow."

"Go for it. I'll hang here and flag down our dinner group."

"Good enough." She ordered a Heineken, refused a glass, and wrapped a cocktail napkin around the perspiring green base. There must have been twenty-or-so people crammed in the bar area. Some talked amiably, some heated, like they'd just stepped away from a day in court. Others had formed small groups. She recognized the agent she wanted to meet. His picture on the internet must have been several years old, but he was still a good looking, middle-aged man. She was about to head his way when she spotted a well-known memoir author. That genre held no fascination for her so she hadn't paid much attention to his bio. He looked like he might delve into the romance genre as well, maybe under a different name, with his dark, wavy hair, gold bracelet, and casual GQ attire. His cigarette waved about as he talked, maybe his way to maintain breathing room. Women pressed around him in a tight circle. He and the woman at his side sipped martinis; red silk clung to her body and her hair molded to her head in a dramatic gold sweep that twisted and tucked to an elegant finish in back. *No – no – no.* Mattie stumbled, almost lost the small leather clutch pinned beneath her arm. *What the hell is she doing here?*

She changed course not wanting to come face-to-face with Carol Ann again. She moved to the edge of the group that surrounded the agent she wanted to meet and kept her back to Carol Ann. When the group dispersed, she introduced herself to the agent and said she looked forward to their critique session in the morning. That done, she skirted the room and rejoined her new acquaintances at the bar.

* * *

The next morning, Mattie was too excited to sleep. Check-in for the conference wasn't until nine thirty, so she threw on her running clothes and headed to the lobby. The hotel offered a courtesy bus. She had the driver drop her on Kelly Drive behind the Art Museum and asked him to pick her up in an hour in front of the museum at the Rocky steps. It was barely light, but the sidewalk along Kelly Drive was busy with walkers, joggers, bicycle riders, and roller bladers. Rowers were the main action on the Schuylkill River where the main attraction was Boathouse Row where the whisper-thin rowing shells were housed along the river in historic boathouses built in the eighteen-hundreds. As hard as she tried to be in the moment to absorb Philadelphia, her head replayed a beach weekend during her senior year at Georgia. A group of friends had gone down to St. Simons Island to celebrate the end of final exams. She'd been dating Skeet Van Leer at school for about six months and thought things were going well. The group on the beach wanted to grab lunch. Skeet was nowhere around. She went back to the King & Prince Hotel to see if he was in his room. She knocked. He said, "Yeah," so she pushed the door open. Carol Ann's bare back and that wild mane of yellow hair jerked up from Skeet's bare chest. That was it. Mattie could still hear the loud whack of the door she slammed. She picked up her pace. After thirty minutes out, she turned around and went back then did a quick up-and-down on the famous Rocky Balboa steps in front of The Art Museum.

Back at the hotel, she showered, changed, picked up a cup of coffee as she signed in to the conference, and filled out a name tag. She picked up a list of rooms where different talks would take place; subject matter of several appealed to her: crafting mysteries, how to build suspense, self-publishing, revision. Her critique was at four o'clock with Jack McConnell, so she attended his lecture and several others that morning. At lunch time, she grabbed a salad from a deli down the street and ate outside. After several sessions that afternoon, she went back to her room and freshened up then headed to the floor where critiques took place.

Mattie gave her name and appointment time to the proctor and was asked to have a seat. She took a deep breath. Her rapid heartbeat surprised her. *This is silly. Get a grip.*

The door opened and a serious faced young woman walked out. "Mattie," the proctor said. "You're up. Go on in."

"Good luck," said the serious faced woman who had just exited the room. "He's tough."

Jack McConnell had a manuscript laid out on the table. He didn't look up so she sat in the chair across from him that had been left pulled out. She thought of the chair's former occupant and wondered what she'd been told that had disturbed her. The agent slowly thumbed through the manuscript. She read her name upside down on the top of the page. After several minutes she said, "Um, Mr. McConnell, my name is Mattie Dorsey. I'm your four o'clock critique."

He looked up. "Oh. Hi. Sorry. I got carried away."

"Beg your pardon?"

"Jack. Just Jack. It's your writing. It takes me home."

His accent had edges sharpened by life in New York but the softness of the south was still there. "Virginia, I bet."

"What, my accent?"

"Yes. It's still there. In your vowels."

He smiled. "You sound just like your writing. Georgia, I'd wager."

"That's right."

"I'd like to get back down there one of these days, maybe do a workshop in Atlanta or something."

"Atlanta's too big. Do one on the coast—St. Simons, Beaufort,

Charleston, the lowcountry. If you've never been, you're in for a treat."

"I feel like I have been there. In your writing."

Mattie sat back and let out a long held breath. "So, I got some of it right?"

Jack chuckled. "When are you going home?"

"Back to Atlanta tomorrow. There's a short story contest I want to enter and I've only written half. It's due middle of next week."

"So, you write short stories?"

"I'm trying. They make me write tighter. And faster."

"Send me that too."

"Too?"

"Didn't I say?" She shook her head. "I want to see your full manuscript." He pushed his business card across the table. There was a knock at the door. "I guess time's up."

Mattie stood. Jack handed her the material she had sent him and stood. "I made a few notes on here you might want to take a look at. Mostly comments about what I really liked, some where I thought you could go deeper. See what you think, but don't change anything in your manuscript until I've had a chance to look at all of it, okay? No tweaking or any of that stuff. I want to see how you write, unedited."

Mattie grinned and nodded. "As-is then. You got it." She headed toward the door then turned back. "I have my computer with me. I could send it to you...today."

"I figured as much. You're a writer. Send it to the email address on the card. It will go straight to me."

"Will do. Thanks, Jack."

* * *

Mattie was beside herself. Fully prepared to pitch her novel when she'd arrived, Mattie took the elevator to her floor and zipped off an email to Jack McConnell with a thank you and her full manuscript attached. She hit SEND. "Hot-doggone-damn."

Sessions were over. Tonight was for fun. Craft beers and appetizers would be served from four-thirty until six in the bar to be followed by the grand finale, billed as a TALENT QUEST. Attendees had been invited to submit the first five hundred words of any of their manuscripts, any genre, ahead of time. Works would be splashed up on a screen and commented on by a panel composed of the entire group of attending agents and publishers. Mattie threw on her favorite jeans and cotton sweater and headed down.

Conversation was already loud and lively. She selected a beer from the selection listed on the chalkboard at the end of the bar. Several from her dinner group huddled together and pulled her into their circle when she walked up. One of the men said, "You're from Atlanta, right?"

"Yes," Mattie said.

Two of the women in this group were memoir writers. They'd been sharing how their session had gone that afternoon. "So I suppose you and Carol Ann Van Leer are in the same writing group in Atlanta," one of them said.

The Van Leer surname attached to Carol Ann caught Mattie off guard. "Van Leer did you say?"

The woman turned her head slightly and pointed from hip level. "The blonde over there chatting up Mr. Memoir."

Mattie followed the point. Carol Ann was as close to nose-to-nose with the man as she could get. "Oh, her. We were at the University of Georgia together. She's from Savannah." *That bitch. Snakes my boyfriend. And marries him, apparently.*

"Ah. Close, anyway. Lucky you, being in school with her."

Mattie rolled her eyes. "Why. What did she do?"

"Took over our session. The agent hardly made a point before she asked a ridiculous question. Apparently she had a critique with him today."

Another woman said, "And she was intent on continuing their private meeting in the hour he was supposed to present to us. She's got a lot of nerve."

"That's putting it mildly," Mattie said. *Conniving bitch.*

"So you know her pretty well," the first woman said.

"Well enough to know she's out for one thing. Carol Ann."

"Her questions were pretty direct. Sort of familiar," the woman said. "She embarrassed me and I don't embarrass easily."

"We'd better grab something to eat before the vultures get it all," one of the men said. "I want a good seat at the talent show."

They topped off their beers, filled small plates with appetizers, and headed to the large conference room where chairs had been lined up in rows. There was a long table at the front of the room for agents and publishers; on the wall behind them was a large, elevated screen. Mattie and her group occupied the front row. Each of them had submitted, so there were "ughs" and "uh-ohs" when the work of one of them came up on the large screen. Though each had met privately with an agent, this was the first time the conference's entire group of agents and publishers was able to read and comment on a work. The Quest proved both interesting and humbling.

Mattie scanned the next manuscript. *I know this one.* She looked around the room. *He would have told me if he was coming to this.*

An agent on the panel began to critique the writing. He was highly complementary, as was the publisher who commented next. Mr. Memoir was the final one to speak. "I got a sneak preview of this work earlier today. In my opinion this author shows great promise." His gaze was behind Mattie and to her left.

Mattie looked over her shoulder. Carol Ann sat at the end of a row; her eyes were locked on Mr. Memoir's. Her smile was suggestive, bed-roomy if there was such a thing.

Mr. Memoir said, "This panel voted almost unanimously that this piece by Carol Ann Van Leer wins the Best Manuscript Submission award for this workshop. Come on up, Carol Ann." He held a framed plaque. There was vigorous applause at first but as soon as Carol Ann stood, the claps dimmed to merely polite.

"I'll be damned," Mattie said.

"What," the fellow to her left said.

"That's not her work."

"What do you mean?"

"That's not hers. I know who wrote it."

As soon as the panel broke up, Mattie headed straight for Jack McConnell. "Jack, may I have a word?"

"Uh, sure, Mattie. What's up?"

"That last piece. By Carol Ann Jones from Atlanta."

"Van Leer, you mean?" Jack looked confused.

"Yes, well, she was Jones when I knew her. We were at Georgia together. I was in a small writing group. There was a very talented fellow in the group from Sapelo Island, Georgia, a small island just south of Sea Island. His work was brilliant but unpolished. The work Carol Ann submitted was his. I'd know it anywhere. He worked it over and over in our group until he nailed it. Well, you saw. It's beautiful. He has an amazing voice. Sam Greer wanted to be a writer more than anything in this world, but his father split and left Sam head of the household. Like I said, he was brilliant. He had to support his mother and siblings so he became a lawyer, graduated the University of Georgia Law School. He's in my brother-in-law's firm in Atlanta now. He never got to be a writer."

Jack stared at her. "Interesting. I had a difficult time believing a woman wrote that piece. I didn't vote for it for that very reason. She was in one of my sessions and, well, let's leave it at that."

"You need say no more. You know."

"I got a pretty good idea," Jack said. "You can prove this?"

"You bet I can."

"Well hell, Mattie. Let's go." Jack had copies of all the manuscripts that had been submitted. He pulled out Carol Ann's and he and Mattie headed to the front desk. On the way, Mattie called her brother-in-law and told him what was up. He gave her everything she needed.

* * *

The next morning as Mattie and her new group of writer friends waited for the hotel's courtesy van to drive them to the airport, a cab pulled to the curb. When the rear door opened, a slim-fit blue-jeaned leg and a red leather stiletto heel emerged and found the curb. The blonde hair that followed had lost its poof. Carol Ann's smeared, angry eyes found Mattie's. "Well big effen deal. It's all a crock, you know," Carol Ann said.

Mattie and her group watched as Carol Ann stumbled and wove her way into the hotel then disappeared inside. "Ooph," one of the men said. "Rode hard."

"And damp dried," a woman added. A van pulled to the curb.

"Nice try, Carol Ann," Mattie said. "Gotcha."

IN HIS IMAGE

Joel Shulkin

"I cannot imagine a God who rewards and punishes the objects of his creation and is but a reflection of human frailty."
— Albert Einstein

After years of wandering, suffering heartbreak after heartbreak, Samuel was ready to face the Creator. He stood beneath the mainsail on the galleon's deck and scanned the horizon. The ship groaned as it surged forward. Lightning crackled, illuminating the night sky, leaving the tang of ozone to linger in the salty air. Two nautical miles ahead, the waters roiled and thrashed.

A gust of wind struck the young man's chest.

His hand shot out. Clamped onto the mast.

The ship rocked side to side.

He dug in his heels and leaned in against the wind, gritting his teeth.

Gale forces whipped at and around him. His feet lifted an inch off the deck.

He gripped the mast. Clung with all his strength.

At last, the wind died. His feet dropped back onto the deck. The ship settled back into its slow, cradle-like rocking. The young man allowed himself to smile as he gazed at the sky and whispered, "Nice try."

"Samuel! Y'all right, lad?" The voice of Barnaby, the ship's captain, exploded from the cabin moments before the man himself emerged, his belly straining against his hastily buttoned vest. He brushed an errant lock of coarse blond hair away from his eyes and grabbed the rail for support. "That guster came outta nowhere."

"I'm fine, Captain." Samuel swept a strand of seaweed off his stiff wool jacket. "But I suggest you warn the crew. There'll be more than a few puffs of air in store for us."

The corner of Barnaby's lip twitched. "We're with you fer the long haul, lad. We owe you that much fer what you done back in Halloway—but you sure this is what you want? No one's ever gone against the Creator and returned to tell the tale."

Before Samuel could reply, a bundle of blankets stirred at his feet. Snickering, he crouched and unfolded them to reveal a shivering ball of white fur. A single blue eye appeared, followed by another. When it spotted Samuel, it leaped and latched onto the boy's chest with needle-like claws. Its long tail flicked side to side.

Samuel laughed and stroked the creature's back. "Easy, Moog. The storm's over for now."

Clucking his tongue, Barnaby eyed Moog. "A cayfel killed my uncle. Blamed fool thought he could tame one'a them beasts. I got no idea how you bonded with one."

Moog popped its head up, sniffed the air, and glared at Barnaby. A sound somewhere between a purr and a growl rumbled in its throat. The captain retreated.

"Shush." Samuel rubbed the fur between Moog's ears. The creature closed its eyes and quieted. "He lost his family, just like me. I felt his pain, as he felt mine. We're in this together until the end."

Barnaby watched Samuel caress Moog's head and grunted. "Look, I know you got a cargo hold's worth of questions about yer life, but in all yer years of wandering, did'ja ever stop to think maybe the Creator don't want you to know the answers?"

Samuel gave Moog's back one more stroke before turning to the sky. "He should've thought of that before creating me in his image."

* * *

"Sam." The woman's voice penetrated the heavy door, ripping the writer from his thoughts. "Are you ready yet? I told Susan we'd be at the party in twenty minutes."

It took a moment for Sam to remember he was in his bedroom and not on a ship's deck. Cursing, he hit 'Save' and shouted, "I'm not feeling good, Aunt Sarah. Can I stay home?"

"What?" The doorknob rattled. "Samuel Miller, unlock this door."

"Don't come in. I'm not dressed." Sam snatched the blanket off his bed and draped it over his lap. "I'll go to the next party. I promise."

"That's what you always say. Are you writing stories again? You promised you'd stop."

His cheeks flushed. "No. I just need to finish my science homework and then I'll rest."

"You'd best not be lying to me. If I find out you're obsessing over those stories again…"

"I'm not writing." His ears burned. "God, why don't you just leave me alone?"

"Don't you use the Lord's name in vain! If your parents were alive —"

"Well, they're not and going to that stupid party won't bring them back!"

Her sharp intake of breath confirmed he'd hit the right nerve. She shuffled her feet, probably deciding what to do. They'd had this argument dozens of times, and it always ended the same. Later, he would regret hurting her, but, at that moment, all he cared about was getting rid of her, so he could get back to work.

In a hushed voice, she said, "Escaping into your stories won't bring them back, either."

The words slammed into Sam's chest like a gust of wind, stealing his voice. When he could again speak, he said, "At least it makes me feel better."

"You've barely left that room in months, Sam. God helps those who help themselves."

"God doesn't help anyone!" Sam pounded his fist on his desk hard enough to make his computer shake. He had to stop himself from smashing his fist through the screen. Slowly clenching and unclenching his fingers, he choked back a sob and said, "Just go."

Silence followed for several heartbeats. Long enough for Sam to wonder if this time she might try harder, say something that showed she had even a glimmer of understanding of what he was going through.

Instead, her footsteps disappeared down the hall.

Sam lowered his head and sighed. Yes, they'd had this argument dozens of times, and it always ended the same. Exhaling through his nose, he tossed the blanket aside and repositioned his wheelchair in front of his computer. He read aloud the last few sentences.

"That's weird. I meant to have Samuel say, 'I still have to try.' Why did I write this other stuff?" His hand moved to the delete key. He stopped and read the words again. He shrugged. "I like this better."

Sam started typing again.

* * *

Long after the crew had retired for the night, Samuel tossed and turned on his cot. Moog slept fitfully by his side. Every time the boy moved, the cayfel startled, its short legs bicycling until it calmed back to sleep. With a hint of a smile, Samuel tucked the blanket around Moog and lay back to stare at the ceiling.

For all his bravado, he feared Barnaby might be right. No one knew for certain if the Creator existed. In the desert city of Agnocia, a race of 'scientists' claimed the universe was ruled not by a powerful being, but by the random collision of 'atoms'. They made a strong enough case Samuel considered abandoning his quest for the first time in five years. That is, until a tidal wave flooded the desert, killing everyone. Everyone except Samuel.

Samuel pressed his hand against his forehead and sighed. How many cities had he visited? Fifty? A hundred? An invisible thread tugged at his chest, dragging him to each town, each village, each metropolis. Fighting against the pull caused excruciating pain. Only by following its lead could he find peace.

Peace. Right. He may have found many things, but peace was never one of them. In every town, someone needed his help. Each time he found a clue to the Answer, a monster attacked, or an earthquake struck, or a magician cast a devastating spell. Each time someone died. But not Samuel. No, Samuel always survived. Samuel, the Wanderer. Samuel, the Fearless. Samuel, the Blessed.

Cuddling Moog, Samuel closed his eyes. Some blessing. Barely fifteen yet he'd already lived ten lifetimes. Samuel wasn't even his real name. He'd changed it erase his past. After so many years, he couldn't even remember his real name. It didn't matter, anyway. He was no longer the same person he'd once been. He tried so hard to do good work, to help others, yet all he earned in return was pain and loss. What more did the Creator want from him?

Moog stiffened. A low, gurgling growl spilled from its muzzle.

Samuel bolted upright. "What's wrong?"

The cayfel sat back on its haunches, hair on end, staring at the wall. It growled again.

"Easy, Moog. There's nothing there."

Samuel reached out to stroke Moog's fur. A jolt ran through his fingers and up his arm. He yelped and jerked his hand back.

"What was that?"

Moog turned to him. Shadows swirled in its blue eyes.

Slowly, Samuel looked over his shoulder. A wraith floated in mid-air, stretching and shifting but never taking shape. The hairs on Samuel's arms stood on end. He understood why Moog was on high alert. Great power emanated from the wraith. This was no ordinary spy.

Samuel drew his sword. "Who are you?"

The wraith flickered and morphed.

"Whom do you serve?"

The vapors coalesced into the upper half of a boy. A face stared back at Samuel before sinking back into the amorphous blob. Samuel's face.

Anger surged through Samuel's veins. He'd faced countless threats before. At least they had the decency to face him directly.

"No more games," he shouted. "Show yourself."

* * *

"Show yourself."

Sam startled. Who said that?

He looked around. The room was empty.

Sam shook his head and returned to the computer.

He jumped again, this time nearly falling out of his wheelchair. Impossible.

There, on the screen, were the words he'd just heard.

"No way." Sam scratched his chin and re-read the last few sentences. As he did, he could picture Samuel huddled next to Moog in the cramped cabin, shouting directly at him, as if he knew Sam was there.

Sam pressed his palms against his eyelids. "Get a grip. He's a character in a story. Your story. He's not real. You're letting the story run away again. Getting so absorbed you're hearing it in your head." He frowned. "And now you're talking to yourself. Again. Fantastic."

With a sigh, Sam repositioned himself before the keyboard and cracked his knuckles. Time to set this story back on course.

* * *

"Show yourself," Samuel shouted as he held Moog close. "What do you want?"

The wraith seemed to startle. It faded, nearly vanishing for a moment, and then solidified again. Wispy hands reached for Samuel.

"Stay back!" Samuel flattened himself against the wall. "Don't touch me."

The wraith's fingers wriggled. They danced and jerked, moving faster.

"Stop that." Samuel could take no more. He leaped away from the wall with his sword raised over his head and shouted, "That's enough."

The wraith jabbed its index finger downward.

An explosion rocked the ship.

Samuel staggered and fell. He caught himself by grabbing onto the crossbeam. The ship swayed. Moog barked and howled.

The wraith vanished.

Another explosion. The ship buckled. Someone screamed outside.

"Fantastic." Samuel snatched up Moog and dashed topside.

The stench—a foul mix of blood, vomit, and fish intestines—slammed against his nostrils the moment he threw open the cargo hatch. He staggered.

The ship rocked again. Samuel slipped and fell. His head cracked against the deck. Everything around him turned gray.

Distantly, he heard Moog barking. He peered through the haze. Captain Barnaby stood over him, mouth moving.

Samuel forced away the ringing in his ears. Focused on the captain's lips.

"—half the crew," Barnaby was saying. "You gotta get up, lad."

"Okay." Samuel grabbed Barnaby's hand to pull himself upright. He scanned the deck. His heart sank.

The mainsail was on fire. Two of the deck hands scrambled to put it out. Four more searched the waves near the port side.

"What attacked us, Captain? Pirates?"

"Nay, nothing so mundane." Barnaby shivered and glanced over his shoulder. "In all my years at sea I never seen a beast like that."

"Like what? What was it?"

"I don't know!" The sea captain's eyes smoldered in a haunted way Samuel had never seen. His cheeks reddened, and he tugged at his hair. "It was like facing Death itself."

Before Samuel could reply, the ship rocked once more. One of the crew flew through the air, screaming. He splashed into the ocean.

Moog began barking wildly.

Something blotted the moonlight overhead. Samuel and Barnaby looked up.

A massive tentacle streaked toward them. They rolled in opposite directions. The jagged claw at the tentacle's end crashed through the deck. Shockwaves rippled through the hull.

Samuel leaped to his feet. Hefted his sword.

"Run, captain," he shouted. "Get the crew to the longboat and row to safety."

"We're not leaving you, lad." Barnaby drew his cutlass. "This is still my ship."

Together, they hacked at the fleshy tentacle. Gelatinous ooze sprayed in all directions.

Pained screams filled the night sky. The tentacle squirmed and wriggled.

Samuel peered through the deck boards. The claw was wedged between two crossbeams, snapping open and shut.

They raised their swords. Swung down. Sliced through the tentacle.

A deafening bellow reverberated in the darkness.

The ship heaved. Something huge splashed.

Samuel clung to the railing. Moog huddled at his feet. It looked up and began growling. Samuel glanced over his shoulder.

Another tentacle dived toward him.

"Run, lad." Barnaby sprang forward. His sword struck the tentacle.

Metal clanged against metal.

Barnaby staggered backwards, eyes wide, mouth open in a dumbfounded expression, clutching his shattered sword.

The tentacle gleamed in the moonlight, scratched but intact, having turned harder than steel. It whipped around. Slammed into Barnaby's chest. Heaved him across the deck. Pinned him against the cabin.

"No," Samuel shouted. He scooped up Moog. Lifted his sword over his head. Dashed to rescue Barnaby.

Another tentacle flashed through the darkness. Swatted Samuel aside.

He crashed against the railing. Moog yipped and clung to his chest.

A sailor shouted. Another screamed.

Samuel staggered to his feet. Peered through the darkness. His gut twisted.

Six tentacles danced a grotesque ballet. At the end of each, a jagged claw grasped a crew member. Each time a sailor struggled, all six claws tightened viciously.

Anger boiled in Samuel's chest. He felt under his shirt for the Amulet of Mercutio. It burned hot in his hand.

Moog whimpered and squirmed in Samuel's arms.

"I am Samuel, the Fearless," he shouted against the wind as he held the amulet high, reciting the incantation the Oracle of Turin had taught him. The amber stone in the amulet's center pulsed softly. "I command you to release my friends and this vessel."

The sea began to boil. Rumbling laughter swelled from the ocean's depths.

A ball of light surrounded the ship, glowing brighter in time with the pulsating amulet.

"You dare command me with a trinket?" A fiery skull rose above the ship's bow. One blazing eye glared down at Samuel. Its sharp beak snapped, blood and ooze trailing from its mouth. "You can't order me around like a pet, foolish child. Nor can you outrun me. I have come to claim what is mine."

"You can't have them." Samuel tightened his grip on the amulet. The stone glowed brighter, hotter. "If you value your life, monster, let them go."

A leathery tongue slid across the beak. "Let's see how much you value life, boy."

The tentacles lifted from the deck and entwined with each other. The claws closed tighter. Barnaby and the crew cried out in agony.

"Use your precious amulet to save yourself but know these men will die a horrible death." The beak twisted into a horrifying grin. "Or surrender to me and I will spare them."

Uncertainty crawled under Samuel's flesh. His grip on the amulet slackened. "Why should I trust you to honor your word?"

"This isn't about me, fool. This is about you." Its beak snapped as it leaned closer. "Do you understand honor?"

"Don't do it, lad," Barnaby groaned. "You have to finish your quest."

"Silence!" Another tentacle wrapped itself around Barnaby's mouth. "What do you value more, Samuel, the Fearless? Your quest... or the lives of these men?"

Samuel's heart pounded as he scanned the faces of the crew, one by one. Their eyes pleaded with him.

Slowly, he lowered the amulet. He knelt and placed Moog on the deck. The cayfel snuffled and pawed at him.

"No, Moog. I have to go alone." A tear streaked down his cheek. He brushed it away. "I need you to be safe."

The little creature's blue eyes stared up at him. It whimpered once and then buried its muzzle under its paws.

Standing, Samuel said, "I'm ready."

The monster's beak contorted again into a gruesome sneer. "So be it."

The tentacles lowered and untwisted. The crew thudded onto the deck in a heap, coughing and gasping. The tentacles lashed out and wrapped around Samuel, hoisting him into the air.

"Samuel," Barnaby shouted as he struggled to stand. "What've you done?"

"What I had to," Samuel said, even as the tentacles began to choke off the circulation in his arms and legs. "Take care of Moog for me."

"Simpleton," the monster said with a bitter laugh. "You share a bond with your cayfel that nothing on this world can break. Where you go, it goes."

A tentacle dived toward Moog. The cayfel hissed and skittered under a bench.

"No," Samuel shouted and fought against his restraints. "Leave Moog alone."

The tentacle slithered across the deck. Moog growled and barked at it.

"Monster!"

Samuel's fist shot out. The amulet in his hand burned bright. He slapped it against the nearest tentacle. The appendage flashed white and crumbled to dust.

The monster roared in pain.

Samuel finished off a second and then a third. The remaining tentacles uncoiled. He fell to the deck. Landed on his feet. Raced toward Moog.

"Stop," the beast roared. Its tentacles lashed themselves around the ship. "There is no honor in cheating death."

"Death has no honor."

Samuel jumped over a tentacle and slid across the deck. He grabbed Moog from under the bench. Flipped onto his back. Pointed the amulet at the monster.

"Be gone!"

The light of a thousand suns radiated from the amulet. A blazing fireball enveloped Samuel. Lightning streaked from the heavens and struck the beast. It screamed in pain. Electricity coursed through its body, down its tentacles, and into the ship.

An explosion sent rays of light in all directions.

* * *

BANG!

Sam jumped. His heart pounded.

He scanned the room. Nothing.

Another bang. Outside. Not as loud.

He wheeled away from the desk and over to the window. He pulled back the curtain.

Bang! The neighbor across the street slammed his car door with his foot and wobbled up the path, juggling his armload of groceries.

Sam stared at the car. A shiny red Honda Accord. Just like his Dad's.

Truck headlights flashed. Metal crunched. Glass shattered. His father's lifeless eyes…

Sam clenched his fists and forced away the memory. No time for that. Not when he had a world at his fingertips.

Puffing his chest, he rolled back to the computer.

* * *

Smoke and pitch drifted upward from a ring of flames, darkening the sky. Demons of all sizes danced and jeered.

As if moving through water, Samuel turned in a circle, sword drawn. Peering through the flames, he spotted Barnaby and the crew lashed to a wall, wailing in torment as demons flayed their hides. Their gazes locked with his between whip lashes. Judging him. Accusing him.

Rage burned through his veins. He gripped his sword with both hands and shouted, "Be gone, demons. Leave my friends alone."

"Friends?" a booming voice said. "Really?"

A massive shadow fell over Samuel. He looked over his shoulder. His jaw clenched.

The flaming skull of the sea monster stared down at him. Its beak opened. Cruel laughter poured out.

"These men were nothing more than your pawns," the monster said. "Where was your concern for them when you chose your quest over their lives?"

"You tried to cheat me." Samuel's grip on his sword tightened. "It's not my fault."

"It's never your fault, is it?" The beast laughed again, the flames circling its skull blazing bright. "Whose fault is it, then? Theirs? Your parents'? The Creator's?"

"You don't deserve to utter the Creator's name. You're a monster."

"I may be a monster, but who do you think created me?"

Recoiling, Samuel nearly lost his grip on his sword. "What do you mean?"

"The ravenous death-stalker that devoured your mother's home village. The tsunami that destroyed Agnocia. Me. The Creator made all of us." The monster towered over Samuel and grinned. "The same Creator you believe will reward you with the Answer."

"You lie. Why would He create a monster like you?"

"You can't accept that, can you? Because that would mean the Creator killed your parents. That's why you fear Him, isn't it?"

The words slammed into Samuel's gut. He searched for a brave retort, some truth that would dispel the monster's lies, but he found none.

"No need to answer." The monster lowered its face inches from Samuel's. Its eye sockets smoldered with a crimson glow. "Your eyes say it all. Samuel, the Fearless, fears only one thing. That He will never give you the Answer."

"You're wrong." Samuel lashed out with his sword. The blade passed through the skull as easily as through a cloud. He hacked again. Same result. "I will face the Creator. I will find the Answer."

"Then prepare, boy."

Massive tentacles shot out and wrapped around Samuel. He snapped his eyes shut and grunted as they squeezed tight. The tip of one tentacle stroked his cheek.

"If you continue down this path," the monster whispered, "Death will always follow."

"No!"

Samuel's eyes flew open. The monster was gone. Clear blue sky filled his field of vision. Waves crashed nearby. The demons and the crew had vanished.

Something touched his cheek. He bolted upright and snatched up his sword.

Moog yipped and retreated, then cowered with its paws splayed, tail drooped.

Placing a hand against his forehead, Samuel sighed and drank in the fresh air. He'd had nightmares like this before, but never so real. The oracle had warned him about the Dream State, a side effect of using the amulet. If Moog hadn't awakened him, he might've been trapped forever while his body wandered the earth, possessed.

"It's okay, Moog." Samuel held out his hand. "I'm still me."

Moog eyed Samuel's hand suspiciously and sniffed at it.

"I promise. You saved me."

With a cheerful bark, Moog hopped forward and rubbed its head against the proffered hand, purring. Samuel stroked Moog's fur while he surveyed their surroundings.

The ocean lay to their left. A forest waited on the right. Jagged mountains poked out above the trees, all but blotting two of the three noon suns. No houses or docks. No sign of the monster or the ship.

Samuel sighed and stood, brushing sand off his trousers.

He froze. The invisible thread was tugging at his chest, pulling him toward the mountains.

"This is where we're meant to be," he said to Moog. "Think you can keep going?"

Moog barked twice and wagged its tail.

"Let's get moving, then."

They walked together for the rest of the day. When night fell, they camped on the sand dunes. While Moog slept, Samuel sat by the fire, stoking the kindling. A spark flew onto his pant leg. He brushed it away. As he did, he felt the rough skin underneath the cloth. He hiked up his trousers, revealing a deep scar over his kneecap.

Unbidden, his hand caressed the bumpy-smooth surface of

the scar. His thoughts drifted back to the cave, so long ago. He remembered passing through the darkness, sliding one hand along the wall, gliding over the protrusions.

"The tunnel's getting lighter," his father had said as he led the way. "A few more turns and we should be safely out."

"I'm sorry for making you come after me," ten-year-old Samuel said. "I didn't think I'd get lost."

"Shush," his mother said. "We'll discuss it when we get home—along with your punishment."

"Yes, Ma'am." He trudged in silence for a few more feet and then stopped. "Oh, no! I dropped my glopper back there. I have to find it."

"Forget it," his father replied and grabbed his arm. "Your toys got us into this mess."

"You don't understand." He yanked away his arm. "You never understand."

"No, you don't understand," his father shouted. "Life isn't about playing gloppers and bobs. You have no sense of responsibility."

"Stop it." His mother stepped between them. "We'll deal with him when we get home."

"You always take his side." Samuel shoved his way past them. "I hate both of you."

"What are you doing? Come back here."

"No!" He ran, stumbling down the tunnel. Their footsteps echoed behind him. "Stay away from me. I don't want to see you again."

"Hush your voice. You're going to cause a—"

"Leave me ALONE!"

The walls shook. The ground fell away under his feet. He tripped and fell. His knee exploded in pain. He cried out.

The cave trembled again. The ceiling cracked. Rocks thudded into the dirt around him.

"No!" It was his mother's voice. "Oh, my—"

A deafening crash cut off her screams.

"Mom?" He tried to stand. His knee flared. He fell onto his back. "Mom! I need help."

More sickening thuds and cracks.

"Mom!" He scrambled to his hands and toes. Something warm and sticky trickled down his leg. "Dad! Where are you?"

The tremors ceased. Fewer crashes now.

The walls closed around him. He crawled through the darkness. His head cracked against something hard. He reached out. His hand bumped into a wall that wasn't smooth like the others.

He slid his hands side to side, up and down. He found no break, no opening.

"Mom," he screamed at the wall, panic flashing white in the back of his mind. "Dad! Can you hear me?"

He pressed his ear against the wall. All he heard was his own racing pulse.

"I'm sorry," he whispered. "I'm sorry I said I didn't want to see you again. I didn't mean it. Please come back."

Tears singed his cheeks. He struggled to breathe. Dust settled around him. He'd laid his hand against the wall. "I promise I'll do what's right. I promise to be responsible. I promise…"

"I promise," fifteen-year-old Samuel repeated as he stared into the campfire. He remembered the primary sun blazing down when he finally crawled out of that cave. It had brought him no joy, that light. It only reminded him of what he'd lost.

He sighed and stoked the fire. He remembered little about his parents before that day. The Worst Day. The day he began his search for the only one who could answer the question burning in his heart. The invisible string pulled him toward the mountains. He was so close now. Soon, very soon, he would have the Answer, and his quest would at last be over.

Soon he could ask the only question that mattered.

"Why?"

* * *

"Why?"

The word slipped past Sam's lips. He withdrew his trembling hands from the keyboard. His eyes blurred as he stared at the screen.

"Where did that come from?" he said aloud. "He's supposed to ask the Creator to make him forget what happened, not to ask why…"

Mom yelling. Brakes squealing. Metal crunching. More screaming.

"No." He pressed his palms against his ears and snapped his eyes shut. "I don't want to remember that. Stop it."

The memories faded.

Sam's heart pounded. He took slow, deep breaths. He opened his eyes. The computer screen stared back at him.

"Stick to the story," he ordered the computer. "This is about Samuel, not me."

The cursor blinked next to the word: Why?

"Because I decide what happens."

Blink, blink. Why?

Bile roiled in his throat. "Because I'm the Creator."

Now it was his turn to blink. He blinked at the screen. He blinked at his hands.

"That's right," he whispered. "I'm the Creator."

His fingers flew over the keyboard. No more stories running wild. No more being told what to do. It was time to prove who was in control.

* * *

The next day at noon, Samuel and Moog entered the forest. Thin beams of light shone between gnarled branches, casting dizzying patterns across the undergrowth. It was quieter than anyplace Samuel could remember.

An hour later, they stopped. The path disappeared into a thicket so tightly overgrown no light could infiltrate. Something howled in the distance. Moog whined.

"Don't worry," Samuel said. "There's nothing in there we can't handle."

Moog's eyes met his. Dark, foreboding colors swirled in the cayfel's irises. Dread and despair crept into Samuel's chest. The colors tossed and swirled. The demon's voice whispered in his ear, *You'll never succeed. You're too afraid.*

Samuel ripped away his gaze. The voice faded. He tightened his hands into fists. "I'm not afraid of anything."

Samuel drew his sword and marched into the thicket. "We haven't survived this long only to die in this forest." He hacked at the brush. "If we stick together, nothing can stop us."

Moog followed, whimpering.

They continued until they found a clearing. Creatures croaked and squawked and chirped all around them. Samuel's pulse quickened. He couldn't see over the trees, but he knew in his heart they were nearing the mountains. Soon, this would all be over.

The earth shook.

Birds streaked from the treetops. Small animals bounded from their hiding spots.

Samuel tightened his grip on his sword.

Another thud, then another. Faster. Louder.

The creatures dashed past Samuel and Moog without stopping.

Wood splintered. Trees fell and crashed to the ground.

A vicious roar echoed through the forest.

Samuel stood ready, holding the blade in his line of sight. Moog cowered behind him.

The pounding stopped. The roaring stopped. The forest was silent again.

Samuel scanned the treetops. The hairs on his neck pricked.

Something hissed. Behind him.

He whirled around.

A dark blur thumped into his chest. He flew over the brush. Slammed into a tree. His sword plummeted to the ground.

He groaned. Forced his eyes to focus. His chest tightened.

Yellow eyes glared over a set of deadly fangs. A mane of gnarled fur, dark as night, ringed a thick, scaly neck. A massive tail twisted and darted snake-like on the ground. The creature sniffed the air and grunted. Slobber and foam spilled from its mouth.

It could only be the dreaded leoverine. No other beast was so colossal yet so stealthy. Some claimed it could travel between worlds, but each world only once every ten years. Of course, no one could prove it. No one had ever faced a leoverine and lived.

For the first time in many years, Samuel felt afraid.

A high-pitched howl cut through the air.

The leoverine startled. It turned away from Samuel.

Little Moog crouched on the other side of the clearing. Its fur bristled. It growled and snapped at the leoverine.

"No, Moog," Samuel shouted. "Get away."

The leoverine spun back to face Samuel. Its lips curled into a snarl.

Moog pounced. Its claws dug into the leoverine's back.

The monster screeched. It thrashed and shook. Moog held tight.

Frantically, Samuel searched the bushes. Where was his sword? Where was the amulet?

The leoverine reared up on its haunches. Threw itself backward.

Moog sprang off at the last second.

The beast crashed against a tree. It staggered, stunned.

Moog lunged again. Its claws buried into the base of the leoverine's neck.

The creature roared in fear and agony. Its tail smashed into the tree, inches from Samuel's head.

Moog sank its teeth into the monster's flesh.

Howling, the leoverine vanished, taking Moog with it.

"No!" Samuel leaped to the spot where the monster had been. "Come back. Moog!"

He sank to his knees. He clawed at the earth. Maybe Moog was buried there, somewhere.

He reached out with his heart, his mind, his soul. Moog was bonded to him. Nothing on this world could break that bond. He couldn't be gone. He couldn't.

"Moog!"

The only answer was the wind blowing through the trees.

Tears streamed down Samuel's cheeks. He couldn't feel Moog anywhere. The cayfel was no longer on this world.

He clutched his chest, clawing at the empty void where his heart had once been. Throwing his head back, he screamed. When he had no voice left, he pressed his forehead against the ground and sobbed. His only friend was gone.

* * *

Sam stopped typing. It hurt to breathe.

"How?" he asked himself, afraid of the answer. "How could you write out Moog? What were you thinking?"

He forced himself to re-read the words. A lump formed in his throat.

"No. I can fix it. I'll make Moog chase off the leoverine."

He started to type, and then stopped. That wouldn't be fair. True, he may have written more than he intended because he was angry, but this was how the story needed to go. Samuel had to lose Moog in order to learn humility. He knew when he first started writing. Hadn't he?

Sam blew on his fingers and rubbed them together. No matter how painful it might be, the story had to go on.

* * *

Minutes passed. Samuel refused to move from his spot. His tears soaked the ground.

The skull-headed monster appeared in his mind. It whispered, "I warned you. Your fear was too great."

"I don't care," Samuel said without raising his head. "Go away."

"Death will always follow you down this path." The flames in the monster's eyes sockets dimmed. "And you must continue your quest."

The monster dipped and bobbed in mid-air. A sour taste formed in Samuel's mouth. He spat it out. "My quest is over. I've lost everything I care about."

"Isn't that what this was all about? To ask the Creator for what you had lost?"

Samuel flinched but remained silent.

"You never expected to succeed." The flames circling the skull flared. "Of course. How did I miss that? It's not the Creator you fear at all." It drifted closer, the flames licking at Samuel's skin. "What you fear is that there is no Creator."

"That's a lie."

"Afraid the Creator will hear? If He doesn't exist, what does it matter?" The monster chuckled with the sound of rolling thunder. "How deliciously tragic."

"Of course, there's a Creator." Samuel wanted to punch the monster's face but knew it would do no good. "It's because of the Creator I'm still alive."

"Yes, you've survived some incredible, impossible, horrible events, haven't you? And that's convinced you there's a supreme being protecting you." Its eye sockets gleamed. "Nothing happens in this world unless the Creator wills it. Isn't that you believe?"

Frost formed inside Samuel's chest despite the heat from the monster's flames. He knew the answer but dared not say it.

A crimson glow radiated from the monster's skull. "Name one instance where something wonderful happened—a miracle, if you will—that proved the Creator gives a damn about you or anything else."

Ice numbed Samuel's bones. Froze his blood. "He kept me alive."

"That he did. But for what purpose? To suffer loss after loss after loss?" More cackling laughter. "Face it, boy. There are only two possibilities. Either there is no Creator, and everything in your life has been devoid of meaning..." The monster leaned close, snorting, but no breath fell on Samuel's face. "Or you're nothing but a puppet."

All desire to move, to fight, to continue the quest died. Even the invisible string snapped.

"You're right," Samuel whispered. "I've lost everything. There's no reason to go on."

The skull's jaw twisted into a vicious sneer. "So, now you'll return home."

"No." Samuel lifted his head. The cold, haunted look on his face made even the monster retreat. "I'm never moving from this spot again."

* * *

"What?" Sam pushed back his wheelchair. His stomach twisted. "He can't do that. Samuel has to keep going. Without him, there's no story."

The words lurked on the screen, taunting him.

"No, he needs to find answers. He can't stay in one place. He's a man of action." He clenched and unclenched his fingers. "I'll make him act."

* * *

How long since the monster faded away? Minutes? Hours? At first, Samuel tried to guess time by counting the flickenbug's clicks, which the hillside monks claimed were perfectly timed every five seconds. After two hundred and fourteen clicks he gave up.

He watched the light reflect off the leaves. Barnaby's crew used to point out shapes and people and creatures hiding in the clouds and stars. No matter how hard Samuel tried, all he saw were meaningless patterns.

Next, he took great interest in the lines and swirls on his fingers and palms. They flowed and swooped as if drawn by an artist. Maybe they told a story, if he knew how to read them.

Night fell. He slept a dreamless sleep. When he awoke, he entertained himself by rubbing together two sticks. His stomach rumbled. He started to stand and stopped.

"I decide if and when I eat," he said. "I choose my own path."

He sat and twisted the sticks together. The rumbling in his stomach intensified. He ignored it, concentrating on the sticks. Gradually, the rumbling faded. He nodded to himself as he traced patterns in the dirt with one of the sticks. Quietly, he said, "I choose my own path."

* * *

"Get up," Sam shouted at the screen. He pounded his fist against the desk. "This is becoming the most boring story ever."

He read the last paragraph. His breathing rate increased. Samuel choosing his own path—what crap was this? He had a plan for Samuel. How dare Samuel refuse to cooperate?

"No," he said. "He can't refuse. He can't sit there forever, not in my world."

Gritting his teeth, he typed.

* * *

A light breeze rippled the leaves. Insects chirped and clicked. Samuel sat cross-legged, blocking out hunger pains and muscle cramps. His fears were gone, along with hope. All he had left was bitter determination to hold his ground.

Distant thunder rumbled. The air grew heavy. A storm was coming.

Samuel held still. *Let it come.*

The rumbling grew louder. Wind whistled through the trees. Rain splattered on his head.

He straightened his back. Raindrops rolled down his cheeks.

Lightning crackled. A tree exploded. The smell of burnt wood drifted through the air.

Samuel closed his eyes and breathed slowly. He would not move.

Wind whipped through the trees. Branches flew and crashed.

Beasts of all sizes leaped from the forest, growling and snapping.

He did not grab his sword. He did not fend off the creatures with his bare hands. He did not run as fast as his feet would carry him.

He remained still, hands by his sides, eyes closed.

Hot breath fell on his face. A putrid mix of sweat and decay invaded his nostrils.

Samuel did not move.

After another moment, the beast snorted and ran off. The wind died. The rain stopped.

Opening his eyes and staring straight ahead, Samuel said, "Is that the best you can do?"

* * *

"Damn it." Sam banged the heels of his palms against his temples. "Why did I make him so stubborn?"

He played scenarios in his mind. He could destroy the island. Samuel would have to flee.

But what if he didn't? If Samuel died, the story was over, and what would be the point?

He could write Samuel's parents back into the story. What could be more miraculous?

No, that would be cheating. And if he had his parents back, he wouldn't need his quest.

Sam sighed. He'd written himself into a corner. There was only one thing left he could do. It was a cop-out, but at least it would get the story back on track.

* * *

A thin beam of sunlight cut through the forest canopy, blanketing Samuel in warmth. Particles danced and floated around him. He looked up at the sky.

The primary sun drifted closer, growing larger, more radiant. Never had he seen anything more beautiful. A man's face formed on its surface. Stern. Benevolent. All-knowing.

"Hello, my child," it said, its voice both commanding and nurturing. "You have waited long enough."

"Who are you?"

"Look upon me and know me, for I know you." The face smiled. "I am the Creator."

Samuel stared, wide-eyed, unable to move, unable to speak. He no longer felt his heart beating or heard his own breathing. Every memory, every dream, every thought swirled in his mind and coalesced into this one eternal moment.

"You've shown great strength, courage, and loyalty," the Creator continued. "You've earned your place in my kingdom."

"Your kingdom? I don't care about that. I just want—"

"You want to understand why."

Samuel nodded.

"One pebble dropped in the middle of a lake sends ripples that affect everything around it." The light surrounding the Creator intensified. "You are that pebble, my child. Wherever you go, you change the world around you. You are the key to my plan."

Samuel's chest tightened. "What is that plan?"

"I can't tell you that. If one cell knows its fate, the act of knowing might alter its destiny and that of all others."

"Enough about pebbles and cells. I sacrificed everything. My parents. My friends. Moog." His voice choked off. It took every ounce of strength to whisper, "At least tell me why."

The heavenly light dimmed. All life collectively held its breath. At last, the Creator said, "In a temple on the far side of the ocean is an ancient scroll, older than any other document in existence. Find it, and you will have your Answer."

"No." Samuel folded his arms across his chest. "No more quests."

"You dare defy me?" The Creator swelled, nearly filling the sky. "Don't you know what I can do to you?"

"Do your worst. Oh, wait. You already have." Samuel lifted his chin and stared directly into the Creator's eyes. "You've taken everything that matters except my life. Without Moog and the others, I no longer need that."

The Creator's mouth gaped open. It stared silently for an endless moment. Finally, it said, "Samuel, this isn't how this works."

A chill ran down Samuel's back. "What did you call me?"

The Creator blinked. "Samuel?"

"That's not my real name. If you were truly the Creator, you'd know that."

"Well, of course, I know that…"

"Then what is it?"

"It's...It's...You're trying my patience."

"You don't know. You don't know because you're not the Creator."

"I AM THE CREATOR!"

Solar flares burst from the Creator's surface, setting the forest ablaze. Lightning arced through the sky, striking the ground inches from where Samuel knelt.

The boy flinched but didn't move.

Fire streams erupted from the Creator in all directions, incinerating everything they touched. Wind swirled, spinning and growing into a raging cyclone, sucking up all in its path.

The Creator stared down on Samuel and roared, "I gave you life. You repay me with disrespect. Now, feel my wrath!"

The sun exploded.

* * *

"No," Sam whispered. His hands fell away from the keyboard. He stared at the last three words he'd typed. He could barely breathe. "What have I done?"

Beads of cold sweat formed on his brow. His heart thudded against his ribcage. He couldn't have just done what he'd done. He couldn't.

Something flipped and flopped in his stomach like a beached fish. He grabbed onto the desk and bowed his head.

"Samuel's dead. He's really dead."

The nausea passed. He lifted his head. He caught his reflection on the monitor.

"You mean, you killed him. This is your fault. Everything is your fault."

He pulled back his fist, ready to smash his reflection.

He stopped. His hollow eyes stared back at him.

He lowered his fist. Turned back to the computer.

"I can fix this." His fingertips hovered over the keyboard, quivering. He squeezed them. His nails dug into his palms. It was the only way the story could end. He'd fought against it for too long.

After taking a deep breath, he began to type.

* * *

The fire raged, sending tendrils high enough to lick the sky. The forest cried out in agony. Smoke and ash blotted the remaining two suns.

Clouds appeared overhead. Rain tumbled down. Wind swept through.

The flames strangled and died. The smoke evaporated.

All that remained was a vast stretch of scorched earth.

At the heart of the devastation, a dust cloud lifted to reveal a shimmering red dome. It cooled to a fiery orange, then to yellow, and finally silver. The dome retracted into the earth, revealing a young man curled into a ball.

Samuel opened his eyes and sat up, turning his head side to side. His heart grew heavy as he surveyed the destruction.

"I survived," he said, voice devoid of relief. "Again."

A twig snapped. Samuel whirled, instinctively reaching for his sword before remembering it was lost.

A shadow lurked near a burnt-out stump.

"I see you," he said. "Show yourself."

The shadow drifted closer. As it moved, its shape became clearer. A young man rolled forward on some sort of wheeled chair.

"Who are you?" Samuel asked.

"I am..." The young man seemed to gather his courage before saying, "I'm Sam."

"Sam?" Samuel tilted his head. "How did you get out here, Sam?"

"This is my world." Sam rolled closer. "I go wherever I want."

"What does that mean?" Samuel studied the young man's face. His heart beat faster. "And why do you look familiar?"

Sam gripped the armrests of his wheeled chair. "Because I created you in my image."

The words surged through Samuel's veins like acid. "You— you're the—is this some sort of trick?"

"No tricks, Samuel. I am the Creator."

"No!" Samuel paced back and forth. "This can't be right. You..." He stopped and turned to the young man. "This must be a test, right? A test of my humility, my worthiness."

With a sigh, Sam said, "It's not a test."

Sweat beaded on Samuel's forehead. He wiped it off. Breathing slow and steady, he said, "If you're the Creator, then what's my real name?"

Sam snickered. "I never gave you one."

"That's not true. Everyone has a name."

"Really? Then, tell me. What is it?"

Samuel frowned. "I don't know."

"Because you're not supposed to know. Remembering your past would only keep you from moving forward."

"Why would it do that?"

"Because I—because that's what happens."

Samuel stared at Sam again, his gaze sharp and relentless. "So, how did I remember?"

"I don't know that, either. You've somehow developed into something way more complex than any of my other characters."

"Other characters?"

"I wrote dozens of other stories before yours." Sam looked down at his hands and wiggled his fingers. "I was writing a really good one about a world filled with robot dinosaurs when that truck crashed into our..." He shook his head. "Forget it."

Samuel puzzled at this bizarre creature before remembering his goal. "If you're truly the Creator, you know what I seek. Tell me now. What is the Answer?"

The two boys stared at each other silently. Each could hear the other breathing. Neither dared blink.

At last, Sam said, "I don't know."

The back of Samuel's neck burned. "How can you not know? You're the Creator!"

"I don't know everything, all right?" Sam threw up his hands. "Look, this was all about the quest. The Answer never mattered."

Samuel's mouth became drier than the desert. He opened it to speak but no words came out. He swallowed hard, running his tongue over his lips and teeth, and tried again. "You claim to be the Creator, yet you don't know the Answer. Do you even know the Question?"

Why? The word simmered in the back of Sam's mind. "You want to know why your parents had to die."

Something stirred in Samuel's gut. As it drifted up his gullet, he realized it was laughter. Bitter laughter. He clutched his belly and laughed and laughed.

Sam scowled. "What's so funny?"

"You really think that's the Answer I seek?" Samuel chortled. "Bad things happen. It's part of life. The moment you flooded Agnocia but let me live, I knew if they hadn't died, I'd never have started my journey."

Surprise jolted Sam upright in his wheelchair. How could Samuel know that? "That's true. I needed you to continue your quest."

"Because you can't." Samuel's eyes gleamed. "Isn't that right?"

Sam stared in shock. "What do you mean?"

"Look at you." Samuel pointed at Sam's wheelchair. "You're nothing but a broken, weak, scared little boy. Does it make you feel strong to control others' lives? Does it make you feel better about your own pathetic, meaningless existence?"

Fire raged in Sam's chest. The sky burned a deep crimson. "You watch your mouth."

"Or what? You'll kill everyone I ever loved?" Samuel marched closer. "The demon was right. Everything that happened to me since my parents died—you were in control. So, now, I want you to tell me the Answer to the question that has haunted me all these years." He bent down so his nose hovered inches away, but what made Sam jerk back in surprise was the pain in Samuel's eyes, the tears that formed and rolled down his cheeks, and the way his lip trembled as he asked, "Why do you hate me?"

"What?" Dark clouds formed both in Sam's mind and overhead. He tried to speak several times and could not. At least, he said, "Samuel, I don't hate you."

"You must. Why else would you keep me alive, force me to hope, to dream, to stagger onward—no matter how much I believed in you, prayed in you, worshipped you—only to make me suffer over and over and over?"

"Because that's what happened to me!"

Lightning sparked overhead.

Samuel stepped back, astonished. Darkness smoldered in Sam's eyes, mirroring Samuel's own fear, pain, and regret.

"I should've died in the crash," Sam said. "It was my fault. I kept talking about my story and the next chapter and then Dad got mad and..." He looked down at his hands. Thunder shook the ground. "I couldn't see Mom, but Dad was there, his windpipe crushed, and I couldn't move my legs. I prayed to God for help, but no one came. He never stopped staring at me." He covered his mouth and whispered, "I should've died. Not them."

Samuel could find no words to speak. Only moments ago, he wanted to hate Sam as much as he imagined Sam hated him, and now he found something else—not quite pity, not forgiveness, but a sort of understanding. At last, he said the one thing he'd waited so long for someone to say to him. "It wasn't your fault."

"You don't know what you're talking about." Sam wheeled around, away from Samuel, so he could stare out over the barren wasteland that had once been his most treasured creation. "They always told me I needed to be more responsible. I should've listened. Just once."

"*I promise to be responsible,*" Samuel whispered. The cave walls closed around him. His parents' last cries for help echoed in his ears. "You gave me your past."

"I wanted you to do things differently than I did." Sam turned his head, catching Samuel out of the corner of his eye. "I created you in my image, but I wanted you to become your own person. That's why I threw so many obstacles in your way. What defines a character is how he deals with adversity. You had to suffer in order to grow."

Years of searching and exploring replayed in Samuel's mind. All that time wasted in search of an impossible goal, all for the amusement of a mad god. His hands tightened into fists.

Before Samuel could speak, Sam turned back to him, his eyes dark pits in a field of sagging flesh. In a heavy voice, he said, "I don't hate you, Samuel. I love all my creations, good and evil. But you're something special. You're what I wish I was." A sad smile crept across his face. "You're my favorite character. The true hero."

The ice surrounding Samuel's heart melted. In that moment, he discovered he'd found the Answer, after all. His life had purpose, even if only to ease the pain of his Creator.

Choosing his words with care, he said, "And what sort of character are you?"

Sam frowned. "What do you mean?"

"You've also faced hardship and loss. Yet you sit in that chair, ruling over others, controlling every life but your own, escaping from your guilt." Samuel stepped closer. "You could've taken any form you chose. Why come to me like this?"

"Because this is how I am."

"This is how you see yourself. This may even be how your Creator made you. You made me in your image and look at what I've become. Scarred but not broken. Flawed but yearning to be more. You said I've developed beyond what you expected." He aimed his finger at Sam's chest. "If a mere reflection of your soul can do that, why can't you?"

The thunder and lightning ceased. The overhead storm clouds dispersed. Twin suns appeared in the sky, shining down on them.

Kneeling before Sam's wheelchair, Samuel looked into his Creator's eyes. "You can create beauty. Love. Hope. Why wallow in darkness?"

As the sunlight shone down on Sam, something warm grew in his chest and worked its way to his legs. Strength surged through his muscles. He looked up at Samuel, who nodded back.

Chest heaving in anticipation, Sam gripped the armrests of his wheelchair. He gathered every ounce of courage he possessed. With a mighty roar he pushed off from the chair and stood.

His legs held fast, bearing his weight. His heart pounded with exhilaration, as if he'd climbed the highest mountain. Sam threw back his head and arms and whooped with joy. Laughing, Samuel cheered with him. Their shouts echoed through the canyons and across the barren fields.

When he'd shouted himself hoarse, Sam turned to his creation, hot tears streaking his cheeks. "You've completed your quest, but I'm afraid I can't resurrect your parents."

Disappointment nipped at Samuel, but he shrugged it off. "I've served my purpose."

"You've done far more than that, which is why I'm giving you something I've never offered any other character." Sam rubbed his hands together and then wiggled his fingers. An ornate wooden door hung in mid-air. "This door will take you back to when your parents were still alive. You can live a different life, as if none of this ever happened." He wiggled his fingers again. A second door appeared a few feet beside the first. "The other will take you to a new, unexplored world. Even I don't know what you'll find there, and I won't make any attempt to interfere. You'll be entirely on your own."

Samuel's skin tingled as he studied the doors. "You're giving me a choice?"

Sam smiled. "I trust you'll make a good one."

After a moment's thought, Samuel set his jaw and approached the doors. He grazed his finger over one and then the other. Thoughts and emotions warred with each other. At last, he turned back to Sam and waved.

Sam waved back.

Taking a deep breath, Samuel turned the knob and stepped through the doorway.

Darkness enveloped him. He reached out with one hand. His fingertips slid across cold, bumpy stone. The sound of his breathing bounced off the surrounding walls.

The walls closed around him. He'd run out of air if someone didn't find him first.

No, Samuel told himself. *This time, I'm in control.*

Gliding one hand against the wall, he began walking. Water dripped, warning him before he crashed into a stalactite. The ground shifted, warning him of sinkholes. Before long, he spotted light ahead. He straightened his shoulders and pressed onward.

At last, he saw the opening. With a victorious cry, he emerged into the sunlight.

All around stretched a magnificent valley filled with lush trees and waterfalls. Birds flew overhead. Flowers sprouted at his feet.

No invisible thread tugged at him. Whatever path he took was his to choose.

He stepped forward. His foot touched down on something soft. He stooped and pushed aside the flowers and grass.

A dark muzzle stared back at him.

Samuel recoiled and fell on his rump.

The creature didn't move.

Crawling forward, Samuel took a closer look. The beast was dead. A mane of black fur drooped from its neck. Blood pooled between glistening fangs. A snake-like tail lay on the ground, covered in tiny bite marks.

The leoverine. It had to be the same one.

Samuel scrambled through the field to a dirt path. His heart beat wildly. Cayfel tracks—he'd know them anywhere.

His chest swelled with hope and joy. With a whisper of thanks to his Creator, Samuel set off to find his beloved friend.

* * *

"Taking a deep breath, Samuel turned the knob and stepped through the doorway."

Sam read the words once more and smiled. Although he had no idea what awaited Samuel in that new world, it'd be one heck of a story.

He studied the keyboard, his fingers twitching as if an invisible thread was pulling them to type just one more sentence. Or maybe a paragraph. Or a whole page.

Instead, he pushed aside the keyboard and shut off the computer. He rolled over to the window and peered outside, where the sun was shining, and children were playing.

His chest swelling with hope and joy, Samuel picked up his phone and dialed.

"Hi, Sarah. I'm feeling better. Do you think you can come take me to the party?"

SWAT!

Katherine Tandy Brown

When she looked out the dining room window, a scream bubbled up from her throat and left her mouth involuntarily. Shaking her head to clear the image, she focused again. *They're here. In my front yard. How could that possibly be?* She hadn't meant to panic. After all, she'd been told about them. But she'd never actually seen one. And certainly not in her neighborhood. She'd assumed the role of ostrich. Total head in the sand. *If I don't think about them, maybe they're not real. Or at least, maybe I won't ever have an "encounter."* That's the word the authorities always used when someone got grabbed. Every time, the TV newspeople described the incident in grizzly detail. *To scare the hell out of everyone,* she thought. And after hearing her first report of death screams, decapitations, severed limbs and bloodless bodies white as seagull poop, she'd "La-la-la" as loud as she could until her thumb found the mute button.

Timothy had always scoffed at her behavior. "You sound just like Scarlett O'Hara in *Gone with the Wind*," he'd say, then add in a syrupy Southern accent, "Ah just won't think about it. Aftah all, tuhmahrrah is anothah day." He'd dissolve in laughter, drawn out when they were with other people, just to embarrass her and make a point. She'd always hated when he did that. Picked on her. Made fun of her fears.

Like global warming. Timothy had railed her endlessly about that "preposterous" idea. His voice echoed in her head, the words livid, nasty, spat out between pulls of beer from a pop-top can as he balanced a bag of greasy chips on his enormous belly. He had repulsed her.

"Pure horse shit," he'd say. "You can't believe all that scientific crap." But ever since she'd read a book about global warming, and how it changed migratory behavior of Monarch butterflies, and how in the end, the story's heroine had watched her farm drown in rainwater, she'd known in her gut that could really happen. It had been a novel, but still birthed in her feelings of dread.

On her 16th birthday, her mother had said, "Recognizing potentially hurtful things is smart." She now recalled every word of shared maternal wisdom imparted on that day her life changed forever. When the authorities came and snatched her mom, committed her to a psych ward, ratted on by a woman who'd professed to be her friend. A week later, her mother had leaped to her death from a window on the institution's third floor. Or so they had told her. But she didn't believe them.

Several years later, after she and Timothy were married, she'd related the incident to her new husband and had been hurt when he'd said her mother deserved it for all her crazy talk about things she herself had known to be true and good. A pregnant woman's choice whether or not to have a baby. Avoiding the use of plastic. Not wasting precious water. Eating organic, pesticide-free food. Re-using, recycling, renewing anything that could be. Working together with people of every race and culture for the good of the earth and for human survival. Especially now, with daily downpours, followed by searing sunshine, insufferable humidity and 100-degree-plus temperatures.

Her spouse had also poo-pooed karma. Guess he'd learned first-hand that was real. All the seeds of hatred he'd planted in dozens of lives—not just hers—had imploded when his friend's DDT-spraying plane exploded in mid-air the day Timothy, a few longnecks, a pack of Marlboros and a little ol' Bic had gone along for a joy ride. Her mother would've been appalled that DDT was legal again, but as her husband had explained, "They've all gotten so big, it's the only thing that'll slow 'em down."

Though he'd put a roof over her head and food on the table, his death had relieved her of a 13-year burden. She found it hard to believe she'd ever been in love with him. He'd been handsome enough back then, with crystal blue eyes that turned down a bit at the corners. Like her dad's. And thick black hair that curled a tiny bit on his neck. She'd thought that was sexy. And he'd been trim. A well-muscled runner. Until he'd taken the desk job at Headquarters and begun tossing back beers with the security agents after work, buying their lies about the company, and becoming a professional brainwasher himself.

How could she not have seen early on how different their perspectives were on the things that really mattered? Love had led her, clouding her vision, and by the time that fog lifted, she was terrified to leave him. The one time she'd mentioned walking out, he'd grabbed her by the hair, popped out his pocket knife, held it to her throat, and told her how sorry she'd be if she even tried. She'd believed him, kowtowing, telling him what he wanted to hear, giving him what he demanded, hiding books that told the truth and sneaking a read at night, to his buzz-saw snoring.

The shattering of glass in her living room picture window jarred her back to the present. She knew what had caused it and that she should run out the backdoor to the garage, hop in her armored vehicle and drive like hell. That's what she'd been warned to do. These beasts were the reason armor was required now. But the spectacle in front of her was mesmerizing. A proboscis the size of a fire hose snaked its way around her living room. It seemed to be sniffing. Like Timothy's pit bull in a stranger's house. Her grandmother's hand-painted lamp splintered as it crashed to the floor. She gazed at chunks of porcelain skidding across the polished pine. The snout emerged from a head the size of the green exercise ball she'd used as a desk chair the past six months. Her lower back pain had eased since she'd switched to it.

Segmented legs followed, seemingly careful to avoid sharp glass shards jutting from the window frame. Graceful as a ballerina's, a right leg long as a vaulting pole stepped onto her blue-and-green braided rug, the one she'd crafted as a teenager. A left leg followed. Then another right, left, right and left. Her jaw dropped as she witnessed the delicate placement of the—what were they anyway?... feet?... leg extensions? She'd often wondered about this when observing mosquitos around the lily pond in the backyard of her childhood and when she swatted at one that had invaded the privacy of her bedroom at night. Could a creature of this size know about stepping with a measure of care on foot-long feet?

Covered in brownish scales reminiscent of chain mail, the narrow body stretched nearly the length of her front hall, with parchment-like wings folded against it. And she noticed an odor, a kind of stench that reminded her of the blood meal her grandpa used to spread around his tomato plants to keep out the deer.

But it was the eyes that held her fast, somehow forbidding her to move. Holding her captive but not against her will. Fascination overcame fear, and a calm relaxed every tensed muscle. Then she remembered what a man who'd miraculously escaped, the only known survivor of an attack, had said. He'd had to endure a lengthy transfusion afterwards but recalled being "spellbound" by the insect's gigantic, "welcoming" eyes. Within a week, however, the poor fellow had died from a blood infection.

Before her, the massive head cocked to one side, as if studying its prey. She saw her reflection many times over in its bulging, compound eyes. *Like a creepy fun house mirror,* she thought. Delicate as peacock feathers, antennae on either side of the proboscis flitted in constant motion, seemingly searching, searching, brushing first lightly over the cedar chest coffee table and its stacks of *South Carolina Wildlife* and *Biology Today*; then the sofa bed where Timothy's brother used to crash when he was too drunk to drive home from Boondocks; and finally, the cherry corner cupboard, its bevel-edge windows showing off her mother's wine glasses. She jumped when the lengthy proboscis smashed the viewing panes and treasured crystal in one swoop.

I should run, I should run, played over and over in her mind but still she stared in disbelief and awe at the monster before her, disgust and enchantment continuing to render her rigid. She caught a flash of movement outside. A quick dart of her eyes revealed the word "SWAT" in huge red letters on the side of a government tank. *The DDT truck,* she thought. *I'm saved.*

But the relief that flooded her mind was quickly displaced by confusion, when her abdomen—exposed beneath the hem of a short, lacy, summer blouse—abruptly grew cool and tingly, then a pain like a hard pinch shot through her midriff. She looked down. The behemoth mosquito had poked its proboscis into her navel. Its outer reptilian protective sheath was folded back on the surface of her skin to reveal a hard, round shaft of needles buried in her belly. With lightning speed, the hollow tubes began to turn red. Horrified, she realized her own blood was gushing into the mosquito. The skin around her gut was morphing to an opalescent white that spiraled out from her navel. Her innards felt as if an industrial vacuum cleaner were sucking them dry of blood, tissue, oxygen. Ripping out every fiber. In excruciating pain, she sought a return to comfort from the compound eyes, but now each of the dozens of chambers glowed a livid, evil red.

This time, the scream began in her lungs. Like giant bellows, they pushed it out with every remaining liter of air. The horrific, primal sound reverberated in her ears, her brain, her spine, as life erupted from her. *Oh god oh god oh god oh god.*

* * *

Clad in full HAZMAT gear, the four-man SWAT team had uncoiled the DDT hose, aimed at the vulnerable rear tip of the humongous vermin's abdomen and were ready to open the nozzle when they heard a prolonged, hideous howl from inside the red-roofed, whitewashed cottage. Each froze in position.

One pronounced the words they were all thinking. "Shit. That was Timothy's wife."

The captain's head dropped for a few seconds before he resumed command. "Call the coroner, then finish off the bastard." His sigh was audible. "Okay, let's go."

A REAL MOTHER

T.D. Johnston

Three weeks after Kerry Tisdale graduated from college, she took the trip to Europe her parents awarded her as a graduation gift, with a second week added for making Phi Beta Kappa. While in Paris, then Tuscany, then Rome, then Venice, then back west to London before flying home to Atlanta, she enjoyed great food and drink, visited many historic sites, observed classic works of art and architecture, and fell in love with a handsome man named Khalid, whom she met on her second tour of the Louvre. Khalid was an artist. He was twenty-seven years old, had studied at the Sorbonne, was currently trying his hand at Monet-style impressionism, and was brown. Khalid was also Muslim, but Kerry tried not to think about that when they made love in Khalid's small but well-appointed apartment above a quaint café the night before she left for Italy. By not thinking about that, Kerry invited Khalid to accompany her to Venice and then London, an invitation Khalid accepted. While in Venice Khalid painted a Venetian canal scene that Kerry insisted Monet would proudly have hung on his dining-room wall.

Kerry Tisdale was the only child of very Republican parents, and the fourth Republican grandchild of very Republican grandparents. The family's Republican loyalty was so powerful that all members of the living generations of Tisdales and Harrisons (Kerry's mother being from Houston) voted in 2016 for a man they each loathed, as told in commiseration that Thanksgiving. Kerry's membership in the College Republicans for the past four years had been expected by Tisdales and Harrisons alike, and she did not disappoint.

In London, on the eve of her return flight to America, Kerry considered for the first time that Khalid, a magnificent artist and generous lover, a kind man with a dry sense of humor that Kerry could picture making her laugh on their fiftieth anniversary, would be a problem on the other side of the Atlantic.

So at dawn on the final Friday of her graduation trip, while Khalid slept after a night of passionate lovemaking at a London hotel, Kerry took a cab to Heathrow Airport. Later, while enjoying surf and turf for lunch in first class miles above the deepest trenches of the Atlantic, Kerry unfriended and blocked Khalid on Facebook. She deleted the selfies of the two of them which Khalid had posted on her timeline last night before opening their second bottle of wine. She regretted having to block him, but she wanted to avoid the hurt of seeing his smiling face again. There had been zero likes on the photos when she deleted them. She was in the clear. When the in-flight movie about a brave female DEA agent fizzled into mindless action after about forty minutes, she dozed off and on for the remainder of the flight to Atlanta.

Back at her parents' home in Buckhead, Kerry began to pack for her move to Memphis, where on July 1st she would begin her fast-track sales management career with one of America's leading consumer-goods companies. For six months she would learn the strategic ground-level relationships with supermarket chains and big-box retailers, before being promoted into brand management if all went well. A month ago she had located a nice two-bedroom apartment on a home-hunting visit with her mother. Furniture was being delivered on June 29th, so she had about ten days left at home to spend with her friends and family.

On June 26th, while in Midtown for an evening with friends, she saw a young man who looked a lot like Khalid. The man was wearing a tight grey tee shirt and khaki shorts, and was laughing with two young black women in seventies-style halter tops. An image flashed of Khalid painting in Venice, then an earlier vision of Khalid leaning in to kiss her for the first time while they sat out a rainstorm with café crème and warm croissants under a table umbrella next to a cobblestone side street in Paris. Suddenly she desired the man at the bar with the two haltered women. She fought the urge to steal him, battled the greater urge to remember Khalid, and drank another Fat Tire toast to the brilliant futures she and her companions each individually possessed. The world really was their oyster. It really was.

The morning of June 28th arrived too fast. Kerry wished she had a few more days to transition into the oyster part of her life, but furniture was arriving in Memphis tomorrow, and she had to be there with the key she would pick up from the apartment complex's manager this afternoon at five. She had an early-morning breakfast with her mom and dad, savoring her mom's poached eggs for what absurdly felt like the last time. Sitting in sudden sad silence with them, she found herself wishing she had said goodbye to Khalid, or that she had somehow left the door open for something more. She pictured him with another woman, maybe not this soon but soon still. Or maybe even right now, locked in rolling ecstatic passion. The concept bothered her, as did the awful certainty that the latter was the reality. If she wanted him, so did other women. They would have him, and he would have them. For the first time in her life, a man Kerry Tisdale dumped was a man Kerry Tisdale wanted back.

But just as suddenly she knew that the fling was just that, merely and only that, a dalliance with a man who would not be welcome at the Church of the Apostles, where she would get married because that's what her parents expected of her. Kerry valued practicality. No, she thought, actually she valued pragmatism, recognizing the distinction as she sipped her orange juice on this goodbye morning. She had learned much about the usefulness of pragmatism in her minor field of political science, which interested her far more than her major study in economics. She had pragmatically made the only viable decision in London, fortunately after satisfying and therefore removing the temporary temptations of desire, one last delicious time, an hour before tiptoeing to the hotel-room door.

Kerry excused herself from the dining table and went upstairs to brush her teeth and pack toiletries into her final suitcase. Everything else was in her car, a late-model grey Volvo SUV that her father had researched and chosen for its high crash rating and durability. As she brushed her teeth, she began to feel sick to the stomach. Too much beer last night, she knew. The feeling passed. She examined her shoulder-length dark brown hair in the mirror, ran her fingers through the lush locks, contemplated makeup while knowing she didn't need it, and spit in the sink after swishing for thirty seconds. She put her toothbrush and toothpaste in her toiletries bag and turned to exit the bathroom when the sick feeling returned. It was nausea. This time she stepped to the toilet, descended to her knees, and threw up her poached eggs and English muffin. *Great*, she thought as she wiped her mouth with toilet paper. *Sick for the endless drive to Memphis.*

She did not know then that she was pregnant. Knowing that she was pregnant would have made for a particularly rough drive to Memphis, particularly because Kerry's family was particularly opposed to abortion, their particular opposition to abortion being due to their particular position, shared by many, that abortion was murder. Kerry had said so herself at more than one meeting of particularly like-minded College Republicans. So it was good that she did not know she was pregnant during her drive to Memphis. It was good that she did not have to consider that the baby's father was a kind, funny, artistic black Muslim man named Khalid living on the other side of the big pond the day before her furniture would arrive, and two days before she would start her career in a world that was her oyster. By the time she and the Volvo crossed over the north Georgia border into Tennessee en route toward I-40, the nausea was a thing of the past, the Bose was blasting variously from fifteen pre-set satellite channels, and Khalid had moved on from her mind, replaced by her excitement about the tan velvet living-room furniture, the beautiful maple dining suite, and the king-size bed that she would break in to-morrow night before starting her new life as a budding corporate executive-in-training.

Pulling into a McDonald's off the highway outside of Chat-tanooga, Kerry parked and entered the fast-food restaurant, stretching her legs rather than sit in the drive-through lane. While in line at the one open cash register, the nausea returned. She left the line, hurried to the women's restroom, and discovered that the lone stall was occupied. She was annoyed. She cleared her throat, not to be obvious but to sound sick, which she was. Then she whispered, in case the occupant of the stall was oblivious, "Oh my God, I'm going to be so sick." She pronounced the last word slowly, and waited for the woman in the stall to respond with an obligatory "I'm so sorry" and an emphatic roll of the toilet-paper holder.

Silence.

"Excuse me," Kerry said. "But I'm going to be sick."

Silence.

"I'm sorry, but I think I'm about to throw up." It was the truth. Surely the woman would understand that.

A raspy voice came from the stall.

"Sink's got a hole in it."

Kerry gaped at the stall door.

"Excuse me?"

"Sink's got a hole in it. You deaf?"

The woman sounded like a black grandmother. The accent was uncultured, maybe Alabama or south Georgia. Kerry consid-ered a response that the woman wouldn't like, but thought better of it. The urge to vomit was powerful, the result imminent. She sighed with calculated exaggeration, and advanced to the sink in time to give in to the rising tide, which consisted first of fluid reminiscent of the morning's orange juice, followed by several violent dry heaves. Gasping, she turned on the water to drain her deposit, washing her hands thoroughly with soap from a dirty Dial dispenser. She reached for the paper-towel holder to the right of the sink. It was empty. She turned and scanned the back wall. No air dryer either.

Shaking her hands over the sink, she felt a sudden rage at the woman in the stall. Surely the old lady had heard Kerry in her mis-ery, and yet sat there unconcerned. *Jesus. What a freaking selfish—*

"You with chile, honey?" The voice was softer than before, almost friendly.

What did she just say?

Kerry stopped shaking droplets off her hands.

"Excuse me?"

"You heard me, honey."

"Pardon me, but I am not your honey and I am definitely not with *child*. I was out late last night with some friends. Too many beers." Kerry finished drying her hands by wiping them back and forth on her khaki shorts.

"Beer ain't got nothin' to do with it, chile. You pregnant. You take good care uh dat baby now. Dat begins right now. Don't be drinkin' no more beers."

Kerry stepped to the stall door and placed her right palm against it. "I am not pregnant, and you can mind your own business. I am not your daughter. Mind your goddamn business."

"Chile, best you not be usin' words like dat. God's name in vain. Who been raisin' you?"

"Not you, whoever you are. Don't you have some pickaninny grandchildren to worry about?"

"Chile, diss is the third decade of the twenty-fust century. White women ain't supposed to call children pickaninnies no mo. You must be related to ol' Jeff Davis."

Kerry was appalled. Rage welled in her gut, then subsided. The old woman was just trying to get her goat. Probably sat in this stall all day to mess with women who were productively on their way to somewhere much better. Unlike the old woman. But no matter; Kerry would take the high road.

"Look, ma'am. I am not pregnant and I am *not* racist. Sorry about the word choice. You're just getting on my nerves. I hope you're proud of yourself. Goodbye."

Kerry pulled open the bathroom door just as the toilet was being flushed. The sound of the rushing water was like a sonic boom, surprising her in its power and then in its duration. Suddenly she wanted to be far away from the bathroom, this restaurant, this exit, this part of Tennessee. She did not want to see this woman emerge from the bathroom, and especially did not want this woman to see *her*. When she reached the restaurant exit, she paced impatiently as a white family of five entered single file, the father holding the door open for his wife, his three laughing kids, and then for Kerry, who thanked him under her breath and ran to her Volvo. She buckled up, started the ignition, set the satellite channel to the Beatles station, backed the vehicle out of its space, and stepped on the gas, not looking toward the restaurant lest she make eye contact with the black woman and give herself away.

Worry began to tug at her. Why did the woman so rudely speculate about Kerry being 'with chile'? She'd said it as if it weren't speculation. And that nonsense about Kerry using her mother's term for cute black children. Mom had always meant it as a compliment. Kerry had simply used the word in a moment of anger, with a woman she would never see face to face, so of course she didn't need to worry about it. But still… the woman had gotten to her, as if… well… as if she actually knew something.

That was ridiculous, naturally. Kerry set the cruise control at eighty-one after merging onto I-40. It was just an encounter with an old woman who had never been anywhere, whose favorite daily activity was sitting in a bathroom stall waiting for white women she could aggravate. For a moment, Kerry remembered Hattie, the family's black maid for the duration of Kerry's childhood. Hattie had doted on Kerry and her older brother, Erskine. But even as a kid Kerry had noticed conflict between Hattie and Kerry's mother. In retrospect, Hattie's comments about the family's comings and goings had been risky, like the time the family was packing for a trip to Hawaii. Hattie was cleaning the house, and soon would be watering the plants and managing the family's pets for a week in the Tisdales' absence. As Hattie helped Kerry's mother pack toiletries for the kids, Hattie said "Must be nice, goin' to Hawaii. Some day, lord. Some day."

Kerry's mother had stopped right then and replied, "It's called a vacation, Hattie. Erskine works very hard at his business, sometimes upwards of fifty hours a week. He deserves a trip like this from time to time."

To Kerry her mother's words had sounded like a rebuke. Kerry stopped working on the Disney crossword puzzle on the floor outside the master bathroom and did some math in her head. She knew her dad golfed on Saturdays and Sundays, usually with Mister Edwards and a couple of other friends from the club. On weekdays he liked his first martini at 5:30 sharp, with water crackers and extra-sharp cheddar cheese, which Hattie would set out every day before taking the bus home from the corner of West Paces Ferry and Dunlap. Dad enjoyed Mom's poached eggs before going to work every day, and those eggs were always on the plate at eight, before Mom took Kerry and Erskine to school. So her mother's response to Hattie resulted in Kerry's employment of the math. Her father's 45 hours away at the office each week were about the same as Hattie's hours splitting time between the Tisdales' home and the Edwardses' three houses down. Ever so briefly, Kerry had thought that maybe her mother was out of line. Hattie wanted to go to Hawaii someday, and Mom's response had suggested that such a thought was either ridiculous or inappropriate or both. Either that or Mom's response meant that she thought Hattie was trying to make her feel guilty. Kerry had felt the awkwardness of the silence that followed the rebuke. That silence had lasted for the next hour or so, interrupted only by the occasional "Ma'am, do you want Erskine's boat shoes to go on the trip?" or "How many flip flops does Kerry like to bring?" Mom's answers were terse on such days. And yet Hattie more and more frequently made comments that Kerry's mother didn't like.

Sometimes Hattie's comments were actually questions, but came off like comments. For example, there was the day the straw broke the camel's back. It was mid-summer. Kerry was sitting at the kitchen table eating a PBJ and doing her eighth-grade summer reading of Elie Weisel's *Night*, while Hattie was emptying the dishwasher and Mom was catching up on the *Parade* magazine from the previous Sunday. Hattie's question, as she settled a plate onto a stack in the glass-front cupboard to the right of the sink: "Kerry, where's that fancy private school sending you to college some day?"

Before Kerry could answer the question, her mother snapped the magazine shut. "Hattie, I am tired of you taking shots at our lifestyle and how we are raising our children. If you could afford it, you would do the same thing."

Then came Hattie's mistake, in which she was clearly out of line.

"Ma'am, if you and Miz Edwards paid me more, I could afford it. And my Thomas could go to school with your Kerry and Erskine, and Thomas wouldn't have to mow no more lawns when he could be doin' more homework to get ready for not cleanin' other people's houses when he's forty-six."

Kerry had squeezed her eyes shut. And then came her mother.

"You're done, Hattie. That's it. Get your things and leave. I will mail you your final check."

"Ma'am, I didn't mean nothin' by that. Maybe you and Miz Edwards can't afford more than the ten bucks an hour. I can appreciate that. Didn't mean nothin' by it. I do need my job. I'm very—"

"I said, get out now!" Kerry's mother had stood, flipping the magazine to the floor. "Every year, you get more and more bold, Hattie. Your job was to clean and help out around the house. If you didn't like the pay, you shouldn't have taken the job. Here or at the Edwardses, who are fine people and just as generous as we are. Now go."

Kerry had watched Hattie leave in silence, retrieving her purse from the granite countertop next to the refrigerator. Kerry examined her book, as if a spider were crawling across the front cover. She didn't lift her gaze until she heard the clap-clap of the kitchen screen door shutting behind the departed Hattie, who had always been instructed to use the kitchen door in coming and going. Kerry hadn't liked her mother in that moment, but this was her mother and this was Buckhead, not Lithonia, to which the bus would take sweet Hattie. Hattie had been unwise, Kerry knew. Now, en route to Memphis and her corporate future, Kerry remembered what her father had said when he learned at the dinner table what happened with Hattie: "Kerry? Erskine? Look at me. You learn something from this. Never disagree with the person who signs your paycheck. The world works just like your allowance. Now eat your asparagus if you have designs on dessert."

Kerry and her little brother ate their asparagus and drank all their milk.

As I-40 continued to flatten into the westward horizon, Kerry avoided the nagging, gnawing question. Was she with child, like the nasty old woman said from a graffiti-marred stall? If she was, Khalid was somewhere in Paris, the father of her first child now generously pleasuring another innocent American college graduate celebrating Phi Beta Kappa and hooking herself on café crème. She considered his obvious selfishness, his meaningless art, his self-obsessed passion for all things unpragmatic. He would never leave that life for the responsibilities of fatherhood. Never. She was certain of it. The bastard couldn't be bothered with protection. So why would he bother with raising a child? What a mother-f—

Her cell phone bleated on the center console. Kerry turned down the radio and looked at the phone. It said 'Unknown Caller.' She picked up the phone and answered, putting it into speaker mode. "Hello?"

"Honey, you need to take care a dat chile."

Kerry hit the brakes, swerving onto the right shoulder before correcting the Volvo back onto the road. She said nothing as her heart pounded.

"I know you can hear me, honey. See a doctor and call dat chile's daddy. Call your folks too, now. You got to take responsibility. Your life doan belong to you no mo."

She was imagining this. Had to be. That old woman was still at McDonald's, and probably didn't even own a cell phone. Kerry was panicking was all, imagining this call the way she had imagined conversations with Hattie over the years. She pressed 'End' and refocused on the road.

It was the kind of thing Hattie would have said. Not to Kerry or Erskine, but to their mother. It just wasn't wise. What if Kerry turned around, headed east back to the McDonald's, spoke to the manager, charged the old woman with harassing a customer? The old woman was lucky that Kerry had to be in Memphis well before five o'clock.

Kerry changed the channel to First Wave, which was playing Billy Idol's "Eyes Without a Face." She tried to sing along:

"Eyes without a face... you got no human grace... you're eyes without a face... such a human waste... you're eyes with—"

The phone rang again. Kerry let the song continue. Surely the old woman wouldn't like Billy Idol. She answered and hit Speaker.

"How did you get my number?"

"Turn the music down, chile. You need to concentrate on dat road."

"How did you get my freaking *number*, you—"

"It was on the stall, chile. Right there on the stall. You put it there, remember?"

The old woman was insane.

"Why would I put it there, you old biddy? You are *crazy!* Leave me *alone!*"

"You know why you put it there, my darlin' chile."

Kerry pressed the brake when she realized she was about to pass a state trooper. She settled the Volvo into the right lane behind the cruiser.

"Darling *child?* I don't even know what you look like. Why are you harassing me? I don't deserve this. I'm just trying to get to Memphis to start my new job."

"I ain't harassin' you, chile. I'm helpin' you."

Kerry allowed silence to be her answer.

"Chile?" came the voice, sounding more and more familiar. "You know zactly why you put your number on that stall. You even put your name there for me."

This was ridiculous, Kerry knew. Maybe it was part of being sick. Delusions. Had she gotten enough sleep? Had someone slipped something into one of her beers last night in Buckhead? Either way, she knew she hadn't written her phone number on any effing bathroom stalls at that pit of an exit back there somewhere.

"Okay, old biddy. So tell me. Why would I do that, after you wouldn't even let me use the toilet to throw up? Why? Why would I *do that?*"

Silence again, this time chosen by the old black woman. Kerry pictured her, an old fat woman with an Aunt Jemima bandana in her hair. And then the old woman whispered something. Kerry barely heard it, the words somehow traveling audibly through Billy Idol's last descending notes.

"Because you want a real mother. Don't you, chile?"

Kerry stared ahead at the rear of the trooper's cruiser.

"I have a real mother," she said.

"You've come to me, chile. I can be your real mama. What say?"

"I'd say I have a future that starts at five o'clock in Memphis. Go away and leave me alone."

Kerry listened. She turned down a song by the Clash. There wasn't a thing about today that had anything to do with rocking a casbah. Maybe there never would be again. She pictured Khalid. He was older now, nursing a café crème. He was seated at a café table, a small child on his knee eating an ice cream cone. It looked like chocolate. A woman, maybe the child's mother, sat with her back to Kerry, oblivious to Kerry's longing to be in that picture, in that café chair, sipping her own café crème, soothing the child's younger sibling in her lap. An ache grew in Kerry's throat as the Volvo drifted closer to the rear of the state trooper's cruiser.

"Chile, your future ain't in Memphis. Not *dis* way. Cincinnati neither. Your future's where you's honest and happy. Come home to see me, chile. Jes' for a while. Come home and see your mama."

Tears welled in Kerry's eyes, blurring her focus on the police car in front of her. She tapped the brake, falling back.

"I did give you my number. Didn't I, Hattie?"

Kerry held her breath. There was only one answer she wanted.

"Why, yes chile. Course you did. I'm your mama. Turn around, sweet baby. Come home to me. After we get you some rest, and some pie, and maybe do a Disney crossword puzzle, how 'bout you call that fine young man? Give him the fabulous news. He's got a gorgeous little girl comin' into dis world. And dat little girl's goan have a darlin' great mama."

Kerry pulled the Volvo onto the shoulder and stopped. She wiped her eyes with the backs of both hands.

"Will you teach me, Mama?" For the second time, she held her breath.

"I already done did, chile. Just promise me dis one thing."

Kerry smiled, tasting salt at the corners of her mouth. "What's that, Mama?"

"When you and that lovely man a yours take that chile to Hawaii..."

"Don't you even finish that thought, Mama."

Silence.

"Mama?"

"Yes, chile."

"That was going to be *my* idea," Kerry said, pressing the gas to re-enter traffic and reverse her direction at the exit up ahead. The bridge over the highway looked new, and so did the McDonald's. After all, she was starting to feel sick again, gloriously sick, already tasting the thick chocolate milkshake that would carry her east toward all her tomorrows.

Lightning Source UK Ltd.
Milton Keynes UK
UKHW010223270223
417717UK00005B/16